W9-CIL-731

THE REMNANT TRILOGY | BOOK 2

NOAH

MAN OF RESOLVE

TIM CHAFFEY &
K. MARIE ADAMS

Thank You

While our names can be found on the front cover, we recognize that many others played a significant role in helping us complete this book.

The team at Master Books, we can't thank you enough. Tim, thanks for choosing not only to read a work of fiction, but to publish it as well. Brittany, Laura, Katie, and others, you've been a delight to work with, and you make even the mundane fun.

Reagen, thanks for taking the manuscript we sent you and making it shine. Thanks for challenging us in every area of writing fiction and for applying your editorial expertise to produce a consistent, dramatic, and engaging story.

Casey, thanks for the long walks of plot discussion, the living room chats of character dissection, and the countless bowls of popcorn. We rely so much on your understanding of English grammar and your attention to details. We'd say you have a thankless job, but here you are being thanked . . . and you completely deserve it.

Ben, thanks for putting up with a word guy and an artsy girl. You take our spoken ideas and particles of thought and make them come alive on canvas in ways we couldn't have even dreamed. Knowing many will judge the book by its cover, we're so glad that you are the one helping us stand tall.

Janice, thanks for your countless prayers, words of encouragement, and happy reminders of ways we can make many details even better. Tony, thanks for the brainstorms on the plot. Steve, thanks for your editorial assistance in the nonfiction sections.

To all those in our lives, who shape our writing by walking out the experiences of the day to day with us, we love you and thank you.

Most of all, we thank our Lord and Savior, Jesus Christ. Thank You for dying in our place and then conquering the grave. Thank You for revealing so much about who You are through Your word and world. Thank You for godly examples like Noah and for growing our own faith and understanding of You as we wrote this novel.

First printing: June 2017

Copyright © 2017 by Tim Chaffey and K. Marie Adams. All rights reserved. No part of this book may be used or reproduced in any manner whatsoever without written permission from the publisher, except in the case of brief quotations in articles and reviews. For information write:

Master Books®, P.O. Box 726, Green Forest, AR 72638
Master Books® is a division of the New Leaf Publishing Group, Inc.

ISBN: 9781683440741
ISBN: 978-1-61458-601-2 (digital)
Library of Congress Number: 2017940467

Cover design by K. Marie Adams; cover illustration by Ben Iocco

Unless otherwise noted, Scripture quotations are from the New King James Version (NKJV) of the Bible, copyright © 1982 by Thomas Nelson, Inc. Used by permission. All rights reserved.

Please consider requesting that a copy of this volume be purchased by your local library system.

Printed in the United States of America

Please visit our website for other great titles:
www.masterbooks.com

For information regarding author interviews,
please contact the publicity department at (870) 438-5288.

Contents

Dear Reader,

Thank you for joining us for another look at what Noah may have been like in the years prior to the Flood. In the first book, we followed Noah on a coming-of-age adventure when he left home to work as a shipbuilder's apprentice. He faced many challenges along the way as he learned more about the world beyond his hometown. He stood for justice, met his wife, resisted temptation, and faced a growing evil in the land. Book Two picks up right where book one ended.

As we mentioned in the opening of the first book, we realize that so much of the story we are telling is made up. The Bible provides scant information about the world in which he lived and what Noah was like before God instructed him to build the Ark. Our story is rooted in those small details revealed in the first six chapters of Genesis.

We certainly do not want to be guilty of adding to Scripture, so we have spent considerable space near the end of both novels explaining why we depicted people, places, and events in certain ways. We stated in the first novel that one of our objectives in writing these stories was to use fiction to help readers learn to discern between fiction and biblical fact. That may sound like a strange goal for a novel, but stories can be used as powerful teaching tools. One need look no further than the parables taught by Jesus. While our story is not a parable or an allegory, it is intended to teach biblical truths in the context of fiction.

We have intentionally avoided many of the stereotypical views about Noah that are not spelled out in Scripture in an effort to challenge the reader to pick up the Bible and pay close attention to what it actually states. The nonfiction section in the back of the book is also designed to help the reader distinguish between fact and fiction, as well as highlighting areas where the novel intersects with exhibits that can be seen at the Ark Encounter theme park in Williamstown, Kentucky.

Welcome aboard for another journey as we respectfully imagine what life may have been like for our great, great . . . grandfather Noah.

Sincerely,
Tim Chaffey and K. Marie Adams

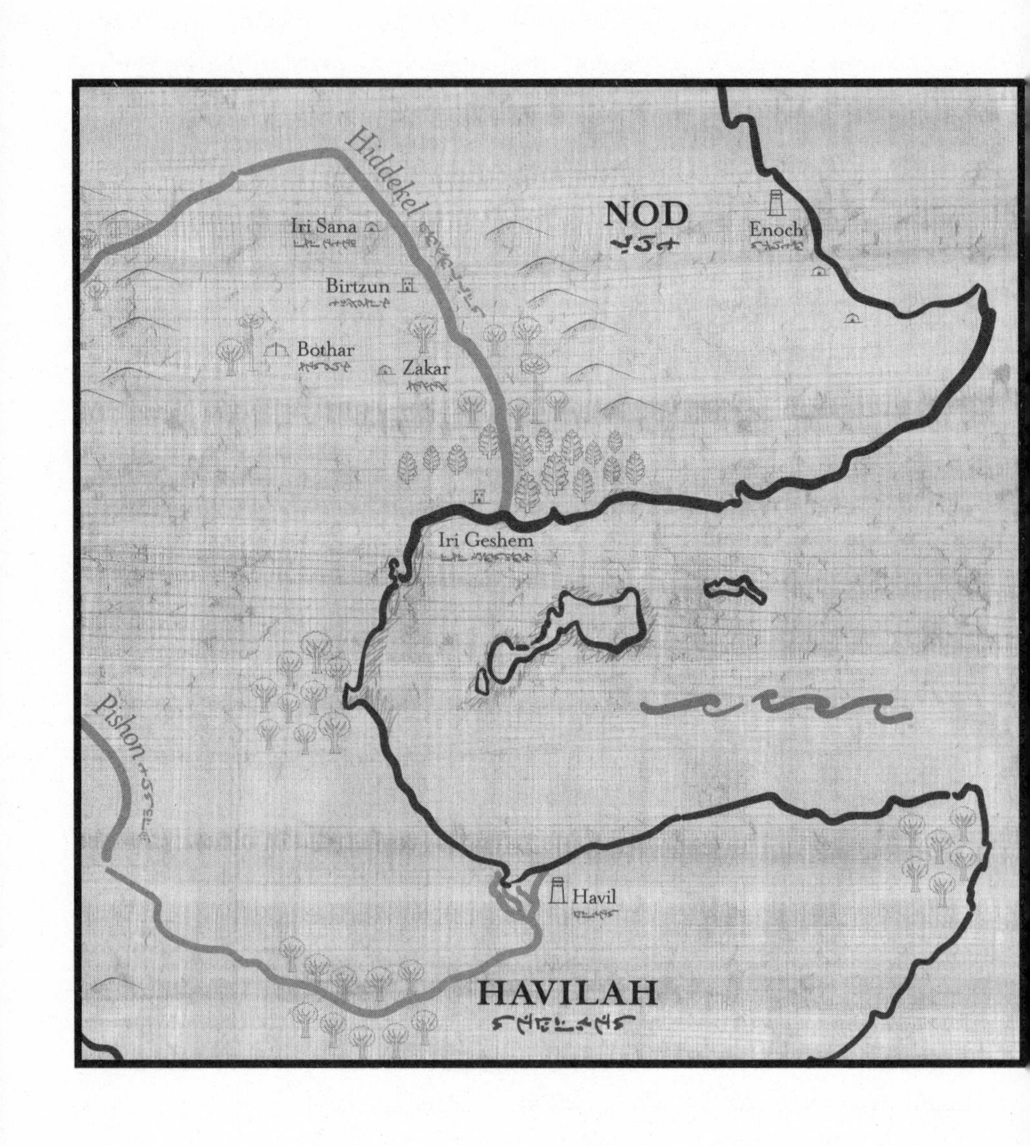
Hiddekel
Iri Sana
Birtzun
Bothar
Zakar
NOD
Enoch
Iri Geshem
Pishon
Havil
HAVILAH

Chapter 1

Havil — Noah's 46th year

Emzara sprinted behind Noah, her eyes on the flap, flap of his robe as they fled the courtyard and the golden stare of the serpent idol Nachash. Her weary mind ran circles around the events of the day: the excitement and pleasure of exploring a new place with her new husband, his enjoyment at her delight when she picked out Tubal-Cain's extravagant surprise gift. And later, the knock at the door, the guards grabbing Noah, the dread that he had been killed. And now this: Noah returned safely and the guards saying it was all a misunderstanding. *So why the rush?* As sickened as she was by what she had seen tonight, the sensuality and godlessness of the ceremony didn't pose a serious threat to their lives, right? *Why won't he look me in the eye?*

Without warning, Emzara crashed into Noah's back as he halted in the middle of the street. She grabbed onto him to steady her balance. "Sorry."

Unfazed, Noah reached out his arm and stopped Zain. Pointing to one of the guest homes, he whispered, "I sent Farna straight to the boat, so tell his crew to pack everything immediately and meet us there as soon as possible."

"What happened?" Zain asked. "Why are we in such a hurry?"

"We have to leave before that ceremony ends. Naamah's preoccupied for now, but Garun told me I'm not safe in this city. Be on alert for her guards."

Zain gave a curt nod. "Is it something you've done?"

"No, quite the opposite actually." Noah glanced back down the road. "I'll explain later."

"Let's hope they've already resupplied the ship for the return trip," Zain said.

"Indeed."

Zain paused and looked back toward the city square. "One more problem. We have no idea where Ashur is."

"Ashur." Noah sucked in a breath through clenched teeth. "Now what?"

"You two grab our things," Zain said. "I'll tell the crew to get going, and then go look for Ashur."

"With that crowd?" Emzara's voice shook.

"What choice do we have?" Zain's question hung in the air for a moment before he continued. "You get to the boat. The important thing is to have you leave safely. If I'm not back, go without me."

Noah held up an arm. "But . . ."

"You're the one in trouble, not me or Ashur. We'll find our own way back, if necessary. Let's go."

Noah reached out and gripped the councilmember's arm, delaying his momentum. "May the Creator guide and protect you."

"And you, my friend. Now go."

Grimly, they made their way to their luxurious quarters. Zain hustled to the house on the left, while Noah and Emzara entered their lodging. The room was completely dark and unguarded.

Emzara turned to light a wick, but Noah stopped her with a hand over hers.

"No, let's work in the dark."

She frowned, peering up into his face and wishing for the light just so she could read his expression. "Very well."

Hurriedly, they grabbed their belongings. Emzara laid one of Noah's tunics on the ground in a long rectangle and arranged their folded garments on top. Strands of piks and pikas, clothing, and a few toiletries gave shape to the growing mound.

In her haste, she bumped into Noah, and a bottle of ointment flew from her hand. It shattered in a far corner, filling the air with the sharp scent of herbs and spices. "Sorry."

Already turning away to resume his work, Noah said, "Leave it. Are you hurt?"

"No, but look at me." She put a hand on his arm, her eyes searching out his. "Please tell me what happened."

For the first time since he had been returned to her, Noah held her gaze. "I promise I'll tell you everything, but there's no time right now." He bent down and kissed her forehead, muffling his voice against her skin. "We need to hurry."

* * *

Naamah twirled, her bare feet tracing the same intricate steps to the dance that she performed earlier in the evening. Tap, tap, tap-tap-tap. In the final steps of the choreography, her toe gracefully patted against the sandstone flooring that lined the gardens on top of the palace. She dipped her left shoulder and glanced over it to where the seer lagged slightly behind, his lanky frame dark against the backlighting of the torches. Laughing, she ran back toward him and swirled around several potted kalum trees, enjoying the spicy aroma their flowers gave off.

"How did I do tonight?" she asked, looking up at him and hoping he approved.

"Very well, my child." The old man lightly patted her cheeks, as a father who was proud of his child would do.

"Did I?"

"Yes, your singing mesmerized the people. Hearing your talent in person was greater than I imagined."

"I'm so glad." Unable to keep still, she spun as they walked toward the waist-high parapet marking the edge of the expansive rooftop garden.

"You're a natural leader, and tonight you received some of the recognition you deserve."

Naamah glowed under his high praise and leaned against the low stone wall. "There were so many people. Look at all the lights below, even this late at night."

They both peered out at the city, which still bustled. Pockets of people moved about the streets below, laughing with their companions and calling out good-naturedly to other groups that passed by. The sheer number of lit windows indicated that the celebratory atmosphere moved beyond the streets. Music and drumbeats sounded out from a variety of places.

She flung her hands wide. "Isn't the city magnificent?"

"It's quite a sight. And you are its only princess."

"Yes, I am. Everyone got to watch me."

"And as priestess." He stroked the serpent image atop his staff. "Introducing them to Nachash was your greatest achievement tonight. Against the backdrop of your talents, the people saw the beauty in following him."

Naamah pressed her hands together and trembled with excitement. "I can't wait for next year's celebration. I'll dazzle them even more."

The seer gave a patient chuckle. "I have no doubts, but listen to me." He grabbed her hands. "Tonight was only a first step for you. With my guidance, you can achieve power you've never dreamed of. The success you now feel — and deserve — is only a glimpse of what is to come."

"More?"

He swept his arm out. "All that you see here — the might of your father's soldiers and the skill of your craftsmen." He shook his head slowly. "It's nothing compared to the power available through Nachash."

Intrigued, Naamah looked up and rubbed her chin, pondering the implications.

"The first time we met I saw greatness and giftedness in you. And power — that few can possess and even fewer will be able to resist."

Naamah leaned in closer. "Show me. Teach me everything."

A crooked smile spread across his lips. "Patience. It takes time. I'll guide you in the ways of Nachash, and as you learn, your power and wisdom will grow."

Hearing the rustle of leaves, Naamah stepped back as she glanced around. "Who's there? Speak."

Nivlac stepped forward from the foliage into the well-lit patio area, accompanied by Tsek, a mountain of a man. Nivlac bowed. "Princess, the king's captain has a message for you." Nivlac retreated to his post a short distance away.

Tsek bowed. "Evening peace, Princess. I'm here on behalf of the king. He wishes to inform you that he's pleased with your part in the festivities. Because of your efforts, the people learned how great a leader they have. Now they have a god worthy of the leader who has done much to build this city into what it is. And you, Naamah, played a part in that."

Naamah stiffened as Tsek droned on. *It's just like Father to take what should've been a simple compliment and make it all about himself.* Discouraged, she looked up at Tsek's strong jaw line as she waited for him to finish. *Power? Can I really be as powerful as the seer promised? Could I turn Tsek's loyalty to me instead of my father? Imagine that. His own captain following me.* She grinned.

"I'm glad that you're pleased with your father's report of the evening's successes."

Pulled suddenly from her reverie, Naamah blinked quickly, attempting to speed up her brain's responses. "Of course. I'm happy as long as my father is happy."

Tsek bobbed his head. "Do you have anything you want me to take to the king in reply?"

She looked at the seer, who had taken a seat a short distance away, while she searched for the right phrase. Stepping close to Tsek, she brushed an imaginary speck from his broad, tanned shoulder, being sure to let her hand linger longer than necessary. She cast him an alluring look as she backed away. "Tell the king that my victory rests in his vast accomplishments."

Tsek searched her face before replying. "I shall relay that. And may I say that, personally, I thought you were the highlight of the evening."

She flashed him a broad smile. "You are most kind, Tsek. Thank you for bringing words from my father." She dismissed him with a small wave of her hand.

He bowed and looked back at her twice as he walked through the garden.

The seer rejoined Naamah, wearing a slight frown. "That was not the type of power I was alluding to."

With a flip of her head, she tossed her hair over her shoulder. "Oh, I care nothing for him, but it wouldn't hurt to have his complete loyalty." She turned around to look at the city again. "There is, however, someone that I'd like to bring to his knees before me. Do you think you could help with that?"

"Perhaps. Tell me what's on your mind."

"A man slighted me twice. He dismissed me once a while ago and again just today." She let tears gather at the corner of her eyes, playing the role skillfully and without hesitation.

"Would this be the man your guard mentioned this evening? Noah? The shipbuilder?"

She bit her lip and nodded.

"And just what do you want to do?" He gently touched her shoulder.

She wanted vengeance. *But how?* "I — I . . . never mind."

"Capture this man's wife so that he has to beg you for her life."

Once hidden in the recesses of her mind, her darkest thoughts became clear. And yet, the seer spoke them calmly and with even tones, as if he were simply discussing what would be served for the next meal.

Naamah's eyes widened. "How — how did you know?"

The seer looked steadily at her. "I've been trying to tell you that the power I can teach you is beyond anything you've imagined."

Still awed by his ability, she stared into the wrinkled face before her.

"If you're bent on making this man pay, then call your guards to go get his wife. But I must say, you're setting your ambition too low."

She shook her head, brushing off his disapproval. "Maybe I am. But if I put this behind me, then I can focus more fully on what you have to teach me." She raised her voice so that the sentry stationed on the terrace might hear her. "Nivlac!"

Her most dependable guard hurried across the roof and stood before her. "Yes, Princess."

"I have an urgent mission for you."

Chapter 2

"About halfway there," Noah said as they crested a rise in the road. "Are we going too fast for you?"

"No, I'm alright." Emzara ducked behind Noah's broad shoulder, thankful for his presence. The whole moon was bright and cast many shadows over the cobbled streets they raced through. Since Havil was built into hilly terrain, several retaining walls rose up, supporting other roads that followed the curvature of the landscape. The way the roads crisscrossed over each other reminded Emzara of a braided hairstyle in which lengths of hair looped and intersected and were tucked out of sight behind other strands. *I sure hope Noah knows where we are.*

Her lungs burned as she followed Noah down yet another hill, but the distinct sound of the waves slapping the shore told her they were close. Suddenly, Noah stopped and gently moved her against the stone retaining wall that towered over their heads on the left. Little bits of grass poked brazenly between the edges of some of the rocks. The cool grit grated against her skin as she looked up at her husband's face. Making no noise, he jerked his head in the direction of the wall, signaling her to move toward it, before flattening himself against it.

Emzara tucked herself even farther into the protective shadows. "What is it?"

"We're close to the shore. I just want to make sure we can reach the boat without any interference." He leaned forward and scanned both directions. "Looks clear from here. Come on."

They walked quickly toward the beach. Finally reaching the gravel road that ran parallel to the water, she spotted the gentle curvature of the peak which formed the bow of their boat. The light hanging from the edge was lit. *Farna and the crew are on board!* Rejuvenated, Emzara readied herself to burst toward it, but Noah stopped her and pointed.

Four guards sat where the dock met the shore, blocking the path. Emzara shrank back and followed Noah, ducking out of sight behind a large building. She looked at him wide-eyed, wondering if he would come up with a solution.

He blinked. "So what now?"

"I'm scared." She ventured the words as quietly as she could.

Noah pulled her close and she clung to him. "Hang in there," he whispered against her ear, tendrils of her hair brushing against his cheek. "It's not over yet."

"What can we do?"

"I don't know." Noah let out a breath of frustration.

"Are they from Naamah?"

"Hard to say, but I don't think so. They're not paying too much attention." Noah ruffled his hair. "How do we get through?" He lightly pounded his forehead with his fist, as if such an action could speed up his thoughts.

Be brave. Don't give up now. Suddenly, an idea came to mind. She placed a hand on his chest and looked at him with a gleam in her eye. "Let's go swimming."

"What?"

"Well, you're not as fast as Aterre, but we don't need speed, just silence. Forget about using the dock. Let's swim to the boat."

"They'll see us for sure." He stared at the sky. "Unless those clouds block the moonlight." He pulled his head abruptly back down and looked at her. "Wait. I didn't know you could swim."

"I grew up on the water, with a shipbuilder for a father. Of course I can swim."

Noah shook his head and tightened his grip on her, pride and amazement spreading over his features. "I could just kiss you right now."

She tilted her head and studied his eyes as he looked into hers. His love and admiration shone back at her without a trace of deception or guilt. Whatever had happened earlier with Naamah, his conscience was clear. She smiled. "Well, since we have to stay here for a bit, what are you waiting for?"

He eagerly accepted her offer. Suddenly pulling away, he looked at her closely.

"Em, you should know what happened earlier tonight. And I'd rather tell you sooner than later."

"Very well."

"Here." He led her parallel to the water, circling around to approach the boat from the other side. Hiding behind an outcropping of trees, they made their way close to the shoreline, putting them more than two hundred cubits from the guards.

"There, I can see them between the leaves of the brush."

"So tell me about today." She nestled close to him.

"Em. . . ." Noah paused, looking serious. "This whole thing . . . the arrest. . . . All of it was a setup. Naamah, she, uh, offered herself to me."

"What?" Emzara took a step back so she could see his face.

"She staged the execution so she could pretend to rescue me. She wanted. . . ." He stopped.

Emzara gently rested her hand on his cheek, and he drew a deep breath.

"The whole point," he went on, "was to get me to her room where she did her best to seduce me. One moment we were talking about the ceremony, and the next I had to keep my eyes closed."

The gaze he fixed on her showed no deceit, but she couldn't stop the question hovering on her lips. "So nothing happened?"

"Absolutely nothing. She repulses me."

Emzara balled up her fists while she turned and glared at the ground. *How dare she! How dare she try to take my husband!* For a long moment she stood there, warring with the anger at Naamah and, she realized, even at Noah.

Closing her eyes, Emzara pulled in and released a deep breath. No. She could not blame Noah for being pure, for being blind to Naamah's trap. Unsure of what to say, she softly leaned her head against her husband's chest.

"I got out of there as soon as I could. Garun was on duty, and he helped me reach you at the ceremony. He also cautioned me that she may not give up and might seek revenge as soon as the ceremony's over."

She shuddered. "I need to know. Were you ever attracted to her?"

Though she wasn't looking at him, she felt Noah shake his head. "I can't deny that she's beautiful and talented, but she could never measure up to you in any way. You completely captivate me."

Straightening her shoulders, she turned back to face him. "I trust you. It's hard to hear, but I'd rather know than not."

Noah nodded. "And I wanted you to know right away, but not in front of the others."

The two sat together in the silence as Noah watched the sky. She closed her eyes and silently thanked the Creator for giving her a faithful husband. After some time, Emzara's thoughts drifted to home. She imagined walking hand-in-hand with Noah near the waterfall where he had proposed to her, but her brief reverie ended as Noah kissed her forehead. "It's as dark as it's going to get. And you have some swimming skills to show me."

Emzara reached up and brushed his face with her hand. "Do you really think this is a good plan?"

Noah nodded. "We'll make it."

She pursed her lips and turned away. *Why are you always so optimistic?* Then she shook her head, realizing that his confidence was one of the many aspects she admired about him. "Well, either way, we're in this together." She hitched up the loose fabric that hung around her ankles and wove it into the sash in the middle of her garment, noting that her husband was fully aware of her preparations. Queasiness struck her as her mind pictured his earlier encounter with Naamah, but it dissipated as she reminded herself of his faithfulness to her. "Ready?"

The two eased slowly into the cool water, packs strapped around their waists. They paddled noiselessly into deeper water, and she could feel the tug of the extra weight from the soaked belongings. Kicking harder and keeping her nose above the water, she concentrated on the safety of the boat. Noah kept close to her as they made slow progress. *Just a few more strokes.* She kept her limbs beneath the water, ensuring silence and minimal splashing.

"Stop!"

She slowly turned toward the dock, still paddling in place to keep her head above water. The guards now stood and blocked two figures from stepping onto the dock.

Noah gestured for her to hurry. "I don't know what's going on, but let's take advantage of the diversion."

When the side of their vessel loomed above them, Noah pulled himself aboard, then turned to haul up the sodden bundles Emzara handed to him. She held up a hand, and he lifted her from the water with a gush of sound that made her wince. Across the deck, a crew member turned.

Emzara held up a finger in front of her mouth, and the man's lips snapped closed as he recognized her. A familiar voice rang out from the shore, causing the crewman to spin in that direction.

Ashur!

"Look, we simply want to get onto our ship. That one." There was a pause, as if the unseen speaker were pointing. "We've no interest in the other. Why would we try to steal the king's vessel, when we're with the company that brought it?"

"He speaks truth." Farna's strong voice joined the conversation. "You may let them pass."

"You know this man?" one of the guards asked.

"Of course," Farna said, sounding almost bored. "He came with our delegation. Ashur, what are you needing this time of night?"

"We couldn't sleep after the festival, so we decided to pay you a visit."

It's Zain! Emzara slid behind a large cargo crate, squatting so Noah could crouch over her as they both peeked around the corner to see the action on the dock.

"Do they have your permission to proceed then?" the guard called.

"Sure." Farna chuckled. His sandals made a hollow slap as he jumped onto the dock and strode toward the cluster of men. "Well, maybe not the shorter fellow. You may want to detain him."

One of the soldiers reached for Ashur but was stopped by his leader's hand on his chest. "He was being sarcastic, Kotic."

"Sorry about that." The guard pointed to the other side of the dock, where Lamech's boat rocked in the gentle swell. "The king wants to make sure his new acquisition is protected."

"Can't be too careful," Farna said. He led Zain and Ashur to the boat and helped them climb aboard. Keeping his voice down, he said, "Now we just need Noah and Emzara."

Noah shifted and stuck his head out from behind the crate, speaking barely above a whisper, "We're here."

"How did . . . ?"

"We saw the guards and didn't want to risk it."

Farna took in their soaked state and then looked at his crew. "Get us moving now." He turned back to Noah and Emzara. "Two of those men are the ones I've been teaching to sail the ship. But I'm glad you played it safe."

Noah turned to Ashur. "I can't believe Zain found you so fast. What happened?"

Ashur shrugged. "I was having a good time when I looked up and noticed that you had all left. I made my way through the crowd, toward the guesthouses, and ran into Zain."

Zain shook his head. "I'm just thankful I didn't have to wade through that mob again." He shot Noah a sober look. "Naamah was already gone, and things were rapidly getting out of hand."

Farna gestured with his hand and stated in a husky growl, "Loose the ropes, men. Let's get out of here."

The crew jumped to obey, freeing the boat, then grabbing pushpoles to shove away from the dock.

"You there!"

Emzara looked up to see about a dozen men with torches approach the dock. The leader called out again. "You! Guards!"

The four soldiers stood at attention as Emzara ducked out of sight.

"Have you seen a man and a woman come this way? We're under orders from the princess to find them."

"No woman, sir. Just the captain and crew and a few of the delegation."

"Be on lookout. No one gets on or off that ship."

On the deck, the puddles left by Emzara and Noah now glowed faintly gray as the first flush of dawn eased over the horizon. "Guess it was worth that swim."

He flashed a grin. "Completely worth it."

"Why is that ship moving?" the leader of the newcomers asked.

"It's — hey! Stop!"

"Move." Farna barked the order, and their sail shot up, flapping then stretching taut as the wind filled it. The ship jerked forward.

Emzara wrapped her arms tightly around her middle as the men on the dock rushed into the king's ship.

Farna glared at the sail. "Come on," he muttered, rapidly tapping his fingertips. "From where they sit, they can still cut us off."

Emzara stood with the others, watching breathlessly as the bow of the Havilite ship pivoted, facing theirs. A few hard shoves from the shouting men would make Farna's warning a reality.

Suddenly a long screech accompanied by a dull groan filled the early morning air. A yell and two distinct splashes followed. Emzara gripped the side of the boat. *What now?*

Farna swabbed his face and let out a laugh. "Looks like they forgot their lessons already."

Puzzled, Emzara squinted toward the other boat. The last upright of the dock was severely bent. In fact, the whole dock looked lopsided, and the stern remained in its original position. *It's still attached!* In their haste and inexperience, the new crew had forgotten to check all of the moorings and the last one held their ship firmly in its grip. Two crewmembers were in the water. One swam for the dock, and the other struggled to stay above water. A guard on the boat quickly shed his armor and jumped in to help him.

Breathing a sigh of relief, Emzara turned her eyes to what she hoped would be her last view of Havil before taking her place at Noah's side.

Chapter 3

Iri Geshem — Noah's 49th year

Noah kissed Emzara on the top of the head and loosened his embrace. "I'll be home in a little while."

Emzara glanced at Tubal-Cain and Adira, who were busy saying their farewell for the evening, and then at Aterre, who rested on a low bench on the other side of the room. Shaking her head at Noah, Emzara curled the left side of her mouth. "Behave yourself."

"Me? Of course." He chuckled and hitched a thumb toward Aterre. "I'm not the one you need to worry about."

"Mmhmm." She gave him a quick kiss. "Let's go, Adira."

"I'm coming."

As Emzara turned to leave, she called back over her shoulder, "Don't let my husband get too silly tonight."

Tubal-Cain laughed. "I'm sure he'll do that on his own."

"Evening peace, Zara." Aterre's playful tone demonstrated he had no intention of heeding her request.

"And that's our sign to leave." Emzara shook her head as she held the door open for Adira. She took a final glance at Noah and smiled. "Evening peace, boys."

Noah smirked and watched her for a moment before closing the door. He picked up his leaf brew from the low table and relaxed on a cushion across from Aterre.

Aterre shifted to make room for Tubal-Cain. "I hate to say it, but pretty soon you won't have to let her go each night."

Sitting down, Tubal-Cain sighed. He put his feet up on the table in the center of the room. "Our wedding can't come soon enough."

"You two complement each other well." Aterre turned up his palms one at a time as if weighing one against the other. "She's pretty and sweet, and you're ugly and grumpy."

Tubal-Cain slapped Aterre's arm with the back of his hand. "You sure you aren't thinking about Zara and Noah?"

"Oh, them too."

"Well, if that's how it works," Noah said, "then I must be all sorts of dreadful things, because Em is wonderful in every way."

Tubal-Cain pretended to gag. "Stop him before I lose my evenfeast."

Noah grinned and threw a pillow at him. "As if you're any better. Lately, it's always 'Adira this' and 'Adira that.' And you aren't even married yet."

"He's right," Aterre said. "She's all you talk about."

Clasping his meaty hands together behind his head, Tubal-Cain reclined. "Beats discussing the weather or blacksmithing." He eyed Aterre before continuing. "She's all I want to think about every waking moment of each day."

"Ugh, you two are intolerable." Aterre held his palms up. "Since when did our game nights turn into this?"

"Since Adira agreed to be my wife." Tubal-Cain let his words trail off as if he were daydreaming about her.

"Not again." Aterre let out an exasperated sigh while the two other men laughed.

"So you really don't care what your father will think?" Noah asked, eyeing Tubal-Cain.

"I wouldn't say that I don't care. Of course I want my father to like her, but we're so far from him, I'm not sure it'll be an issue."

"But isn't the son of a king supposed to marry another person of high status?" Aterre asked.

"I've heard of that in other places, but my father's the first king of Havil, and he hasn't been in that position very long. I'm not sure if he's even given much thought about his successor. That will probably be centuries from now."

"I can't imagine you being the king of Havil," Aterre said.

"Really? Why?"

"I just don't picture you enduring the strict schedule and all the formalities." Aterre tilted his head. "And there's that whole ugly and mean thing."

A not-so-gentle nudge from Tubal-Cain resulted in a lighthearted wrestling match.

Ignoring the two of them, Noah sipped his brew before setting the vessel on the stony floor. Across the room, salty air wafted through the open window facing the beach, carrying a soft chill along with it. To Noah's right, a short hallway led to Tubal-Cain's room across from a kitchen and dining area.

Beyond the outer wall of the house to Noah's left stood Tubal-Cain's busy forge. In just three years, the blacksmith had taken on two apprentices, and he still needed another one to meet the steady supply of orders for his metal implements. Noah himself often came by on days off to learn the basics.

"Your place looks like it's almost ready," Noah said.

Tubal-Cain tried to catch his breath. "And I have you to thank for that. I've told you before, you're the best woodworker I've ever seen."

Noah winked. "I know."

Aterre cleared his throat. "And you have me to thank for getting you and Adira together."

Tubal-Cain laughed. "Yes, I suppose I should thank you for the hundredth time for locking Adira and me in the forge's office so that I'd be forced to talk to her."

"You're welcome," Aterre said. "Come to think of it, Noah, I'm the one that brought you and Zara together, too."

"Yes, and I believe I've already thanked you a hundred times. Isn't that enough?"

Aterre grinned. "Once more would be nice."

"Thank you for embarrassing me in front of Em."

Tubal-Cain stroked the short beard on his chin. "You know, you should open up a shop where you find matches for people. You could call it, You'll Thank Me Someday."

The three men laughed as Noah and Tubal-Cain tried to outdo one another over names for the proposed store.

Noah sat up straight and looked at Aterre. "Wait, I have a better idea. A much better idea."

"Well, it can't be any worse than the last one." Aterre dramatically dropped his head into his hands.

Noah pointed at his friend. "Since you played such a key role in helping each of us find a wife, I think we should return the favor."

Tubal-Cain bolted upright. "That's a great idea. It's our turn to play matchmaker."

Aterre shook his head. "I was wrong. It could be worse."

"No, this is perfect." Noah squinted as he pretended to size up Aterre. "Let's see. I've got just the right person in mind."

Aterre feigned disinterest. "Who?

Noah tried to stifle his amusement. "How about Pohal?"

Aterre crinkled his nose. "No thanks."

"Why not? She's a good baker," Tubal-Cain said. "You'd be well fed and. . . ."

"Not interested."

"Why not?" Noah asked, knowing full well the answer. Aterre frequently complained about her squeaky, high-pitched voice. "Just think, she could sing you to sleep every night."

Aterre snorted. "No, thank you. I'd rather listen to Taht sing a lullaby."

Through momentary breaks in his laughter, Tubal-Cain said, "I've got one."

Aterre rolled his eyes. "This ought to be good."

"What about Bakur's niece, Ehiluel?"

Aterre folded his arms. "Nope. Not interested."

"What's wrong with her?" Tubal-Cain asked. "She's nice. She's pretty. She's intelli — oh, that's the problem. She's smart."

"No, that's not it." Aterre folded his arms across his chest. "I'm just not attracted to her."

"Fine, so you're not interested in the pretty type." Tubal-Cain looked at Noah and shrugged. "Picky picky." He stared at the floor before shifting his gaze back to Aterre. "I know!"

Aterre rolled his eyes. "How long do I have to put up with this?"

"As long as it takes," Noah said, enjoying the chance to tease his friend.

"Fletti, the stonemason's daughter."

"Are you crazy?" Aterre asked.

Tubal-Cain feigned offense. "What? I think she likes you."

"Yeah, she asked about you the last time I saw her." Noah leaned in and winked. "She said she wanted to kiss you."

"Ah, I knew it," Tubal-Cain said. "She's the one."

Aterre shook his head. "Right, like she'd say that to either of you madmen."

Noah angled his head to one side and challenged his friend. "But what if she did?"

Aterre yawned. "I'd rather kiss a grendec."

All three erupted in laughter.

After several moments, Noah tried to catch his breath as an idea came to mind, but it only made him laugh harder. Finally, he held up a hand and fought to put on a serious face. "Alright, I found your perfect match. Last one."

"It'd better be." Aterre's expression showed that he had grown weary of this game.

"Who is it?" Tubal-Cain asked before taking a drink of his leaf brew.

Noah strained to keep his composure. "She lives close by."

"Who?" Aterre asked.

"You're comfortable around her. She's got several qualities to make the ideal wife and . . . she's not *too* much older than you."

Noah waited to allow the tension to build. When he could no longer hold it in, he blurted out, "Nmir!"

Aterre stared at Noah in disbelief. "She's probably 600!"

Tubal-Cain sprayed the contents of his mouth all over the table as he keeled over in raucous laughter. Stoically, Aterre crossed his arms until he cracked and joined Tubal-Cain's merriment.

Noah reared back and howled until his stomach hurt.

The cacophony almost drowned out a knock at the door. Being closest to the entrance, Noah barely heard the sound and pulled himself up, desperately trying to gather his wits.

Another knock sounded, followed by a woman's voice. "Hello? Are you still open for business?"

As if he had been bitten, Aterre jerked to his feet and pushed his fingers through his hair. "I'll get it."

Tubal-Cain blocked his path. "She's asking for the blacksmith. That's me." Tubal-Cain walked to the door and opened it. "May I help you?"

"Evening peace." The woman's soft voice stood in sharp contrast to the male jocularity moments earlier. "I'm sorry for disturbing you this late at night, but the latch to our bovar pen broke, and we need it repaired as soon as possible."

Tubal-Cain took the damaged copper part from her. "Certainly. Please, come inside."

Noah started to introduce himself, but then he recognized her as Jitzel, Cada's daughter. No longer the little girl who brought water to her father's farmhands on hot days, Jitzel had transformed into a beautiful young woman. Standing nearly as tall as Aterre, her braided brown hair dropped to the middle of her back beneath her broad shoulders. Her strong, dark arms reminded Noah of his mother's arms — arms that had labored outdoors for countless days.

Her light brown eyes blinked. "Oh, hello, Noah. I haven't seen you in so long, but Aterre talks about you from time to time."

Noah nodded. "It's good to see you again."

Jitzel looked past Noah and quickly glanced away. "Aterre. What are you doing here?"

Aterre hurried to join them near the door. "Evening peace. It's um . . . I, uh . . . what happened to the gate?"

Jitzel peeked up at him and blushed. "I'm not sure. All I know is that Father wants it fixed right away. And I . . ." She looked at Aterre again. "And since I was already planning to head into town, here I am."

"You came to the right place." Tubal-Cain bent down to tie on his sandals. "I can bend this piece back into shape, and that should last you for a little while. But give me a few days, and I'll make one that's much stronger."

"Wonderful." Jitzel turned away from Aterre and faced Tubal-Cain. "Father will be so grateful."

"I like when the boss is happy," Aterre said. "Jitzel, what . . . why were . . ." He took a deep breath.

Noah had never seen his friend flustered like this before. *Is this what I was like around Em? Oh, this is going to be amusing.*

"Why were you planning to come into town tonight?" Aterre finally asked.

Jitzel smiled and looked away again.

A knowing grin crept across Noah's lips, and he wished his friend would look over to catch his expression, but Aterre was too absorbed to notice.

"I wanted to pick up a few supplies." She gestured to the small pack slung over her shoulder. "And I haven't been across the river in a long time. I guess I missed seeing different faces."

Tubal-Cain stepped past her into the doorway. "The tools I need are in the shop. Anyone want to join me?"

Although longing for some playful revenge, Noah decided not to embarrass Aterre. At least for now.

"I'd like to see your workplace," Jitzel said before following him outside. She glanced over her shoulder. "Are you coming too?"

"We'll be right there." Noah put a hand on Aterre's shoulder to prevent him from rushing after her. Keeping his voice down, he asked, "Would you rather continue stammering in here, or do you prefer to make a fool of yourself in the shop?"

Aterre tensed. "Don't you dare say anything."

"No wonder you weren't interested in any of the women we mentioned." Noah grinned.

"I mean it, Noah."

"So now you know how it feels to be on the other side. It's not easy, is it?"

"I hate it. I wish I could say the right words around her."

Noah chuckled. "I could do it for you."

"Don't. I work for her father, and. . . ."

Noah raised his eyebrows. "That didn't stop you from embarrassing me in front of Em."

Aterre's eyes widened. Noah had rarely witnessed this level of desperation in his friend. "Please. I'm begging you."

Sighing, Noah held the door open. "I'll behave."

Aterre eased his shoulders. "And in return for that, I promise never to set you up with anyone ever again."

"Haha. Deal."

They stepped outside, into the fading light, and Noah spotted Tubal-Cain and Jitzel close to the forge. "Come on, Aterre. Don't let her get away." He jogged to catch up to them, Aterre on his heels.

"Jitzel," Noah said, "it's already getting pretty dark, and this will take a little while." He grinned at Aterre. "I think one of us should make sure you get home safely."

"Thank you, Noah," she said. "That's very sweet of you, but . . ."

"I'm sure Aterre wouldn't mind, would you?"

Aterre scratched the back of his neck and looked at her. "No, um, I mean, I'd be happy to walk you home." He inhaled. "That is, if you don't mind."

Jitzel blushed. "I'd like that. Thank you."

Aterre flinched and bit his lip.

"I think that's his way of saying, 'You're welcome,' " Tubal-Cain said.

Jitzel looked away. "I know. He doesn't talk much."

"Who? Him? He talks all the time." Tubal-Cain paused and then slowly lifted his head as he seemed to grasp the situation.

"Does he?" A bemused expression crossed Jitzel's face, and she laid a hand on Aterre's forearm. "You're so quiet at work when I bring you your midmeal."

"That sure is strange." Noah caught Tubal-Cain's attention. "Any idea why he'd be so quiet at work?"

Tubal-Cain looked straight at Jitzel. "I can only think of one reason." He held up the broken latch. "I'd better repair this so you two can enjoy your evening together. Just the two of you. Walking and talking."

Aterre froze and Jitzel stared at the floor. But she didn't let go of his arm.

CHAPTER 4

Ara's shoulder and arm muscles flexed as he strained to pull the recently secured beam out of position. Shifting his stance, he grunted as he pushed against the wood. Finally giving up, he sat down on the deck and looked at his son-in-law. "These new brackets from Tubal-Cain are much better. The joints are as strong as a superglider's bite."

Noah nodded, eyebrows raised. "Didn't I tell you that?"

Ara stretched his fingers before curling his arm up to show off his bicep. "You did, but they needed to be tested by a strong man."

Noah snorted. "Hmm. When Tubal-Cain gets back, I'll ask him to check. You're getting too old for this."

"Too old? I'm not even 300. Just reaching my prime."

"That's good timing then. If these new joints hold up in the water, I think business will really take off."

After guzzling his drink, Ara set the jar down and stared across the beach toward town. "We might be able to double, even triple the size of our boats."

"And what about crossing the sea?"

"I think it might be possible for our next model." Ara turned to Noah. "But I'm not sure anyone here is anxious to do that anymore."

The image of the massive serpent idol on the platform in Havil flashed through his mind, followed by a memory of Naamah in her room. Noah shook his head to banish the recollections. In spite of the inauspicious trip to Havil, he still craved adventure. He wanted to take

Emzara on a long voyage to explore the world's unknown wonders. "Perhaps not anywhere near Havil," he said, "but I think the world might be a bigger place than we've imagined. I want to see it."

Noah stood and jumped from the boat onto the sand. He thumped the partially constructed hull with his palm. "So how big do you want to make the next one?"

Ara joined Noah and they walked toward his office. "We'll need to do a lot of planning, but we'll probably start with something about 50 percent larger, and if that works, we'll gradually increase the size. We have to work with the ratios still to make sure it's as sturdy as possible. You aren't the only one who'll want to cross the sea. We're going to have trouble filling all the orders once word gets out that the ships are strong enough." Ara stopped and looked back at the water, saying nothing for a long moment as he stared off across the waves.

"Is something wrong?" Noah asked.

"Maybe. Speaking of stronger boats, Zain told me that Bayt is back in town."

"Bayt? Is he the man who wouldn't listen to you and nearly drowned?"

Ara nodded. "Then he came back here and tried to destroy my business. Hopefully, time has calmed his anger."

"That would be . . ." Noah broke off as he spotted something out in the bay, far beyond Ara's ship anchored in the shallows. "A boat is heading this way." He pointed to the vessel. "Who do you suppose it is? Not Farna — he would come from the river."

"And he's not due for another week at least." Ara held up a hand to block the glare. "Could be from one of the coastal towns I've worked with in the past."

The men continued watching as the ship steadily came nearer. At last Noah could make out a yellow banner above the sail. A sinking feeling hit his stomach. "That's the boat we made for King Lamech." Noah sighed. "And just when I hoped we were finished with that wicked place."

Ara narrowed his gaze at the boat. "Should we be worried?"

Attempting to count the number of people on board, Noah squinted. The light from the morning sun reflected spectacularly off the water, making it impossible to discern individuals yet. "I'm sure there's no threat of attack. But I'd definitely be concerned about the influence they might have here. And if Naamah's there, I'd rather not stick around."

"Emz told me about that." Ara put a hand on Noah's shoulder. "I'm proud of you. Thank you for honoring my daughter and the Creator."

Noah nodded. "I believe the Most High protected me that night." He shuddered and looked Ara in the eye. "Thank you for raising Em to follow the Creator."

Ara tightened his grip. "If our trust in the Most High is to be tested by the Havilites, I'm glad to have you by my side." He looked up and down the empty beach trail. "I think we're going to have to be the welcoming party. Stay with me?"

Nodding, Noah walked toward the point on the shore where the boat would likely land. Using a hand to shade his eyes, he strained to make out the figures on board. "I see the king, and it looks like he has about four guards with him, as well as some women. But I don't recognize them." He let out a deep breath. "That's good."

As the ship neared, about a dozen curious townsfolk arrived on the beach. Noah motioned for them to come over and then spotted Emzara leaving her office. He waved to get her attention.

Emzara hurried to join him. "What's everyone doing?"

"Looks like King Lamech decided to pay us a visit."

"If Naamah is here . . ." Emzara balled her hands into fists.

Noah stepped close to her and rubbed her shoulder tenderly, lowering his voice. "I don't see her. But no matter what happens, we need to stay calm and treat our visitors with respect."

"With the same respect she showed us?" Emzara mumbled under her breath before slowly turning to Ara. "Baba, you're on the council now. Can't you just tell them to leave?"

He shook his head. "Not without consulting the rest of the elders. And I don't think it would be wise to make enemies. We'll greet them and be respectful. Let's take this opportunity to show them how followers of the Most High live." He put an arm around his daughter. "Imagine what could happen if their king started following the Creator."

Relaxing her shoulders, Emzara nodded.

Noah and Ara approached the water as the craft reached the shallows. Noah raised his voice and held up a hand. "Morning peace, King Lamech. I'm surprised to see you."

Dressed in a blue-trimmed golden wrap, the king smiled broadly from his place at the bow. "Ah, young Noah. Morning peace to you. How good to see you again."

Noah stepped into the water and caught the rope a guard threw down as the vessel slid to a halt. He looked up at the king and pointed to his left. "Our pier is over there on the river. But this should be fine here until the tide rises late in the day." He held a hand out to the king. "Let me help you."

Ignoring the proffered hand, Lamech leapt down with a splash that sent water halfway to Noah's chest. He stretched his arms out and yawned, making the scar on his right cheek bunch into a knotty red line. "It feels good to be on land again. Took me three days to get used to all the motion."

"I know what you mean." Noah chuckled.

Lamech glanced back at the Havilites on the boat. "Do you mind if they come ashore as well?"

"Of course not." Spotting Garun among the group, Noah gave him a quick nod. It settled his heart a bit to know at least one person on board followed the Creator. He hoped for an opportunity to talk to him soon.

A half-dozen splashes sounded as several men jumped into the shallows, each holding a bundle above his head. When Garun and another guard had debarked, they turned to help a slight, middle-aged man and the three young women hop from the deck. Even wading through the shallow water, the girls moved with a grace that reminded Noah of the dancers who had performed with Naamah in the king's dining hall during his first visit to Havil.

One of the remaining guards stepped to the bow. "Sir, do you want me stay here with the boat?"

Lamech pointed to the river. "You and Bachamel take it to the pier and tie it up." He turned to Noah. "If that's alright with you."

Noah nodded. "It'll be more secure there. So what brings you to Iri Geshem?"

"Oh, I got tired of sitting in Havil all the time. I needed to get out and see some of the world. What good is a ship if you never sail it? So I thought I'd tackle a few tasks in one trip. Put the new ship through its paces, travel the world a bit, and stop in here to see how my son is doing."

He glanced at his surroundings and patted the ship's hull. "And this must be the place where you built my boat."

Noah gestured to Ara. "Actually, this is the man who designs and makes the boats. I work for him. This is my father-in-law, Ara. Ara, this is King Lamech of Havil."

The king grinned. "You invented these incredible vessels?"

"I did. I trust yours is sturdy."

"Indeed, it is. I'd like to talk to you about ordering several more."

Without warning, a bitter laugh sounded from somewhere in the small crowd. "Why would you want to do that? You're lucky to be alive, riding in one of Ara's boats."

Noah spun to locate the source of the angry voice, and it did not take long to recognize the speaker. A short man with a long, scraggily beard pushed his way to the front of the group of villagers. A ragged wrap wound about his wiry frame, and a long dagger hung from his belt. His wild eyes, full of hatred, shot Noah a glance before locking onto Ara. He looked very much as Noah imagined he would. Apparently, time had not cooled Bayt's anger.

Noah pointed at the man and stepped forward. "If you had followed Ara's directions, then. . . ."

Ara put his hand on Noah's chest to stop him. "Don't worry about him. My work speaks for itself."

Noah took a deep breath, nodded, and then moved back to stand by Em.

Lamech measured Bayt for a moment before shaking his head. He faced Ara. "As I was saying, I'd like to talk to you about ordering several more ships."

Ara raised an eyebrow. "Sounds like a discussion for later." His words came out slowly, and when Noah caught his eye, he could clearly read the reluctance there.

Lamech, too, seemed to sense Ara's hesitation. His gaze shifted from the older man to Noah, and then to Emzara. "And you must be Noah's lovely wife he spoke so highly of. I remember seeing you sitting by my wife, Adah, during the ceremony."

Emzara smiled, but Noah could tell it was forced. "Yes sir. I'm Emzara."

"A beautiful name for an even more beautiful woman."

Some of the coolness left Emzara's smile as Lamech took her hand. "Thank you."

"You and your husband are always welcome back in Havil." Releasing Emzara, he turned to Noah and gestured to Tubal-Cain's workplace. "Is my son around? That looks like a forge over there."

"You have a keen eye. That's his shop, but he isn't here today." Noah bit his lip and looked down. He knew Tubal-Cain wanted to share the news, but this unforeseen situation changed things.

"I suppose he's out looking for ores around here," Lamech said.

Noah chuckled. "He'd better not be — at least not right now. He wanted to be the one to tell you this, but he just got married. He and his wife, Adira, planned to be away for a few weeks to celebrate. They should be back within a week."

Lamech's eyes narrowed, and for the briefest instant, Noah thought he glimpsed anger in the flinty eyes. "Married? Tubal-Cain? Without sending word to me?"

"Adira's perfect for him." Emzara took a step forward, and Lamech's mask slipped back into place as he turned to meet her sparkling eyes. "She's smart, funny, beautiful, and is completely devoted to your son. You should see them together. And she follows the Creator. . . ." Emzara flinched and broke eye contact with the king. "And she, uh, she's my best friend. Everyone loves her."

Lamech arched an eyebrow and smiled. "Well, if she's anything like you, then I'm sure my son will be very happy."

"That he is." Noah tilted his head toward the boat he and Ara had been working on earlier. "Would you like me to show you around the shipyard?"

"Maybe later. I wonder if you might show us a place where we could lodge while we're here. Perhaps that friend of yours has space? I'd like to rest in a bed that isn't rocking on the waves."

Noah looked questioningly at Ara.

"Sir, allow me to take you to Ashur's," Ara said. "Noah has an errand to run, and then he can catch up with us in town."

"Thank you." He held out an arm and smiled at the gathered townsfolk. "Please, lead the way."

"Certainly. Come with me." Ara took several steps before stopping. "Ah, just a moment. I've forgotten. . . ." He hurried back to Noah.

"An errand?" Noah kept his voice low.

"Yes. We'll take a longer route. Run and inform the council members about this." He turned to leave and raised his voice so the king could hear him. "Meet us at Ashur's when you're finished."

"I'll see you there."

Ara hustled to catch up to the unexpected guests, and most of the bystanders followed the entourage toward Sarie's Bakery on the road that Noah and Aterre had taken to the shipyard during their first visit to Iri Geshem.

Emzara sidled up to Noah. "I'm coming with you."

Noah squeezed her hand. "I hoped you would." He led her to the road to Ara's house, which would allow them to take a shortcut into town. "As soon as we're out of view, we'll need to move quickly."

"I don't like this," she said. "Lamech — coming here. I don't like it at all. Did you see his face when you told him of Tubal-Cain's marriage?"

"I did, and I don't like him coming here, either. I don't want anything to do with Havil anymore — especially their serpent god." Noah picked up the pace a little. "I hate what he stands for, but I must admit, he's never been anything but kind to me. He can be quite convincing, can't he?"

"He's very cunning. I can see why people follow him." Concern spread across her face. "You don't think Baba will fall for his lies, do you?"

"Never. He's the last person that would. He's not happy about this surprise visit either."

They turned off the road and ran past Ara's house. The trail led through the grove of milknut trees and next to their own home before ending at the beach where Aterre had embarrassed Noah in front of Emzara years earlier. As the sand penetrated his sandals, Noah smiled inwardly, recalling the awkward moments that led to his first sunset with Emzara.

The sun had nearly reached its zenith, and the morning's coolness had given way to warmer air. Sea birds squawked as they flew overhead, while others trotted along the shore, pecking at the moist ground after every wave. Noah and Emzara ran west along the shoreline until they reached the path that led straight to the middle of town. They turned at the second crossroad, and from there a short jaunt took them to Zain's residence.

A well-groomed trail wound through a wide array of colorful flowers that gradually gave way to rows of large niti trees. Tucked away in the shade, Zain's two-story, mud-brick home was one of the oldest in town.

A narrow path to the left led to a well that always reminded Noah of the one on his father's farm.

Noah knocked on the door. "Zain, are you here?"

Moments later, Zain stood in the entryway. "Ah, Noah and Emzara, morning peace. What a pleasant surprise. Please come in." He stepped aside and gestured for them to enter.

Piles of folded garments separated by color rested on shelves along the back wall. Seated in the middle of the room, Zain's wife, Kmani, skillfully slid a shuttle through the strands on a large loom. She stopped and stood, motioning for them to enter. "Welcome." She started to step over a pile of garments, but seemed to have second thoughts about her ability to clear the pile with her short legs. After zigzagging around piles of fabric, Kmani met Noah and Emzara just as they stepped inside, giving Emzara a warm hug.

After shutting the door, Noah put a hand up. "We'd love to stay and visit, but there's no time. I have troubling news. King Lamech and nearly a dozen Havilites just arrived."

Zain's eyes opened wide. "What? Here?"

Kmani looked up at Noah. "What does he want?"

"He said he wanted to try out his ship and visit Tubal-Cain, but he may have other motives. We weren't sure how to handle the situation. It was such a shock."

Emzara pulled her hair back and tied it up as she spoke. "Baba thought it'd be best to be on our guard while extending hospitality to them."

Zain pursed his lips. "That's probably wise. No need to start a feud with Havil. Where are they now?"

"They're taking the long way to Ashur's," Noah said. "Ara wanted me to inform the council members immediately and meet him there. You're the first one on the way."

Zain's eyes shifted to Kmani, and he took a long breath before turning back to Noah. "You two go and warn Ashur. That should give him a little time to get ready for visitors. Let him know that I'll be there soon with the other council members."

Noah nodded.

Zain turned and kissed Kmani's forehead. "I'll be back as soon as possible."

Chapter 5

Ashur's eyes grew wide. "The king is in Iri Geshem? Now? And he wants to stay here?"

"Yes, he'll be here very soon," Noah said.

"How many people were with him?"

"About a dozen, including several guards and a few women."

"That's wonderful. Imagine, the king staying at my inn." As if realizing what he'd just said, Ashur frowned. "I mean, that's terrible. I'm not ready for such an important guest."

"What can we do to help?" Emzara asked. "We don't have much time."

Ashur's gaze darted around the dining hall. Several customers were scattered about the room, savoring their meals and enjoying one another's company. "Noah, can you clean the empty tables and straighten the chairs?"

"Of course."

Ashur pointed down the hallway to his left. "Emzara, would you mind preparing a couple of the guest rooms?"

"I can do that," she said. "Which ones?"

"I'll show you in a moment. I'll be right back." He hurried through a door in the back.

"He seems rather excited about it." Emzara bit her lip. "Almost too excited."

Noah kept his voice low. "I think he really enjoyed himself in Havil. I'm not sure he agrees with the rest of the council on this matter."

Emzara crossed her arms and leaned back slightly. "Certainly that can't be true. How could anyone from Iri Geshem want anything to do with Havil after seeing that ceremony?"

Noah shrugged one shoulder. "What if that someone didn't really follow the Creator?"

"You think Ashur doesn't . . ."

"I'm just thinking out loud, but sometimes he seems too interested in wealth and pleasure. Havil has plenty of both. I think your father suspects as much too."

Emzara opened her mouth to speak just as Ashur re-entered the room.

Ashur tossed two cloths to Noah and set a bucket of water on the table beside him. "These are for tidying up out here. Emzara, come with me, and I'll show you which guest rooms you can prepare."

Noah plunged a rag into the water and wrung it out while Emzara followed Ashur up the stairs to the second floor. The establishment boasted four guest rooms on the second floor and four on the ground level. Widely considered the best place to eat in town, the spacious dining hall often filled to capacity in the evening. Noah turned his attention to the nearest unoccupied table and wiped it down, all the while keeping an eye and ear out for the group from Havil.

Before long, Ashur led a couple down the stairs and then to the last room on the right. "I'm sorry about the inconvenience. You can stay for half price tonight."

Noah finished cleaning the tables and set the bucket near the door to the kitchen. He planned to ask Ashur what else needed to be done, but decided to check outside for the Havilites first. Looking out the front door, Noah saw a large crowd of people across the town square with Ara and Lamech at the front. He moved quickly to the landing and called to the second floor. "They're almost here."

A door slammed shut. "Coming." Ashur hurried down the steps, his sandaled feet slapping against the wooden boards. "Thank you, Noah. I owe you one."

"You're welcome. They're still on the other side of the fountain, but I thought you'd want to greet them outside."

Ashur nodded. "Thanks again."

"Do you mind if Em and I use the back exit? I'd rather not be here for this meeting."

Ashur shrugged. "I suppose if you want to. I need to go." He took a deep breath and darted out the front door.

"He sure was in a hurry."

Noah spun around at the sound of Emzara's voice. He crossed the floor and took her hand. "I am too. Let's get out of here."

He picked up the bucket and set it inside the kitchen. Ashur's kitchen hand was busily kneaded a pile of dough while, to his right, a large iron soup pot simmered above coals, giving the room its pleasant aroma. "Smells great, Enika. Ashur said we can use the back door."

"Oh, I didn't even see you. Be sure to stop in again sometime."

As they stepped into the narrow alley behind the inn, Emzara's hand flew to her stomach and then to her mouth. "Whew, I don't feel well all of a sudden. I hope I'm not going to be ill."

Noah gently rubbed her back. "Are you alright?"

"Yeah, I think so." She inhaled slowly and leaned against the building. "What do we do now?"

"After they arrive, we'll join the crowd from behind and observe." Noah wiped sweat from his forehead. He cast about and spotted a large wooden box under a nearby tree. "Do you want to rest over there for a while?"

"That sounds good." She took his hand and followed him to the shade.

Noah sighed as he sat down. "This is much better."

She reclined against him as he wrapped both arms around her. Grinning, she locked her dark brown eyes onto his. "No, *this* is much better." She closed her eyes, a contented smile etched across her tender lips.

As she rested, Noah caressed her cheek with his thumb. Her eyes moved beneath her eyelids and her nostrils flared ever so slightly with each breath. Leaning in, Noah kissed her forehead, taking in the spicy sweet fragrance of the oil she used in her hair. He tilted his head back and closed his eyes. *Creator, thank You for Emzara. What have I ever done to deserve her?* The sound of the approaching crowd turned Noah's thoughts away from his wife. *Most High, please give our council members wisdom regarding this unexpected visit. May we always seek to serve You.*

Emzara sighed. "Did they have to get here so soon?" She sat up. "We'd better go."

Before leaving the alley, they peeked around the corner and saw roughly 40 people gathered between the fountain and Ashur's inn. Ashur stood before Ara and the king, exchanging pleasantries, while the people fanned out in a semi-circle beyond them.

"Are we trying to hide?" Emzara asked.

Noah furrowed his brows. "No, but I got the impression that your father wants us to be cautious, and I agree. Let's just observe from the back. If we get a chance, I'd like to talk to Garun too."

"Oh, I didn't realize he was with them."

"Makes sense. He's been here before, so he could teach them about our city and practices." Noah took her hand and stepped out into the street. "I'm glad Nivlac isn't here."

She wrinkled her nose and frowned. "Me too."

Noah looked down the road toward the sea. *No sign of Zain yet.*

Noah and Emzara slipped into the crowd, maneuvering themselves just close enough that they could hear what was being said at the front.

"It's an honor to host you and your group during your stay," Ashur said. "Would you like to see the rooms now?"

The king put up a hand. "Thank you. My daughter spoke highly of your inn, and I am looking forward to a fresh meal. But first, I would like to address the citizens of Iri Geshem." He paused and his gaze shifted from Ashur to Ara and back again. "May I?"

"Of course." Ashur held out his hands and raised his voice. "Brothers and sisters, King Lamech of Havil would like to speak to you."

The crowd quieted, and Lamech turned to face them, taking a step back as his gaze swept from left to right across the group. With shoulders back and chin up, the king's posture matched his regal position, the dark brown scar stretching from his right cheekbone to ear only adding to the aura of fierce strength he exuded. "Men and women of Iri Geshem, thank you for kindly welcoming me and some of my people to your city. We have traveled a long way to visit you and to thank you for the marvelous ship made by my new friend, Ara."

Without a smile, Ara nodded once in acknowledgment.

"Just as you have learned about metalworking from my son, Tubal-Cain, we would like to learn all we can from you." The king looked directly at Noah, whose height caused him to stand out behind the three rows of people in front of him. "Noah may have told you that we've constructed a place of learning, what I call the House of Knowledge. I've dispatched scribes to cities throughout our region to record any of the wisdom and discoveries they find. Just imagine what we might accomplish for the good of all people if we could learn from each other."

Lamech smiled broadly and opened his arms wide. "With your blessing, of course, I'd like to learn what we can from you." He tipped his head toward one of his subjects, a man dressed in a fine silken wrap, much like the one Noah had worn in Havil. "To show our appreciation for your cooperation in this endeavor, I have prepared a bit of a gift and a brief demonstration of a fraction of what Havil could share with you."

The man opened a small chest and pulled out a handful of golden piks. Excitement grew as he handed out a small gold ball to each person in the crowd.

"I understand that you may not be familiar with gold in Iri Geshem," the king said, "but Havilah has the finest gold in the world. A beautiful metal and so easy to shape, I am sure you will find endless uses for it."

The townsfolk chatted excitedly as each received his or her gold. "It is beautiful," a woman next to Noah said as she stared at her gift. Meanwhile, Ara spoke to the king, but the commotion prevented Noah from being able to hear him.

After a few moments, Lamech held up his hands and the crowd quieted. "I hope you are pleased with that gift. Ara has informed me that I'll need to speak to the town council before any official arrangements are made. But, in the meantime, I'd like you to enjoy a small demonstration of Havil's beauty and talent."

The three Havilite women stepped forward. Joining them were three men dressed in matching blue wraps. One held a stringed instrument, another a wooden flute, and the third carried a drum. In perfect harmony, the women allowed their overwraps to drop to the ground. Two wore light blue silken gowns and the third's was a royal blue. The dresses were much more modest than the ones worn by the dancers in Havil, but still accentuated their attractive bodies.

As the musicians played, the women danced and clapped along to the tune. Thankfully, this show was also more reserved than the performance that exuded sensuality during Noah's first trip to Havil. After a few moments, the dancer in the darker outfit started to sing. Her strong voice perfectly accompanied the music.

She looks like one of the dancers Ashur spoke with at the king's table. Noah glanced at Ashur, who was engrossed. Noah put an arm around Emzara and looked into her eyes. "I'd rather watch you."

A strong hand gripped Noah's arm, distracting him from Emzara's answering smile. "Did you inform the councilmembers?" Ara asked.

Keeping his voice low, Noah said, "We told Zain and Ashur. Zain said he'd get the others immediately."

"They'd better hurry," Ara said. "I think our fellow citizens like what they see from Havil. We need to stop this before it goes on too long, but I don't want to act alone."

"What about Ashur?" Emzara asked. "He's on the council."

Noah snorted. "Look at him. Do you really think he wants any of this to stop?"

"He's right, Emz. Ashur refuses to see Havil as a danger."

The music came to a stop, and the entertainers returned to their former places. Two guards armed with black staffs stepped forward, each clad in Havil's customary light brown leather tunics partially covered by metal armor. They moved about 15 paces in front of the crowd and roughly five cubits apart before turning to face each other. In unison, they looked at the king, who responded with a nod. Both men assumed a fighting pose similar to the one Aterre had shown Noah years earlier. Following a brief pause, they tapped the two staffs together between them.

Without warning, the guard to the right yelled and spun toward his opponent with blinding speed. His strike would likely have broken the other man's leg, except that the second guard deftly blocked the blow with his own staff. A flurry of attacks, blocks, and dodges ensued. The men moved so quickly, effortlessly, and skillfully that the action soon mesmerized Noah. *I wonder how Aterre would fare against these men.* He glanced at Garun, who was positioned near the man who handed out the gold. *Can Garun fight like that?*

As the crowd grew, a few newcomers asked if anyone was going to stop the fight, but they were quickly shushed and informed that it was a demonstration.

The soldier who blocked the first attack intercepted an overhead swing and then ducked and swept the legs out from under the other man. In one continuous motion, he finished the sweeping stroke and spun completely around, swinging his staff high above and then down with reckless velocity at the other guard's head. He hit the ground when the tripped soldier moved at the last possible instant and then kicked the attacker in the chest. Still on his back, he sprang to his feet in one sudden motion and raised his staff above his face just in time to thwart another blow. The two men squared off and slowly spun in a circle, studying each other's movements.

Lamech clapped. "Excellent!"

The guards stood tall, nodded to the king, and then tapped their staffs together. As they moved back to their position near Garun, the assembly applauded.

"There he is," Ara said, pointing to the road to the beach.

Zain ran to them. "What's happening?"

Ara kept his voice down. "They are winning over the people. We need to do something."

Zain nodded. "Right. Let's talk to the king."

Ara and Zain walked around the crowd and joined Ashur near Lamech.

"King Lamech, I'm surprised to see you again," Zain said.

"Ah, Noah's steadfast companion — Zain, I believe it is?"

"That's right. I am one of the council members of Iri Geshem." Zain swung his arm out, palm up. "As are Ashur and Ara."

The king beamed and put his hand on Zain's shoulder. "Perfect. We have much to talk about."

"Indeed we do, but we cannot decide on these matters without the rest of the council," Zain said. "I just spoke with two of the other members, and we will not be able to meet together until tomorrow evening."

"Oh, believe me, I understand what that's like." Lamech looked around the town square. "That's just fine with me. As I mentioned before you got here, I want to learn all I can from your people."

Zain dipped his head and pointed to the town hall at the end of the square. "Our meeting will take place in that large building over there."

"I look forward to it." The king yawned. "Now, if you don't mind, I'd really like to see just how comfortable one of Ashur's rooms is."

Ashur chuckled. "I'm sure it'll seem just like your own room at the palace — when you close your eyes."

The king laughed and cuffed Ashur's shoulder. "I like it already. I hope the food is good too." He turned and called his subjects over. "Come. Let's see where we'll be staying."

Chapter 6

Noah and Emzara crossed the square toward the front of the council building. The air held a trace of coolness. The sun hung just above the horizon, causing the looming shadow of the building to stretch far across the grounds. He whistled lowly at the sight of the throng of citizens waiting to enter the structure. "I think we're in for a long night."

Emzara slipped her hand into his. "Looks that way."

"I sure hope we can find a peaceful resolution to this situation." Noah cleared his throat. "I really don't want to be part of this."

She pulled his hand up and kissed it. "You'll do great, if they even ask you to speak. Whatever happens, I'll be right there with you."

"Then I have nothing to worry about."

To avoid the cluster of people at the portico, Noah and Emzara turned left before the building and headed for the side door as Ara had instructed.

As they slipped into the hall, Noah glanced at the growing mass of people trying to enter through the main doors. "There's no way everyone will fit in here."

Extra benches and chairs occupied every available spot inside the hall, but they were filling up fast. Seated at the front of the room behind the large wooden desk, Iri Geshem's elders conversed quietly among themselves. As chairman, Akel had settled in the middle seat. To his right were Ashur and Oban, a farmer from across the river who was well into his 500s. To Akel's left sat Zain and Iri Geshem's newest councilmember, Ara.

As Noah and Emzara found their reserved spots in the front left row, Emzara waved to Ara.

"I don't see Aterre." Noah bit a fingernail as he watched the room fill up, although the bench to their right remained empty, having been set aside for the contingent from Havil. The overflowing crowd pressed up against the back and side walls, and their hushed conversations indicated that Noah was not the only nervous citizen. The doors stayed open to allow people in the lobby to witness the meeting.

Akel stood slowly and stretched out his arms for silence. "Please, let us begin our meeting by seeking the Creator's favor." He lifted his hands up near his face. "O Most High, Maker of heaven and earth, we ask for Your guidance during this meeting. Give us the wisdom to follow and honor You."

The old man eased himself back into his chair. "I know many of you are excited about our guests, while others are not too thrilled about their visit. Before we invite them into the hall, I'd like to ask that you treat them with respect, and please let us conduct this meeting in an orderly fashion. If you have questions for the Havilites, there may be an opportunity for you to ask them near the end of our time. Thank you."

Akel signaled to two men standing at the main doors. Moments after exiting, they reappeared with Lamech and some guards. Gesturing for the Havilites to enter the hall, each attendant stepped to one side.

In his typical manner, Lamech strode into the room with head held high and shoulders pulled back. Unlike his public appearances in Havil, the king was not wearing his crown and royal robe, but his blue and red silk wrap still stood out from the linen garments worn by the locals. His eyes scanned his surroundings before focusing on the council members. He stopped at the front of the room. "Council members of Iri Geshem." Holding out an arm, he turned toward the audience. "And citizens of Iri Geshem. Thank you for kindly hosting us in your fine city. I bring you greetings from the great city of Havil, the jewel of the sea."

"Thank you for agreeing to meet with us in this setting." Akel motioned to the empty front row. "Please, be seated."

The king nodded and allowed two of his soldiers to enter the row before him. Two more followed him, including Garun, and they all sat down in unison.

Akel cleared his throat and spoke loudly. "We have called this special session of the council to discuss your arrival." He looked at Lamech. "I know some of our citizens may have questions they'd like to ask. I've informed them that they may have the opportunity later, if you find that agreeable."

The king stood again and smiled broadly while surveying the crowd. "Of course. I'd be happy to answer any question or address any concern you may have."

"Thank you," Akel said. "And I'd personally like to thank you for allowing Tubal-Cain to live with us. He's a fine young man, and his skills have greatly benefited our people."

Lamech nodded. "Nothing pleases a father more than knowing his children are such a help to others."

Emzara squeezed Noah's arm and whispered in his ear. "Too bad the same can't be said about his daughter."

Akel continued, "I know you spoke to several people yesterday in the city square, but would you mind explaining to the council your purpose for coming here?" Akel leaned back slightly. "I want to make sure everyone has the same information before we proceed."

"Council members." Lamech's focus swept from the right side of the table to the left. "Once again I thank you for receiving us. I'm pleased to see that your hospitality has not waned since the last time I visited your lovely town."

Akel scratched his cheek. "You've been here before?"

"Long before I was king of Havil, I passed through with my father. I believe we were here only for an evening. It was much smaller then, but delightful nonetheless.

"But let me speak about this trip. Our purpose is fivefold. First, I had a desire to try out our fine vessel made by your very own councilman, Ara."

Lamech turned to the audience. "Second, I wished to visit my son." He chuckled. "But my timing seems to be off for that.

"Third, I wanted to see more of the world. Meet new people, as well as visit old friends. With such a magnificent boat, I can discover the unknown wonders of the coast from Havil to Nod."

He paused, steepling his fingers before his lips as if considering his next words. "Which leads me to my fourth reason for coming here — I started an initiative nearly four years ago — a House of Knowledge. It's a massive building." He scanned the walls and ceiling of the hall. "You could probably fit 50 of these rooms in it."

Gasps and chuckles filled the air, while from somewhere behind him, Noah heard an accusation of exaggeration.

"You think I'm joking?" Lamech raised his voice over the general murmur. "It's as large as my palace. Ashur, do you think 50 of these rooms could fit in my palace?"

Ashur laughed. "I wouldn't be surprised if you could fit a hundred of these rooms in it."

The king snorted. "You see, I am not jesting. Havil is a magnificent city, grander than anything you've ever seen. But I'm getting ahead of myself." He looked up as if trying to recapture his previous thoughts. "This House of Knowledge — our goal is to fill it with the world's combined wisdom and knowledge. I have sent scribes throughout Havilah and the surrounding lands to record what people have learned regarding medicine, agriculture, animals, religion, metallurgy, music, and technological advancements. Just think what we might be able to accomplish if we worked together and combined all our understanding." He pointed to Ara. "Thanks to your ships, we can already travel farther and faster. Imagine being able to sell your wares to a distant land. What if we could find a cure for the sicknesses in our world? We might even witness men or women live for over a thousand years. The possibilities are endless."

Akel raised an eyebrow when Lamech mentioned an extended lifespan. "Do you really believe that?"

Noah scratched above his ear. *Several people have lived into their 900s. Why does a thousand years seem so strange to Akel?*

Lamech shrugged. "I don't know the limits of what's possible. But I am willing to work hard to make this world a better place." After an awkward silence, Lamech continued. "Our final reason for coming here is that we'd like to establish official trade relations between Havil and Iri Geshem. At this point, with so few ships, I doubt there would be much trade, but I'm looking toward the future when travel between our cities could take place regularly and perhaps be much quicker."

Folding his arms over his chest, Lamech fell silent, though he continued to stand.

"Was there anything else you'd like to say before we deliberate?" Akel asked.

"No, but I'll gladly clarify anything, if needed."

"I'm sorry you missed your son. It is a pity, after you have come so far." Akel put both hands on the desk in front of him, pausing as if to further convey his sympathy. "It seems to me that we really only need to discuss your last two reasons — our potential contributions to your House of Knowledge and the question about a trade agreement. I think it would be fair to let you know that before we sent our first group to Havil, we'd decided against establishing official trade relations with your city. We'd heard rumors about certain practices, and we would like to keep those influences out of Iri Geshem." Akel glanced both ways down the table at his colleagues before fixing his sights on Lamech. "That was a few years ago, and today we have a better understanding of what your city and people are like. At this time, I'd like the other elders to share their concerns, now that you're here to address them."

Lamech's stoic expression changed little during Akel's discourse. When the elder finished speaking, Lamech bobbed his head once and then walked several paces toward the council. "Rumors you say? I find it strange that a wise and upstanding person like yourself would make a decision based on rumors."

Glancing around, Noah saw several townspeople nodding their agreement as Lamech continued in an almost injured tone. "I confess I hadn't dreamed you'd be so accusatory after everything I've done to show my goodwill toward you all."

Ashur leaned forward and addressed Akel. "Well, since I've been to Havil twice now, perhaps I should speak. That way you'll all know I'm speaking about truth and not rumors."

Noah took a deep breath and squeezed Emzara's hand. *Please let this go well.*

"Just a moment." Akel held out a hand toward Ashur and then directed it at the king. "Would you have a seat and make yourself comfortable?" The words were more of a declaration than an invitation, and for the second time, Noah caught a glimpse of anger on Lamech's face. It was slight — nothing more than a glint in the king's eye — and it vanished in a heartbeat.

When Lamech had settled on his bench, Ashur addressed the crowd. "On our first voyage to Havil, we were concerned about the impact certain practices could have on Iri Geshem, particularly activities we had heard were prominent in Havil. It's true that the Havilites, by and large, don't follow the Creator, as most of us do, but I believe that the potential benefits of trading with them outweigh the risk." He glanced at the king. "I've learned much from them during my two trips, and I hope they might learn from us as well, including, perhaps, the value of obedience to the Creator."

Oban, the beardless elder whose name Noah forgot during his first visit to the council meeting four years ago, shifted in his seat to face Ashur. "I remind you that such an agreement would stand at odds with our previous decision, which was not based on pragmatic concerns about business opportunities but on a desire to remain true to the Creator."

Zain set down his pen and pushed a small scroll to the side. "Like Ashur, I have also visited Havil twice." He looked at Lamech. "And while I thank you for your hospitality toward us, I don't believe it would be in our best interest to establish official relations. We certainly don't wish to make enemies of anyone, particularly with those who have shown us kindness. Our desire is to live at peace with all of our brothers and sisters throughout the land. My concerns are primarily based on what we observed at the ceremony, which directly opposed our beliefs. Here, we worship the Most High, the Creator. But you openly encouraged your people to worship the Serpent, the Great Deceiver. I don't believe such an action is something we can simply overlook."

"I'm glad you mentioned that, Zain." King Lamech brushed his robe, looking as comfortable as if he were ordering his next meal from a servant. "I've learned much in my time as king. When I started, I believed that I needed to use religious ideas to win the support of the people. That whole Serpent religion event was a mistake, a means to an end, if you will. I've since learned that the best way to lead my people is through setting a good example."

"Are you saying that your people no longer worship the Serpent?" Zain asked.

The king shrugged. "There are probably some who still hold those beliefs, but it wasn't too long after that ceremony that we stopped promoting them."

Noah studied Garun's face, but the guard sat perfectly still, his pose hiding any emotion.

"That would be a step in the right direction." Zain leaned his elbows on the table.

Ara cleared his throat. "I have a question that pertains less to your ability to run your city and more about the way you run your family. As anyone here can testify, Tubal-Cain is a fine young man. Many of us had the opportunity to meet your daughter as well when she visited, and she seemed to get along well with folks. But I've heard many disturbing things about her since she's returned to Havil."

The king held up a hand. "If you're referring to her role in the ceremony as priestess, I can assure you that this is another area where things have changed. You're correct, Ara, my daughter should never have been involved in something like that."

Ara took a deep breath and slowly let it out. "I was not referring to her role in the ceremony, but to her actions just prior to it."

The king opened his mouth to speak and then tilted his head to one side. "What actions?"

"She used your guards to arrest Noah, and they even detained Zain for a time. When Noah was brought to her chambers, she attempted to seduce him, though she knew he was a married man. Why would your daughter act that way?"

"I have not heard of this until now." The king slowly shook his head and looked at Zain. "You were really arrested by my guards? Did they mistreat you?"

Zain's eyes narrowed slightly as he nodded. "After they stormed into the guest house, threw Emzara on the ground, and said they were going to execute Noah."

"What?" Lamech turned toward Noah. "This is true?"

"It is." Though he wasn't thrilled about being brought into the conversation, Noah twisted halfway around so that both the council and audience could hear him. "I'd rather not discuss all the details in this setting, but it is true that Nivlac barged into our quarters, made false allegations, and threatened to execute me. After the soldiers dragged me to the courtyard, they acted like they were going to sacrifice me to the Great Deceiver. And that's when Naamah stepped in. She stopped Nivlac, but I have reason to believe that was part of the setup to have me brought to her room."

Lamech tilted his head back and closed his eyes as if coming to a realization. "I had no idea, but that explains much. When I found out that our dock had been damaged, I asked around and learned it was because she sent guards to detain you after the ceremony. She never gave me a straight answer about why she had done it, but now I understand."

Lamech faced Noah. "If she really did all that you said, then I'm very sorry for her behavior. I'd have put a stop to it immediately, if you had let me know, but I will certainly deal with this upon my return."

"I'm glad to hear it, sir." Ara sat up straight. "However, the fact remains that her actions reflect negatively on your leadership. Since you're the one who put her in a position of authority, which she abused, it calls into question the decisions you make as a leader. All the more reason for us to be reluctant to establish an arrangement with your city."

"Holding one person responsible for the actions of another is a harsh standard, council members. However," Lamech sighed, "I don't believe in blaming others for what happens under my watch. What my daughter is accused of doing is clearly wrong, and as I said before, I'll certainly deal with it upon my return. I'm afraid there is little else I can offer at the moment. If Noah had brought it to my attention at the time, we might have avoided this whole unpleasant conversation."

Ara strummed his fingers on the desk, his scowl deepening. "Not to belabor the point, but your daughter said it would make sense for Noah to have two wives because you, her father, also have two wives. The Most High created marriage to be between one man and one woman. What makes you think it's acceptable to violate the Creator's standard for marriage?"

Lamech sighed. "I do have two wives, but I only took a second wife after her husband died. She needed someone to care for her. Before I was made king, there was considerable violence around Havil. I helped bring an end to that." He rubbed his eye. "One of the many unfortunate consequences of such violence is that when married men are killed, many widows are left without a means of support. You may not agree with my decision, but I believe this was a way for me to care for a woman and her family."

Ara stroked his beard and then leaned forward. "Intentions, no matter how good they may seem, do not justify disobedience to our Creator." His face reddened slightly and his voice rose in volume.

"Oh, Baba, be careful," Emzara said under her breath.

"Zain told me that you also eat the creatures of the sea." Ara looked unflinchingly at the king. "Another direct violation of the Creator's standards."

Lamech held Ara's gaze. "Who's to say that those old stories about the first man and woman are even true? I've heard other myths about our origins that included no such prohibition. Are you really willing to negate what could become a very profitable trade agreement between us for the sake of your religious traditions? This would just be a business arrangement and has nothing to do with what the Creator may or may not have commanded us to eat."

Ara hit the table with his fist, making more than one person in the hall jump. "These things are never just business!" He rubbed his eyes with the fingers of one hand, and said more quietly, "In any trade agreement, ideas are exchanged, and it's precisely the types of ideas that you've admitted to that we don't want in our city."

Akel stood and held up both hands. "Please, everyone pause for a moment." He glanced at Ara and then the king. "There's no need to let our emotions, no matter how justified, get in the way of reaching a well-reasoned conclusion."

"My sentiments exactly," Lamech said.

Ara let out a deep breath. "Forgive me if I've allowed my feelings to color the council's decision."

Akel slowly shook his head. "There is nothing to forgive because there's nothing wrong with being passionate about these matters." Akel turned to address the crowd. "However, I question whether we're right to require adherence to our rules from those who do not share our view of the Creator." He shrugged. "Why should we expect someone to hold to our standards if they don't believe in our God?"

During a prolonged silence, Noah's insides twisted. *We might not hold them to our rules, but I wonder if we should trade with them so that we can try to help them understand the Creator's ways.*

"Are there any more questions for the king?" Akel asked his colleagues. When no one spoke up, he continued. "The council has no further inquiries. However, I'll now allow others to speak."

Murmurs spread through the audience, but no one spoke up.

Akel rubbed his forehead. "If there are. . . ."

"I have a question."

Noah and Emzara exchanged glances and turned to look toward the back of the room.

Aterre stood near the door, barely visible in the crowd standing behind the rows of benches. "I'm sorry it's not directly on point. I was going to save it until later, but since he mentioned the violence from several years back, I decided I'd ask now." Aterre stood on tiptoe so he could look at Lamech, but the king remained seated. "I'm from the land of Havilah, not very close to your city, but in the region."

"Yes. I figured that out right away." The king grinned but only turned his head enough to see Aterre from the corner of his eye. "It's good to hear familiar speech. Well, almost. You sound like you're from the western lands."

"Indeed, my accent usually gives it away." Aterre chuckled. "Anyway, my question has to do with my family. You see, about ten years ago, my village was raided in the night. My family was taken, and, from what I saw before fleeing, many people were killed. But I've never stopped wondering what happened to my mother and sisters. Do you know if there are slave traders in the region? And if so, would there be anyone you know who could help me find my family, if they are still alive?"

Lamech bowed his head. "I'm sorry to hear about this. What's your name?"

"Aterre, sir."

The king's back rose as he inhaled deeply. "Aterre." He said the name as if savoring the taste of a fine drink. "I know there's been some slave trading, particularly in the west. We've been trying to put a stop to it. I will look into this matter for you." He put a hand on the shoulder of the guard to his left. "Talk to Bachamel here and give him all the details you can. In fact, you'd be welcome to return with us to search for them."

"Thank you, sir. Maybe I will be able to go soon." His head popped up over the crowd again, and he smiled at Noah and Emzara. "But I have some important matters to take care of here first."

Akel waited for a few moments before speaking. "Thank you, Aterre. I pray that your search will not be unfruitful." He cleared his throat. "Regarding the matter of official relations with Havil, I suggest that we refrain from making a decision at this time until we can see for ourselves that the reforms Lamech mentioned are moving forward. Any objections from the council?"

The council members offered their agreement, although Ashur failed to hide his displeasure.

"Then it's decided. King Lamech, I appreciate your willingness to endure our questioning."

The king nodded. "I fully understand your decision. You show much wisdom in not rushing into these matters without all the necessary information. If you'd like to see Havil for yourself, you're welcome anytime."

"Thank you." Akel sat up straight. "Now, regarding the other matter. I think there's an easy solution. You say that you've sent scribes throughout your land to record information."

"Yes."

Akel put his palms together and pointed his hands at Lamech. "Then I assume that you've brought a scribe with you on this journey."

"Yes, we did," Lamech said. "Bedin is our most gifted scribe. I'm sure you could learn much from him, just as he could learn from your citizens."

"For the sake of clarity, are you simply seeking to leave him in Iri Geshem for a certain amount of time to record what he learns from us?"

"That's mostly correct. I'd like to leave one of my guards here as well." Lamech looked at Garun, seated to his left at the end of the bench. "Garun would be perfect for the job. He was here before, and I believe many of your citizens already know and like him. And you won't have to provide for them. They'll cover their own expenses."

"Please give us a few moments." Akel stood and motioned for the other elders to gather around him.

Noah looked at Garun, still practically motionless, as if he were a statue. He leaned close to Emzara's ear. "It'd be great to have Garun here again."

She rested her head on his shoulder. "Do you think they'll agree to it?"

"Not sure. Four of the five elders don't like Havil, but this request doesn't seem to be asking a whole lot. However, I'm not sure Lamech truly has the best intentions."

"I was thinking the same thing."

"May I have your attention." Akel eased himself down in his chair. "The council has unanimously granted the request of the Havilites to leave Garun and a scribe in Iri Geshem until the scribe completes his work."

Lamech stood and bowed slightly. "Thank you. It's my sincere hope that you'll soon see for yourselves the changes being made in Havil and that we might trade openly in the future."

"We shall see." Akel leaned over and spoke briefly to Oban.

Oban stood and raised his voice. "At our normal council meetings, we'd ask if anyone has any new business to bring up, but this was a special meeting to address the requests of the Havilites, so no further business will be discussed tonight. Evening peace to you all."

Welcome to the

Trenton Veterans Memorial Library

The library staff is always
available to assist you
in any way they can

Books

fiction, best sellers,
informational, large print,
books on CD, books on tape,
talking books for all ages,
DVDs, videos,
music CDs,
magazines,
pamphlets

Services

School group tours
Interlibrary loan
Internet access

Programs

Book Discussion Group
Storytimes for toddlers,
preschoolers & families.
Craft activities,
Computer Classes,
Special programs for adults

Check us out!

27900 Westfield Road
Trenton, MI 48183
(734) 676-9777
www.trenton.lib.mi.us
Media & Book Drop open 24 hrs.

HOURS:
Monday - Thursday
10:00 am - 9:00 pm
Friday and Saturday
10:00 am - 6:00 pm
Sunday
1:00 pm - 5:00 pm

DONATED BY
THE FRIENDS OF THE LIBRARY

Chapter 7

The sea breeze ruffled Noah's hair as he watched the vessel from Havil drift out of view on the right side of the bay. Hidden for much of the morning by gray clouds releasing a steady drizzle, the sun peeked through a clear patch in the sky, hinting that the afternoon might grow warmer. Sea birds squawked and screeched as they glided over the coast, dipping and rising in their chaotic flight patterns.

Noah folded his arms as his eyes traced the movements of one of the larger birds. "I'm glad that's over."

"I am too." Emzara smiled. "I'm surprised they left so soon. I thought he'd at least stay until Tubal-Cain and Adira returned."

"I thought so too. Perhaps Lamech was more annoyed about the council's decision than he let on."

Emzara pushed a stray lock over her ear, and the wind immediately whipped it free again. "Well, I'm happy they aren't here anymore."

They stood there in silence for a moment while Noah studied her face, a half smile creeping over his lips as his mind wandered back to the day nine years ago when they had stood in this very place and he had finally worked up the courage to tell her how he felt about her. After a time, she looked at him, her delicate brows puzzled. "What?"

"Nothing." He sighed. "I suppose I should go do some work on my day off. Thanks to our unexpected and uninvited guests" — Noah cast an exaggerated glance at Garun — "I'm behind on my work."

Garun chuckled. "And I was beginning to think you were just lazy."

"Not me, but that describes him pretty well." Noah nudged Aterre, who stood beside him, digging one toe into the sand.

Aterre looked up from the ground. "Huh? What did you say?"

"Were you even listening?"

"Sorry, no."

"Is everything alright?" Emzara asked.

Aterre bit his lip and stared at her for a moment. "Yeah, I'm fine. Listen, I need to get over to Cada's."

Emzara tilted her head. "I thought you had the day off too."

"I do, but I need to. . . ." Already walking away, Aterre turned and called over his shoulder, "there's something I need to check on."

"Will we see you later?"

Aterre just raised a hand in reply, and Emzara turned to Noah with a questioning smile. "Is he alright?"

Noah shrugged. "I don't know. He's been distracted like that for a little while."

Bits of metal clinked as Garun shifted his position. "Maybe he's thinking about finding his family. King Lamech did say something about helping him."

Noah's pulse quickened at the thought of a rescue attempt, but his excitement rapidly dampened. "But if I'm going to help him, as I promised I would, that would mean. . . ."

Emzara looked down and fidgeted with her bracelets. "Another trip to Havil."

"Maybe I can go in your place," Garun said. "When I get home, I can do some checking around. Do you know his mother's name?"

Noah stared across the bay at nothing in particular. He slowly shook his head. "I don't think I've ever asked him before. I'll find out."

Emzara pressed her hands together. "Forgive me for changing the subject. Garun, I never had the chance to thank you for warning Noah to get us out of Havil immediately."

Garun turned toward her with a small bow. "It was the least I could do after learning what Naamah planned. I was relieved when I heard that your group escaped." His prominent cheekbones rose as he smiled. "One thing's for sure. You'll never need to question Noah's love for you. The way he withstood Naa —"

"I know." Emzara's features softened as she glanced at Noah. "He told me what happened." She stepped forward and lightly kissed Garun's cheek. "But thank you for the reminder of my husband's faithfulness."

Noah smiled at Garun and gestured to Emzara with his chin. "I knew I was married to the most wonderful woman in the world."

Emzara drew back and pointed at him. "And don't you forget it." She took his hand and gave it a squeeze. "I have to check on Baba. He wasn't feeling well this morning. Enjoy the shipyard. I'll see you at even-feast. Garun, would you like to join us?"

"I'd love to, but I need to get back to Ashur's soon. Maybe tomorrow night?"

"I look forward to seeing you then." Emzara held Noah's hand against her cheek for a moment, then sighed and let it go. "Until this evening."

Noah watched her walk down the hill toward the trail through the milknut trees. As she moved out of sight, he joined Garun close to the edge of the hilltop. "Tell me something."

"What is it?"

"How can your king be so likeable at times?" Noah scratched the back of his neck. "He's been so nice to me, and offering to help Aterre. . . ." He shook his head. "But then there was the serpent ceremony and Naamah . . . and every now and then, I would catch this look. . . ."

After scanning every direction, Garun's eyes met Noah's and his countenance turned serious. "Because he's very good at what he does. He tells people what they want to hear, and when they're not paying attention, he uses his power to do whatever he wants anyway. By the time the thing is done, people rarely challenge him."

Noah held up a palm. "So was he just telling the council what they wanted to hear?"

Garun nodded and frowned. "Much of the time. He told several outright lies last night, but I couldn't say anything then. He would have exiled me and my family, sold us into slavery, or worse."

"Executed?"

"Possibly. It wouldn't be the first time he's gotten rid of someone who disagreed with him." Garun looked down. "He lied about the serpent ceremony. He hasn't put an end to it. If anything, it's grown larger each year. And he hasn't stopped Naamah from participating." He pursed his lips. "She's more involved in Nachash worship now. Ever since . . ." His gaze drifted to Noah and his eyes glinted. "Ever since that night you were there, she's been following the teachings of a strange man, a seer."

"A seer?"

"He's supposedly able to communicate with spirits."

"The spirits of those who have passed on?" Noah stroked his chin.

"More disturbing than that." Garun said. "I've heard some of the ideas he teaches her. He says that the Creator is just one of many spiritual beings, or gods, who run this world. They believe Nachash is the most powerful god, so they follow him. They think he'll reveal secrets about this world that will allow them to become the most powerful people on earth."

"Do you think these spirits exist?" Noah asked.

Garun breathed deeply. "I wish I could say that I thought it was a hoax."

"But you don't."

"No. They've learned things that no one should be able to know." He looked away. "But I think it's come at a cost. Naamah is different. She was always spoiled, but she used to smile and have a good sense of humor. Now. . . ." He shook his head. "She's cold and — I'm not sure how else to put it. But it's sad and, at times, more than a little frightening."

Noah put a hand on Garun's shoulder. "I'm sorry to hear that. Tubal-Cain will be unhappy to hear it as well."

"I'm sure he will. He was always so good to her. But I think when he left, and" — he cast Noah an apologetic look — "when you rejected her, she stopped caring about anyone else. Now she just craves power and control."

"Just like her father." Noah folded his arms again.

"Yes. They make a dangerous team." Garun tugged on the sleeve of his tunic to straighten it under his armor. "I was wrong about her sending the guards after you that night."

"What do you mean?" Noah asked. "The guards did come after us."

"Yes, but they were sent to capture Emzara."

"Em? Why?"

"For revenge. She wanted to make you beg for Emzara's life."

Noah put his thumb on his upper lip as he pondered this new information. "Does she still want that?"

Garun shrugged. "I don't know. I haven't heard her mention either of you for quite some time. As I said, ever since you left, she's been obsessed with this seer and the power he offers. She spends her days in the House of Knowledge for the most part."

"I guess that's a good thing." Noah adjusted his stance. "There isn't much we can do about it anyway, except take great care if we ever return to Havil. Which, judging from what you're telling me of Lamech, I'm not sure we'll ever do. What were some of the other lies he told at the council meeting?"

"His whole story about taking a second wife was false. Taking a second wife allowed him to flaunt his rebellion against the Creator's ways and show the people that he could do it without any consequences." Garun snorted his disgust. "His cant about leading his people by example was spot on, though. His example emboldens them to act wickedly too."

Noah shook his head. "He sounded so convincing."

"That's one of the reasons he's the king. He knows how to manipulate people into doing exactly what he wants."

"Even if it means worshiping the Great Deceiver."

Garun let out a breath as he nodded.

"So what about the scribe?" Noah asked.

"Bedin? What about him?"

"Is he really here to study our culture, like the king said, or is he here to spy on us?"

"I think he is here to record what he learns." Garun shrugged. "That's one thing Lamech didn't lie about. He really is pulling together knowledge from all over the world. He's determined to discover the path to longer life."

Noah looked askance at Garun. "How?"

Garun chuckled. "I don't know. But maybe it isn't as crazy as it sounds. According to the old stories, Greatfather Adam and Greatmother Eve were created to live forever. Maybe there's a way to at least prolong one's life."

Noah considered this, but Garun went on before he could comment.

"When I was a boy, I remember when our town received word that Greatfather died. They said he returned to the dust, just as the Creator said he would." Garun crossed his arms. "At the time, my grandfather told me what had been passed down to him by Ma'anel — one of Greatfather's sons. He said that the Most High created Greatfather from the dust of the ground and Greatmother from one of his ribs. They lived in a beautiful garden, but they were only there for a few days until the Serpent deceived Greatmother and she ate from the forbidden tree. After they sinned, the Creator banished them from the garden and cursed the ground."

"Only a few days?"

Garun shrugged one shoulder. "That's what I was told."

"My grandfather told me many of the same details, but I never heard that part," Noah said. "Also, he said that Greatfather was 930 years old when he died."

"That's what I heard too. In fact, I think the king is determined to live longer than that, so he can be seen as greater than the first man."

"He's definitely full of pride."

"Yes he is." Garun snorted. "But what he doesn't know is that he'd have to surpass 985 years to outlive Ma'anel. Then again, maybe he does know that, since he mentioned something at the council meeting about living over a thousand years."

Noah bent down to pluck a long blade of grass from the hillside, wondering about Lamech's statement. *Did the Creator set a limit on how long people could live? If He did, how could Lamech ever hope to break it?* Cupping the grass between his hands, Noah lifted it to his lips and blew a long whistling note.

He grinned at Garun's startled look. Suddenly, his thoughts shifted away from pondering such mysteries and to the man before him. "How did you ever become one of Lamech's guards?"

"Before Lamech came to Havil, I was part of the city guard. I trained men to defend themselves and to fight. But I always taught that fighting was only for self-defense." Garun bent and plucked a blade of grass of his own, but instead of raising it to his lips, he began shredding it, his mind on the past. "When Lamech arrived, he brought Sepha's teachings with him. He joined the guard and quickly rose through the ranks — you've seen him. He used his considerable charisma to entice our men to Sepha, promising not only skill and discipline, but power. Before long, he joined the town council." Shaking his head, Garun tossed the wad of shredded grass onto the ground, where the breeze tickled the strands, teasing them apart and scattering them across the hillside. "They never knew what hit them. Lamech — when he knows what he wants, he's like a force of nature, inexorable and undeniable. With the support of most of the guards, he eventually assumed control of the city and made himself king. He assigned me to guard Tubal-Cain and Naamah."

A quiet bitterness tinged with self-recrimination had crept into Garun's voice as he told his story. Noah watched the fibers of Garun's grass dance and twine among the still-standing blades, trying to figure out how to ask his next question without causing his friend more pain. "Why did no one stand up to him?"

"I ask myself that all the time. I wish I had done something right away, but I was blind. I don't think anyone could have imagined how quickly he'd rise to power and how wicked he really was."

"So what was Havil like before he arrived?"

"I'm sure it wasn't as good as I like to think it was. I can't blame the king for everything." Garun gazed across the water and rubbed his hand over his chin with a sound like sand blowing across stone. "We had problems to deal with, like violence and theft. You don't have that many people together in one place without some trouble. But since Lamech, people seem to be unashamed of their evil acts." A contemplative smile crossed his lips. "You know, I think I might take you up on your offer."

"What offer?"

"To move here."

Noah raised an eyebrow. "You'll want to collect your family, of course." He paused. "I know someone who has a boat."

Grinning, Garun gripped Noah's shoulder. "Let me give that some more thought. For now, I should get back to Ashur's to help Bedin. We're moving into that guest house today."

Chapter 8

Emzara pinched another piece of dough and arranged it with the others on the thin clay dish. Fussing over the placement, she ensured the proper spacing, then she turned to stoke the coals at the base of the stonework oven, readying the temperature so that it would be just right when she placed the tray inside.

She replaced the cover on her starter for the next time she made bread and wound the leather cord tightly on the lip. As she raised it to the shelf, she bumped it against the edge and her other hand rushed to protect and steady the clay pot. With her second attempt, she succeeded in carefully replacing it on top of the dark-stained wooden ledge.

After grabbing the broom, she glanced at the corner where a bowl sat upon a crate. *Not yet.* Shaking her head, she tried to focus on her methodical sweeping, which sent dirt and bits of food swirling around her bare feet.

The small house Noah and Aterre built had started out relatively plain, but Emzara's touches soon made it a home. After the wedding, Aterre moved in with Ara, and Noah expanded the kitchen and dining areas. It was more rustic than her childhood home, but it was theirs. *And it takes less time to sweep.*

She flicked the broom twice more before losing resolve. *I need to know.* Dropping the handle, she rushed over to the bowl. She barely flinched when the broom hit the ground behind her. Picking up the container, she stared at the contents. There was no mistaking it. Cradling the little hollowed-out bowl of sprouting grain pods, she danced around the room. She moved into the bedroom and placed the bowl next to their bed before pirouetting back through the doorway and into the well-lit main room.

Moments later, the smell of fresh bread brought her whirling thoughts back down to earth. *Alright, Em. You've had your reward. Now it's time to get back to work.* She grinned, and placed the fresh bread rounds into a square cloth. She tucked the edges of the fabric in and tied up the four corners, then set the packet on the table as she scooted her feet into her sandals and bound the straps around her ankles. Taking up the warm bundle and balancing it on her head, she left the house and joined the familiar path to her father's place. Looking to her right, she tried to spot Noah and Garun where she had left them earlier on the scenic overlook, but they were gone.

It still felt foreign to knock at her old home, but Emzara forced herself to rap on the front door before she stepped in. "Baba." Her eyes quickly adjusted to the darker space, and she realized he must have heard her approaching because he already hovered near the door.

"Emz! So good to see you." Ara pulled her in for one of his embraces.

She soaked in the comfort of her strong father and her soul warmed, knowing he was always there for her.

"I don't often see you away from the shipyard anymore." He winked. "Now that there's another man in your life."

A sympathetic smile tweaked the corners of her lips as the two of them walked into the house. "Baba, I know you weren't feeling well this morning, so I brought some bread rounds for you. And it gives me an excuse to stop by and give you some care as well."

"Ah, how you spoil me. I'm doing much better. I could've even worked today, but . . ."

"But someone who is very wise and who loves you very much gave you orders to take it easy."

"Well, we've always called you 'Boss' for a reason." His eyes crinkled up at her as he eased his body back into a pile of soft cushions near a low table in the main room.

Emzara set her bundle down in front of him and reached for an empty cup. "Here, you try one of these while I get you more water."

She made her way to the kitchen. *It's still so hard to believe. I just want to burst with this secret.* Beaming, she placed the dipper into the drawn bucket of water and refilled the mug. After forcing herself to pause and allow her facial expression to return to what felt normal, she hurried back to her father.

"Here's your —" Before she knew what was happening, she bumped into a low table and lost her footing. Awkwardly trying to right herself, she flailed for a moment and tumbled into a heap next to her father. The contents of the cup shot forward in an arc, as if at a slowed pace, and deep spots formed on the cushions and on the front of her father's tunic. "Oh, how clumsy of me!" Losing all control of her emotions, Emzara burst into tears.

Ara snorted. "It's completely fine, Emz." He laid a hand on her shoulder, causing her to sob harder. "With the balmy afternoons we've been having, this will dry in no time." He waved the worst part of his damp garment before her, emphasizing his words of comfort.

She wiped her filmy eyes. "I — I'm sorry!"

"What's wrong? You're not usually like this."

"I know." Emzara sniffed, trying to regain control of her emotions. *What is wrong with me?*

Rubbing her back in little circles, he tried to peer into her face. "This isn't about spilled water, is it? Tell me what's going on."

"Well . . ." Unwanted tears pricked at the back of her eyes again and made their way to the corners. She blinked. "I've thought it may be possible for a while, but as of today, I'm pretty sure I'm carrying your grandchild." She looked sheepishly into his face.

Now tears formed in his eyes and he hugged her tightly, muttering barely discernable prayers of blessing and thankfulness under his breath.

It's more real telling someone else. She shook her head in renewed wonder, awe, and disbelief at the joy that flooded her heart.

"Tell me more." Ara pulled back, looking ready for one of the heart talks they had so often shared when she was a girl.

"Well, a while ago Kmani and Nmir told me early signs to be looking for." She flushed a little and bypassed the specifics. "I noticed some and wondered, but felt so unsure. I — I didn't want to be wrong." Emzara shrugged before continuing. "So I tried wetting kernels of certain grains that Nmir showed me with — well, you don't want those details. Anyway, if they sprout, then that's a good indication. I waited as long as I could before checking today, and here we are."

Ara's wide grin matched her own. "So there will be a new little one here in several whole moons. Does Noah know?"

She shook her head. "I haven't had a chance to tell him yet."

"Finding out that you'll be receiving a gift of life from the Creator is a unique joy. I remember when your mother first told me her news about you. I jumped up and shouted. She laughed that bubbling laugh of hers, like bangles making music together. We were so happy. Although," he touched her cheek and smiled, using his thumb to wipe away a tear that lingered there, "it definitely made her cry more quickly as well."

"What happened next?" Emzara pulled her knees to her chest, cherishing every detail about her mother.

He closed his eyes and spoke slowly, as if savoring every word of the precious memories. "In the whole moons to come, we talked and planned as if your coming was the first and only of its kind on this earth. She worked to prepare linens for you, delighting over each. We'd guess what you might be like and talked often about you — even until just before daybreak. I was almost 200 and she was just a little younger, but we felt as giddy as 20-year-olds, yet as endowed with all the responsibility and respectability of people who are 900." Ara paused.

"What else about Amma?"

"We had this game together. I'd made a little wooden bed for you — so tiny. She'd hide it each day, and I had to find it when I came home from work. Some days it'd be in the kitchen. Another day, I found it on a branch in one of the trees outside. She was very creative. Sometimes it was with the animals, or even tied to the coastline as a little boat. Each day I'd bring it back and as I cleaned it, she'd tell me a story about you. With the kitchen, it was about how you'd be a great cook. When it was on the water, the tale was all about the many adventures you'd have. The last place she hid it was on our pallet. She whispered to me that you'd come into both of our hearts and lives to stay."

Emzara felt full, hearing how much her mother had delighted in her while she was still in the womb.

"You know, she left us too soon," Ara said. "Nmir was there to help with the birth, but once you came, your mother struggled to recover. We placed you on her chest and she glowed. I'll never forget the tenderness and love shining from her whole being. But that couldn't defeat whatever was at work inside her body."

He bowed his head in his hands and Emzara wept with him. "I miss her so." Ara cleared his throat and smiled deeply. "You have her hair, her gift for seeing the world for what it can be, and her strength of character. With all she and I discussed about how you'd look and behave, you've surpassed our every dream."

Emzara held his hand. "I wish I'd known her."

"Everything alright? Why all the tears?" Noah's voice filtered into her world, expanding it from the one her father had just shared. She rose to her feet, glided to Noah, and kissed his cheek.

"Yes." She tilted her head up while reaching for one of his hands and placing it on her still-flat middle. "I'm a little emotional right now because, as I just told Baba, someone might soon be calling you Baba."

"What?" His mouth agape and eyes wide, Noah held her at arm's length.

Emzara beamed, nodding.

Ara stood and Noah looked askance at him. "She's — I mean — we're — baby?"

Both father and daughter laughed. Although Noah's words were far from eloquent, his face spoke volumes. He held on to her tightly.

"So you're happy?" She spoke softly into the folds of cloth draped over his shoulder.

"I couldn't be happier." He raised her chin, and she saw a glimmer in his eye that spoke of mischief. "So does this mean I'm going to have to put up with more of this kind of behavior for a while now?" He wiped her eyes and cheeks gently.

Emzara worked to form her lips into a small pout, which wobbled as she struggled to hold back the grin that wanted to burst forth like the morning sun. "And if you are?"

"Worth it." Noah peeked at his father-in-law. "Well I certainly didn't expect to come over tonight and get this news. I was just going to tell you about goings on at the shipyard."

"That can wait." Ara placed his hands on the couple, creating a loose circle. "I've been thinking about this event for some time now. And I want you to have this place. We'll trade. A small house like yours is perfect for an old widower, but with the 40 or so children you'll be having, this will be a much better home for you and all my grandchildren."

"Only 40?" Noah tipped his head to the side and winked at Emzara.

"One at a time. We both come from unusually small families." She reached out to her father. "I can't take your home from you."

"You're not taking it. I'm giving it. Trust me, I've thought about this for a while, long before meeting this fellow."

Noah turned serious. "It's an amazing gift. I — 'thank you' doesn't seem like enough."

"Your care for my daughter is more than enough." Ara paused before adding playfully. "Think about it. If you didn't take her off my hands, this place would belong to her someday anyway."

"Hey!" Emzara placed her hands on her hips.

Noah suddenly reached toward her midsection. "We can't wait to meet you, little one. You're a wonderful gift from our Creator."

Placing one hand over Noah's, Emzara used her other one to grab Ara's hand and situate it near hers and Noah's. "Amen."

"What's this? It's too small to be a community dance." Aterre's sudden entrance broke the close circle, or rather expanded it.

"Aterre!" Emzara extended her arm.

Aterre picked up one of the fresh bread rounds that sat forgotten on the low table. He waved it in the air as he strode over to the group. "Why do you all look as guilty as if you've been caught taking one of these when you're not supposed to?"

The group stared silently until Noah cleared his throat. "Well, maybe it's because I just learned that I'm a father."

Aterre looked quickly back and forth between the couple for confirmation. "You're serious?"

"Yes." Emzara looked down, feeling her cheeks heat up. But then both she and Noah were smashed into a big hug from their friend and everyone was laughing.

"That's wonderful!" He released them. "When?"

"Well," she smoothed the front of her wrapped dress, "it could be anywhere from six to eight whole moons."

Aterre shook his head before clasping his hand firmly on Noah's shoulder. When he didn't speak, Emzara wondered if he was holding back tears. "Well, when he comes," he said at last, the mischief in his voice belying her suspicions, "I'll have plenty of stories to tell him about his father."

"Or she." Ara said as he wrapped an arm around his daughter.

"Oh, I'll be sure she knows too." Aterre took a large bite of the bread.

"We'll have to see that you're far away from here by the time our child is old enough to listen to the yarns you'll spin about me. You'd probably claim to be a faster swimmer."

Emzara grinned as she recalled that special evening.

"But I am," Aterre mumbled with a mouth full of food.

"Or that I ran terrified from a grendec on our journey."

"You tried, but the pace you call running doesn't really qualify. As I recall, you shivered behind Taht for protection."

Emzara laughed, delighted by the banter.

"See? Your stories are so far from reality. My little boy" — Noah glanced at Ara and emphasized his next words — "or girl, needs to know the truth about how strong and handsome and brave I really am. We can't have Uncle Aterre around too much."

Aterre's demeanor suddenly calmed, puzzling Emzara. "Well, you may get your wish. Because it looks like I'll be moving to Cada's farm after the harvest."

All three turned in unison as he scratched his head. "I asked Jitzel to be my wife tonight, and she agreed. I've purchased a plot of land from her father, and we'll be married once the harvest is in."

Emzara squealed, clapping her hands together in excitement. "This is such great news!"

"You finally got up the nerve to ask her?" Noah asked.

"At least I didn't need your help to do it like you did with Zara. That's another story I'll get to tell your child."

"Well there will be plenty of versions to each story with you, me, Baba, and Noah retelling them."

"At least there will be three of us telling the truth about me." Noah sank back into a cushion.

"Hmm, I don't know about that." Emzara flashed him a playful glance as she joined him. "I might have to come up with a version of my own."

Aterre threw his head back, and his infectious laughter compelled the rest of them to join in. Emzara nestled into Noah's side, enjoying the camaraderie and joy that the fellowship of this group brought. She peeked at her father.

Ara, beaming with joy, caught her look. He winked and mouthed the words "I love you."

Chapter 9

Whistling a tune, Noah lifted the large hatchet from its hook on the wall of the shipyard's supply room. He walked out of the building and across the beach. The half moon and stars provided more light than the pinkish glow on the eastern horizon signaling the coming morning. The ever-present lapping of water on the shore blended with squawks of seabirds searching for their first meal of a new day.

Usually asleep at this time, Noah rose early after tossing and turning throughout the night, unable to contain his excitement over the announcement of Emzara's pregnancy. He had spent a long while watching his wife rest peacefully while he imagined what their child would be like. Finally, he gave up on any illusion of slumber and decided to get an early start at work. Despite the lack of rest, Noah still felt fully alert. *Creator, thank You for giving us a child. Help us to raise him,* Noah chuckled softly, *or her, to love and serve You.*

He set the heavy tool down and started to turn back to get more supplies when a faint orange glow farther down the beach arrested his attention. *Is he back?* Moving quietly toward the glimmering light, Noah smiled when he heard the unmistakable sounds of the blacksmith's forge. He hurried to the building and peeked through a thin gap between two boards in the outer wall. Tubal-Cain, back to the door, was bent low feeding chunks of charcoal to the furnace. Noah gently pushed the door open just enough to sneak through it. Stealthily, he entered the shop and tiptoed across the floor until he stood a few cubits behind the blacksmith.

"Hey!"

Tubal-Cain jolted. He scrambled to catch his balance and spun around, wielding a metal bar above his head.

Noah held his hands up. "Whoa! Easy. It's just me."

Tubal-Cain paused for a moment before recognition spread across his face. With a deep breath, he set the tool down. "Noah." The blacksmith stepped forward and embraced him. "It's great to see you. What are you doing here so early?"

"That's what I was going to ask you. I didn't realize you were back."

"We made it home late last night." Tubal-Cain leaned against a worktable. "I needed to check on the shop since I haven't been around for a few weeks."

"Everything look alright to you? From what I've seen, your apprentices have been doing a fine job."

"I think so."

"So, how was it?" Noah asked.

"Our trip?" Tubal-Cain smiled broadly. "Zain was right. That place is the most beautiful spot on earth. You'll have to take Emzara there sometime. There was a massive waterfall that you could walk behind, and the trees." He stretched his arms out wide. "Noah, some of them had trunks bigger than this shop, and they must've been more than 200 cubits tall."

"Sounds amazing." Noah glanced to the side. "But you missed all the excitement around here."

"What excitement?"

"Your father showed up. In fact, you just missed him. He left yesterday."

Tubal-Cain's smile faded. "What did he want?"

Noah sat down and filled Tubal-Cain in on the details, carefully avoiding the disturbing specifics he had heard from Garun the day before.

"I wish he'd stayed for one more day." Tubal-Cain bit his lip and stared at the wall for a moment. "You know, we were never very close, but it still would've been good to see him."

Noah gazed out the window at the back of the shop. Even though this angle hid the water, the early sunlight revealed a blue sky with a few wispy clouds. A playful smile crossed his lips. "That wasn't the most exciting news though."

Tubal-Cain cocked his head. "Really? What was?"

Noah shrugged. "I guess I should tell you before Aterre does. Let's just say that it won't be long before Baby Noah is here."

"Baby Noah?" His eyes shot wide open. "You mean Zara's . . . that's great!" Tubal-Cain enthusiastically clapped Noah's shoulder.

Wincing a bit, Noah tried to conceal the discomfort caused by the hard hit. "I guess we might have Baby Emzara instead."

"That's fantastic. I can't wait to tell Adira." He paused. "No, I'm sure Zara will want to do that."

"I think you're right. Maybe the two of you can join us tonight and Em can tell . . ."

A gut-wrenching wail rang out in the distance.

Tubal-Cain looked around. "What was that?"

Noah jumped to his feet and bolted for the door. With Tubal-Cain right on his heels, Noah raced down the beach road toward the sound of the cry. As he rushed past the shipyard office, he spotted Emzara staggering down the path from Ara's house. "Em!"

She glanced up, dropped to her knees, and screamed. Her hands and robe were dappled with blood and tears streamed down her face.

Noah's heart sank. He sprinted to her and slid to his knees, catching her as she collapsed in his arms. "What's wrong?"

She dug her fingernails into his back and gasped for air. "They . . . he's . . ." She moaned in agony, unable to force another word out.

"This blood. Are you hurt? Is it the baby?" Helplessness filled Noah's body. He held her out in front of him as he checked her for any injury. Finding none, he brushed aside a stray piece of hair from her eyes. She hid her face in his chest, sobbing. He looked up in confusion at Tubal-Cain.

With concern etched across his face, Tubal-Cain said, "I'll check it out." He ran toward Ara's house.

Emzara pulled back a little and her terror-stricken eyes met Noah's momentarily. She opened her mouth to speak but quickly buried her face into his shoulder, her body wracked by sobs.

Holding her tight and unsure of what else to do, he stroked her head softly as she attempted to gather herself.

At the sound of hurried footsteps behind him, Noah turned his head. "Nmir."

"What's wrong?"

"I don't know."

The old woman knelt beside them and rested a hand on Emzara's shoulder.

Emzara slowly turned toward Nmir. She let go of Noah and her lower lip trembled. "Ba . . ." Whimpering and shaking her head, Emzara fell into Nmir's arms.

Tubal-Cain stepped out of the house, his face downcast.

Noah stood and ran to him. "What happened? Where's Ara?"

Wiping his eyes with a blood-streaked hand, Tubal-Cain bit his lip and looked away.

His mind racing to make sense of the anguish of Emzara and Tubal-Cain, a miserable thought sprang into Noah's mind. "No. Please, God, no."

Tubal-Cain turned back to Noah and shook his head. "He's dead." He held up his hand to show the blood. "Someone killed him."

Noah's stomach contorted into a knot and he bent down, putting his hands on his knees. Through hot tears he glanced back at Emzara, who was being cradled by Nmir.

Tubal-Cain put a hand on Noah's back. "That's not all."

Noah groaned from deep within his being.

Tubal-Cain pursed his lips and looked to the sky as he stammered and covered his mouth. His grief-stricken eyes met Noah's and he voiced the name on Noah's mind. "Aterre too."

"No!" Breathing seemed impossible as he dropped to his hands and knees. Overwhelmed by sorrow and pain, he felt as if his heart had been ripped from his chest. Time seemed to slow. The milknut trees blurred in his vision, and everything went silent except for the throbbing pulse inside his ears. He heaved, but only air came up.

His gaze locked onto Ara's front door. He reached for it as his grief turned to anger. Forcing himself to his feet, he balled his fists as his anger turned to rage. Seething through clenched teeth, Noah started for Ara's house. "I need to see."

Tubal-Cain blocked his way. "Don't. Go to your wife."

Noah plowed into him, but the blacksmith stood his ground and wrapped his brawny arms around him.

“Let me go.” Noah thrashed against him. “Let go.” He twisted, but could not break free. “Let me . . .” Noah moaned and slumped in Tubal-Cain’s grasp, his fury draining.

“There’s nothing you can do for them, but Emzara needs you, and you need her.” Tubal-Cain let him go.

Noah nodded and shuffled over to Emzara. He lowered himself to the ground next to her.

Emzara let go of Nmir. She hugged Noah and they wept together.

Chapter 10

Eat this now, both of you."

Noah groggily lifted his head off Emzara's shoulder. He blinked, trying to orient himself. *How long has it been since. . . .* Unable to finish the sentence in his mind, he glanced at the sun, which was well past the peak of its path.

"Eat." Nmir held out a platter filled with bread slabs topped with honey and dried vinefruit. The commanding tone of her voice pulled him from what seemed like relentless waves of thought threatening to pummel him into mental unconsciousness. The scent of her savory flat-seed stew added a welcome greeting, further drawing him from his grief-tossed haze.

Limp, he watched as she set the tray on a flat grassy section at their feet. Awareness finally took root after she took out three bowls.

"Em, here." He guided her gently to the ground. She moved slowly, almost as if she were a child, discovering certain motions for the first time. As they ate, some of his strength returned. *Where is Tubal-Cain? I've never had someone close to me die before. Who could've done this?* The image of Bayt and the long dagger on his belt flashed through his mind. Clenching a fist, Noah felt his temperature rise, and the urge to race off and find the man filled his body.

Breathing shallowly, he glanced at Emzara, and he knew he needed to stay by her side for now. She had managed to consume a half a piece of bread, but her bowl of stewed flatseed lay untouched, slightly askew in the grass. He reached over her lap and held the bowl out. "Please."

Tears welled up in her eyes and, understanding her mute plea, he set the bowl back down. He looked helplessly at Nmir. "Thanks for this. I . . ."

She fidgeted, twisting the overwrap that was tied to her midsection. "I had to do something." Dried trails of darker brown traced down her cheeks like the crooked texture left behind in the wet sand from a retreating breaker.

"Come." His voice cracked and he tried again. "We share this sorrow."

She took his extended hand and sat across from them. Time stretched on before she finally spoke. "There's much to be done before nightfall. Time for grief will be later."

"I don't know what's next. I've never done this before."

Emzara looked up slowly, a distant look in her eyes. "I can only remember going to one burial. It was for the old innkeeper. I was only 15, but I remember them lighting the torch and the family standing huddled by it."

"Torch?" Noah asked.

"It's placed at the head of the burial mound and is kept lit for seven days in honor."

"If you ask me, it's to give the family something to do," Nmir said.

Emzara's wry, half-smile almost appeared. *Trust Nmir to see the practical side of things. She's often right.* Noah tapped his nose with the broad side of his thumbnail, and his wife responded to their secret communication with a soft smile, declaring her love for him as well.

Gone. Ara and Aterre. They're gone. The realization hit him afresh and anguish tore through his midsection. He had needed that lightness of spirit even if just for a moment, but the pain at remembering almost undid any good from the temporary reprieve.

Suddenly, Tubal-Cain's strong hand squeezed Noah's forearm. Standing next to him were Zain, Cada, and Garun, each with a shovel in hand. "We've come to prepare for the burial." Tubal-Cain's voice was deeper than normal, revealing that he had been weeping.

"Let's get this over." Cada's flat voice matched his expression.

He lost his best worker, a friend, and his soon-to-be son. Noah shook his head in frustration, realizing for the first time all the suffering that would stem from this tragedy.

"Here's a shovel, if you're up to it." Zain handed the tool to Noah.

"I'm coming too. I need to focus on something else." Emzara stepped forward, face flushed, but Nmir grabbed her.

"I need you. We'll have to fix up a meal for those who come to mourn, and I can't do it alone."

Tubal-Cain nodded. "Adira's back at your house, Zara, with Kmani. They've got the linens for wrapping Ater —" His word caught in his throat, so he lowered his head and buried it in the palm of his hand.

"And Jitzel will come later with the rest of my family." Cada's stone face barely moved as he spoke. "She . . . needed some time still." He leaned his head back as a tear ran down one of his dark cheeks.

Emzara nodded slowly and Noah dropped his gaze, finding it difficult to imagine what Jitzel was going through. *What would I have done if something had happened to Em?* He shook his head, trying to banish the dreadful thought from his mind. "Thank you all for coming. We . . ." He gulped and gestured to Emzara and Nmir. "We couldn't do this without you."

The group turned and the men made their way around the side of the house. Noah fell into step behind Garun, thankful for the momentary silence. Stopping beside the low grassy mound that marked the grave of Em's mother, Noah pointed to the ground adjacent to it. "Right here."

"And the other one?" Zain asked in a somber tone.

Forcing his thoughts to the task at hand, Noah glanced at Cada. "Here or at your place?"

Cada's puffy red eyes looked away. "Here. I think it would be too tough of a reminder for my daughter at our place."

Noah nodded. "Over here then." He walked several cubits beyond the first mound, plunged the sharp blade of his shovel into the ground, and hoisted a scoop of fresh soil to the side. He simply watched the blade slice into the soft sandy soil and cleanly come up again. Slice. Lift. Drop. Slice. Lift. Drop. The repeated action consumed his mind as he zeroed in on the sounds and the fresh memory of Bayt's crooked grin. The tool dove deeper with each thrust, allowing Noah's anger to fuel his work. With each load his frustration grew and tears dropped freely from his eyes. Soon, the rhythm from his implement was joined by a second scoop as Tubal-Cain joined him. When Noah stopped to catch his breath, he scanned the group. *Where's Aterre?* He dropped his shovel as the pain stabbed him anew and cut through him just like his spade had pierced the earth.

* * *

Wind from the sea just beyond rippled through his hair and whipped across his face. The salty fragrance brought Noah a measure of peace, and he inhaled desperately. The sun hung low on the horizon, but for the first time the radiant oranges, pinks, and purples brought no joy.

Deep within his soul, he silently pleaded with his Maker. *Most High, You have made all things. Surely nothing is too difficult for You. Oh, how I wish the sun would return in its course to last evening and You'd stay the hand of the murderer and spare the lives of Your faithful followers. I don't want to face another day without them.*

Noah paused before placing a shovelful of earth over Aterre's grave. The two fresh mounds joined the older grass-covered one. Each berm stood about knee-high and was several cubits in length, although much narrower in width. The bodies of his friends rested on separate wooden planks and were wrapped with linens. Aterre had been placed first, and then Ara, so that he was right next to Biremza's resting spot. Silently, the men steadily piled soil on top, grading the surrounding landscape and packing it in tightly.

Using his forearm, Noah wiped sweat from his brow and resumed his work, eager to finish the task before losing the sunlight.

Emzara sidled up to him, an unlit lantern in her left hand held aloft. "This one's for Baba. We're almost ready to begin."

Cada carried a similar lantern toward him. "This is for Aterre."

Hand in hand they stepped to Ara's mound. Letting go for a moment, Noah drove the lantern's post deep at the head of the rise, making sure it would stand. He paused, remembering the face that had looked so kindly upon him when he and Aterre first arrived. The face that had been firm but patient with him as he picked up the new trade and learned the skills needed for shipbuilding. The face that shed tears of joy as he gave his daughter away in marriage. The face that only yesterday had been so happy to hear of the new life. Uncontrollable sobs wracked him and he reached out for Emzara's hand. Instead, her body crushed him with a fierceness born of deep pain, love, and even desperation.

A wail pierced the descending twilight. Then another one rang out. Soon several voices rose in their loud expressions of grief. The deafening sound caused Noah to hold Em even tighter as they too, joined in. Oddly, the incredible closeness of friends and family mixed simultaneously with the sorrow of separation. As the cries continued, a bucket of cool mud was passed to them. Emzara smeared streaks of it down Noah's arms before marking her own. "This is to remind us that Greatfather Adam was formed from the ground, and we are made from the same substance. And because of his rebellion, we each die and return to that ground."

In the dim light, people from town followed suit and covered themselves in long stripes of mud from their cheeks, down their chest and arms, to their legs.

Zain stepped forward, his streaked face illuminated by the torch in his hand. He spoke loudly, accentuating his words while lighting the two lanterns. "I light these lamps this evening to honor Aterre and Ara. They were our dearest friends, our family, and we loved them. And we know they loved us deeply in return. Our town wouldn't be what it is today without Ara's vision in his work or his wisdom on the council. And who of us hasn't laughed along with Aterre, whether through his quick wit or his playful spirit. He gave us joy in life. To Noah, Emzara, Nmir, Cada, and Jitzel, you have our support."

Zain hung the torch on the stake Noah had placed. Raising his hands, he continued, "Creator, receive these two men and enable us to be better because of their examples of faithfulness in serving You. We are again reminded of the ultimate price for disobeying You." His voice softened. "We are also thankful for Your mercy that allows us to live each day."

Sounds of assent murmured through the crowd and then died down as each paused in a lengthy silence. An old, bulky man stepped forward from the gathered throng. It took Noah a few moments to recognize Akel with the streaks of mud across his body. He carried a large wooden crate and placed it before the two newly raised places of earth. "Let each person here take a flower cutting from this box and place it on the sites where our dear friends lie. When you have finished saying farewell, the women have prepared evenfeast at Noah's and Emzara's home. You are welcome to gather there."

Noah twined his fingers through Emzara's. "Almost done. Can you make it?"

She looked up at him gratefully, her red eyes shining with tears in the light of the torches. "I have you." She squeezed his hand, and together they moved to lead the procession in placing flower cuttings on the graves.

Chapter 11

Carefully guided by the hand of an expert, the carving knife slid gently along the side of the wood, trimming a thin strip from the block. After several more passes, the back of the large-eared tusker began to take shape. Noah set the piece on the table next to the fresh shavings. He brushed the dust from his fingers and used the back of his hand to rub his eyes, which were sore due to the countless tears shed over the past week.

Noah blinked and took a deep breath, fighting the urge to start weeping again. Whittling helped take his thoughts away from the recent tragedy. *And another carved animal may brighten Em's spirit a little.* Normally, the shipyard would be the perfect place to find sanctuary for his weary mind. But with Ara gone, Noah could not bring himself to head to work today. Everything about the place reminded him of his father-in-law.

He stood and lifted the hatch on the wall that faced east, propping it open with a small beam he had fashioned. Breathing in the warm morning air, Noah looked through the window at the grove of milknut trees. He grimaced when he heard hammering in the distance. *Bakur and Fen must be back at work. The mourning period is officially over.* He shook his head. *I need to get over there.*

Noah spun quickly toward a couple of soft knocks on the door. It had been four days since anyone had stopped to check on them. Emzara was still in bed, as she had been for nearly the entire week since the burials. She had only eaten bits of a few meals and was inconsolable at times.

The knocking started again. "Noah, are you home?"

A partial smile tugged at his lips as he recognized the voice. "I'm coming." Noah opened the door. "Zain, it's good to see you."

Zain's expression showed sympathy. He held out a basket bedecked with flowers and filled with bread rounds and a couple of small, covered clay bowls. "Kmani wanted me to deliver these." He tipped his head toward the bowl closest to Noah as he handed him the goods. "She made your favorite berry spread."

Noah gladly took the basket, and his stomach grumbled, reminding him that he had not eaten since midmeal the day before. "Please thank her for us."

Zain nodded. "I will." He looked off into the distance and then down at his feet before back up at Noah. "I'm sorry to disturb you, but you really need to get to the town hall immediately."

Noah tilted his head. "Why? What's going on?"

"It's Garun. Some of the people are blaming him for . . ." He paused as if searching for the right words. "For what happened. And they want the council to meet to decide on his punishment."

"Garun?" Noah tapped a finger against his lips. "I don't think he would ever do that."

"I didn't believe it either," Zain said.

"Wait. Why do you need me for a council meeting?" He ran his fingers against the stubble on his face. *I haven't shaved in a week.*

"I'll tell you on the way."

"Alright, I'll be right back after I let Emzara know where I'm going." Noah walked toward his room, setting the basket on the table along the way.

He opened the bedroom door, and Emzara rolled to her side and looked up at him through despondent eyes. Kneeling next to her, he gently rubbed her shoulder. "Kmani sent us some food. I think you should try to eat something." He slid his hand to her belly and smiled. "Our child is probably hungry."

Her eyes glistened as she forced a smile. "I'll try." Her gravelly words barely surpassed the volume of a whisper.

Noah bent over and kissed her forehead. "I need to go to the town hall. Garun's in a lot of danger, and Zain's waiting for me." He stood to leave.

"Noah, wait." Emzara cleared her throat as she pushed herself into a sitting position and slung her feet over the side of the bed. She reached out and hugged him around the waist. "Be careful."

He softly stroked her head. "I will, and I'll be back as soon as I can. I love you, Em."

She let go of him. "I love you too."

Noah hurried into the front room and quickly strapped on his sandals. He dipped a piece of bread into the berry spread and made for the door. Stepping into the sunlight, he squinted in Zain's direction. "Let's go."

Walking at a brisk pace across the beach, Noah devoured his snack in three large bites. The food combined with the wind in his face and the exercise invigorated Noah. For the first time since the murders, the mental fog lifted from his mind. Savoring the last morsel in his mouth, he said, "Kmani's bread was tremendous."

"It always is." Zain turned onto the path that led away from the beach and to the center of town. "You asked me to ask about Bayt to see if he might've committed the crimes. I was told that he was on his way out of town the morning you saw him on the beach. No one I talked to has seen him since that day."

Noah breathed in through a clenched jaw. "But he might have decided to stay out of town until that night so that we wouldn't suspect him."

"That's possible, but why would he even bother showing his face at all? If he had planned to murder Ara, it would make more sense if no one knew he was around."

"Or that's just what he wants us to think."

Zain shrugged. "Maybe, but I have my doubts. It's no secret he didn't like Ara, but I don't think he wanted him dead. Besides, I'm not sure he's capable of beating Aterre in a fight."

Noah remained silent while trying to weigh this new information.

"You should know that the council wishes for you to fill Ara's position."

Noah pointed to himself. "Me? I'm so much younger than everyone else."

"You make it sound like I'm so old." Zain chuckled. "I thought you knew that our rules say that if a council member dies, his heir has the right to replace him until the next choosing. So, for now, that makes you his successor. The next term comes around in eight whole moons. If you want to continue, and if the council believes you're a good fit, then you could become a permanent member."

"That's quite an honor. I'll need to speak with Emzara about it."

"Of course. But depending on how things are going with Garun, you may need to fill that role as soon as possible." Zain stopped and grabbed Noah's arm. "The people accusing Garun and Bedin are out for blood. They believe that since the crime committed was murder, then the penalty should match. They are talking about executing them."

Briefly, Noah clenched his jaw and fists. "In many ways, that sounds like a fair punishment, though I don't know if I could ever make the decision to put someone to death." He pulled free from Zain's grip. "But Garun's innocent."

Zain let out a breath. "That's how I feel too. But you are in a unique position."

"How so?"

"You were close to both victims. As Ara's son-in-law, only you or Emzara could bring formal charges against the suspected killers. That being said, you were also Aterre's best friend, and since he and Jitzel weren't married yet, you'd be the natural person to bring charges for him as well."

Noah stared straight ahead, processing Zain's words. "So you're saying that people might listen to me, if . . ."

"If you can get them to calm down, and especially if you're on the council."

"And you'll help me?"

"In any way I can."

As they neared the town square, raised voices echoed off the buildings. Noah sprinted to the end of the road to the source of the cacophony. On his left, at the steps of the town hall, approximately 30 people stood, raising their fists and shouting at the two men bound closely together to one of the pillars Noah had carved.

Noah dashed toward the gathering. Ashur and Oban stood helplessly on the top step. Garun and Bedin seemed to be unharmed, but probably not for much longer. The whole scene looked similar to the way Noah pictured a disciplinary sentencing in Iri Sana that his father described to him during his childhood. A man's wagon beast had died, so he stole one that belonged to his neighbor and dumped the dead one in its place. His crime was eventually discovered. As penalty, he was tied to a post in the street and whipped 20 times. Then he had to return the animal and pay a fine.

But they don't want to only whip Garun. Noah swiftly picked his way through the crowd and climbed the five short stairs.

"Murderers!" Ethlin, from the front of the mob called out and pointed in Garun's face.

Stepping between him and Garun, Noah raised his arms to the side and gestured for the crowd to calm. "Please, my brothers."

"They murdered Ara and Aterre." Ethlin's voice maintained its volume.

Noah held up his hand, palm out. "Please, let's talk calmly."

"But your friend and father-in-law," said a man to Noah's left. "These men should be put to death."

Noah closed his eyes and breathed deeply, struggling to keep his emotions in check. "Please." He directed a thumb at Garun and the scribe. "They aren't going anywhere. Let us discuss these accusations in a peaceful manner."

Zain called out, "Let's listen to what he has to say before we make any sudden decisions. After all, he was close to both of the men who were killed." Slowly, the crowd quieted.

"Friends and neighbors," Noah said. "Thank you for honoring the seven-day mourning period and for your desire to see justice done." Scanning the crowd and confident they were willing to listen, Noah continued. "Believe me, no one wants justice for the tragedies more than I do. Aterre was my . . ." He averted his eyes and sucked in a breath through his mouth. *Creator, help me.*

Noah stood up straight, facing the group again. "He was my best friend for nearly ten years, and he was the best friend a guy could ever want. I could tell you so many stories about him." He smiled and shook his head. "But now is not the time. And Ara was my father-in-law, my mentor, and my friend. Apart from my wife, no one will miss him more than me." Noah brushed away a tear from his left eye, but his confidence rose with each completed sentence. Talking about them in this setting helped ease the intense ache inside.

"So what do you think we should do with these men?" Ethlin asked.

Noah turned and faced the accused men for the first time. Bedin's eyes were wide with fear, and Garun smiled grimly as he looked Noah in the eye, before shaking his head and dropping his gaze.

Noah slowly turned back to the group and sighed. "I think we should set them free."

"What?" Ethlin asked, and many others echoed his response.

"I agree that the person, or people, who did this deserve death, but I don't believe Garun is guilty."

Ethlin put a hand on his shaking, bald head. "No one's ever been murdered in Iri Geshem until these two showed up."

Noah nodded and out of the corner of his eye caught a glimpse of Tubal-Cain quickly approaching the scene. "I know the timing looks bad, but if they were guilty, then why would they stick around during the mourning period? They could've easily snuck out of town to avoid being accused and captured."

"That's true, but maybe they knew we'd think about that, so they decided to stay," Ethlin said.

"Maybe, but that's quite an unnecessary risk to take." Noah's thoughts drifted back to the day King Lamech arrived. "Let me ask you something, Ethlin. Did Garun put up a fight when you seized him?"

Ethlin smirked. "No, but there were four of us."

"You're lucky then." Noah returned the smirk. "Garun could've easily defeated all four of you. He's trained many of Havil's guards, and you've seen what they're capable of."

Ethlin's grin vanished and he took a step back, looking unsure of himself for the first time. Suddenly, his countenance brightened. "So he would certainly be capable of the murders."

"No doubt, but he has proven his good character to me." Noah considered mentioning the fact that Garun had probably saved his life in Havil, but decided to keep those details hidden from Bedin. "If he says he didn't do it, then I believe him. And if he can vouch for the scribe, then I'll take his word on that too."

Noah looked at the Havilites. "Garun, were you involved in murdering my father-in-law and friend?"

Garun returned Noah's steady gaze. "I promise that I had nothing to do with it, and I don't believe Bedin did either. We were in the guest house your town provided that entire evening."

"Is there anyone who could verify your claim?" Ethlin asked.

Garun paused before speaking. "Bedin met with a farmer that night, and their meeting went very late. But the man wasn't there all evening."

Noah motioned for Zain to join him. "Since you're the ranking council member gathered here right now, I wish to express that I have no intention to accuse these men of murder. I ask that you set them free. However, I want to stress that I plan to do everything I can to find the murderers, and if we find any evidence that leads back to Garun or Bedin, then I'll reconsider my decision."

Zain put a hand on Noah's shoulder and addressed the people. "I believe Noah has spoken wisely. Are there any further objections to this plan?"

"If we set them free and someone else gets killed, then what?" Ethlin asked.

"We're all new at this, so I understand your reluctance to set them free. If something else happens, then we need to investigate and try to find the killer, just like we should be doing now," Zain said.

Ethlin's chest heaved a couple of times as his demeanor softened. "That's all well and good, but we need someone to keep an eye on them for now."

Zain adjusted the wrap slung over his shoulder. "I think that's fair." He looked at Ashur. "Do you still have a room available for them?"

Ashur bit his lip before nodding. "Yes, I have room, but I can't keep a close eye on them at all times."

Zain clapped his hands together. "Very well, they stay at Ashur's, and if they want to leave the inn for any reason, they need to notify him first. Does that work for everyone?"

Ashur frowned and no one else objected.

Oban stepped away from Ashur and whispered something in Tubal-Cain's ear. Tubal-Cain looked confused at first, but then his eyes lit up with understanding.

Zain gestured to Garun and Bedin. "Free them."

Chapter 12

This whole situation makes me nervous." Ashur scowled at Garun and Bedin, both of whom were stretching their limbs after Noah loosed their bindings. "How much longer do you plan to be in our city?"

Bedin shrugged. "Perhaps two more weeks before I complete my interviews."

Ashur harrumphed. "I'll go prepare their room."

"We'll take them to collect their belongings from the guest house," Zain said. "That ought to give you enough time."

Ashur walked away and acknowledged the plan with a dismissive wave of his hand.

Noah waited until Ashur was out of earshot and then tilted his head toward him. "What's he so mad about?"

"I don't know," Zain said. "If he thinks they really are the murderers, then I could see why he'd be nervous."

"Then why didn't he speak up when he had the opportunity?" Noah asked.

Tubal-Cain reached the top of the stairs and stepped into their small group. Speaking quietly he said, "I think I might know the answer. Oban just told me that Ashur's been secretly housing a guest ever since the day after the murders."

"Who?" Noah's mind raced.

"You think it's the murderer?" Zain asked.

Tubal-Cain shook his head. "I don't know, but Oban says that arrangement will explain why Ashur doesn't want these two to stay with him."

"Noah, you go with Tubal-Cain. I'll stay with them." Zain pointed over his shoulder to Garun and Bedin. "We'll get there as soon as possible."

Garun grabbed Noah's arm as he turned to leave. "Thank you for trusting me. You saved my life."

Noah tipped his head and half-smiled. "I guess that makes us even." Though his words were light, inside, his bruised heart ached anew. When had life become this series of life debts earned and redeemed?

Garun snorted. "Let me know if I can help."

"I will."

His mind churning over what awaited them at Ashur's, Noah hurried across the square with Tubal-Cain at his side. "Any ideas about who this guest is?"

Tubal-Cain shook his head. "No, especially since Oban seemed pretty certain he's not the murderer. I just don't understand why anyone would want to . . ." Tubal-Cain flinched. "Sorry. I don't mean to keep bringing it up."

Noah gave him a grim smile. "It goes around and around in my head like a calic chasing its tail. Sometimes I feel like I'll never escape it, and not because you keep bringing it up." He straightened his spine, turning his mind away from futile regrets. "But the only thing I can give to Ara and Aterre now is justice, so I'm focusing on figuring this out."

"Well, since Ashur's in a foul mood, let's make sure we use some tact."

Noah chuckled. "You don't think I should just march in and demand that he deliver the murderer to us?" Laughing felt good, but at once guilt stabbed him, as if he had disrespected the dead.

Tubal-Cain winked. "That's probably not the best idea."

Noah pulled the door to the inn and held it open for Tubal-Cain. After following his friend inside, he moved to their favorite spot in the nearest corner. The large open room was sparsely populated, indicating that midmeal had not yet been served. Wafting out of the kitchen, the unmistakable scent of Ashur's mouthwatering bread reached Noah's nostrils and reminded him of his hunger. Noah waved over Ashur, who stood behind a counter, wiping down drinking jars.

Ashur avoided eye contact until he reached their table. "Noah, I'm really sorry about Ara and Aterre. They'll truly be missed."

"I appreciate that."

"If there's anything I can do to help, just let me know. Would you like some midmeal? Enika just made Momma Kylel's stuffed specialty."

"Smells great, but not right now," Tubal-Cain said.

Noah raised his eyebrows. "He may not want some, but I sure could use it."

Ashur brightened and leaned toward Tubal-Cain. "You sure you don't want any?"

Tubal-Cain shrugged. "Adira will have something for me when I get home."

"We actually came to talk to you about something important." Noah rubbed his growling stomach. "But we can discuss it while I eat."

An uneasy look passed over the innkeeper's face, and he twisted the cloth in his hands. "Of course. I'll go get your plate."

Tubal-Cain lifted one finger from the table, pointing at Noah. "So do you want to bring it up, or do you want me to?"

"It's probably best if I do it." Noah grinned. "After all, you suggested we use tact."

Tubal-Cain smiled. "Well, then I'll be the muscle if we need to make him talk."

Lowering his voice, Noah ran his finger along the smooth wood of the round-topped wooden table. "Actually . . . he sure likes your father and your city, so he may be willing to talk to you."

"Maybe. When I first moved here, he talked to me quite a bit. But over the past two years or so, he hasn't said much."

Through the kitchen door to Noah's left, Ashur appeared with the meal. He crossed the floor and set down a plate laden with spicy baked pebble beans piled under two large halves of a tangy green vegetable, each filled to the brim with an assortment of grains, beans, and vegetables. Two chunks of bread completed the arrangement. The delicious aroma made his stomach rumble in anticipation. Ashur handed him a clay vessel. "And here's some water."

"Thank you. It looks so good, as always." Noah held out two copper piks.

Ashur reached for the pieces but then withdrew his hand. "This one's on me. Enjoy." He turned to leave.

"Wait, Ashur. I need to talk to you for a moment." Noah motioned to a nearby chair at an empty table. "Please, join us." As Ashur grabbed the chair, Noah shoved a few of the hot, sand-colored pebble beans into his mouth and savored their spicy flavor.

Ashur sat back from the table and crossed his arms. He glanced nervously at Tubal-Cain and then at Noah. "What is it?"

Noah folded his hands together and looked out the square-cut windows that faced the main street of the town. "At the town hall we discussed the need to figure out who killed Ara and Aterre and why they did it."

"And you're certain it wasn't your friend Garun?" It seemed as if Ashur emphasized *friend*, but Noah chose to overlook any insinuation.

"I really doubt it. Garun helped us all escape Havil the last time we were there."

Ashur rubbed his beardless chin. "So what does that have to do with what happened here?"

"It speaks to his character. I trust him. Besides, what would he stand to gain by their deaths? He had no quarrel with them." Noah scanned the room then focused again on Ashur, satisfied that the three other customers were far enough away to not overhear him. "I've heard that you've been keeping a certain guest here since the day after the murders. Is that true?"

The innkeeper fidgeted and glanced at Tubal-Cain.

"So it is true," Noah said. "Who is it?"

Ashur shook his head.

"Ashur, tell me. We need to figure out who the murderer is, and even if you believe your guest to be above reproach, he might have seen something." Noah kept eye contact with Ashur until the chiseled-faced man looked down.

After releasing a deep breath, Ashur pointed at Tubal-Cain. "Not with him here."

Tubal-Cain raised his eyebrows. "Me? Why won't you say it in front of me?"

"Yeah, what's wrong with Tubal-Cain?" Noah asked.

"Nothing, but I just can't say anything with him here." Ashur turned away. "You'll understand why when I tell you, Noah."

Tubal-Cain stood, towering over Ashur. "You'd better tell him when I leave."

"Don't worry. I will. It's nothing against you, but you must trust me on this."

"Fine." Tubal-Cain reached across the table and snatched a portion of bread from Noah's plate. "Now, I'll go." He smiled at Noah as Noah slapped at his hand but missed.

"Hey, thief, get your own bread." The memory of meeting Aterre seared Noah to his core, but he blinked and willed himself to move on.

Tearing off a huge bite with his teeth, Tubal-Cain walked out of the building.

Noah turned his gaze from the door to Ashur. "Now tell me about this guest of yours."

"I think I'd better show you." Ashur slid his chair back across the wooden floor. "I'll be right back." He stood and headed toward the staircase to the upper rooms, and Noah wondered for a brief instant if Ashur would try to flee. *Guess that's where Tubal-Cain comes in as the muscle.*

Noah took a couple of deep breaths as he imagined what he might do or say if Bayt returned with Ashur. *But why would he make Tubal-Cain leave?* Shaking his head to clear his thoughts, he returned to his meal. After a week of barely tasting a morsel, the hearty, flavorful assortment of vegetables, the warm bread, and spicy baked pebble beans reminded him how much he appreciated food. He closed his eyes and breathed in deeply to relish the flavors. *Creator, thank You for the delicious foods You've made for us to enjoy. Please help us find the murderer and may justice be done.*

A creak on the stairs jolted Noah. He tried to hide his surprise when a lovely young woman followed Ashur toward the table. She wore a long wrap with a red border stitched into the edges. Her dark hair was pulled tightly back and then dropped behind her neck. Tilting his head, Noah wondered where he had seen her before.

Ashur directed her to his recently vacated chair, and then he sat in Tubal-Cain's spot. Scooting his seat close to hers, he made introductions. "Noah, this is Navea."

"Noah." She bowed her head slightly.

"Hello." Noah furrowed his brow. "You look very familiar."

She flashed a wide, beautiful smile. "That's not surprising. You've seen me a couple of times."

"I have? Where?"

"The first time was in the royal dining hall in Havil," Navea said.

Noah raised his chin in acknowledgment. "That's right. You were one of the dancers that dined with us."

She bit her bottom lip and nodded quickly.

Noah pointed toward the city square beyond Ashur's front door. "And you were one of the dancers that performed out there when the Havilites arrived in town?"

"Yes."

Pleased with his recall, Noah popped a succulent, red orb into his mouth. Suddenly, he leaned forward. "Wait, what are you doing here? How did you get here? I watched your whole group leave on the boat. Well, everyone except Garun and Bedin."

"That's why I wouldn't bring her out here until Tubal-Cain left," Ashur said.

"Um," Noah rubbed the back of his neck. "I'm not following you."

"Let her explain."

Noah turned to Navea but she sat quietly, her eyes downcast as she played with a strand of her hair. "So how did you get here after I saw you leave on the boat?"

"It's alright." Ashur put a hand on her arm. "You're safe here. And Noah deserves to know."

"I did leave on the boat, as you said." Navea paused and took a deep breath. "We sailed until your city was out of view, and then the king ordered our crew to move the boat close to shore. We sat there at anchor all day, then, early that evening, King Lamech and three of his guards jumped into the water and swam to shore."

"What were they doing?" Noah asked, though the truth sat like a rock in his belly.

"I don't know. They didn't say." As if by habit, she glanced over her shoulder and then relaxed a little. "They were gone for a long time, well into the night. When I realized no one was watching, I slipped into the water and swam for the beach."

"Why?" Noah tilted his head as his eyebrows scrunched together.

Navea rubbed her arm and gave Noah a look that made him feel like a child, naïve and foolish. "You don't know what it's like to work for the king. For years now, I've been free in name only. To Lamech and Naamah, I've been a slave, kept for their pleasure like a caged songbird. It used to be different, at least, with Naamah. We used to enjoy each other's company. I thought . . ." Her eyes glistened, but she clamped her lips into a hard line and swallowed. "I thought we were friends. But then her father made her Nachash's priestess." The bitterness in her voice made Noah wince. "It was like he was pitting us against each other, using me to manipulate her."

She paused, staring out the window as if seeing something other than the street outside. "I didn't care about the honor or the ceremonies, but Naamah wouldn't believe me. She's changed so much — and the changes aren't good. She only cares about power. She's just like her . . ." Navea closed her mouth and shook her head.

Noah nodded. "So what happened after you came ashore?"

"I made my way back here."

"Why here?"

She shrugged and glanced at Ashur. "It seemed like the right thing to do. Ashur always treated me very kindly, so I thought he might be willing to take me in and give me work."

"Did you see the king or the guards again?"

Navea shook her head. "No. I got a bit lost on my way here. I ended up sleeping in the forest and then found my way in the morning."

Mind churning, Noah shuffled through and picked one follow-up thought. "Do you believe they came back here that night?"

She massaged her temple with her thumb. "I'm not sure where else they might've gone, but I don't know this area."

Noah clenched his jaw and studied Navea for signs of deception. "Let's assume they did come back. Do you have any idea why they'd kill my father-in-law and friend?"

She didn't seem shocked at the idea, but met his eyes calmly. "I don't know. If I had to guess, it probably had something to do with the council meeting. Before that, he acted like he always does. He was outgoing and" — she checked over both shoulders — "and arrogant."

"And afterward?"

"After the meeting, he didn't say a word to any of us except his guards." Navea bit her lower lip and stared at the ceiling. "Even on the boat, when we were all in pretty tight quarters, he only spoke privately with his men. It was very strange."

Noah and Ashur exchanged a look, and Ashur shrugged one shoulder. "Ara *was* aggressive in his questioning."

"Yeah, a little," Noah said. "But he wasn't rude. Certainly nothing that would warrant such a violent reaction. And he wasn't the only one to question the king."

"No, but he was the last to speak," Ashur said. "Maybe the king thought Ara was responsible for the rejection of his trade proposal."

Noah's thoughts tossed from one to the next like waves in a stormy sea. The king's kindness toward him in their personal interactions made it hard for Noah to imagine him carrying out such atrocities. But based on Garun's insights, he saw the possibility. He fixed his view on Navea. "Do you believe he'd respond that way to some basic questions?"

"Some disrespectful questions." Ashur held up a hand toward Noah to let him finish. "At least from the king's point of view."

Navea trembled and fear stole into her eyes. "Promise me you won't tell the king about our conversation — or that I'm here at all."

Noah arched an eyebrow. "I don't plan on ever seeing him again. But yes, I promise."

Navea pushed her hands into her lap and lowered her head. "Yes, I think he'd be willing to kill someone he thought was getting in his way."

Fury rose inside of Noah, and he fought to control his emotions. "But why Aterre? What did he ever do?"

"Seems like he was just in the wrong place." Ashur let out a breath and ran his fingers through his dark wavy hair. "Noah, you should know what Zain told me. When they cleaned up Ara's house, it was apparent there was quite a struggle that night. Ara's body only had a couple of wounds, but Aterre's. . . ." Ashur looked away and swallowed hard. "But Aterre was slashed all over. It seems like he gave his life trying to protect Ara."

Noah slammed a fist on the table, causing some food to spring off his plate. Burying his head in his hands, he wept. The agony wrenched his body. "Why?"

Ashur put a hand on Noah's arm. "I'm very sorry."

After a few moments, Noah slowly lifted his head and glared at Ashur through tear-filled eyes. "Why didn't anyone tell me this before?"

"Because of the mourning period." Ashur smiled sympathetically. "And because we knew how hard it'd be for you to hear it."

Noah tipped his head toward Navea. "And her. Why didn't you say something sooner?"

Ashur nodded and repentance showed in his eyes. "I know I should've. But for her safety, I didn't want to say anything the day she showed up." He scratched the back of his neck. "And then I didn't want to interrupt your mourning. And then it became more difficult each day, since I should've said something right away. Trust me, I wasn't trying to keep anything from you, but this morning, when I saw the mob going after Garun and Bedin, I didn't want the same thing to happen to her."

"That would explain your attitude this morning," Noah said.

"Yes, I'm sorry for my rudeness. I knew that having them here would force me to say something before I was ready."

"Noah," Navea said, "I'm very sorry if my presence here is adding to your grief."

Noah closed his eyes and took a few deep breaths. *I need to speak with Garun and Tubal-Cain.* He unclenched his fists and held her gaze. "No, it led to this information. If I think of anything else to ask, should I look for you here?"

"I think so," she said.

"At least for now," Ashur said, patting her hand. "Once things quiet down, I'd like to help her find a more permanent arrangement."

"I understand." Noah stood. "Thank you for the meal and the information."

He strode purposefully across the floor and shoved the door open so hard that he nearly hit Zain with it. The council member jumped back, bumping into Bedin, who followed closely behind, his arms full of belongings. A little ways down the street came Garun, lugging a cart loaded with items.

"Sorry," Noah said.

Zain smiled. "No harm done."

"I have to go right away, but you need to talk to Ashur. He's just inside." Noah pointed to Garun. "And I need him to come with me."

"Is everything in order?" Zain asked, suddenly serious.

"Not yet."

"We'll take Garun's things in. Remember our agreement this morning. You'll be responsible for him."

"Understood." Noah put a hand on Zain's shoulder. "Thank you."

Chapter 13

Can't you just tell us who was at Ashur's?" Tubal-Cain asked as he walked with Noah and Garun past the shipyard.

"Not yet. I don't want to explain it more than once, so we'll wait until I can tell Em too." Noah smiled inwardly at the irony of his situation. His suppressed anger smoldered against Havil and their king, yet now the two people whose help he needed most were the Havilites walking with him.

Typically, while staring across the sea to his left, he contemplated the adventures that lay beyond, but today was different. Today, the surf softly splashing the shore brought no delight and only reminded him of the long days working on the beach with Ara. He turned his eyes away from the water. The long road to Sarie's Bakery steadily rose as it reached into town. Memories of his first jaunt down that hill flooded his mind. The excitement of taking in a new city, the satisfaction of reaching his destination, and the hope of soon becoming an apprentice shipbuilder caused a short-lived smile to appear on his lips. It quickly vanished when he remembered that Aterre had been at his side through it all. It seemed no place in Iri Geshem was safe from memories of Ara or Aterre. *Will this hurt ever go away?*

"Noah?" Tubal-Cain nudged him with his elbow.

Noah lifted his eyes. "What?"

"Garun asked you something."

"Oh, sorry." He looked at Garun. "What is it?"

"I just wondered if you or Emzara would like me to help with anything — get food, do some chores, you name it." Garun held out a palm. "I want to help."

"I can't think of anything like that right now, but I'll need you both to help me with something else soon enough."

They continued straight ahead as the main road turned north. The trail through the milknut grove led immediately in front of Ara's house before reaching the small home he shared with Emzara. *The home I built with Aterre.* He gritted his teeth and stared at the sparse canopy above. *I can't escape them. Do I want to?*

Averting his eyes as they passed Ara's dwelling, he cringed. Ashur's words stung all over again. *It seems like Aterre gave his life trying to protect Ara.* "Why wasn't I there to help?" The words came out louder than he intended.

"You were where you should have been. In your home, with your wife. You can't blame yourself for what happened," Garun said.

Tubal-Cain frowned. "And you probably would've been killed too. And where would that have left Zara? She needs you to be strong."

Noah forced a smile. "It's just . . ." He froze. Laughter emanated from his home, which lay just ahead of them. His heart leapt at the sound of his wife's joy. "That's Em." He spoke softly and put his arms out to halt his friends.

"Adira too." Tubal-Cain put a finger to his lips. "Let's not spoil the moment."

As the group slowly crept forward, the discussion in the house became clearly discernable.

"Remember that time when Aterre told Noah that he had developed a new kind of bean brew and Noah took a huge drink of it?" Adira's voice carried beyond the delicate fabric coverings that hung over the square holes in the walls to allow light into the interior.

"And it was really just bean brew made with seawater." Emzara giggled. "He spit it out all over the table."

Laughter resounded from both women, and Noah gave a lopsided smile. "How was I supposed to know?" He spoke softly then shook his head at the memory of the taste. "It was like drinking brown salt."

Garun put a hand over his mouth to suppress the snicker that crinkled his eyes.

"What about when Baba and Noah challenged Tubal-Cain and Aterre to a race in those two-man boats," Emzara said. "And they gave them one that leaked."

"And they sank right in the middle of the bay." Adira forced the words out in between giggles. "Tubal-Cain was embarrassed because it happened in front of the large crowd that had gathered for the Harvest Day celebration."

"And Aterre wouldn't even talk to Noah until the next day." Emzara chuckled and then sniffled. "And now it makes sense why — Jitzel was watching."

"Serves him right," Adira said. "He always took every opportunity to embarrass us around the men or vice versa."

"Yeah." Emzara dragged the word out. "I miss them so much."

"Oh, I do too. Come here."

Emzara's muffled sobs barely reached Noah's ears. He motioned toward the front door. "Let's go."

As Noah approached, Emzara asked, "Remember when Aterre hid in the kitchen?"

Noah swung open the door. "And he startled Adira."

Both women jolted.

As Noah entered he said, "And she broke the tray over his head."

Smiling at her husband, Emzara hurried to him and wrapped him in a tight embrace.

"He deserved it," Adira said with her hand over heart. "And so do you." She winked.

Noah pulled Emzara's head against his chest and breathed in her familiar scent. He looked at Adira. "And what I wouldn't give to have him here so you could do it again."

Adira smirked. She stood, placing her hands on her hips and tilting her head saucily. "I'd be more than happy to do it too."

Tubal-Cain crossed the floor and kissed his wife. "Sounds like you two are having a good time."

She sighed. "We've been trying to remember all the hilarious moments with them."

Noah released Emzara. "Any time with those two was a good time."

"It sure was." Emzara turned to Adira. "I'm glad you came over. I really needed it. Oh, Garun. You're here. I didn't even see you. Welcome."

Noah held up a hand. "Adira, can you stay a while? I have some news to share with everyone."

"About what?" Adira asked, returning to her seat.

Noah pointed to the few low benches that lined the walls. "Why don't all of you have a seat." He grabbed a chair from the table, as well as the basket delivered by Zain earlier that morning. Sitting down across from the group, he placed the food between him and the others. "Help yourselves."

Noah waited until each person had taken a snack. "What we discuss in here is private. I may want to bring Zain into it at some point, but for now, it stays among the five of us. Agreed?"

"Sure," Tubal-Cain said, and the others nodded.

"Oh, and one more thing. We'll need to talk about Havil, so Garun and Tubal-Cain, you two need to decide if everyone can speak freely about these matters without fear of repercussions."

"What do you mean?" Tubal-Cain squinted and shook his head. "This sounds serious."

"It is. Look, I trust both of you. But there are some sensitive things to discuss. Given your positions in Havil, a prince and an important palace guard, I want to be clear. If one of you says something that reflects poorly on your city or some of its residents, the other one won't seek retaliation."

Garun glanced at Tubal-Cain and spread both hands out, palms up. "Say whatever needs to be said. As you mentioned, this is a private meeting."

Tubal-Cain nodded. "Same goes for me. But you need to tell us who was at Ashur's."

"I will, but just not right away." Noah searched for a place to start. "Garun, except for Adira, we've all seen how Tubal-Cain's father acts in public. What's he really like behind closed doors?"

Garun stroked his chin with his thumb and index finger. "What specifically do you want to know?"

"Do you trust him?"

Biting his lip and sneaking a peek at Tubal-Cain, Garun slowly shook his head side to side. "Only to do what he thinks is in his best interest."

"And what if someone gets in his way?" Noah asked.

"Then I wouldn't want to be that person."

"What do you mean?" Noah worked to draw out his answers, noting that the guard understandably spoke much less freely in Tubal-Cain's presence.

"Well, they usually end up imprisoned." Garun looked at the floor. "Or worse."

"Where are you going with this, Noah?" Tubal-Cain asked. "What does my father have to do with anything?"

Noah turned and met Tubal-Cain's stare. "We've been friends for about four years, and our wives are best friends. You know I wouldn't ask these things if I didn't believe I had good reasons for it."

"I know. I'm just confused." He set aside his plate of food and drummed his fingers on his knee.

"Fair enough. Just a couple more questions and then I'll explain." Noah leaned forward. "Do you believe your father would do almost anything to get his way?"

"He's very ambitious." Tubal-Cain reclined and ran his fingers through his hair. "There are some pretty bad rumors about him. Some say that he's killed a bunch of people. I've even heard someone say that he killed his own father, my grandfather, on the way to Havil." He took Adira's hand. "But I've never seen any of that."

"But do you think he is capable of doing it?" Noah asked.

"Capable? Definitely." Tubal-Cain shrugged. "But willing? I'm not sure. Maybe? If he were angry enough. Why are you asking about him? You said he left town early in the morning well before the murders."

"He did." Noah glanced at Garun, "But what if he came back to go after someone that had gotten in his way?"

"Are you insinuating that my father killed Ara and Aterre?"

Noah took a deep breath. "After you left Ashur's, he brought his secret guest to meet with me. I was very surprised to see her."

Tubal-Cain raised his eyebrows.

Emzara's eyes narrowed. "Her?"

"Yes, one of the dancers from Havil. Her name is Navea."

"Yeah, I sort of know her," Tubal-Cain said. "She's a friend of Naamah's. Or was."

"Didn't she leave on the boat?" Garun asked.

"She did." Noah took a deep breath, then recounted Navea's tale about the king and his guards swimming to shore and how she ended up at Ashur's.

When he finished, Tubal-Cain stood and began to pace. "Did she accuse my father of the murders?"

Noah shook his head. "She said she never saw them again after they left the ship, but she did say that his whole demeanor changed after the council meeting."

"But that doesn't prove anything," Tubal-Cain said.

"No, it doesn't. But it raises some questions. Why did his attitude change from that point on? And why did he and three of his guards swim ashore and disappear for a long time?"

"I don't know. What possible motive could he have? What happened at the council meeting?"

"Baba stood up to him." Emzara sat up straight and her dark eyes snapped. "He questioned him about having two wives, eating animals, and the lack of wisdom in putting your sister in a position with so much authority."

Garun leaned forward. "I overheard him that night telling a fellow guard that the shipbuilder wrecked the opportunity for a trade agreement. He wasn't happy."

Tubal-Cain's wide eyes met Noah's and then shifted to Emzara. "If my father did this" — he lowered his head — "I'm so sorry."

Adira put her arms around her husband.

Noah paused to give them a moment. "If he did this . . ."

"Then he alone is responsible for it." With tears in her eyes, Emzara walked over and put a reassuring hand on Tubal-Cain's shoulder. "We'd never hold this against you."

Tubal-Cain nodded his thanks, then his eyes narrowed. "We need to find out for sure."

"How do we do that?" Adira asked.

Tubal-Cain sighed. "We go to Havil and ask around. I have several people I trust who would tell me if they've heard anything."

"I do too," Garun said. "There are a couple of palace guards and many others in the city that do not approve of the king."

Tubal-Cain held out his hand. "You should stay with Bedin. If my father secretly brought guards to Iri Geshem then I say we go to Havil in secret."

"Is it safe for us?" Adira asked.

Tubal-Cain pulled her close. "As much as I'd like you by my side, I'd prefer that you stay here. If my father hears that we're in the city, he may demand to meet you. And if he's the murderer, then I don't want you near him."

"If you think I'm just going to let Noah walk around Havil after what happened last time —"

"He wouldn't have to." Tubal-Cain held up a hand to interrupt Emzara. "We have a small beach home outside of the city. It doesn't get used anymore, so we could stay there while I check around."

"And while you do that, Noah could find my family and help them pack up to move here." Garun smiled at Emzara. "Don't worry. My place is also outside of the city."

"Are you sure you still want to move here?" Noah asked. "After this morning?"

Garun met Noah's eyes. "Even more so. Those people were misguided, but they thirsted for justice and they listened to reason. And justice and reason should always go hand in hand. I want my family to live in a place like this, under leaders like you and Zain."

"It's settled then. I'll help with the packing too." Emzara stepped to Noah and put an arm around his neck. "You aren't going without me."

Noah pulled her down so that she rested on his lap. "Why do I get the feeling that I won't be able to convince you otherwise?" Peering at Tubal-Cain, he asked, "When do we leave?"

"Since we don't want Bedin to know our plan and alert my father, we leave right after he finishes his work here. Garun, you'll need to take him to the next town and return here when you can. We'll be back with your family soon after."

Chapter 14

Havil — Noah's 49th year

Looking upward and into the sunlight, Naamah inhaled deeply. She paused, allowing the warmth to cradle her darkened skin. She loved the seemingly slower trek the sun made during the warm season. Completely alone, she reveled in the center's open-air design. *Mmm, my House of Knowledge.* Her fingers traced their way down one of the gilded stone columns. Three intricately carved intertwining serpents gracefully wound their way around the curvy forms of vinefruit. The light stone was smooth and cool to her touch. Brushing her cheek against it, she closed her eyes and enjoyed the contrast of the sun's heat to the staunch pillar's chill.

The sound of a bird calling from outside disturbed her quiet enjoyment of simple things and she hastened on her errand. Her sandals slapped against the stone floor as she made her way from the center toward one of the adjacent rooms. The House of Knowledge stood two stories high, but the ceilings of each floor were tall enough that a man standing on another man's shoulders would not be able to touch the brilliantly hued, frescoed top.

Naamah loved the way this massive square structure made her feel so small. Fourteen rooms on each floor surrounded the atrium, and they acted as entryways to smaller nooks. Two large open entrances stood on either end. This place awed her. The sheer number of scrolls able to be carefully organized and stored in the 84 rooms tingled her sense of anticipation. After just a few years, nearly 4,000 documents filled a tiny fraction of the edifice, and they beckoned to her to not remain small and insignificant in her world.

She gazed at a freshly painted map of the known world; the land shape resembled a semi-circle with an opening on the right side. Her city stood in the middle of the lower half and much of the land in its immediate vicinity was charted. Directly above Havil to the north she spotted Iri Geshem. *Just across the Great Sea.* To the west stood a large region marked as "unknown." *What of Nod at the northeast tip of the map, or the wild lands north and west of Iri Geshem?* She ached to know more of the secrets they held.

Realizing she had daydreamed long enough, Naamah passed through the expanse of that area to the room beyond, where high, thin windows allowed light to peek its way through. Square shelves about two cubits in length formed a geometric pattern on the walls to either side of her and each stored a number of scrolls. After rolling a small, wooden staircase over, she climbed up and reached the place where she had last left off. Clutching the three scrolls from that cube, she made her way back down and then eased onto a plush cushion near the window. Unfurling bits of the rolled papyrus, she skimmed the looping and curving text for information about Sepha.

Aha. Here we go. She reclined in her seat and became absorbed in reading until a light appeared beyond her scroll. She blinked, shaking herself from her reverie, and turned her head slightly toward the sound of soft-padding footsteps. In the now-dim room, a human outline appeared. She sat up straight, and her muscles tensed without warning. As the figure lit a hanging lantern, the visage of the seer came into focus.

"You've been here awhile. Anything to report, my princess?" His soothing tones calmed her the way her mother's soft caress on her cheeks used to when she was a small child.

"I've learned much." She beckoned with her hand, and he lounged on the cushion next to her.

"Tell me."

"This scroll talks of lands that have practiced Sepha since the dawning of days."

"Ah, very good."

"There's a place called Bothar. Apparently, they're very far to the north and west. It seems as if their large city was much like Havil, but there's a strange mystery about it."

The seer nodded, encouraging Naamah to continue.

"A scribe from the west met someone who spent several years living there. Some of what he wrote is . . . well, it makes me uncomfortable." Her tutor's eyes displayed concern, and she plunged ahead. "The people of that town are allowed to . . ." Her eyes scrunched as she held back tears. "The men as an act of worship will go to a temple, where young children are waiting . . . in special rooms . . ." She buried her face in her hands, not wanting to continue.

"Hush, child. I'm surprised that bothered you so."

Her head jerked up, her eyes wide. "Why would you say that? The children. . . ."

"Did you read about the results?" At her silence, he went on, "What did it do for the devotion to Sepha?"

"It increased greatly. The amount of people coming to the temples tripled in a single year."

"Yes." His voice savored the word, drawing it out. A smile played about his thin lips. "I'm shocked that you don't see the great benefit. With all you've done to get our people to follow Nachash, I'd have thought you'd be excited with learning a new method to increase their devotion."

"But the young children."

"They got to play an incredible role in nurturing the people's devotion. Don't you see the honor they held?"

"Yes, but why so young?"

"How would you do things differently?"

"What about someone like me?" She spoke quickly. "Wouldn't it be better if we could get women my age who long to play a greater role in promoting devotion to their god?"

He gazed at her face and frowned. "Someone *like* you, yes. But not you. You're the princess."

"But, why not me? If I could give myself wholly to the cause of Nachash, I would!" Her passionate voice echoed against the dim walls. "It'd be my greatest act as princess."

"No!" He sat upright with a jerk.

She recoiled slightly at his volume. "No?"

The seer cleared his throat. "I want something greater for you."

"What could be greater?"

He settled back and calmed his voice. "Think of how pleased Nachash would be if you were in charge of this idea of yours. You'd accomplish so much more if you were responsible for bringing this to Havil. I'd be so proud."

Her face flushed in pleasure at being back in his good favor. *And something like this — which would add ardent followers — would certainly please our god.*

She longed to hear his praise again. "You like my idea?"

"Certainly. Continue to learn more about how you could implement this here." He tapped the scroll on her lap.

"Oh, that reminds me" — she glanced down at the flowing text — "there was a mystery surrounding Bothar."

"Go on."

"Well, a number of years after beginning this new temple practice — here, let me find the place." Naamah rolled up the right side of the scroll and unraveled the left as she searched for the details. "Ah, here's what the informant told the scribe."

> I have always stayed on the edge of society, watching, recording, but never taking part. However, just today, twelve more have given up the inner spirit and left their bodies to this world. There is wild speculation about what is causing the sickness. It seems that death usually arrives within two weeks of the first symptoms. As a precaution for my own safety, I have settled in a small abode much farther away from the city and have spread word that I have perished. I shall continue to write about the strange death toll in the city from here.

Naamah moved her finger down the page, searching for the part she wanted to show the seer. "And there's a tragic ending here."

> The entire city of Bothar is no more. Within the span of just a few whole moons, the city went from a thriving cultural center to being abandoned. More people were needing to be buried than those who felt well enough to accomplish the task. The stench of burning piles pervades the city. I have watched from

my secret place this week as the last remaining citizens have succumbed to the strange sickness that caused both young and old to leave their life here on this earth.

Naamah looked up into his deep-set eyes. "What could cause all that?"

The seer remained silent, but his expression implored her to speak her mind.

"Do you think it's because of what they did to those children?" Naamah shuddered. "Because, if so, we should never bring this to Havil."

"Nonsense, you should have more wisdom than that. You yourself called it a mystery, and if the scribe had known the cause, he'd have recorded it. Instead of trying to link the deaths in Bothar to their practices, think about how great those customs made their devotion. Don't forfeit great advancement and power because of the unknown." The irritation in the seer's typically calm voice alerted Naamah to his displeasure with her question.

Naamah stared at the scroll as she contemplated his words. "You're right." She straightened up and tossed her head back, forcing her straight dark hair behind her shoulder. "I'll start working on this program then. It's just . . . well it's just too bad that . . ."

"That what?"

"The annual ceremony is in two whole moons. I wish I had discovered it sooner so that we could be ready by then."

"I'm certain there's enough time. You can use your influence with the palace. Don't forget to practice those incantations I've taught you. If you promote it properly, women will beg to be priestesses of Nachash."

"You really think so?"

He stood and offered her a hand. "I know it. Now, let's talk about how."

Chapter 15

The crowded city streets bustled. Emzara craned her neck to see the tops of the buildings. The towering stucco edifices were taller than she remembered. *Guess they've been busy in the last four years.* She tripped on a gap in the cobblestone roadway, causing her to look down at the broken surface, pockmarked as it was with holes where stones were missing. *Maybe they should have put some of that construction effort into repairing this road.*

Noah's strong back just in front of her comforted her among the unfamiliar sights all around. She'd expected to recognize more, but the city seemed utterly alien. *A lot has changed here in Havil. Although, maybe it's just my focus that has changed. I was paying attention to Noah last time, and this time we're on a dangerous errand. Or maybe it's because we're on the outskirts of town that I don't recognize all this.*

On some level, she knew the rationalization for what it was: an attempt to make sense of something that bore no logic. The city was more different than her four-year absence could justify. Yet the fact of it remained, and she could do nothing but walk on, following Noah as they headed to Garun's house. Shaking off her unease, she took in the brilliantly colored signs announcing in bright paint a variety of shops: weaponry, woven and wrapped cloths, and jewelry.

She gave a wide berth to another large gap in the street and nearly ran into an elderly woman. Turning, she said, "I'm so sorry," but the woman had vanished. Puzzled, Emzara held her baby close, protecting the tiny form as she scanned the street. There was no sign of the old woman, and Emzara dropped a kiss on the soft fuzz of her baby's head. "Tera." She whispered the name aloud. A perfect combination of *Ara* and *Aterre* for her perfect little one. She smiled as she remembered her father telling her that *Emzara* was a combination of his and her mother's names. Tera barely shifted in the tightly wrapped cloths that served not only to hold her close to Emzara but also to keep her arms free for other tasks.

"Em, are you coming?" Several steps ahead, Noah paused and looked back. She hurried to catch up. The shops thinned out and soon the cobblestone road turned to dirt and became noticeably narrower. Squat dwelling places stood tucked together on either side, with very little room in between. *If this is where Garun's family lives, I'm glad they'll get to move to Iri Geshem soon.* The wind moaned through the branches of a tall tree, sending a chill through her body.

As if on cue, a voice called out from behind them. "You two, stop!"

Noah turned around and grabbed her right hand with his left. "Run!"

She sprinted after him, but based on the sounds coming from behind them, they were not making much headway. Her breath came in short gasps, each one like a knife in her side. Somehow Tera was still sleeping, even with the extra jostling. *Thank you, Most High.*

"Stop or you'll wish you had." The voice from behind them rang with authority.

"Noah, I — the baby . . ."

"We'd better do what he said." Noah's pace slacked and he turned to face their pursuers, pivoting so that she was shielded behind him.

"Noah and Emzara," a man with an evil grin said. His eyes were in shadows, giving his face a ghastly hollowness that struck terror deep within her. "We've been looking all over for you, and here you wander right into our city." Eight guards walked around their leader and encircled the young family, cutting off any hope of escape.

A weight settled within Emzara, like a milknut dropping from a tree and hitting the sandy ground below with a thud. But something about his words struck her as off. They'd been looking for her and Noah? But Lamech had been to Iri Geshem — surely Naamah knew where to find them.

"What do you want with us?" Noah asked.

His boldness both pleased and scared Emzara.

"Step aside." Another voice sounded from behind the guard.

Emzara adjusted her shoulder wrap to further conceal Tera. *Where are all these people coming from?*

Lamech appeared and headed straight toward her.

"King Lamech! But — I — I thought these were Naamah's guards." The words escaped from her mouth before she could stop them.

"Naamah's guards are also my guards, of course." He stepped closer, forcing her to return his gaze. The power and hate in his eyes revealed at once that he had killed her father and Aterre. She swallowed hard. *And now it's our turn.*

"Why have you stopped us, sir?" Noah asked.

"You have something that we want. Something we need."

"What's that?" Noah's voice growled low and instinctively Emzara knew he was readying himself to protect them with his life if need be.

"We've been looking for her." The king pointed directly at Emzara and she quaked inside.

"Me? Why?"

"Get away from her." Noah stepped directly in between his wife and the king.

Before she even saw them move, two soldiers were there, restraining Noah and yanking him out of the way.

Lamech stroked Emzara's cheek with the back of his hand.

She twisted away, being careful to protect her child.

Lamech laughed. "Not you."

Confused, Emzara drew Tera closer to her body.

He sneered. "The child. Take her." Noah broke free and lunged at Lamech, but the king shoved Noah aside as if he weighed nothing at all. The two guards seized him again and one struck him with a club, rendering him unconscious.

Crying out, Emzara struck at Lamech's hands as he reached for Tera. When he brushed aside her blows, she came at him again, this time going for his eyes, her fingers bent like the claws of an animal.

Stars exploded in her vision as he struck her across the cheek, sending her to her hands and knees in the dirt. Pushing aside her outer wrap, Lamech wrenched the cloth wound around Emzara's torso and seized the baby.

"No!"

Awakened by the noise and rough treatment, Tera's loud cries mingled with her mother's sounds of anguish. Still too dizzy to rise, Emzara clung to the king's robe with all her strength. "You can't have her! Not without me!"

Lamech flashed a grin, his large teeth gleaming. "You're welcome to come along." He handed Tera to a guard and with a flick of his wrist beckoned two other soldiers. They hauled Emzara to her feet and shoved her toward the city, back the way they had come.

Somehow, in a blur, they were standing at the base of the middle steps of a large edifice Emzara recognized as the central structure of the ceremony on their first visit. Tears blinding her vision, Emzara stumbled as a guard shoved her up the stairs. The edges dug into her shins and she clamored behind Tera and Lamech, trying to reach her dear baby girl. "Where are you taking her?"

A woman's loud cackle echoed across the expansive courtyard, pulling Emzara's focus to the top of the platform. There stood Naamah, dressed in one of Emzara's own gowns. *Where did she get that?*

"Oh look, it's Emzara." Naamah stepped forward and stared into Emzara's eyes. A wicked grin spread across her face. "The one who has so captured my Noah over there that he won't even look at me, but I'll soon fix that. Once you're gone, he'll have nowhere else to turn."

Emzara followed Naamah's gaze. Held up by two armed men, Noah slumped against a low wall, his head lolled to one side.

"And there's the new symbol of your love. A child. Bring her to me!" Naamah beckoned a nearby guard.

Emzara could barely stand to look as the woman held onto Tera. She clutched at the baby awkwardly as if she had never held one before. "Wake him."

A guard picked up a pail and pitched its contents in Noah's face. The water splashed against him and he shuddered. His eyes slowly registered consciousness, and a look of terror crossed his face as he saw Naamah with his child.

"Look at me, Noah. Now will you have me? I'm dressed for the part in this rustic dress. I'm even carrying your child."

Her laugh drove shivers of fear through Emzara. "Please." Emzara uttered the only word that would come out of her mouth as she fell to her knees in a feeble attempt to reclaim her baby.

Naamah held Tera out with two arms and inspected the child. "Well, it's too late. Now you'll regret ever refusing me." She stood in front of the large serpent statue so its head curved over hers.

"Finally, I have all I need." She held Tera aloft before placing her on a golden altar. "Remember those children Noah rescued before he even met you? Well, Nachash desires the blood of innocents, and your child will take the place of those Noah stole."

Emzara shrieked and struggled to wrench herself away from her captors, but she was no match. They stuffed a cloth in her mouth and held her face in the direction of Naamah.

Naamah closed her eyes and hummed an eerie tune. As her volume rose, the molded head of the serpent grew in size and started swaying. Emzara froze in terror — such a thing could not be. But before her eyes it morphed from a statue into a moving golden being, the head raised and poised over the writhing form of her daughter. Tera's high-pitched cries pierced her mother's heart. As the serpent moved to strike, Emzara screamed with all her might.

"What's going on, Em?"

Someone was shaking her and she sat up, narrowly avoiding collision with Noah's face as he hovered over her. "Where's Tera?" She gripped his upper arm and clung to him as if her sheer force would result in a faster answer. A cold sweat drenched her forehead and her heartbeat raced.

"Who's Tera?" In the semi-darkness, she saw the confused look on her husband's face, and anger at his stupidity stabbed through her heart.

"Our daughter! Is she — is she dead?" The painful word barely crossed her lips.

"Em, you were having a dream. You're still pregnant." He stroked her cheek, and she relaxed her grip on him slightly. "You're safe here in the ship's quarters."

"A dream." She breathed deeply, trying to shake off the sick horror of what she'd seen, but the vivid memory was still etched in her mind. "It was so real." She rested against him, silent for a while. "Do you think it's wrong for us to be traveling to Havil?"

Noah kissed the top of her head. "No. We're going to find answers. If we discover that Lamech is truly to blame, we need to protect others from being hurt or killed by him — his crime must be punished. We're also getting Garun's family to safety. It's just your fears coming out while you're sleeping."

"I guess you're right. But, Noah" — she grabbed his hand and placed it on the growing bulge in her midsection — "I want you to promise you'll be careful. This baby becomes more real to me each day. There are times when I think I can feel her inside of me, moving around. And we need you." Her gaze found his. "Even if it was just a dream, we know Havil is a wicked place. I have a terrible feeling that something evil grows there. And it's *seen* us."

He moved to wrap her in an embrace, but he didn't try to reassure her again. Instead, she felt his stubble scrape her ear as he nodded. "I know."

He shifted so they were both lying on the narrow bed, with her head nestled on his chest and his hand on her belly. For a long time they were silent, allowing the fear to dissipate into the darkness and peace to return.

Noah's chuckle rumbled under her ear. "Her, huh?"

Emzara smiled. "Well, I have no way of really knowing. I just keep thinking of this baby as a girl." She looked up at him. "I kind of like the name Tera."

Chapter 16

This is probably my favorite part of the journey," Noah said as he watched the waves crash into the shore hundreds of cubits away.

"Sitting and staring at the water?" Tubal-Cain asked. "Looks pretty boring to me."

Noah yawned and pointed at a small gap in the distant forest. "See that opening there?"

"Between the trees?"

"Yeah."

Tubal-Cain slid a crate along the deck and sat on it next to Noah. "What's so exciting about that?"

"There's a small river flowing through there." Noah shifted in his seat to face his friend. "I like to imagine what it'd be like to travel up that waterway with Em and do some exploring. Do any people live there? If so, what are they like? What animals live in the forests? Em would love to discover new creatures. And what about those hills way back there? Is that where the river starts?"

"You know what I think about when I see those hills?"

"The metals you might find there?" Noah asked.

"Exactly."

Noah snorted. "Your musings aren't as exciting as mine."

"Maybe not to you." Tubal-Cain leaned back on his hands. "Since you like sitting and thinking so much, I've got a serious question for you."

Feeling the prick of exhaustion behind his eyes, Noah longed to head below deck and fall asleep next to Emzara, but he already expected very little rest on this secret mission. Emzara and Tubal-Cain assisted in the seafaring responsibilities where they could, but they relied upon Noah's growing expertise to captain the vessel. Yet, despite the somber cause for their voyage and the long days and nights, he had largely enjoyed the first 12 days of the trip.

"Okay, just a moment." Noah pretended to write something on the large scroll spread out on a bin to his left.

"What are you writing?"

He glanced at the map. "I'm adding details about those hills. It says, 'Tubal-Cain's metals' right there." Noah tapped the page.

Tubal-Cain stretched his neck to see and chuckled, his amusement spreading to form laugh lines around his eyes. "No, you didn't."

Noah smirked. "I've just been updating it from our previous trips. There are still some blank areas because we've sailed past them at night." Noah rolled up the map and wrapped a string around it. "What did you want to ask me?"

Tubal-Cain scratched behind his ear. "Do you think we'll ever see them again?"

"Those hills?"

"No." Tubal-Cain shook his head. "Aterre and Ara."

Noah's smile disappeared.

"I mean, do you think there's more than this?" The blacksmith waved his arm from left to right, indicating the whole world.

Noah watched the mildly undulating water distort his long, early morning shadow, enjoying the light, cool breeze as it passed through his unkempt hair. He sighed and stretched a hand out toward Tubal-Cain. "What do you think?"

"I'd like to assume there's something after this life. Some of the older people in our city say we were made from the ground, just like the people of Iri Geshem believe. But they say that we return to the ground and that's it."

"They think the person just ceases to exist?" Noah asked.

"Some of them do."

Noah tilted his head. "That might explain why so many people in your city live the way they do."

Furrowing his brow, Tubal-Cain asked, "What do you mean?"

"Well, think about it. If this life is all we have — if there's nothing after it — then you may as well live however you want. Seek pleasure and power, instead of serving the Creator and helping others."

"I can see what you're saying, but I think you're overstating it a bit." Tubal-Cain looked up and squinted. "Some of those people are very kind to others. They don't just live for pleasure and power."

"Hmm." Noah rested his chin on his fist. "I guess I could argue that they desire to have others think well of them and that's selfish, but I'd rather not judge their motives, particularly since I don't know them."

"Well, that's good. I'd hate to think you pretend to know everyone's motives." Tubal-Cain stared across the water. "After all, couldn't someone turn it around on you and say that you serve the Creator for selfish reasons too — that you're hoping to somehow get His favor?"

"I guess it could look like that from someone else's point of view," Noah said. "But the main reason I serve the Creator is to thank Him for giving me life."

"I can see that, but we're getting away from my initial question. What do you think happens after death, if anything?"

Noah slowly drew in a breath. "I'm not really sure. I've heard several ideas about it."

"Like what?" Tubal-Cain leaned forward.

"Well, remember the Zakari people I told you about?"

"The ones whose children were kidnapped?"

Noah nodded. "Their elder told me that the people who stole their kids, the people from Bothar, practiced the dark arts. They tried contacting spirits, either people who had already died or some other kind of spiritual being."

"So if they contacted the spirits of people who had died, does that mean after death we just roam around the earth and no one can see us?" Tubal-Cain scratched the prickly growth on his face, which seemed to be growing in twice as fast as Noah's attempt at a beard. "Doing what?"

"I'm not sure — waiting to give advice to those who contact them?" Noah shrugged a shoulder. "I guess that's what the people of Bothar believed."

Tubal-Cain drew back. "That's really weird. What did you mean about the other kind of spiritual being?"

"Garun told me . . ." Noah stopped and quickly regretted mentioning his earlier conversation with the king's guard.

"Told you what?"

Noah shook his head. "Never mind."

Tubal-Cain crossed his arms. "No, not never mind. Tell me."

Pulling a tiny sliver of wood from the rail above the hull, Noah said, "I'd rather not."

"It's about my sister, isn't it?"

Noah slowly turned and nodded.

The distinct clinking and scraping of copper and silver reached Noah's ears as Tubal-Cain fidgeted with the leather money pouch that hung from his belt. "Just tell me."

"Garun told me that he's heard her mentor — they call him a seer — telling her about the spirits that he communicates with. The seer told her that the Creator is just one of many spiritual entities. Originally, He made the world that we see and another realm that we cannot see — one that's inhabited by spirits or gods. The Creator was the most powerful spiritual being." A frown grew on Noah's face. "But as time went on, and as more people turned away from Him, other gods, like Nachash, turned against Him and became stronger. Apparently, this seer thinks that Nachash is now the most powerful, or that he can become the most powerful spirit if he has the most followers."

"Do you think she buys into that?" Tubal-Cain asked.

Noah let out a deep breath and spoke softly. "I have a feeling that she'll believe it if it means more power."

Tubal-Cain's forearm bulged as he tightened his grip on the leather bag. "And do you think these spirits actually exist? Besides the Creator, of course."

"Garun thinks they're real because the seer knows things that he shouldn't be able to know. He didn't give me any examples, so I'm not entirely sure what he meant."

"And do you believe that Nachash is becoming more powerful than the Creator?" Tubal-Cain asked, his dark, heavy eyebrows nearing each other.

"I sure hope that isn't happening." Noah lowered his face into his hands and massaged his forehead. "I guess I can see how it might look like that, especially to people in Havil, who think that the city's become so grand because they follow Nachash. But it doesn't really make sense to me that one of these spirits could become more powerful than its Maker. If the Most High created these spirits, then it seems like He could just as easily destroy them."

"That makes sense, but we got off subject again." Tubal-Cain huffed and pointed to Noah. "What do you believe happens when we die?"

Noah thought back to childhood conversations with his father. "I've always believed that the Creator will reward those who faithfully serve Him."

"What sort of reward?"

"My guess is that we'll get to live with Him."

"As spirits?" Tubal-Cain said. "Obviously, our body remains here."

Noah raised his gaze to the sky. "I'm not sure. I think we'll have some sort of body."

"Really? Why?"

Noah chuckled. "You ask a lot of questions." He faced his friend. "My grandfather's father was a man who walked closely with the Most High. He used to warn people that the Creator was going to come to earth someday and judge the wicked people."

Tubal-Cain smirked. "My father said that where he grew up, there was a man like that who visited the city several times, and many of the people mocked him for his rants. As my father told it, this man would walk through town and shout about the coming judgment that never came." A grin spread on his face. "Everyone made up labels for him. They didn't want to use his real name because it was the same as the name of the city, and they didn't want to be associated with him."

Noah looked at Tubal-Cain, then the ship's deck, and then back at his friend. "Wait. Your father is from the land of Nod, the city of Enoch, right?"

"Yes."

One side of Noah's mouth turned up slightly. "That's the name of my grandfather's father."

Tubal-Cain's smile disappeared rapidly. "You mean, the man who warned the city of Enoch about judgment . . ."

"Is my grandfather's father." Noah nodded.

"Forgive me. I didn't mean to disrespect your family."

"You were just repeating what your father told you. I know you wouldn't intentionally say something bad about my family."

"Nah, just you." Tubal-Cain slapped Noah's shoulder and laughed. "So why did you bring up your grandfather's father in the first place?"

"He decided to visit the land of Eden with Berit, my father's —"

"The cursed land?" Tubal-Cain held up both palms. "Sorry, interrupting again."

Noah smiled at his large muscular friend apologizing like a child. "You've heard the rumors, too. Well, I think this might be why they started." Noah adjusted his wrap to cover his shoulder. "As they approached the land, Enoch simply disappeared."

"What do you mean 'disappeared'?" Tubal-Cain asked. "Did he wander off and become lost?"

Noah shook his head. "No, I mean he vanished. One moment he was walking with Berit, and the next moment" — Noah snapped his fingers — "he was gone."

Tubal-Cain stared through wide eyes.

"My father believes God just took him from the earth."

"Why?"

"Our best guess is so that he wouldn't have to face any more of the evils in this world."

"And because of that, you think he's living with the Creator and that we may live with Him after we die?"

"That's right."

"And since his body was taken too, you think that we may have some sort of body when we're with the Creator?"

Noah shrugged. "Like I said before, it's my best guess."

Tubal-Cain sat up straight. "Well, it makes sense to me, and I like it."

"You do?"

"Of course. It would mean that Aterre and Ara are with the Creator right now."

Noah nodded and forced a tight smile. "I like it even more now."

An anguished cry came from below deck, and Noah tensed and spun toward the opening. "Em?"

He hurried to the stairs and made his way down to the low-ceilinged quarters under the deck. Ducking to avoid crossbeams, Noah blinked several times, trying to force his eyes to adjust to the dark quarters lit only by an oil lamp affixed to a nearby shelf. "Em, what's wrong? Where are you?"

There was no figure on the bed, only tousled blankets. A low moan emanated from the foot of the knee-high cot. As he rushed there, Noah's breath caught at the sight of his wife huddled on the floor.

"Em . . ."

Emzara rocked quietly back and forth. Her ebony curls clung to her cheeks. Her long lashes were pinched between her tightly closed eyelids. Even in her discomfort, her beauty gripped Noah's heart. Another subdued moan escaped from her. Her leg violently shot out and she gripped the base of the bed as if in extreme pain. He rushed to her side. Her labored breathing worried him. "Em, what's going on?"

She grabbed his hand with her free hand and for a few moments squeezed with a grip he did not know she possessed. Pain surged through his fingers, reminding him of one of Toman's intense greetings. "Em?"

Suddenly her features relaxed. She released her grasp and reclined against the wall, limp.

Is she dead? The thought vanished as instantly as it came to mind when she took a deep, shaky breath. Noah breathed a sigh of relief.

"I . . ." She held up a bloodied cloth. Combined with Em's pain and heavy breathing, the pieces came together. He had been only a boy when his second sibling was born too early, but he remembered the day vividly. It was not until the birth of Misha a few years later that the light in his mother's eyes finally came back. But the unknown child was never forgotten.

Returning to the needs in front of him, he held Emzara tenderly as she sobbed. Then together they wept over yet another loss.

Chapter 17

Land of Havilah — Noah's 49th year

Holding a bag of supplies in his right hand and with his left gripping one end of a large basket stuffed with clothing, Noah trudged through the shallow water with Tubal-Cain, who held the other end of the oversized container. As they neared the shore, Noah handed Emzara the sack. "I think this is the last of the items that we'll need for now."

Emzara placed the bag on top of a small crate on the beach and arched her back. Silently she took in their surroundings.

Needing a rest after three trips from the boat, Noah walked toward his wife and placed a hand on her shoulder as he took in the clean, glimmering sand and listened to the water gently lapping the shore.

She shrugged off his caress. "Leave me be."

Sighing, he turned and went to sit on the sand beside Tubal-Cain, facing the sea. Noah couldn't resist feasting his gaze on the display of God's creation before him. "It's very beautiful." Enticed, he stretched a foot back into the refreshing liquid.

"Indeed. I spent a lot of time in this water as a child." Tubal-Cain tilted his head toward the nearby woods. "I used to find the slimiest creatures under rocks or logs in that forest, and then I'd put them in my sister's hair."

Despite his revulsion of Naamah as an adult, Noah tried picturing her as a young child like Misha, and struggled to stifle a laugh. "I'm sure she loved that."

"She squealed like a baby, and I'd get in trouble every time." Tubal-Cain leaned back on his hands and chuckled. "It was worth it."

Noah watched Emzara from the corner of his eye to see how she would react to the discussion about Naamah, but she never flinched. She remained the stoic shell of herself that she had become in the past few weeks. A band of longing tightened around Noah's heart, and he ached to see her usual good humor and ready smile return. Losing her first child would have been difficult enough, but going through it just weeks after losing her father and close friend had been nearly unbearable. Surprised by her lack of tears in the first few days after the loss of their baby, Noah did his best to comfort her. But her demeanor eventually shifted from plain apathy to occasional outbursts of exasperation. While he didn't like that she vented her anger at him, at least she came alive during those moments. In between these explosions of anger, she retreated. Not sure what to do, Noah eventually stopped trying to console her, and she rarely spoke to him. Privately, he wondered if she blamed him for everything.

He sighed and watched the boat, anchored about 50 cubits away, as it bobbed softly on the surface. The broad-leafed trees of the forest lined both sides of the narrow lagoon. Noah recognized most of them, but he spotted a couple that seemed foreign to him. *I'll have to check those out with Em.* He let out a sigh, realizing the futility of that now. Colorful flowers topped low-lying plants near the water's edge, their cheery petals a marked contrast from how he felt. A variety of animal chirps and clicks called out through the still morning air. "It's a good thing we arrived at this point during the daylight, or I fear we may have sailed right past that little inlet."

"We would've realized our mistake soon enough," Tubal-Cain said. "The lights of Havil aren't too far away."

"We're that close?" Emzara asked, taking sudden interest.

Tubal-Cain shrugged. "It's a pretty long walk, but close enough for me to get there, check around a little, and return before it's too late this evening."

Emzara paced back and forth. "And you're sure your family won't be visiting this place while we're here?"

"I really doubt it. If they're planning another Serpent Ceremony three days from now, like Garun said, then they'll be too busy making arrangements for that."

Noah climbed to his feet and motioned to their belongings. "Let's get all this inside."

Two quick jaunts up a sandy trail from the shore to the beach home completed the task at hand. Noah set his second load on the wooden floor of the main room.

Emzara dug out some supplies from the largest container. "I'll fix firstfeast right away." She pointed at Tubal-Cain. "That should give you the energy you need for a long day."

"Where should we stay?" Noah asked.

Tubal-Cain tipped his head toward the hallway that began in the middle of the back wall between the front room and the kitchen. "First chamber on the right."

Noah took his time moving their supplies to the guest room. Frustrated by his inability to provide solace for Emzara and by her seeming indifference toward him, Noah tightened his grip on the door handle and pushed harder than necessary. He stepped inside and closed the door. After dropping his physical burden, Noah moved to the large, low-lying pallet adorned with multiple cushions and sat down, determined to release his emotional burdens. Emzara had every reason to sulk, but so did he, and sooner or later, she needed to break free from her mood. He did everything he could think of to be there for her, but she seemed disinterested in all of it. A tear formed in his eye as he pictured her smiling face on the evening she told him he would be a father. *Em, I need you back.*

Noah lay back on the bed and stared at the ceiling. *Creator, forgive me for my reluctance to speak to You these past weeks. I don't understand why You've allowed all of these terrible things to happen recently. I can't bear this pain alone. I know You're here, but I want Em by my side too. If I've done something to hurt her, please help me to make it right.* He closed his eyes and wiped the tears from the sides of his face. A strong sense of conviction washed over him. Gathering his thoughts, Noah continued to pray. *Although I don't understand all that is going on, I trust that You will always do what is right. Even if it hurts.*

After letting out a deep breath, Noah stood and dried his eyes and cheeks. As he stepped into the hallway, he overheard Emzara asking Tubal-Cain something about the house. He entered the main room and Emzara's countenance immediately dimmed; being run through with a grendec's tooth would have hurt less.

"So many memories in this place," Tubal-Cain said as he breathed in deeply. "It still smells the same as I remember."

Noah offered him a weak smile. "How often did you come here?"

"Only about twice year. But I haven't been here since" — he scratched his head — "maybe about 12 years ago. Once I started working with the smiths on a regular basis, I didn't have the free time."

"Firstfeast is ready." Emzara spread three plates on the table between them. "It's not much, but I'll bake some bread today, and we'll have a grand evenfeast tonight."

"And maybe I'll bring some food back from the city," Tubal-Cain said.

Noah glanced at the assortment of nuts, dried fruit, and sliced vegetables on the tray, and his stomach growled. Ever amazed at her gift for making an inviting feast out of even the slimmest of provisions, he selected a few from each of the options and dropped them in the bowl in front of him. After stirring them together, he paused before taking a bite. "This looks wonderful, Em."

She looked down at her bowl and started eating.

Noah suppressed the urge to vent his frustration and glanced at Tubal-Cain, who returned a sympathetic half-smile.

"Well, as soon as I finish, I'll head into Havil with my new disguise." He grinned and rubbed the beard he had grown during the voyage. "I'll check with some people I trust to see if they've heard anything about what happened in Iri Geshem."

"And you'll make sure they don't say anything about the three of us being here?" Noah asked.

"Of course." He shoved another fruit slice into his mouth and talked around it. "Just wait for me here, and I'll be back before you know it."

"What if someone recognizes you and tells your father?" Noah asked.

Tubal-Cain nodded. "I've thought about that. If my father finds out, then I'll act as if I were planning to pay him a surprise visit. If I get caught up in the city, I'll send word to you through someone I trust."

Conversation lagged and the three fell silent as they ate. *Em, I miss your lively banter during a meal.* Suddenly, his once-hungry insides changed on him and tightened. He lowered his spoon and pushed his bowl away.

"Is there anything you want us to do while you're gone?" Emzara broke the quiet as she combined all the leftovers onto one plate.

Tubal-Cain stood and swiftly rewound his wrap over one shoulder. He grabbed Emzara's hand and put it in Noah's. "Yes, talk to each other and rediscover the love you've always had together." He whirled and moved toward the door. "I'll see you tonight."

"Be safe," Noah called out as he squeezed Emzara's hand and watched her.

She slowly raised her head and met his gaze. Looking away, her lip trembled. "Noah, I . . . I . . . don't . . ." Emzara slipped out of her seat and slid over to hug him. "I'm sorry."

Noah stood and held her tight. Afraid to spoil the moment, he silently waited for her to speak.

Emzara brushed his cheek with her lips and backed away, wiping her eyes. "Can we go for a walk?"

Noah lifted her hand and kissed it. "Of course."

Without another word, she led him outside. Turning toward the beach, she whispered "Which way?"

Noah pointed to the west side of the lagoon where some trees that he did not recognize stood. "Over there."

They left the trail to the beach and waded through long grasses until they reached the edge of the woods. Watching Emzara, Noah smiled to himself as he thought about their different perspectives on life. A setting like this inspired him and ignited a need to examine all the various types of wood around him. But she would normally be on the lookout for any animals that might cross their path. Her fascination with God's creatures had grown with each passing year, and now he hoped that these new surroundings would rekindle some passion in her.

"I'm sorry that I've been cold." Emzara pushed her hair back with her free hand. "I just. . . ." She shook her head. "You didn't deserve that."

Noah put an arm around her shoulder and pulled her close. "Em, I don't know what I did wrong, but you know you can always —"

"You didn't do anything wrong. You did everything you could to cheer me up." She stopped and put her hand against his cheek as her eyes welled up. "I've never felt so lost, so helpless, and I never should've pushed you away. Forgive me."

He nodded and placed his hand over hers, keeping it on his cheek.

"I was so focused on my own anguish that I barely even thought about the pain you were feeling." She leaned in and rested her head against his chest. "Every time I saw you, it made me think of our baby and that it was my fault — that I was inadequate to be a mother or to be your wife — and all the heartache rushed back in."

Holding her tight as she wept, Noah kissed the top of her head. He wanted to tell her of his suffering as well, but he decided to remain silent and allow their embrace to begin healing their wounds.

Emzara finally pulled back slightly and looked into his eyes. "I'm still working through my feelings and thoughts, but I'll try to include you when I can. It might take some more time though."

He cleared a tear from her cheek with his thumb. "Em, I love you."

Her eyes flashed their old sparkle. "I love . . ."

Embracing her tightly, Noah dipped his head and planted an impassioned kiss on her lips, which she returned. Weeks of grief seemed to retreat, and the joy they once shared flooded back into his soul. With their lips still pressed together, he slid his arms around her lower back and stood to his full height, lifting her off the ground in the process.

Emzara pulled back first. Noah loosened his grip, allowing her feet to slowly drop to the ground. "Promise me something."

"What?"

"That whatever tragedies arise in our future, we face them together." He tucked a strand of her hair behind her ear. "I need you more than ever in those times."

She bit her lip and looked at her feet. "I'll . . . try."

A loud cracking sound in the distance drew their attention.

"What was that?" Emzara asked.

"Not sure. Let's go see."

Noah quietly led her through the forest toward the disturbance. A snort and then some stomping filled the air. Suddenly, the crashing noise rang out again.

"Over there," he said as he shifted course.

Unrecognizable sounds emanated from an animal as it bellowed and snorted. Emzara wet her lips and slowed her pace slightly as they closed in. Movement in a small clearing ahead made Noah dart behind a wide tree several cubits in front of them.

"What are those things?" Emzara asked.

Noah shook his head, which she probably didn't see, since her attention never left the two brownish-green creatures. He craned his neck to get a better view. Staring each other down, they stalked about on two legs in a large circular pattern. Noah estimated they stood about Emzara's height but were at least twice that long from head to tail. Their most unique feature was the large bony mound on the top of their heads.

The animal closest to them stomped, reared back, and then charged its foe. The other beast lowered its head and dashed in. The spectacular collision echoed through the forest, and the two combatants slowly returned to the edge of the clearing. A snort from one creature triggered an angry blast from the other.

As they marched around their ring, Noah peeked at Emzara. As if she sensed his gaze, she glanced back at him, eyes full of wonder and an ear-to-ear smile etched on her face, before turning back to the observe the confrontation. The stomping of feet signaled another dramatic charge. This time Noah kept his focus on his wife, relishing her reactions as she marveled at the Most High's creativity.

She winced at the thunderous crash that generated a moan from one of the beasts. Noah turned back to the battle, but it was clearly over. The creature on the other side of the clearing raised its head in the air and let out a victory cry. The other staggered away, hanging its head.

Ducking back behind the tree, Emzara gripped Noah's hand and leaned close to his ear. "Incredible."

"Have you ever seen anything like that?"

Emzara shook her head. "Not quite like that. Some male bleaters spar with each other but never so violently." Her eyes lit up. "I can't wait to draw them."

A settled feeling returned to Noah's soul, as her apathy faded. While neither of them would ever be the same, he hoped that this was the beginning of a new normal.

Chapter 18

"I'm worried about Tubal-Cain." Emzara paced across the floor and peeked out the front door of the beach home. "It's getting pretty dark, and he should've been back by now."

"He'll be fine. Besides, looking outside repeatedly isn't going to get him here any sooner. There are better ways to pass the time." Noah patted the cushion next to him on the bench. "Come here."

She closed the door and leaned against it, folding her arms in front of her. Scrunching her face, she considered his invitation before slowly making her way to him. She paused, grabbing a piece of cloth from the table.

"So here's what I drew," she said as she sat beside him. Her fingers gracefully smoothed the fabric piece over his lap. The clear lines she had sketched caught the moment of impact. Looking at the colliding animals, he could almost hear the crash of skull meeting skull. "I feel like this often lately." She pointed to the smaller one on the left. "He's the few little pleasures left in life." She shifted to the larger creature and Noah saw the detail in the hardened features about the face. "And he's the pain. Even when they meet, everything hurts."

Noah held her and massaged her head. His insides warmed as she melted in his embrace and a tiny smile appeared on her lips. He tilted his head back, and with his eyes, he followed the wooden trim near the ceiling to the closest wall and then toward the hallway. *Nice craftsmanship*. The house easily outsized their own place, but it was not as grand as Noah had anticipated, based on the king's dwelling in Havil. Other than a couple of small woven tapestries on the front wall, the space was rather bare.

"So tomorrow is when we get Garun's family?" Emzara asked.

Noah's focus returned to his wife. "That's the plan, unless Tubal-Cain has something else in mind." A faint, yet familiar voice from outside arrested his attention, but he furrowed his brow when it was joined by an unrecognized female voice. "Speaking of Tubal-Cain, I think he's back, but it doesn't sound like he's alone."

The woman's words grew louder as she neared the house, and Emzara stiffened. "That's not Naamah, is it?"

Noah placed a reassuring hand on her knee and shook his head. "Doesn't sound like her."

A couple of rapid knocks hit the door before it opened. "I'm back." Tubal-Cain stepped inside and located Noah and Emzara in the meeting room. "I didn't plan on bringing someone with me, but if anyone can help us, she can." Tubal-Cain held his hand out and welcomed his guest into the room.

"Hello, Noah. It's been a long time." The woman pulled the wrap away from her head and let it drop down her back, revealing her long black hair. Her face was oval with pronounced cheekbones, giving her a refined and dignified appearance. A lone freckle graced her left cheek.

Noah stood and leaned forward as he struggled to recognize her. "Hello, it's good —"

Emzara leapt to her feet. "I've seen you before. You sat in front of me at that ceremony."

The woman smiled at Emzara. "Yes, I remember you." She spoke in low tones, even and confident. "You were the pretty girl looking around for your husband." She dipped her head toward Noah. "It looks like you've found him."

Emzara grabbed Noah's arm. "I did." She released Noah and stepped toward their guest. "We were never introduced. I'm Emzara."

The woman tilted her head forward slightly. "And I'm Adah. It's very nice to meet you."

Adah? Noah shot a look at Tubal-Cain. "Adah? Queen of Havil?"

She sighed. "Please, just call me Adah. There's no need for formalities here."

Tubal-Cain closed the door and held a hand toward Adah. "She's my father's second wife."

Noah raised his eyebrows as he stared at Tubal-Cain.

The blacksmith held up a palm. "Don't worry, we can trust her."

"Tubal-Cain has told me briefly why you three are here." She blinked twice and opened her mouth as if to say something else, but then closed it.

Emzara brushed Noah's forearm reassuringly and looked at Adah. "Can I get you some water?"

"No, thank you, dear, I'm fine."

Noah and Emzara returned to their spots on the bench while Tubal-Cain moved two chairs across from them.

Once everyone was seated, Tubal-Cain gestured to Adah. "She'll be staying here for a few days just as if she were on a small retreat, and I've asked Kenter, her personal guard and my friend to keep watch. We haven't had a chance yet to talk many specifics, but I think you'll find what she has to say interesting. Adah?"

"So you want information on Lamech?" She placed her hands elegantly in her lap, all emotions masked.

"Why don't you start with what you noticed when he got back," Tubal-Cain said.

Sitting perfectly upright, Adah said, "He was a little frustrated about your council rejecting his trade proposal, but he didn't seem all that upset — not nearly as angry as I would have expected since things didn't go his way. Usually when he's rebuffed, he completely loses his temper." She glanced at the floor. "I thought he might've calmed down on the long trip, but Kenter told me something else."

"What was that?" Emzara asked.

"It seems that Lamech bragged to Zillah — Tubal-Cain's mother — that he'd carried out a bit of revenge before leaving the city."

Noah moved to the edge of his seat and his heartbeat raced. Aware of the pain rekindling in both him and Emzara, Noah pushed onward. He needed to know. "Did he specify what that revenge was?"

Adah took a deep breath and let her gaze drift toward the ceiling. "He killed two people, a troublemaker and someone else who was just in the way."

Tubal-Cain sat up straighter. Obviously, this was news to him, too.

Emzara put a hand to her mouth and tears filled her eyes. "Oh, Baba."

Noah embraced her, and his neck and head grew hot. He had expected a stream of emotions if he discovered the identity of the murderer, but he was not prepared for the anger that flooded his mind. He imagined the king slipping into Ara's house with a team of guards to carry out their attack. Closing his eyes, he breathed deeply and focused his thoughts on Adah. "Those people were my best friend and my father-in-law."

"How could you marry such a monster?" Emzara glared at Adah.

Adah shook her head softly, saying nothing. Finally she offered Emzara a sympathetic expression. "I'm sorry to hear it was your father." She turned to Noah. "And your friend."

"How?" Emzara buried her head in her hands.

"It's not what you think." Adah rubbed her forehead and looked down. "I didn't have a choice. I already had a family. One night, a group of raiders attacked our village. They killed all the men, including my son. And I still don't know what happened to my daughters. They were tied up and led away. I assume they were sold into slavery."

Noah held his head in his hands and shuddered. "Did you get your daughters back? How did you meet Lamech?"

"He led the group that attacked the village."

Emzara's jaw dropped momentarily. "And you married him?"

Noah winced at her tone, and the queen's eyes flared with long-simmering anger. "Not all weddings come from love. I was forced to marry him. It was marry him or die." Adah's gaze slid out of focus, and she stared blankly at the wall behind them. "At that point, my only thought was to stay until I could find out what happened to my girls. But my plans changed when I gave birth to twins." She gave a bitter laugh, and Noah's heart clenched as he recognized a strong sense of resignation and self-loathing that he had recently caught glimpses of in Emzara.

When Adah continued, her smooth voice had changed, carrying a hiss of rage as she spat out the words of her story. "And I've hated nearly every moment of it. If it weren't for my boys, I would've run long ago. But I'm afraid of what they'll become with him as their father." She sighed. "Oh, what I wouldn't give to be free of him." Her voice grew quieter. "He even bragged about murdering the young man."

Noah felt his heartbeat quicken. "Excuse me. Did you say that he bragged about killing a young man?"

She nodded. "Isn't that what I mentioned earlier?"

"No." Noah shook his head. "You said it was a troublemaker and someone who got in the way."

Adah lifted her head in understanding. "Oh, well yes, the troublemaker was the young man. Kenter specifically told me that Lamech boasted about killing a young man who had injured him. I didn't know what he was talking about because he didn't have any injuries when he came back."

Emzara's eyebrows scrunched together as she faced Noah and mouthed, "What?"

"Are you sure?" Noah asked.

"That's what Kenter said."

Emzara's gaze flicked from Noah to Adah and back again to Noah. She spoke softly. "So Baba wasn't the target."

"No, that would mean that Aterre was," Noah said. "But what did he . . ."

Adah leaned in and tilted her head to one side. "What did you just say?"

"I was just confused because we were sure my father-in-law was targeted, but it sounds like they were after my friend instead."

"Yes, but what did you call your friend?"

"His name was Aterre."

Adah sank back in her chair. "I thought that's what you said." She forced a smile. "I haven't heard that name in a long time. That was my son's name too."

Noah's mouth dropped open as memories tore through his mind. *Aterre's village was attacked and so was Adah's. His mother and sisters were taken. Aterre slashed the face of the man who grabbed him, and Lamech has a huge scar on his face. And Aterre's accent was the same as Adah's.*

Noah steadied himself and turned to Adah. "When you first met Lamech, did he have that scar on his face?"

Adah drew back at the strange question. "No, it was a fresh wound." She paused and her lower lip quavered. "What are you saying?"

Noah trembled as he took in a breath through his mouth. "My best friend was also your son."

Sobs rocked the queen's body. All of her austere mannerisms fled. "No!"

Tubal-Cain paused before putting a hand on her shoulder, but Emzara hurried around the low table between the bench and the chairs and knelt beside Adah, reaching for the older woman.

The queen bent down and welcomed Emzara's embrace. She composed herself after several moments and faced Noah. "So Aterre survived the night our village was attacked?" She dried her cheeks with the shoulder portion of her gown. "How did he ever run into you since you live so far away?"

Noah thought back to his first encounter with Aterre and smiled. As Emzara held Adah's hand in support, Noah recounted some of his favorite memories with Aterre, with Tubal-Cain and Emzara adding details along the way, and the queen laughed and wept throughout.

When Noah finished talking about Aterre's relationship with Jitzel, Adah said, "I'm so glad to know that he escaped that night and met all of you. As you said, he always was full of mischief. Did he ever mention us?"

"He always wondered what had happened to you and his sisters," Noah said. "In fact, after his wedding, he was planning to come here to look for you. He even asked the king about help . . ." Noah clenched his jaw and slammed his fist on the table.

"What is it?" Emzara asked.

Noah's breathing increased and his face flushed. "That's how Lamech figured it out." Noah pointed at Adah. "Aterre asked about his mother and sisters at the council meeting. The king even talked about recognizing his accent."

Having recomposed herself, Adah held onto her placid, stately demeanor, but her shaking hand reached to clutch Emzara's.

Noah scrambled to his feet and paced the room. "What a wicked . . ." He grabbed a cushion and threw it against the wall and yelled in anger. "He needs to pay for what he's done."

He turned back to the women to find Emzara staring at him with wide, sympathetic eyes. Tubal-Cain moved toward the door and waved his hand to instruct Noah to join him. "Let's get some air. I have an idea."

Noah followed Tubal-Cain a short distance from the house. The cool, fresh air greeted his lungs, and he took it in greedily. Suspended just above the treetops ahead of him, the nearly whole moon lit up the evening. The dew-drenched grass soaked Noah's feet as he walked. "So what's your plan?"

Tubal-Cain stopped and faced Noah. "The annual Serpent ceremony is in two days. What if we told the crowd that my father murdered two innocent people in Iri Geshem?"

"How would we do that?" Noah pointed to the house. "Emzara won't let me go near the city."

Tubal-Cain stroked his beard. "I can do it. I could interrupt the beginning of the ceremony. I'm sure the people would be surprised to see me and allow me to speak for a few moments."

"You would openly stand against your father?" Noah crossed his arms. "I appreciate your desire to expose his evil deeds, but you might end up dead too."

"I don't think it would happen."

"Why not?" Noah asked.

"Because I think the crowd would turn against him if they knew what he was really like."

"And what if they didn't?"

Tubal-Cain blew out a breath. "That's a risk I'm willing to take."

"You need to think about Adira now, too. What would she do without you? And what do you think she'd do to me if I came home without you?"

"She'd probably kill you." Tubal-Cain slapped Noah's shoulder. "See, it's a good plan."

Noah laughed and sensed some of his anger settle. "Do you really think the people of Havil care what he did? They seemed quite willing to follow him the last time I was here."

"Yeah, but not if they knew what kind of man he really is. They believe that he's just a man who helped expand their city, but I don't think they would put up with him murdering innocent people — especially when they find out he killed the son of his second wife."

"I know I wouldn't follow him." Noah stared at the ground. "It still seems quite risky."

"That's because it is." Tubal-Cain adjusted his wrap. "But do you have any better ideas?"

Noah tried to come up with another strategy to turn the people against the king. "Are there others who would stand with you?"

"You mean besides you?" Tubal-Cain chuckled but let it fade when Noah remained quiet. "I know this is serious. You and Zara don't have to take part. I'm sure we'd have the support of the guards Garun talked about, along with Adah. And I've got several friends in the city who would join us and tell others too."

"I don't think Emzara and I can lose another friend right now."

"Look, maybe this will work, maybe it won't. But I've got to try something. As much as I'd like to deny it, he's family and so I'm partly responsible. I may be the only one who can stop his evil influence."

"What if this crazy plan of yours succeeds, then what? Would you take over as king?"

Tubal-Cain drew back. "Whoa. I never even thought of that. I don't have any interest in ruling." He rubbed a hand over his eyes, thinking it through. "I'd probably appoint a group of trustworthy elders to run the city."

Noah sat on a nearby stump. "Look, we still have a day to think this over. It'll give us something to do on the way to Garun's."

Tubal-Cain took the spot next to Noah. "That's right. I almost forgot about that. If we do this, I'll need to go into the city again tomorrow, and you can go to Garun's."

"Okay. Obviously, I'd like to see what Em thinks."

"Definitely. I'm open to other ideas, too." He looked in the direction of Havil. "We just need to be careful who hears about it. I don't think my father would go easy on anyone conspiring against him."

Noah looked over his shoulder at the house. "Maybe Adah will have some ideas. She certainly doesn't seem to care for your father. I'd imagine she's contemplated turning against him."

Tubal-Cain nodded. "Let's find out."

Chapter 19

Noah dodged a large puddle in the trail, but his foot slipped on the soft ground, nearly causing him to fall. Gathering his balance, he scraped some of the mud from the side of his sandal by wiping it in the tall grass that grew alongside the path.

Pausing atop a small rise, Noah studied the route Tubal-Cain had indicated before they parted moments earlier and then surveyed his surroundings. Behind him, the waves of the sea continued their endless ebb and flow. Far to his left, dark rainclouds hovered over Havil as the sun peeked through a tiny gap. On the horizon beyond the city, a single column of smoke rose from one of the high hills. Noah did a double-take. *That's strange. I've never seen a fire emit such a tall plume before. I hope it doesn't come any closer to Havil.* His skin tingled with the memory of the intense heat and smoke during the blaze in the Zakari's barn. He shuddered and took a deep breath, remembering the burning pain in his lungs.

Between him and the strange smoke cloud, the palace climbed above the surrounding buildings, and for the first time, Noah noticed a variety of trees on the building's roof. For a moment he marveled at the architectural prowess that could create such a building. Then his gaze moved on to another edifice. Standing nearly as tall and wide as the king's home, rose a building that Noah guessed to be the House of Knowledge. At the sight, his wonder gave way to a stab of anxiety. *Creator, please protect Tubal-Cain in the city today.*

A warm breeze from the west drew his eye to the lighter-colored clouds rolling in and offered Noah hope that his garment would dry quickly. He faced into the wind toward the wider road he and Tubal-Cain traveled that morning. Thoughts of Emzara prompted a smile to spread across his face. She had risen before anyone else to prepare firstfeast, and by the time Noah and Tubal-Cain left, she was heavily engrossed in a conversation with Adah. *I'm glad Em has someone to keep her company today.*

Noah moved down the narrow path as it meandered past a handful of farms, through a small meadow, and then entered a grove of trees. A couple of bushy-tailed rodents scurried about before him, while a scattering of chirps, peeps, and squawks filled the air. A buzzbird zipped past his head and hovered over some blossoms to his right. The tiny radiant bird mesmerized him as it flitted quickly from one blossom to the next. *I wonder if planting some of those flowers at home would attract buzzbirds.*

Just as Tubal-Cain had mentioned, the trail split near the far edge of the grove. Noah followed the path to the right and marched purposefully toward the house directly ahead. Nestled between two of the rolling hills and shaded by several tall trees, the large, sturdy-looking wooden home featured two levels and an attached shed. Smoke curled out of the stone chimney running up the near side. *This must be the place.*

Noah checked his wrap's inner pocket and then turned onto a thin trail that led to the front door. He ascended two short steps and knocked. Unsure if he had rapped the door hard enough, Noah waited a moment and then reached to hit it again but stopped at the sound of faint footsteps approaching from the inside. A small rectangular portal, just under Noah's eye level, slid open from the inside.

"Can I help you?" a woman's voice asked.

Noah stooped and met her gaze through the slot. "Yes, my name is Noah, and I'm a friend of Garun, a palace guard of Havil. Is this his home?"

The woman eyed him warily. "It is, but he's not able to talk to you right now."

Noah bowed his head respectfully. "I know. He's across the sea in Iri Geshem, my hometown, and he sent me here with a message for you." He pulled a small scroll from his pocket and, mushing it slightly, slid it through the opening. "Here."

Still peering through the tiny slit in the door, he watched as she took the missive and slipped the rope off one end. After unrolling it, she quickly skimmed its message. "How can I be sure it's really from him? This isn't his handwriting."

"He said he doesn't write well and asked me to do it for him. He knew you'd know it was from him if you read the back."

She turned the page over and her eyes brightened. "Just a moment." The small window closed and after a few scraping and clicking sounds, the door opened. The woman waved Noah inside. "Quickly, come in."

Noah entered the house and she shut the door behind him. The fireplace to his left highlighted a rather plain sitting room. The dining area lay beyond it and a wooden ladder to his right led to the second floor.

"Welcome to our home, Noah." The woman nodded slightly before pushing her dark hair behind her shoulders. Her small face supported a tall forehead, with thin eyebrows, small eyes, upturned nose, and firm lips all spaced compactly. "I'm Laleel, Garun's wife. I guess being married to a palace guard makes me a little wary."

"I understand." Noah placed his hand to his chest and smiled. "I'm sure your husband would be glad to know that you're careful."

Gesturing to a low bench near the fireplace, she said, "Please, have a seat. I'll be right back."

Noah thanked her as she shuffled from the room. He sat where she had indicated and stretched out his legs.

Laleel soon returned with a clay vessel and handed it to him. "Have some water."

"Oh, that's very kind." He took a drink and delighted in the coolness it brought to his mouth and throat.

She held up the note and her brown eyes lit up to match her smile. "Thank you for bringing word from my husband. It's a pleasure to meet you in person. Garun told me about the man that rejected the king's daughter." Laleel's shoulders drooped and she frowned. "It breaks my heart to see how that girl's turned out. She had so much potential, but she's too much like her father."

Eager to change the subject, Noah asked, "So what do you think of the message from Garun?"

"He wants me to bring the family to Iri Geshem with you right away?" She gave him a shrewd look. "What's the hurry? Are we in danger?"

Noah glanced around. "I assume it's safe to speak here."

She slid onto a seat across from him and fixed her gaze on his face. "Yes, it's just me and my girls, and they're in the barn feeding the animals."

"There's nothing to worry about right now. But Garun fears that Havil may soon become too dangerous for followers of the Creator, and he isn't sure how safe it'll be for him to be around the palace anymore."

Laleel leaned back and crossed her arms over her chest. "Yes, we thought this day might come, but I didn't think it'd be so soon. What happened?"

Noah closed his eyes, regret and pain washing over him again. "The king murdered my father-in-law and my best friend." He turned away. "If you don't mind, I'd rather not talk about it in further detail."

Suddenly, the floor vibrated, causing Noah and Laleel to exchange glances. The clay vessel nearly fell to the floor, but Noah grabbed it just before it slipped off the bench. The surface and walls creaked and groaned as the gentle shaking continued for a few moments.

"What's that?" Noah asked. "I don't remember that happening when I was in Havil before."

"I'm not sure, but it's happened a few times this past week." Laleel scanned the room, her shoulders hunched. "I'm really sorry to hear about your loved ones. When do we need to be ready to leave?"

"We have some business to attend to tomorrow evening and plan to leave right after that."

"Business? At the ceremony?"

Noah hesitated. He did not plan to discuss the ceremony, but it seemed Garun's wife's mind was as sharp as her eyes. "It looks that way."

"Garun hates going to those awful events."

"I don't blame him. Once was enough for me."

"And yet you plan to go back?" Laleel asked.

The muscles in Noah's jaw tightened. "We have some unfinished business. It's probably best if you don't know."

She pursed her lips. "I see. Well, if Garun trusts you, I trust you." She stood at the sound of a door opening beyond the dining area. "But there's a slight problem with his instructions."

"And what's that?"

She looked toward the other room. "Come in here, all of you."

Three young girls entered. Noah guessed the oldest was close to Misha's age. The two smaller ones were at least ten years younger, although they looked quite different from the taller girl with a lighter brown complexion. "I thought Garun said he had two daughters at home."

"That's the problem. We now have three." She smiled at the older girl and spun to face Noah. "Will you have room for all of us on the boat?"

"Of course." He found it difficult to look away from the eldest girl; she reminded him of someone, but he could not decide who it was. Her face was turned down, but beneath her long, straight black hair, he saw her delicate countenance. The edges of her eyes trailed back, running parallel along her high cheekbones. Her long lashes lay softly against her skin, and her wide nose protruded only slightly from her face.

Laleel held out a hand and the older girl joined her while avoiding eye contact with Noah. Putting a hand on the shy girl's shoulder, Laleel said, "This is Zedakal, and she just joined our family this week."

Noah raised an eyebrow. "I don't understand."

Laleel flicked her wrist toward the younger girls. "Please go out to the barn for a little while." Once they had gone, she said, "The king's daughter recently implemented a program where they take girls of Zedakal's age, and they prepare them to serve as prostitutes for Nachash."

Laleel's scowl was so fierce that Noah almost wished Naamah were there to face it. Here was a woman who could stand up to the princess, if ever there was one. Zedakal, however, stood with her head down. Her shoulders gave a slight shiver as she buried her face in her hands.

Noah scrunched his nose and averted his gaze at the thought of the horrors she'd possibly faced, understanding now why she shrank from him and clung to Garun's wife. "Naamah is doing this? She needs to be stopped."

"And just how would you do that?" Laleel asked.

Some of the bluster went out of him. "I don't know," he admitted. He looked at Zedakal. "How did you escape?"

As the girl remained silent, Laleel hugged her. "She ran away a few nights ago. I found her curled up in a corner of our barn." She raised her small chin. "I don't intend to let anything else happen to her."

Noah imagined Garun's pride in his wife's actions. "But what about the family she was taken from? Shouldn't you return her to them?"

Zedakal shook her head rapidly and her hair flew about in cascades, like a melad shaking its mane.

"No," Laleel said. "She was a slave. They all were — all the girls that the king's daughter took for this program. I imagine they have people looking for her even now. And that's the reason I was suspicious of you when you came to the door."

Speechless, Noah slowly shook his head and clenched his fist. Sadness mingled with anger until the line between them blurred.

"Zedakal is free now." Laleel lifted the girl's chin and stroked her cheek. "I'd like her to come with us to Iri Geshem, if she is willing."

Zedakal nodded her head and then buried it in Laleel's shoulder.

Laleel gave a tiny smile. "It looks like you'll need to make room for four of us on the boat."

"Gladly."

"We'll be ready to travel tomorrow." Garun's wife held up a palm. "Where would you like us to meet you?"

"I'll return here to help you," Noah said. "Then you can just come with me."

Laleel glanced around the room and shrugged. "That won't be necessary. The girls and I can manage."

"Are you sure?"

She nodded. "It won't take us long. Just tell us where to go."

"Well, ironically, we're staying at the king's beach home. It's a rather long walk down the western road."

Laleel's eyes grew wary. "The king's? Why would you possibly be there?"

"I came here with Tubal-Cain — he's a friend." Noah held out a hand to reassure her. "He isn't like his father or sister at all. He follows the Creator."

Laleel raised her eyebrows. "That's encouraging. I wish he were ruling in place of his father."

"I agree," Noah said. "Maybe someday Havil will be a different place." He considered Zedakal, who darted her glance away when she saw him looking at her. "For now, though, we'd be better off almost anywhere but here."

Chapter 20

"Open up." Naamah's commanding voice resonated from outside the locked door of Adah's room. Clutching the light wooden box to herself and trying not to think about the contents, Emzara spun and looked wildly at Adah. Her new friend motioned to a curtained balcony to the right of her massive bed. After ducking behind the fabric, Emzara crouched down.

Thankful for the height of the railing on the third-level terrace, Emzara stayed low and glanced at her surroundings. Other than a low table, a few benches, and several poles with unlit oil lanterns hanging from them, the balcony held few furnishings. A heavy curtain that hung over the columned entryway back into the room was on her right. That and a large potted plant against the railing were the only means of concealment should Naamah come out here. Her heart pounded. *What are we doing? It all seemed so simple when Adah and I talked in the comfort of the beach home. This isn't simple anymore.*

The holes in the box next to her were necessary, but she hoped they were small enough to keep the contents inside. She shuddered, thinking about how close she had cradled the container against her body. She gently moved it an arm's length away and focused on the conversation inside.

"So this time, you and my mother are to be seated at the top of the main platform, one on either side of Nachash's statue. Da wants everyone to see that his queens are just as involved as his daughter is. Now, here's the order of the ceremony."

Emzara let her thoughts about what had led to this situation drown out Naamah's voice. Was it only this morning that Noah left for Garun's family? And now it must be beyond the time for midmeal. She hoped her insides would remember the few smaller items that she and Adah purchased to munch on as they traveled through the city. A grumbling stomach would be as good as a gong with Naamah standing so close.

Angry footsteps paced inside the large room just beyond her, and she clutched at her knees in an effort to make herself smaller. *Get it together, girl. You'll be in a far scarier place tonight.* Her tense muscles persisted until she reassured herself that Naamah seemed to have no intentions of coming outside.

She rested her head against the curtain, pushing it into the pillar behind it and thought back to the morning. She and Adah had bonded instantly over their shared anguish of losing close family. Adah's ability to understand the loss of a child acted as a balm to Emzara's grieving spirit. However, it was not long until their sorrows were overtaken by another emotion. The words between them repeated in her mind as clearly as when they had first been spoken.

"It's not fair that he can just get away with something that hurt us so badly."

"I know." Adah looked down and twisted a thick bangle on her wrist. "I just wish there was more we could do."

"Like what?"

"Well he took the life of your son. He took the life of my father, and I hold him responsible for the death of my child as well. He deserves more than humiliation tomorrow."

Adah spoke their thoughts aloud. "He should die so that other lives can be spared from his evil."

Emzara nodded. "Yes. But . . ."

A loud slap broke Emzara's reverie. "I don't care that you're the queen. You will not speak to me like that. And yes, you will wear this special garment that was made especially for tomorrow. The seer demands it." She barely heard the faint sound of cloth hitting the stone floor.

"The seer!" Adah's scornful tone rang out. "I will not take orders from him. Even if you try to hit me again." Suddenly the queen's voice softened. "Naamah, I know you and I have always been at odds, and I understand why. But I can't help but be concerned for you. I don't like how you've changed under his influence. He's leading you into some very dark places. You're no longer the happy, beautiful girl I'd occasionally see around this place. You're angry now and too hungry for power. It's going to come back to bite you someday."

Ironic choice of words, Adah.

"You're just envious because my father replaced you with me as first in his affections. And yes, you'll wear this because I'm in charge of the celebration." A chair scooted on the floor.

"We'll see about that. Don't bother me again."

"Oh, I have no intention to. Besides, I thought you were supposed to be at the beach house until tomorrow."

"That was my plan, but I remembered that I'd invited a few ladies to the palace and will be entertaining them for dinner tonight in the main hall."

"Then I'll just inform Da not to concern himself with you tonight. And I'll make sure mother looks her finest." Emzara pictured the flash in Naamah's green-flecked brown eyes. Shaking her head, Emzara knew that comment did not hurt Adah as intended. The door slammed shut.

Moments later, Adah made her way outside and leaned back against the solid stonework that lined the balcony. "Are you okay?" She kept her voice low and her head level. Concern filled her eyes, but anyone seeing her from the town below would just see the back of her head and assume she was alone, enjoying the fresh air.

"Yes, but I'm concerned for you. Did Naamah slap you?"

Adah placed a hand softly on her own cheek. "Yes, but that's not important now. Let's discuss our plan."

"I still can't believe that all just happened."

"I know, but it actually helps us. Now, Naamah will inform Lamech that I'm here and that I have visitors tonight. I'll stay on one of the couches in the main hall, and it'll look like I fell asleep where I was after a long night of hosting."

"But will that really make you above all suspicions?"

"I'll be surrounded by well-respected ladies and several guards all night. There's no way I could legitimately be blamed for anything that happens up here."

As she pondered Adah's words, Emzara stared past her, noticing the beautiful scenery beyond the southern edge of the city for the first time.

Rolling green hills stretched as far as she could see. The telltale patterns of crops interspersed with small patches of wooded areas blanketed each rise. Straight in front of her, a path, wide enough for at least two large wagons to pass each other unhindered, extended from the city wall and divided the landscape in two. Smaller trails broke off from the road, connecting the small farms dotting the countryside.

"Are they still in there?" Adah stared at the box.

Emzara nodded.

"Good. Stay in here until after you hear that his room is empty. If I know Lamech at all, once he hears from his daughter about the ladies I'm hosting, he'll be sure to look his finest before joining us for evenfeast."

"How will I know when it's clear?"

"Don't worry. Because our rooms are adjoining, it's easy to hear any commotion in there." She rolled her eyes in contempt. "And it can get noisy since he makes a grand deal out of even the simplest things."

"That's when I slip into his room?" Emzara asked.

"I don't think so. That's too risky."

"But he deserves to die."

"And I'd rather you didn't. You can hide in here. In fact, come with me." Adah reentered her room. Emzara "walked" forward on her knees, using one hand to keep her skirt from getting tangled, and carefully holding the package away from her body with the other. She stood up once she was inside and the curtain had fallen back in place.

"What are you thinking?" After setting the box on a side table, she arranged some scrolls that had been lying there to partially cover it.

"Here — where is it?" Adah rifled through several long and expensive cloths hanging on hooks. "Ah." She held up a length of cloth the same tawny color as a young bovar. "This is similar to what our servant girls wear. Let's wrap it around you, so that if someone discovers you, they'll think you're one of my maids tidying up in here."

"So I stay here, but what about . . ."

"You'll hear when the king makes it back to his chambers." She walked over to an ornate wooden door to the right of her main entrance and placed her hand on it. "This leads to his room. When you open it, you'll see a little hallway only about six cubits in length, and on his side there's a thin golden tapestry. It's slightly transparent so don't have any lamps lit in here."

"So I wait until all is still and then carefully open this door. Sounds easy enough. Then I'll just crawl and release the contents before coming back here and making sure this door is shut tight."

Adah nodded. "I certainly don't want any of those things to get in here."

"Adah, what if what Naamah said was true? What if her mother comes back with the king?"

Adah shrugged, "I'd be very surprised if that happened. Naamah was trying to upset me, but the king's affections shifted away from Zillah after I arrived."

Later, as Emzara sat in the darkness listening intently for any movement in the adjacent room, her mind raced through memories of her father and Aterre. She placed a hand on the box and imagined the movement inside, aware of the calamity these creatures could deliver. *Am I no better than Lamech? Willing to kill someone just because they wronged me?* She shook her head emphatically, changing the direction of her thoughts. *Don't back down now. There's no comparison. Aterre was only defending himself, and Lamech killed him and Baba for it. A serpent bite is a fitting end for the king. And besides, I'm not really the one killing him.*

Her breath snagged in her throat as she heard the unmistakable confident tread of the king entering his room. He behaved just as Adah described. *You think you're so powerful; well you're no match for the Creator. Most High* — she immediately and instinctually leapt into prayer, but for some reason, she just couldn't ask Him for help. *I guess I'm in this alone.* She sighed internally but then shifted her focus back to her task. *Sounds like the king is alone too. Good.*

After everything grew silent, she waited for what seemed like eternity. Taking a deep breath, she silently opened the door and took hesitant, soundless steps toward the tapestry. She held onto her precious cargo of death, before laying it on the floor. She lifted the lid and slipped back into the hallway.

Chapter 21

They're gone. They're gone. The refrain played repeatedly in her mind as Emzara ducked around a massive needle tree a good distance from the palace. Immense relief rushed through her at not having the box of serpents close by anymore. The thought of having them as her companions for most of the day caused her to shudder.

Although the thick cloud cover kept her hidden from the moonlight as she wound her way through the streets of Havil, it posed other complications. *Let's see, I've passed the big needle tree, so the twisted post is the next landmark.* On their way to the palace in the morning, she took note of things that stood out every so often to aid her on the way back. But the darkness made everything look different. As she veered left, the misshapen tree trunk on the corner of the lot came into view. The shadowy form of an oil lantern still perched atop the odd structure, but as she had suspected, it was not being used.

I wonder how successful Noah was in his errand today. He and Tubal-Cain are probably back already and wondering where I am. She trembled with her whole body, feeling very alone in the darkness. After all her actions of the day, would she still feel alone after she returned to Noah? *Will he be angry? Or will he understand?* Her palpitations continued as she spotted the small grave mound on the edge of someone's property, showing her she was on the right track. A strange sensation coursed through her. Her whole body vibrated again, but this was different than the shivering. *It's like the whole ground is trembling with me.* When the eerie tremors passed Emzara increased her pace.

After what seemed to be the length of a couple night watches, she finally picked her way through the trees and brambles at the edge of the royal beach home. Light from within flickered and danced its way outside the window, giving her a small measure of comfort. Thankful to be back, she also dreaded the explaining that needed to be done. Taking a deep breath, she slowly eased her way through the door and right into a face full of dark textured fabric. She clung to Noah and returned his fervent embrace.

"Are you alright? Where have you been?"

Guilt slithered through her at the fear in her husband's voice. "I'm fine." She gulped, hoping to calm her voice with the next sentence. "I had an errand to run with Adah. I didn't realize it would take so long."

Noah guided her to the sitting area outside of the kitchen then held her on his lap. Clinging to him, she savored the comfort of his nearness and feared that this might be their last moment of closeness after he found out what she had done. He turned her slightly so she nearly faced him and cupped her face in his strong hands.

"I've been so worried about you. Where could you have possibly gone that would have you getting back so long after the deepest dark? And like this too." He brushed at her cheek and a bit of caked dirt landed in her lap.

His touch stung, and she figured that she probably cut herself on the journey back. Fidgeting, she eased her face from his hold and tucked herself under his chin, nestling against him. "I'll tell you," she said just above a whisper, "but please don't interrupt."

Slowly she recounted her day, her chin lowering with each revelation. Hearing their plan aloud and in Noah's presence made her recoil within herself. As penance, she held nothing back, forcing herself to tell him each horrible detail, not even trying to rationalize it as she had before.

"So Lamech is likely dead?" he interrupted for the first time, as she neared the end of her account.

She met his eyes for a moment before dropping her gaze. "I . . ."

She sensed his head turn away. "You murdered the king?"

"What? No, I couldn't go through with it." She gripped the front of his tunic. "I was there, crouched behind the tapestry in his room, the box of serpents in my possession. I pulled the lid off and stole out of the room, but then something came over me. I just couldn't do it, so I snuck back in and covered the box, thankful that the creatures were still in it." She shuddered, waiting for his verdict.

His eyes flashed with an unreadable expression before he pulled her close, squeezing the breath out of her.

She relaxed in his arms, wishing to stay this way forever.

Finally, he sighed. "I'm so glad you're back safely. And I can't tell you how . . . how . . ." He paused and his lower lip quivered. "How glad I am that you didn't let those serpents loose."

"Me too." As she lay there against him, the day's troubles started to fade away, and she savored the rest that they found in each other.

"What made you stop?" he finally asked.

"Two things." She toyed with the embroidered edge she had sewn on the folds of cloth by his neck. "No matter how much he hurt us, and no matter how much I think he deserves to die, I was never entirely comfortable with the idea Adah and I came up with. Eventually, I saw how in my anger and desire for retribution, I was willing to become just like Lamech. Obtaining vengeance would probably feel good, like Adah said, but could I really live with myself knowing I'd murdered a man? Would you ever look at me the same way again? Would you even want to see me?"

He brushed a finger softly over her bottom lip. "And the other thing?"

"I — I tried to pray to the Creator, and it was the first time I ever remember Him feeling so distant. I couldn't seem to reach out to Him. That's when I caught a glimpse of the future if I carried it out." She blinked back tears and verbalized the question at the front of her thoughts. "Do you hate me?"

He kissed the tip of her nose. "Never."

"But what I tried to do was so wrong."

"Yeah," he pulled her head close against his chest. "But it wasn't just you."

"Adah certainly was willing to help. And little wonder with her life as it is now, plus hearing about Aterre. But. . . ." Her large eyes focused on him. "But it was my idea. She simply gave assistance in carrying it out." Her cheeks deepened in shame and her words trailed off.

"I love you."

She looked up, almost shocked.

"Remember, the Creator never treats us how we deserve. Think about Greatfather Adam. Before banishing him from Eden, the Most High offered a sacrifice, allowing our first parents to live instead of instantly carrying out the sentence of death." He kissed her on the top of the head. "I'm proud of your courage. And I'm glad you thought about what the Creator would think, and that you chose to follow Him instead of your own way."

Peace washed over her as the last lingering feeling of isolation faded and she lifted her lips to her husband's.

"Do you really have to do that here?"

Tubal-Cain's voice snapped her back to reality and caused her to blush.

"Can't believe you're still up," he said.

"We're just catching up." Noah grinned as he turned to face their friend.

"Is that what you call it?" He returned a wry smile before scooting up a chair. "Well, as long as we're all still awake, I may as well tell you the little that I've found out about the ceremony."

Emzara stayed silent, allowing Tubal-Cain to talk. But at the moment she cared nothing for the ceremony or Lamech or anything else. For the moment she was content to just be in Noah's arms. Still, she couldn't help but listen as their friend recounted his information.

"It's supposed to be bigger than ever, so my father definitely lied to the town council — what a surprise. There'll be a raised platform for invited dignitaries from all over the land, kind of like where you described being seated last time."

Emzara yawned and reclined against Noah. With her eyes shut, a contented smile crossed her lips as he held her, and before long she lost the fight against the slumber and drifted away.

Chapter 22

Noah awoke for what seemed to be the tenth time during a fitful night. Lying flat on his back, he yawned and rubbed his eyes. Sunlight pushed its way through the dark cloth covering the small window in their room of the beach home.

He turned his head slowly to face Emzara. If his night was restless, hers was even more so. She had tossed and turned, and twice awakened shaking and rambling about another bad dream. Noah smiled at her now resting peacefully. He sighed as he imagined what life may have been like for them if she had carried out her plan the night before. *Certainly, Lamech deserves to die, but what would the Creator think of Emzara carrying out the murder? And how would Tubal-Cain take it? Lamech's still his father.* He shuddered and thanked the Most High for staying Emzara's hand.

Determined to let her sleep, Noah quietly slipped out of bed and dressed himself before heading to the sitting room. Pulling back the cloth to let in some early morning light, he scanned the room, deciding what to do first. His mind made up, he entered the kitchen and dipped his cup into the bucket of water he'd drawn from the well the night before and then grabbed a handful of nuts and a malid fruit from the table. He chomped into the luscious produce and relished its blend of sweet and tart flavor and crispy texture.

He moved back to the open window and stared at the scenery before him. Surrounded by taller trees, a handful of malid trees grew along the dirt trail to the house, and several birds stalked under them in the grass looking for a morning meal. Dozens of colorful flowers had just begun to open their petals to drink in the sunlight of the day.

"Looks like a beautiful morning."

Noah spun to see Tubal-Cain entering the room. "Morning peace. I didn't know you were up yet." He took a swig of water and set the cup on the front room's table before sitting on the nearby bench.

Tubal-Cain took a seat across from him. "I've been up for a while. I didn't sleep well." He snorted. "I guess you could say that I'm a bit nervous about tonight."

"I would be too." Noah tossed a few nuts into his mouth. "It'd be hard enough to stand up to a king in front of such an audience, but the fact that he's your father . . ." Noah shook his head. "I'll pray that the Creator gives you the courage."

"I appreciate that." Tubal-Cain crossed his arms. "Just be ready to back me up if I need it."

"My husband will be doing no such thing." Her hair braided and wrapped in a twisting fashion around her head, Emzara stood in the doorway and looked at both men.

Noah held out his hand, inviting her to join him.

"I get it, Zara. I know you don't want him in danger. Neither do I."

Noah took her hand and guided her to sit beside him. "I didn't realize you were awake."

"I've hardly slept. I just decided to stop trying." She leaned against him and looked at Tubal-Cain. "If there's going to be trouble, I need to be by his side."

"What are you saying?" Tubal-Cain tilted his head.

"*We* will be there to support you." Emzara put her hand on Noah's chest. "If you need it."

Noah drew back and his eyes narrowed.

"It seems like you haven't run this past Noah yet," Tubal-Cain said.

She chuckled. "I just did." She kissed Noah's cheek. "And what does my handsome husband think of the plan?"

Noah scratched the back of his neck. "I don't want you in danger. . . ."

"And you think I want you in danger?" Emzara asked. "Being separated from you the last time we were here made me feel so helpless. I won't go through that again."

"You didn't let me finish. I don't want you in danger, but if Tubal-Cain's willing to risk his position or even his life to see justice done for your father and Aterre, then the two of us sure better be willing to do the same."

"My thoughts exactly." Emzara grinned. "My intelligence must be rubbing off on you."

Noah snorted and turned to Tubal-Cain. "I guess we're in."

"You realize what you're signing up for, don't you?"

Emzara leaned forward. "Death has been our life recently. And maybe it means nothing, but on our way here, I faced death in a dream about Havil. I say we have nothing to lose."

Noah clasped Tubal-Cain's shoulder. "We're in this together."

A knock at the door caused a round of nervous glances. Tubal-Cain spoke softly. "Are we expecting anyone?"

Noah raised his head as he remembered what day it was. Keeping his voice down, he said, "Garun's family."

The banging on the door started again. "This is the palace guard. Open up immediately."

Emzara shuddered. "What do we do?"

Tubal-Cain smiled broadly. "It's not locked, Kenter. Come on in."

The guard opened the door and entered the house followed by Adah.

Emzara's hand flew to her chest. "You scared me, Kenter. Don't do that again."

"I'm sorry, lady. I was hoping to scare your husband. Noah, it's good to see you again."

Noah let go of Emzara's hand before climbing to his feet. "It's good to see you as well."

"What brings the two of you out here this morning?" Tubal-Cain asked.

The queen stepped in front of the guard, but Emzara spoke first. "I think I know." She stared at the floor. "I'm sorry, Adah. I was right there. Everything was going as planned, and then something deep inside me wouldn't let me do it." She studied the wood grain around her feet.

Adah held her head high, but her eyes remained unfeeling. "I've lived with things the way they've been for so long, I can last a while longer. My situation is not your fault."

Emzara stepped back and wiped a tear from her cheek. "Thank you. But what are you going to do now?"

"I'm not sure." Adah looked at Tubal-Cain. "What are your plans?"

"It's better if you don't know. That way, if things don't go well and my father questions you or Kenter, you can truthfully tell him that you knew nothing about it."

"But you're planning something for tonight's ceremony?" Adah asked.

Tubal-Cain pursed his lips and shrugged.

The queen looked at Noah. "Well?"

Noah copied his friend's response.

Adah sighed. "Thank you for considering my situation, but I'm really . . ." She stumbled and Kenter helped her regain her balance.

Noah steadied Emzara as the room seemed to sway a little side to side. As the wooden structure creaked and groaned, a basket of bread rounds fell off the table in the kitchen. Suddenly, the shaking stopped.

Adah patted Kenter's shoulder. "Thank you. Another one of those rumblers."

Noah scratched his chin. "I felt that yesterday too. What is it?"

"I don't have any idea," Adah said. "They started before the last whole moon, but they're getting stronger and more frequent."

Kenter pointed in the direction of Havil. "I've heard some people say that it's because of that smoking hill on the other side of the city, but I don't know how a hill could make the earth shake."

A true earthshaker. Noah smiled to himself as he thought of the mighty beasts with the same name.

An awkward silence settled over the group until a large animal bellowed outside the house.

Noah spun and looked out the window. A massive lunker that reminded him of Meru tugged a wagon full of crates and baskets up the trail. Garun's wife and the three girls walked ahead of it toward the house. "Garun's family is here." He pointed to Kenter. "Can you open the door?"

Kenter pulled the door and moments later, Laleel entered with her two younger daughters.

"Hello, Kenter," Laleel ducked her head as she greeted him. "I didn't expect to see you here." She hesitated upon seeing the prince. "Tubal-Cain, sir, I barely recognized you with your beard."

"It's good to see you, Laleel." Tubal-Cain spread his arms out wide. "Welcome."

She continued to scan the room and froze when she spotted Adah.

"Do not fear," Adah said. "I will say nothing to the king." She flashed a grim smile. "In fact, I envy you."

Wondering what had become of the runaway slave girl, Noah peeked out the window again. There she stood, petting the large animal on its shoulder, then she turned and walked toward the house.

Laleel introduced her two daughters to the group, who greeted them in turn.

Adah turned and put a foot on the edge of the low table so she could retie the leather straps around her ankle.

"And the newest addition to our family." Garun's wife gestured toward the door, imploring the girl to come in, which she eventually did, with her eyes downcast and her face flushed. Laleel said, "This beautiful young lady is Zedakal."

Adah spun around, and her sandal, which she had not finished securing, slipped off her foot. "Zedakal?"

The girl peeked out from beneath the hair hanging in her face.

Adah slowly approached her and bent down to see her face. "Kal?"

The recently freed slave looked up slowly, her eyes wide. "Mam?"

"Kal!" The queen swept the girl into her arms and held her tight.

"Oh, Mam, I missed you so much," Zedakal said as she returned the embrace.

Shocked, Noah stared at the two. *Mam? This poor girl is Adah's daughter?* Noah smiled and grabbed Emzara's hand as he watched the reunited mother caress her daughter and whisper into her ear. Suddenly, Noah's jaw dropped. "Wait."

"What's wrong?" Emzara asked.

Noah pointed at the queen. "If she's her mother" — he shifted his finger toward the girl — "then that would make her . . ."

Emzara squealed. "Aterre's sister!"

Adah and Zedakal, still hugging, turned in unison, each with ear-to-ear smiles on their faces and tears of joy streaking down their cheeks.

Emzara released his hand and bolted toward the girl.

Zedakal focused on Emzara. "You knew my brother?" she asked as Adah stepped slightly back, still leaving her hand on the girl's arm.

Emzara bit her lip and nodded before reaching out and hugging Zedakal.

The girl blinked rapidly. "I don't remember you" — she glanced at Noah — "or him. But I was a lot younger back in the village."

Noah shook his head. "No, we're not from your home. We've known Aterre for the past ten years."

"What? How?" She shook her head as her voice trailed off.

Adah beheld her daughter. "Your brother wasn't killed the night of the attack. He ran far away, and that's how they met him."

"Really? Where is he now?" She frantically looked around the room.

Adah rubbed her eyes. "He was killed recently."

Noah and Emzara explained some of the details about Aterre's life. Along with the others, Noah's emotions ran the gamut from joy and amusement to sorrow and anger.

With tears in her eyes, Zedakal thanked them for the stories. "I'm glad you got to meet him. He used to pick on me and pull my hair, but he helped take care of us when Da left home."

Noah decided not to belabor the fact that Aterre's father abandoned his wife and children, opting instead to keep the focus on happier elements of Aterre's life. "Well, Zedakal . . ."

"You can call me, Kal. Mam always did, and so did Aterre." The sides of her mouth curled up shyly. "He called me lots of other things too."

"Okay, Kal. Well, I couldn't figure it out yesterday, but now I know who you reminded me of." Noah crossed his arms. "You're very much like him. You have the same look in your cheekbones and noses. Your smile is so much like his — well, yours is much prettier — and you have the same accent."

Adah put a hand on Laleel's shoulder. "How did she end up with you? Is she your slave?"

Laleel looked offended. "We don't own any slaves." She nodded to Kal. "Would you tell the story?"

Kal indicated the bench next to Noah. "Do you mind if I sit? I'm a little tired from the long walk."

Noah moved aside. "Please."

Kal sat down as the others gathered around her. She looked at the queen, and at her reassuring nod, began her story. "I was sold into slavery after we were separated. For about eight years, I worked on a farm in the south. My owners weren't too harsh, but it was hard labor. Then a couple years ago, they gave me to a family in Havil to pay off a debt."

She rested her forehead on her hand. "They were terrible people. If something wasn't exactly the way they wanted it, they'd beat me and I wouldn't eat that day. But then it got worse." Looking down at her fingers in her lap, she twisted them nervously and spoke in measured tones as if detached from her own experiences. "The man of the house started to take notice of me. He . . ." She fell silent and leaned against her mother.

Fiery rage spread through Noah's body. He glanced at Tubal Cain, and seeing the tightness in his jaw, Noah knew they both wanted justice to be served on behalf of this young girl.

Kal took in a deep, determined breath. "Anyway, then when the princess started recruiting young women in the city for her new priestess program, I was noticed and taken away to become one of her . . ." Again she stopped.

"One of her what?" Emzara asked.

Like a mother bird protecting her nest, Laleel stepped forward and put a reassuring hand on Kal's bent head. "At the ceremony tonight, Naamah's going to introduce her latest idea. She rounded up over a dozen young women from the city who are going to help her *serve* Nachash."

"What do you mean 'serve'? How?" Tubal-Cain's voice was firm and his eyes narrowed into slits.

"You won't like the answer."

Tubal-Cain folded his arms. "Tell me."

Laleel glanced at the queen, who encouraged her to proceed with a nod. "Naamah will tell the people that the most effective way for them to worship Nachash is to unite with one of her priestesses."

Tubal-Cain's posture turned stiff and rigid. "She's turning them into ritual prostitutes?"

"I'm afraid so," Laleel said, glancing at her two young daughters.

Listening intently, the two girls displayed compassion but no comprehension of Kal's horrors. Their innocent young eyes showed only a sadness that mimicked their friend's reactions.

"What's wrong with her?" Tubal-Cain asked himself before looking directly at Laleel. "Where did you hear this?"

Garun's wife turned to Kal.

"It's true," Kal said. "I was supposed to be one of them, but I was able to sneak away one night."

Tubal-Cain glared at Adah. "Is Naamah really doing this?"

"I think so," the queen said. "I'm not aware of everything going on around that place, but I know she's rounded up a group of young women."

"You were able to sneak out," Tubal-Cain said. "Why didn't any of the other girls go with you?"

"They didn't want to." She looked up at the blacksmith as a tear slipped down her cheek. "We all went from being slaves to being lavished with baths, silken gowns, jewelry, and more food than we'd ever seen. For the first time, we were treated like we were important." She shrugged. "Naamah and a creepy middle-aged man kept telling us what a valued role we were to play in Havil. Most of the girls longed for the chance to feel like they meant something to someone, and to have the princess of Havil telling us that we mattered — it was all very tempting to stay."

"So why did you run?" Noah asked gently.

"Even with all the clothes and food that we could want, it seemed like just another form of slavery, especially when they did this." She slid the wrap up her left shoulder, revealing a sizeable mark similar to the one burned onto Elam's arm. "Plus, I knew that all the comforts in the world wouldn't make up for what was coming." Noah barely caught the whispered last few words as Kal hugged Laleel and buried her face into the woman's open embrace.

"So she ran." Laleel took up the story. "She fell asleep in our barn. The girls found her in the morning, and we took her in." Laleel turned to Adah. "You're her mother and a queen of Havil. Should she stay with you from now on?"

Adah's chin quivered. "I wish she could, but after what Lamech did to Aterre, I can't risk it."

Kal reached out and gripped Adah's garment. "Come with us, Mam."

Adah knelt and hugged her. "I would if I could. But I have two small sons back at the palace. I can't abandon them."

"Then bring them too," Kal said.

"I can't — at least not now. Lamech would never let us go. He would hunt us to the ends of the earth." Adah looked up at Laleel, her eyes wet. "Can she stay with you in Iri Geshem until I can find a way to escape with my boys?"

"Of course," Laleel said. "I'm sure Garun won't mind."

"And we'll help out in any way we can," Emzara said.

Noah grinned and looked into Kal's face. "We'll have to swap more stories of your brother. I have many tales of how his devious ways have gotten me into trouble."

With tears still running down her cheeks, Kal smiled up at him. "Oh, I'd like that." She paused and her eyes twinkled. "And you should know that he always said I was the mischief master."

The whole room erupted into laughter and Noah relished seeing Aterre's good humor and spunk shine through his sister.

Chapter 23

"I look ridiculous." Noah peered at his reflection in one of the four fountains built outside the western gate of the city. He fidgeted with the preposterous cap on his head and wondered how anyone could think it was in good taste to wear one. He snorted as he studied the blue paint Adah had put around his eyes. "I'm sure to blend in with the crowd looking like this — as long as it's a crowd of mimicbirds." Running his fingers through the four weeks' growth on his chin, he added, "And I can't wait to shave this beard."

Emzara slid her hand across his lower back and snickered. "I think you look handsome." She stared into the water. "I'm the one that looks ridiculous."

"You're always lovely." Noah pulled her close and grinned playfully. "Even with all those white streaks on your face."

Leaning close to his ear, she said, "Let's make sure we don't start these trends back home."

"There's no chance of that."

As Noah adjusted his outfit, Emzara wrapped the end of her garment over her head and then down around her chin and tucked it in, revealing only her face. They stepped toward the city gate and fell in line with other travelers. Sentries swiftly checked each person, ensuring no weapons entered the city. After passing the guard station, Noah and Emzara soon found themselves shuffling along the main road through the smiths' section of town.

Noah pointed to a window near the top of the palace ahead and to their right. "That's Tubal-Cain's room, and that large shop over there is where I met him."

Emzara squeezed his hand tightly. "I'm afraid that I'll never see him after tonight."

Trying to mask his own concerns, Noah forced a smile. "He'll be fine."

She rolled her eyes a little and her lips curled up. "You're not very convincing. But thank you for trying."

"You're right. I'm nervous too." He held her gaze. "And not just about him. I don't want tonight to be our last few moments together, but if we're doing the right thing, then it's worth dying for."

She brought his hand up to her cheek and closed her eyes. "I'm sorry for bringing it up. Let's try not to think about those things. We're supposed to look like we're glad to be here."

Noah straightened and put an arm over her shoulder. "Let's go."

The crowd thickened as they drew near the large entrance into the massive courtyard. While walking in silence, Noah thought through their plan and wondered if it was the best approach. Their goal was to arrive early and find a spot close enough to the stage to influence the multitude yet far enough back so as to not be identified by Lamech, Naamah, or anyone else who might recognize them. The fact that the sun still hung well above the horizon in front of them indicated plenty of time before the ceremony's start.

Eventually, they spilled into the courtyard and were able to move faster as the throng spread throughout the grounds. Noah and Emzara walked purposefully toward the palace wall on the right, hoping to find a spot beneath where Tubal-Cain planned to appear.

Four guards approached them from the left. Noah turned his head and reached his arm out to stop Emzara. "It's Nivlac," he said under his breath.

Emzara's eyes grew wide, and after hesitating briefly, she bent down to dust off her sandal, keeping her face turned away from the guards.

Noah flinched when one of the soldiers brushed against him as they passed by. He continued to watch them from the corner of his eye until they were out of range. Breathing a sigh of relief, he glanced up at the palace wall. A silhouetted figure moved past the window in Naamah's room, sending a chill down his spine as his mind flashed back to that fateful night four years earlier. "Let's go."

Keeping their heads down, Noah and Emzara picked their way through an ever-thickening mob. Noah occasionally peeped upward to locate Tubal-Cain's designated spot.

"I don't think we're going to get any closer," Emzara said as they met a wall of people.

Noah scooted behind a taller man who would prevent anyone on the stage from spotting him. "This is probably close enough." Nodding toward the corner of the building, Noah said, "He should be right up there."

Noah and Emzara talked quietly as they waited for the ceremony to begin. A loud group of people to their left passed around a small container and they each took turns sniffing the smoking contents inside. The pungent odor invaded Noah's nostrils and momentarily covered the stench of so many bodies packed together on a warm evening. As the sun neared the horizon, Emzara edged up to him and rested her head against his chest.

Noah put an arm around her. With nothing else to do but wait, Noah's thoughts drifted to his precious wife, so he pleaded with the Most High for her safety and thanked Him repeatedly for the treasure she had been to him. *Creator please protect each of us, frustrate Naamah's plans, and expose Lamech as the murderous villain that he is. I pray that the citizens of Havil would seek to follow You.*

Suddenly, the crowd hushed to an eerie silence. In the distance behind him, a slow but steady drumbeat grew in intensity and frequency. To avoid standing out, Noah and Emzara turned around with those nearby and watched the procession. Beginning at the palace entrance, approximately two dozen girls traipsed toward the lone tree in the middle of the courtyard. Half of them wore white silken gowns, and the other half sported yellow garments. Flanking them on either side, musicians played a variety of stringed and metal instruments and drums. The procession turned right at the tree and moved to the center stairway, where the musicians and women in yellow danced and spun their way up the steps while those in white slowly walked between them. Suddenly, they stopped when the first pair of dancers and corresponding musicians reached the next-to-last stair.

The instrumental tones softened and a woman in a long, flowing black gown approached the top of the procession. Her hair stretched high above her head before fanning out like a fountain. White and yellow streaks hid much of her face, but Noah knew exactly who she was. As the crowd cheered, he turned to Emzara with a disgusted look. "Naamah."

Emzara gripped his hand with strength beyond her size.

Naamah's lovely voice rang out, silencing most of the crowd, and the music grew louder. As she sang, the girls in the procession resumed their routine. Each pair bowed low before the princess when they reached the top step before moving to the stage. The young women in white formed a semi-circle behind Naamah, and the others continued dancing as they made two symmetrical lines extending outward from the tips of the semi-circle.

Quiet at first, shouts of disapproval grew sporadically. Noah spun around to find the detractors then leaned to Emzara's ear. "I guess some people don't care for her or her song."

"I wonder what will happen to them," she said.

"Not sure, but this might bode well for Tubal-Cain and us."

After ending her song, Naamah raised her arms and shouted enthusiastically, "People of Havil. It's my great pleasure to welcome you to another celebration of our great god Nachash."

Someone lit a basin filled with flammable fluid in front of the giant serpent statue. Flames leapt up to illuminate the golden atrocity, drawing loud cheers from the audience.

Once it quieted down, Naamah snapped her fingers, and the girls in white moved closer to her, tightening the semi-circle. "I have a very special announcement to make about these beautiful young women. They've been selected to be the first priestesses to assist you in your worship of Nachash."

She paused as applause erupted from the crowd. "Yes, they are lovely. And for those who desire to devote yourselves wholly to Nachash, you'll have the opportunity to discover just how lovely they are. We've learned that Nachash is pleased when one of his followers engages in an act of sacred union with one of his priestesses."

Emzara leaned close to Noah. "I think I'm going to be sick."

Noah nodded.

Eyes wide, Naamah jerked her head back at the subdued response she received. "Do you not understand what I'm telling you? You'll now have greater opportunities to worship Nachash."

Applause broke out, but it was mixed with a significant amount of jeering, including from several people near Noah and Emzara. They joined the chorus of dissenters.

Naamah held up her hands and laughed haughtily. "Maybe you don't understand what I'm talking about. Give it a chance, and I'm sure you'll see how *special* this opportunity is."

The disapproval sounded louder than the excitement as the mixed responses continued. From somewhere behind them a disgruntled voice yelled. "You stole my slave for this. How is that a special opportunity?"

Noah smiled and looked at Emzara. "I didn't expect this."

Her lips curled up. "I didn't either. Maybe there's hope for this city after all."

Naamah huffed and paced the stage. "Listen to me!" Instantly the crowd quieted. "Apparently, this idea will take a while for you to get used to. Let us move on to the moment you've really been waiting for. People of Havil, please welcome your king." Naamah and all the other young ladies stepped aside to allow Lamech to take Naamah's place in the front of the platform.

Much of the crowd erupted in praise again while Noah searched the corner of the palace above him for any sign of Tubal-Cain.

"My people," Lamech said. "Please welcome your queens, Zillah and Adah."

Four guards carried a richly ornamented throne on which Zillah sat to a place of honor on Lamech's right. On the opposite side, the same procedure was simultaneously done for Adah. In unison, the guards lowered the chairs to the ground.

"People of Havil, we have much to celebrate this evening." Lamech strode to Zillah's chair as he continued. "Our city is thriving, and our House of Knowledge behind me receives new reports every week. This year we'll be sending out more scribes than ever before, and we'll send them even farther."

He paused while the applause roared. "In fact, I just returned from a trip to visit my son and we left a scribe there. So our initiative has already reached north across the vast sea." The king strutted toward Adah's chair next and put his arm on it. "We had a bit of a problem while we were there, but I left them a powerful reminder that they'd better not get in our way."

Noah's insides twisted and he fought to keep his last meal from resurfacing as he stretched his neck forward and caught a glimpse of a man standing on the parapet above. *Tubal-Cain!*

The king placed a hand on Adah's shoulder. "Adah and Zillah, listen to me; wives of Lamech, hear my words. I have killed a man for wounding me, a young man for injuring me." He stepped forward and raised his voice. "If Cain is avenged 7 times, then Lamech 77 times." He raised his arms to the sky. "Yes, this slash on my face was returned 77 times. Hear me! The same thing will happen to anyone who gets in our way!"

As the crowd roared their approval, Noah stood motionless in his shock. *Lamech admitted what he's done and they're cheering. Cheering! Now what do we do?* As the people slowly quieted, a voice above Noah rang out.

"Murderer! The king is a murderer! He slaughtered innocent people!"

Stunned at the audacity of his friend to continue forward with their plan, Noah remained rooted to the ground. Heads spun toward the roof of the palace, and Lamech squinted as he tried to locate the origin of the taunt.

Noah closed his eyes. *Please Creator, protect Tubal-Cain and let the people recognize the truth about Lamech.*

"Guards, seize that man who would dare insult me."

"Murderer! You're a murderer!" Tubal-Cain remained hidden in the shadows as he accused his father. "People of Havil, do you really want a king who murders innocent people?"

Murmurs spread through the crowd and a smattering of jeers rose up.

The king lifted his sword high above his head. "How dare — bring him to me now! No one speaks to me like that. I am the king! I am the most powerful man —"

Without warning, the terrain beneath them shook violently. People on both the ground and the stage screamed and shrieked as they struggled to remain standing. The earth's intense movement reminded Noah of a large wave under a boat. Deafening cracking sounds boomed across the square. A fissure opened up in the middle of the center steps, and Lamech leapt to one side to avoid falling in it.

Huge chunks of the massive wall on the other side of the courtyard fell to the ground. Noah's gut turned. Something snapped above him and instinctively, he pulled Emzara away from the palace's edge. He looked up as the site of Tubal-Cain's defiance collapsed merely cubits away from their previous location, silencing the screams of the people now beneath the rubble.

Emzara dug her fingers into Noah's hand as terror filled her eyes.

Pandemonium ensued and then suddenly, as abruptly as it started, the violent quaking stopped.

"Listen to me!"

Noah glanced up and saw Naamah at the front of the stage yelling loudly, but her voice was muted by the cacophony around them. "Nachash displays his wrath against those who rejected his priestesses. Do not defy him again!"

Noah grabbed Emzara's arm. "We have to find out if Tubal-Cain is alive and then get out of here."

Chapter 24

Noah tried to push through the panicked crowd but quickly found it nearly impossible to make any progress. The collapsed wall of the palace had created a makeshift exit from the square and some of the citizens clambered over the debris trying to escape. Others struggled in vain to lift the wreckage off those crushed under it.

Filled with dread, Noah realized that Tubal-Cain might be among the deceased. Still clutching Emzara's arm, he drove ahead and did his best to avoid being trampled until a massive gray cloud in the distance caught his eye. Noah pointed to it. "What's that?"

Emzara's height hindered her ability to see beyond the crowd. She bounced on her toes, "I can't see it."

Noah's jaw dropped. In the rapidly fading light of the sunset, an immense cloud of smoke shot upward into the sky. *The smoking hill just exploded!*

Minor vibrations shook the ground again. A small chunk of the palace wall dropped on the person next to Emzara, causing her to lurch sideways into Noah, hand pressed to her mouth in horror. Pieces of rock fell as the tremor continued, and many people around them changed course, deciding to head for the northern gate. Just then, a blast of wind swept through the courtyard, nearly knocking Noah to the ground.

Accompanying the wind, a deafening boom, louder than any thunderstorm, rattled through the square, forcing him and others to cover their ears. Undeterred, he forged ahead. Veering right, Noah and

Emzara reached the location where they expected to find Tubal-Cain. His heart sank when he gained a clear view of the devastation. Nothing stirred among the rubble and he climbed over the stones searching for his friend.

The earth continued its trembling, and a group of guards arrived and studied the ruins. "Find the man who spoke against the king," the leader said to the others.

"We don't know what he looks like," another one said.

"Just find someone in this mess who looks like they could've done it. The king ordered us to capture him, and I don't want to come back empty-handed."

Understanding the risk, Noah refrained from calling out the blacksmith's name. Afraid of being identified or caught up in the ever-expanding cloud emerging from the distant hill, Noah turned to Emzara. "We need to get out of here."

"But. . . ."

"I don't think we can help him now."

Defeated, they retraced their steps and, after some initial slow-going, made it to a thinner section of crowd for a while, which allowed them to dodge around the people more easily. After nearing the spot they had occupied throughout the ceremony, they moved quickly toward the western gate. As before, they kept their heads down and did their best to avoid the guards stationed at various points in the square.

Destruction surrounded them. Massive sections of the wall on the north and west sides now rested in ruins. People wailed as they picked through the carnage, and Noah passed two bodies bent awkwardly, lying motionless on the ground. He assumed they had been trampled by the terrified crowd.

As they neared the exit, the motion of the earth finally settled. Noah aimed for the middle of the cluster of people to avoid being spotted by guards. Keeping his hands on Emzara's shoulders to ensure they stayed together in the chaos, he shuffled into the horde trying to leave the square. As their advance slowed, the gravity of the situation engulfed his whole being. He glanced up at the massive arch above the exit. *What if that collapses while we're under it?* He fought the urge to turn back and assist some of the wounded people. *What can I really do for them? I'm not trained as a healer.* Besides, getting Emzara back to safety remained his priority.

They finally passed under the gate, and their pace immediately increased a little, although they dodged several large pieces of debris. Moving in lockstep with the masses, they passed Tubal-Cain's shop and the other forges, one of which had collapsed while another was ablaze. With each intersection they crossed, the crowd dispersed slightly and their speed increased even more. At the outskirts of town, Noah breathed a sigh of relief when he saw the abandoned guard checkpoint.

Once they reached the western road outside of the city, Emzara touched his arm. "I need to stop for a moment."

Noah led her a few steps off the trail to avoid the trickle of passersby. He gently rubbed her back as she bent over to catch her breath. "You alright?"

She turned her face toward him and the moonlight glistened off her teary eyes. "Tubal-Cain is . . ." She sniffed and shook her head.

"You don't know that."

"That whole area of the palace collapsed. How could anyone survive that?"

Noah bit his lip, looked away, and took a deep breath as he struggled to ward off tears and display confidence.

"Do you think Naamah is right, that Nachash did that?"

Noah scowled. "Why would you even think that?"

"I don't know." She wiped her face. "Maybe because the one person brave enough to take a public stand against the wickedness seems to have been targeted in the destruction."

Gazing back on the city, Noah swallowed hard, trying to push away the sorrow of losing another close friend. The stars above the city, so bright and sparkling earlier in the evening, now disappeared one by one behind the thick blanket of smoke spreading across the sky. As another celestial body vanished, so did his hope that Tubal-Cain had survived. Each moment he spent thinking about it, the more distressed he became. He closed his eyes hard and clenched his jaw. *Just get out of here.* Trying to block the desperate thoughts from his mind, he touched Emzara's cheek. "We need to keep moving."

She nodded and followed him back onto the road. "I'm sorry."

Noah reached an arm around her. "There's nothing to be sorry for. If he didn't make it" — he pulled her against him tight — "at least he did what's right. I'm proud of him."

The bright whole moon hovered over the road ahead, spilling its light on the earth. *Won't be long before that smoke blocks out the moon, too.* An eerie silence hung over their trail, with only the sounds of his breathing and the soft crunching of dirt beneath their footsteps.

Eager to break the stillness and force his thoughts elsewhere, Noah pointed to an upcoming road on their left. "That's the way to Garun's house."

Emzara squeezed his hand but kept her face down.

Noah straightened. "What if all that destruction came from the Creator as a judgment against the Havilites for following Nachash?"

She turned her face to him and shook her head ever so slightly. "Then why would He let Tubal-Cain die?"

A large figure stepped out from behind a tree on their left and strode toward them. "He didn't."

"Tu . . ." Emzara released Noah's hand and hugged the man. "You're alive!"

He chuckled. "It appears that way."

Noah waited impatiently for his wife to step to the side before embracing his friend. "It's so great to see you." Noah released him and they continued down the path together. "How did you survive that fall?"

"I didn't."

"Um?" Noah gestured from his friend's feet up to his head. "Clearly, you're alive."

"I mean I didn't fall." Tubal-Cain stroked his beard. "When everything started shaking, I jumped through the window into Jubal's room. The whole wall and some of the floor instantly collapsed behind me. So I sprinted down the hallway and snuck out the side door. Then I came here to wait for you."

"Praise the Most High, you're safe." She sighed and lifted her eyes up to the sky.

Noah grinned at his wife. "Well said, Em."

Abruptly, her arm shot out and she pointed up. "The moon."

Noah drew back as he beheld the evening light. "It's red."

"That's strange," Tubal-Cain said. "Have you ever seen anything like that?"

"Farna told me that there are times during certain whole moons, when the earth moves between the moon and the sun, that it turns a brownish color. But I think this is different." He searched the heavens. "I think that cloud of smoke is causing it to look red."

"When the earth moves?" Tubal-Cain asked. "Don't you mean, 'when the sun and moon move into the right position'?"

"No, it looks that way, but I said it correctly." Noah thought about describing how Farna taught him to use the stars to track the planet's movement and to chart their progress during a voyage, but they needed more space between them and Havil. "I'll explain on the boat. We should go."

"What's that?" Emzara brushed something off her arm.

Noah held out his hand and watched as tiny gray pebbles struck him.

"Is it rain?" Emzara asked. "It doesn't feel wet."

"Amazing." Noah turned back toward the city. "I think it's from that hill that burst into the sky."

"Is that what happened?" Tubal-Cain asked. "I was wondering where all the smoke came from and why the air is like a blast from one of the furnaces in my shop. I guess I was too busy trying to escape the palace."

More small pellets bounced off Noah's arm. "We really do need to move."

Noah described what he had seen as they started for the beach home. Tubal-Cain reminded them of Kenter's statement about the smoking hill causing the earth to rumble, sparking a lively discussion of how a hill could cause quakes and then burst open. As they reached the halfway point, the substantial amount of dust in the air sparked a coughing attack in Tubal-Cain.

"It reminds me of ashes from a fire." Emzara slid the end of her wrap over her nose and mouth to filter the air. She encouraged Noah and Tubal-Cain to do the same.

With their makeshift masks in place, the gray dust no longer hindered their breathing, but it irritated their eyes. Before long, they left footprints in the accumulating, obnoxious gray flakes. Noah urged them to move quickly, motivated by thoughts of sailing away.

After a long stretch of silence, Tubal-Cain pointed to a dim light ahead. "There it is."

With safety from Havil in sight and longing to breathe clear air again, Noah encouraged the others to run the rest of the way. Reaching the front door, he pulled it open and allowed Emzara to enter first. They shook out their clothes and hurried inside. Garun's wife and the three girls sat in the main room.

"Tubal-Cain, I'm sorry about the house," Laleel said. "The ground shook so hard that part of the roof caved in over the bedrooms." She pointed to the kitchen. "And those shelves collapsed."

Noah quickly recounted a few of the events of their evening. Feeling a sense of gratitude for his friend, Noah especially enjoyed telling about Tubal-Cain's boldness in accusing the king of his crimes.

"Well, I'm glad you're safe. But how terrible about the people who were hurt or killed. I wonder if I knew any of them." Laleel glanced at Noah. "Are we still planning to leave in the morning?"

Noah shook his head. "I think we need to leave immediately. We don't know if the king or others will come here to get out of the city. Plus, we have no idea how long that gray dust will be falling. The sooner we leave the better."

"I agree. We've already loaded our belongings on the boat like you asked." Laleel stood and wrung her hands. "There's just one problem. A huge wave hit after the shaking, and it pushed the boat onto the shore."

Noah's eyes widened. "How far up on the shore?"

"Not far," Zedakal said. "A little bit of it is still in the water."

"Let's go check it out." Noah cuffed Tubal-Cain on the shoulder and turned to Emzara. "Make sure all our things are packed."

As he followed the blacksmith toward the water, Noah said, "So the smoking hill bursts and scatters all this ash" — Noah looked around at the falling debris — "the moon turns red, the ground shakes, and there's a huge wave? I don't understand. What could cause all of that?"

"I don't know, but right now I'm not concerned about that. I only want to know that we can get out of here." Tubal-Cain stepped onto the beach. "I think we can push that back in the water."

Noah squinted in the low light. "I hope the hull isn't broken, or else it'll be a short trip." He put his hands on the hull and Tubal-Cain joined him on the opposite side of the bow. "Ready, push."

Noah shoved with all of his strength, and the boat shifted a little in the sand. He adjusted his grip and dug in his feet. "Push!" The ship slid a couple of cubits before moving it became easier, and before long, Noah found himself standing in the shallows with the vessel floating next to him in the lagoon. "I'll get things ready here if you'll go get the women."

Tubal-Cain turned and called over his shoulder as he ran. "Be right back."

Noah climbed aboard and checked all of the equipment. After pulling up the anchor, he found two pushpoles and shook the ash off of them. "This stuff is everywhere." Satisfied that everything was secure, Noah closed his eyes and offered the Creator a brief prayer for safety.

Emzara reached the boat first. She handed Noah the large basket of goods and then climbed onto the deck.

Tubal-Cain assisted Laleel and her daughters up after tossing some of Noah's supplies onto the ship. He reached out, forming a foothold with his hands for Zedakal to step in. "Here Kal, or should I call you little sister?" He shrugged. "Not that I want to take your brother's place, but we are sort of family."

She gingerly put her foot in his hands. "It's been a long time since I've had a big brother."

Tubal-Cain pushed her up and over the side and then scrambled aboard. "Let's go."

Noah handed him a pushpole, keeping one for himself. He stepped to the bow and shoved one end into the sand, pushing them deeper into the water.

"Hurry," Emzara said quietly as she pointed to the house. "Someone's in the house."

Noah spotted the faint light moving around in the home. "Push harder."

They drifted away from the shore, and soon the pushpoles no longer reached the seafloor. Noah ran to the sail and opened it, tying it into place. As the powerful warm wind drove them toward the open sea, a person carrying a torch walked to the shore and peered toward them. "Is someone there?"

Noah tapped Tubal-Cain on the shoulder. "Who is that?"

"I'm not sure. Probably one of my father's guards," Tubal-Cain said.

"Do you think he saw us?" Emzara asked.

Noah shook his head. "I don't think so." He took hold of the rudder control. "Let's get out of here."

Chapter 25

450 years later, Iri Sana — Noah's 499th year

"Farewell, big brother." Jerah grinned as he locked his grip on Noah's forearm and squeezed, his jaw tightening from the exertion.

"Peace to you, little brother." Noah returned the favor, causing Jerah to wince.

Pivi folded her arms. "Still as competitive as ever." She kissed Noah's cheek. "Be sure to greet Emzara for us. We really missed her. What's it been? Fourteen years?"

Noah nodded. "I think so. I know she'd love to see you again. As I mentioned before, you're welcome to visit us any time."

"Maybe we will. Now that Marneka is married we'll have more time available." She looked at Jerah and sighed. "Plus, I'd love to get to the sea again, if I can ever get my husband to leave the farm." She leaned in close. "I think he's just afraid of rumors about bandits on the river."

Noah shrugged. "Well, you do need to be careful, but I've never heard of them attacking the larger boats — they're well-guarded. If you visit, I'll be sure to take you for a small venture on the sea in one of our new ships."

"We'll hold you to that." Jerah helped Pivi into one of the seats on the wagon hitched to their lunker and then climbed into the spot next to her. "Farewell, Noah."

Noah smiled. "May the Creator watch over you until we meet again."

"Always great to see you," Pivi said.

Noah slapped the beast's rump and the animal lurched forward. He watched his brother as they pulled away on their short trip across a few fields to their own farm. Normally, they would walk, but this time a wagon had been needed to haul all the supplies for their daughter's wedding. Shaking his head, Noah's mind drifted back to the marriage ceremony the day before. Marneka, the 31st and youngest child of Jerah and Pivi, made a beautiful bride, but, though the celebration exhibited the traditions acknowledging the Creator, Noah had grieved the lack of sincerity. From his few brief discussions with Marneka's new husband, he had gathered the man had very little interest in walking with the Most High.

The thought made him ache for his wife. His beautiful, godly Emzara, who followed the Creator in spite of all they had endured. He looked at the festive pattern woven into the edge of his fine celebration clothing. Thinking of his wife's efforts in fashioning it made him miss her even more.

Emzara had decided to remain in Iri Geshem to manage the shipyard while he was away, but Noah knew another reason existed. Watching all her nephews and nieces get married broke her heart since she wanted nothing more than to have a family of her own. Four and a half centuries had passed since they lost their unborn child, and Emzara had never conceived again. Yet her faithfulness to her husband and their Creator never waned. *God, would You watch over Emzara too? I know I've asked this countless times before, but please allow us to have a child. Have we not faithfully served You all these years?*

Wisps of despair crept into his mind as he replayed the recent taunts from some of the younger citizens of Iri Geshem. *What's the point in serving the Creator if He never answers? Your God can't even give you a child.* Noah shook his head. "Don't listen to their lies," he said under his breath.

He turned and walked back to his parent's house in the hues of early evening. So much had changed, but some things remained the same. His childhood home had been rebuilt and expanded three times to accommodate his many younger siblings. Yet, as he caught the tangy scent of the familiar springal trees, memories from his early years came rushing back. Even though the row of trees looked different, the thought of chasing Aterre through them remained etched in his mind.

Noah strolled along the stone front wall of the house and entered the large sitting room. On the bench along the far wall, his father sat reading a scroll.

"Son." Nina pulled a slab of braided bread rounds from the oven and placed the hot flat stone on the large table in front of her. "Do you really need to leave so soon? I just baked these for you."

Lamech rose and stood behind her. "You know she doesn't like people leaving here empty handed."

"Or empty bellied." Noah patted his midsection. "Yes, I need to leave now. You know Valur's boat is nearly always on time. Plus, I miss Emzara, and she'll need a break from the shipyard." Eager to hide his frustration with life and people and even with God, Noah stepped forward and embraced her, turning his head so she couldn't read the despondency in his eyes. "I love you, Mother."

After a long hug, she released him. "I love you too, Son."

"It's been great to see you again." Noah smiled tiredly before turning to face his father. "Where's Grandfather? I thought for sure he'd be in here once he smelled fresh bread." Methuselah planned to stay one more evening before returning to his own place the next day.

Lamech rolled up the scroll and set it beside the bench. "Out back, waiting to send you off with his blessing, I suppose." He stood and hugged Noah tightly. "God be with you on your journey."

"Thanks, Father." Noah held him tightly, treasuring the rare moment with his father. He let go and bent to retrieve his bundle of items.

"Here. I also gathered a few things from the feast for you to take with you." Nina held out a bulging satchel, laden with remnants of her good cooking.

"Thank you, Mother. I'm sure this won't go to waste." Noah kissed her cheek before grabbing both bags in one hand and scooping up a couple of fresh bread rounds in the other. He headed for the doorway, nearly as anxious as the first time he had left home and longing to be alone with his thoughts.

Noah walked outside and headed toward the rear yard. He spotted a familiar figure seated near the edge of the house. "Grandfather, I'm headed to the Hiddekel now to catch the boat."

Methuselah stood. "Do you mind if I walk with you?"

"I'd love that, but are you sure? The sun's descent is nearly complete."

"I may be old, but I can still handle a walk like this. It keeps me feeling young. Besides, I want to talk to you."

Noah stretched a welcoming arm out wide and Methuselah attempted to pilfer one of the rolls. It tore apart and less than half remained in Noah's grip. "Hey!"

Methuselah took a quick bite and the bread slurred his words. "I though' you're off'ring one."

Noah chuckled and fell into step with his grandfather. "I suppose you can have it as payment for your company. I always enjoy our talks."

A smile spread on Methuselah's wrinkled face. Although his 870th birthday would come soon, he still displayed the energy and mobility of a man two centuries younger. "As do I."

"What topic should we cover this time?" Noah asked.

Methuselah cocked his head to the side. "Do you remember before you left home all those years ago when I said that my father was the godliest man I'd ever known and that I saw some of that same spirit in you?"

Noah thought back almost half a millennium to his coming-of-age ceremony and how the events of that night led him straight to Emzara. "I remember."

"As you've gotten older, that spirit seems to have grown. You've kept your commitment to honor the Creator." Methuselah put a hand on Noah's arm. "But there's something different this trip. You seem distracted, and I've rarely seen you smile. What's troubling you?"

Noah sighed and tipped his head back to look at the tinged hues of gold and pink beginning to weave their way across the sky. He debated playing it safe by just sharing his everyday frustrations over the growing corruption in the world. In his younger years, those who openly opposed the Creator remained largely confined to certain cities and regions. But as the centuries passed, the immorality of those places had spread like a wildfire and had infiltrated Noah's beloved Iri Geshem long ago. Thankfully, a slight majority of the city's aging council members continued to enforce policies consistent with the ways of the Most High. *But it's only a matter of time.* Noah shook his head. He had shared those concerns with his grandfather before. His recent unease arose from deeper within his soul.

He turned to the wise man beside him. "Is it truly worth it? Following the Creator, I mean."

Methuselah drew back and ran a hand through his thin gray hair. "Of course it is. Why would you ask that?"

"This world. Everything. I don't know." Exasperated, Noah let his arms drop. "I'm nearly 500 years old, and I've followed the Most High my entire life. But what good has it done?"

His grandfather tipped his head forward a little but remained quiet.

"Every year the evil grows in our lands. Nachash is worshiped throughout half the world, and I know many people in Iri Geshem follow that abomination now. And it's hardly any better here. The Nodites' vile influence is all over this region. You saw the marriage ceremony. Marneka and her new husband have very little interest in the Most High. And I don't think it bothers Jerah and Pivi at all." Noah clenched his fists and increased his pace. "If the Creator truly is the Most High, then why doesn't He put a stop to all the wickedness?"

"You wish for Him to stop people from acting as they please?" Methuselah asked.

He knew his grandfather despised the vile behaviors all around them but had learned long ago to cut right to the middle of an issue instead of griping about peripheral matters. Noah huffed. "No. I wish He'd warn them so that they'd know He's real and would follow Him."

"My father used to warn them on behalf of the Creator."

"Grandfather, please tell me the truth. Did he really walk with God?"

"Yes. He was a very godly man."

"I believe that, but that's not really what I meant." Noah pulled his eyebrows together and turned his head away from Methuselah. "Did the Creator actually speak to him? I guess what I'm asking is" — he ran his hand through his hair — "can we truly know that the Most High exists or are we just supposed to hope that our beliefs are right?"

"I never heard the Creator speak to him, but I believe He did. That's why he went to the city of Enoch — to warn the people."

"Right. That was so long ago. Where's the judgment that he talked about?"

"I don't know. I've learned that the Most High does things when He chooses to, and not always when we want Him to. Maybe He's waiting for someone else to warn the people." A coy grin spread across Methuselah's lips.

"Who? Me?" Noah stepped over a small depression in the trail.

With a gleam in his eye, Methuselah nodded. "I told you that you have some of my father's spirit. Why don't you do it?"

"I've stood up for the Creator for centuries, but lately, I've been so . . ." Noah shook his head and his jaw tightened. "Why should I? After all I've done for Him, what has He done for me? We still don't have any children, and we never will. For 450 years Emzara and I have pleaded with Him for a child, and what response have we received? Nothing. Silence. Why should I continue doing what He wants?"

His grandfather hesitated before putting a hand on Noah's arm. "He's given you all that you have. Your life. Your breath. Your health. It's all from Him. And He's given you a wonderful wife. Is Emzara not enough of a gift for you?"

"Of course she is." Noah blew out a long breath and the heat in his face slowly dissipated. "But my frustration is for her too. You can't imagine how much she wants a child. She helped our friends, Tubal-Cain and Adira, raise all 17 of their children, but it's not the same as having your own. The best time we ever spent together was when Jerah and Pivi allowed the twins to stay with us for about half a year. She talks about them so much. And that was over 50 years ago. For once, she had a small taste of what it'd be like to be a mother."

"I'm sorry that you two haven't been able to experience the joy of raising your own children. I truly am. I don't pretend to know how difficult that is." Methuselah pulled Noah to a halt so he could face him. "But let me ask you this. Did you know that many of Jerah's children reject the Most High's ways?"

"Yes, I've heard Father talk about that," Noah said. "It saddens him greatly."

"It saddens me, too, but not as much as it hurts Jerah and Pivi. They were devastated each time one of their precious children walked away." The old man stared at Noah. "Maybe that's why you remain childless."

Noah straightened and rubbed his arms to keep warm. "What do you mean? You think my children would turn away from the Creator?"

Methuselah held up his hand and shook his head. "No, that's not what I was trying to say. I meant that maybe the Most High is sparing you the pain that would come if your children did refuse to follow Him."

"Do you really think that?"

Methuselah shrugged a shoulder and began walking again. "I'm just thinking out loud and trying to give you a different perspective on it. I believe the Creator will honor your faithfulness, but I certainly don't know what He has planned for you."

As Noah massaged his temples and sighed, a tiny spark of hope ignited within. "I wouldn't expect you to know that. I appreciate another viewpoint, as well, but it doesn't really change my situation. This wedding reopened the wound of our barrenness. Look at Marneka. She's not even following the Creator, but she'll probably have children within a short time."

Methuselah remained silent, his eyes sympathetic.

"I know everything I have is from the Creator. And He's blessed me greatly. I could probably sell the shipyard and never need to work another day in my life. Yet I have no one to leave any of it to."

"I didn't realize shipbuilding was so profitable."

"We make the best boats. We get orders from all over world, even though people could order from local shipbuilders for less. But what good is that? I just wish I could do something more meaningful than making boats. To pour my life into raising a child of my own would be so satisfying."

"It is. Well, at least it is until they complain to their grandfather about why the Creator isn't doing what they want Him to do." Methuselah placed a hand on Noah's shoulder. "I'm joking, of course. You're a blessing to me and to everyone else I know. Think of what you've accomplished. Your boats carry food and supplies to people everywhere. What about that long voyage you and your wife took to finish mapping out the earth? Was that not meaningful?"

Noah pursed his lips. Many years earlier, he and Emzara along with Tubal-Cain and Adira journeyed around their enormous land mass. It took much longer than he anticipated because he had misjudged how far they would need to sail. But it had been worth it. Even with all the wicked people, the world still held myriad wonders, and during the voyage he had often found himself marveling at the Creator's handiwork. Emzara had discovered scores of spectacular animals and delighted in studying and drawing them. *We wouldn't have been able to do that if we were raising a family.* He sighed. Even the memory of that fulfilling adventure held no comfort for him now.

Reaching the river's edge, Methuselah stopped. "Let me ask you this. Where do you get this idea that the Creator owes you something?"

Noah stepped back, his eyes wide. "I . . ."

"Do you forget that we're created from dust, just like the stuff that's been at our feet this whole walk?" His grandfather's voice was firm yet gentle. "Is not His forgiveness the greatest gift of all?"

Noah bowed his head, not ready to give up his anger, but understanding the wisdom in his grandfather's words.

"Listen. I understand your frustration. But you need to think about whether you're wholly worshiping the Creator, or if you're worshiping the idea of having a family. We serve Him because of who He is, not because of what He gives." Methuselah turned to face his grandson squarely, gripping both of Noah's arms and waiting for him to look up before speaking again. "You don't have to accept this right now, but you have the strength of character to stand for the Most High in these evil times. Don't let your disappointments get in the way of what He may be calling you to do. Continue to serve Him in spite of how you feel and resolve to follow Him no matter what."

Noah stood up tall. "I have a lot to think about."

"Good. You'll have plenty of time for it on your trip home." He slapped Noah on the back and grinned knowingly.

One corner of Noah's mouth turned upward.

"There it is."

"What?" Noah crossed his arms. "I finally smiled?"

"Nope." Methuselah pointed past him. "There's your boat."

"Grandfather, thank you. I needed this walk."

Chapter 26

Novanam — Noah's 499th year

"As always, it was good to travel with you, Valur." Noah released the old man's corded forearm. During the week, Noah had wrestled with the thoughts that still plagued his soul, though he had also spent plenty of time helping Valur with the physical demands of running a boat. But even as he worked, he felt his soul preparing for peace, drawing nearer each day to the resolution that would sustain his spirit.

The captain's smile revealed a couple of missing teeth, prominent reminders of the story Valur had told Noah about a violent passenger on his boat many years ago. "You're always welcome on my vessel." The man tilted his head. "Or should I call it your vessel, since you built it?"

"Hardly." Grinning, Noah shook his head and slung his bag over his shoulder before stepping onto the gangplank. "May the Creator watch over you."

"And you as well. Be sure to greet your lovely wife for me, and make sure she comes with you next time so I'll have better company."

"I will." Noah pivoted and eyed the bustling town of Novanam. After marching down the long ramp and reaching land, he turned left in hopes of finding a vacancy at his favorite inn.

"Hey, Noah."

Noah looked up to see Valur calling to him from the ship's deck above.

The sailor patted the rail. "Remember, bigger boats."

"I'll see what I can do." Noah chuckled, enjoying their traditional farewell in memory of Recharu. He and Valur had partnered up to take over a share of the business when Deks retired. Then Valur had become sole owner when Recharu passed away nearly a century ago. It was Recharu who had first requested larger boats after Noah's maiden voyage with them as a young man.

After securing a room and dining at the inn, Noah walked through the city streets. Once a brief stop for the river runners, Novanam now boasted a few thousand residents and had grown into a major stop for the increased boat traffic on the river. Noah estimated that only a small percentage of the people there followed the Creator, and it was not uncommon for fights to break out in the tavern district at night, due to a combination of strong drinks and strong men.

Noah steered wide of that area as he headed for a place that had provided him a peaceful respite on a few occasions. Before reaching the top of the hill on the road to Zakar, he turned down a little-used dusty trail to his left. Part of him longed to continue on the main road and visit his friends in the forest village, but he thought back to his grandfather's words and craved the time alone to reflect and continue praying to the Creator.

Ducking under broad leaves and carefully dodging thorny plants, Noah regretted not purchasing a clearing blade in town, but the trail soon opened up. Mature trees surrounded him on every side, shading out the undergrowth until it dwindled into almost nothing. He climbed up a large log lying to his left and sat down. Staring out over the city of Novanam and the river just beyond it reminded him of his childhood years watching the occasional boats and dreaming of adventure. Now, centuries later, he had experienced more adventure than he had ever imagined and built just about every large boat on the Hiddekel.

Noah slowly closed his eyes and took several deep, relaxing breaths as he listened to the birds chirping and forest animals scurrying about. Without a single man-made sound in the air, he smiled and cherished the tranquil surroundings, occasionally opening his eyes to watch the light glisten on the crystalline water far below. His thoughts drifted back to his frustrations and the recent conversation with his grandfather.

He's right. Who do I think I am, that I can force the Creator to bless me? A battle between selfishness and gratitude raged deep in his soul. Absently breaking a small branch into pieces, he wrestled with himself. Noah took a deep breath. *Creator, do You know what I'm feeling right now? I have no legitimate right to hold on to all this anger, but I find myself unable to let it go. Help me.* He paused. *Help me let it go. Forgive me for doubting Your goodness. You have given me so much to be thankful for, and I often take it for granted. Thank you for Emzara and her tremendous love and support over these many years. Help us to serve You in spite of our disappointments.*

Noah stopped as relief spread through him and the burden eased a little. As he breathed in a new sense of contentment, he became keenly aware of the silence. All the animal noises, as well as the gentle breeze, had ceased. The perfect stillness made him a little nervous, and he slowly opened his eyes to something even more alarming. Gone were Novanam, the river, and the opening in the woods before him. In their place, a forest full of tall, straight trees rested on the edge of a large, relatively flat field with the sun high overhead. Having worked with wood his whole life, Noah was certain he knew every kind of timber in the world, but these were foreign to him.

Instead of resting on the log as before, Noah found himself standing, his mouth agape. He blinked hard. *This must be a dream.* He shook his head, trying to clear it. Only then did he sense a presence behind him. Somehow in the midst of silence, he knew he was being watched. He turned slowly, then stood motionless. On the edge of the forest, a babbling stream flowed beside an old, small stone house and an outbuilding he was sure he hadn't passed earlier.

"Noah."

The voice came from his right, although *voice* might not be the right way to describe it. Instead, it sounded like thunder mixed with raging waters. But his name was clearly discernable.

Fear and peace grappled for control inside Noah. Conflicted, he wanted to run away, but at the same time, he longed to turn and see who had called his name. A chill ran up his spine, causing his arms and legs to tingle and his neck hair to stand upright. As he turned, a bright glow appeared in the corner of his view. He closed his eyes, took a deep breath, and faced the light.

As he cautiously opened his eyes, comprehension eluded him. Hovering just above the ground between the two largest trees in the forest, a flame of fire, not much larger than a man, burned brightly, but it did not consume anything around it. Captivated, Noah gazed at the beautiful yet terrifying sight. The light emanating from the flame seemed to pierce his entire being.

"Noah." The intimidating, thunderous voice resounded from the flame.

Instantly, Noah dropped face first on the ground. Fear surged through his frame, and he felt as if every particle of his body would tear apart. Too scared to think, let alone speak, Noah focused on trying to breathe.

"Do not be afraid, Noah, for you are greatly loved."

Noah's fear waned a bit as the voice took on a hint of a whisper that somehow mingled with the thundering. Keeping his face averted, Noah struggled to speak. "Who . . . who are you?"

"I am the God of your forefather Enoch. I am the Most High, the Creator of heaven and earth."

Noah had never imagined how frightening it would be to meet the Creator, and he instantly regretted the times he had wished that the Most High would speak directly to him. The words finally registered in his mind. *Enoch was telling the truth.*

"Yes, Enoch told the truth and walked faithfully in My ways."

Trembling over the realization that the Creator knew his very thoughts, Noah asked, "What happened to him?"

"I took him so that he would not face death."

"Forgive me for being so bold to speak. Is that why You are here now — to take me?"

"No. I have heard your prayers and have come to speak to you. The whole earth has corrupted itself, and the descendants of Adam have grown exceedingly wicked. I am grieved that I made them, so I am going to destroy this world with a flood."

Keeping his face toward the ground, Noah's mind whirled and he managed to ask, "A flood?" *What about all the people?*

"You are concerned about the people. Do you believe that I will do what is right?"

Still trying to come to grips with the situation, Noah nodded. "Yes, I know You will do what is right. What do you want me to do?"

"You are to build an ark. It will be for you, your wife, your sons, your sons' wives, and the creatures that I bring to you."

Noah played the words back in his mind and tried to make sense of them. "Sons? But I don't have . . ." Hope filled his soul, and he fought to control his emotions. "Thank You, Most High." *Build an ark.* "How large will it need to be?"

"You will receive that information when the time is right."

"What should I do until then?" Noah waited for a response, but he sensed that the flame was gone. He slowly looked up and discovered he was back in the clearing. Shakily, he climbed to his feet and scanned his surroundings. The sun hung low in the sky, casting long shadows from the trees, and the log he previously sat upon was about ten cubits away. The unusual trees and little dwelling place were gone. *Strange.* Noah concentrated on committing the Creator's message to memory. "The whole world?" he asked himself.

As Noah turned to leave, he tripped over a rock and nearly fell, dislodging the relatively smooth stone in the process. He bent over, picked it up, and set it in the spot where he found himself after the vision. Hastily, Noah gathered six more stones and set them all up in a pile as a memorial. Kneeling down near the stones, Noah prayed to the Most High and thanked Him for speaking directly to him. "My grandfather's father warned people about Your judgment. I'll warn them about the flood, if that's what You desire."

Near the end of his prayer, Noah's thoughts meandered back to the Creator's words about the ark's future inhabitants. With an ear-to-ear smile crossing his face, Noah stood. *Sons?* He shook his head and laughed. *Amazing.*

Chapter 27

Iri Geshem — Noah's 499th year

The warm wind whipped through Noah's dark, gray-streaked hair as he surveyed the city that now sprawled on both sides of the river. Iri Geshem's population had multiplied many times over, and Noah guessed it was one of the ten largest cities in the world. Elegant three-story homes lined the western shore to his right, while smaller domiciles cluttered the eastern bank.

They drifted past the old wharf where the river boats used to be loaded and unloaded. A few fishing boats were tied to the ancient docks where he had first set foot in town. All cargo ships now traveled directly to the large port near the city's central district. But before reaching their destination, the small river runners needed to pass under the bridge.

Two centuries earlier, Noah had assisted with the construction of a wooden crossing that spanned the broad width of the river. This allowed produce from the farmlands of the east to quickly reach the city. Wide enough for a pair of animal-drawn carts to pass by each other, the structure rested on a series of piers. The trickiest part of the design was creating the system that pulled two significant sections of the deck back in order to permit the boats to sail through without damaging the bridge or the ships.

Noah studied the mechanisms of the lift as they floated by. *Those hinges will need to be replaced soon. I'll let Tubal-Cain know that he should check them.* As he turned his attention to the city to his right, mixed emotions bombarded him. The fact that so many people in the city refused to walk in the ways of the Creator frustrated and saddened Noah, but he changed his focus to his wife. Knowing he was only moments away from seeing her for the first time in nearly two whole moons, he could hardly resist the urge to dive into the water and run down the beach road to reach her faster.

A hand grabbed his shoulder. "You look like a giddy child again."

"I feel like one, too." Noah faced his longtime friend, Farna. "So, just a couple more runs before you turn the business over to your son?"

"Yeah, I'm getting too old for this. I love being on the water, but I'm looking forward to living out my remaining days relaxing on my small farm up the river." Farna signaled to a member of the crew, and the ship turned right as it entered the bay.

"I'll definitely miss having you around. Em and I will have to stop in from time to time."

"I'd like that. We can kick back and discuss the old days before . . ." Farna looked around and spoke quietly, "before the Nachash followers spread everywhere."

Noah sighed. "I hope they turn from their evil ways before it's too late." He waved to the workers at the shipyard as the craft drifted across the bay, but no one returned the greeting. *Must be too focused on their daily work. That's good.* A smile automatically crossed his lips when he saw the hill where he and Emzara had enjoyed their initial sunset together. The boat crept toward the long pier ahead and Noah bounced on his toes in anticipation. He watched the shoreline closely, hoping that Emzara would be there to greet him.

As one of the crew tossed a rope to a dock worker, Noah asked, "You'll have my crate delivered to the shipyard?"

Farna nodded. "As always."

"Excellent."

When they finally docked, Noah said a brief farewell to Farna and his crew and practically leapt to the pier, only to be stopped immediately by a cargo inspector. Moments later, the man finished his examination of Noah's bag, satisfied that it was free of any taxable items. Slinging his belongings over his shoulder, Noah ran to the beach, weaving in and out of crates and cargo wagons along the way. He turned right and hustled across the sand toward the familiar milknut grove, but running through the soft sand tired him out more than he remembered. He slowed to a walk to catch his breath as he reached the trail that led to the house.

Before reaching home, he passed by the once-small place he and Aterre built. It had been expanded over the centuries, but it currently needed several repairs. Garun and his family had lived in it for several years before finding a place of their own. After that, it had served at various times as a home for a few of Tubal-Cain's children, a storage place for shipyard items, and a guest home, but now it was vacant.

Honoring Ara's wishes, Noah and Emzara had moved into her childhood home. Although it was difficult for the first few years to be reminded regularly of the tragedies, they eventually opted to remodel the interior. As the exterior came into view, he reveled in the peace the sight gave him. It looked almost the same as it did when Ara lived there, thanks to Noah's regular maintenance and Emzara's meticulous care of the grounds.

No longer able to contain his anticipation, Noah ran the remaining distance and entered his house. "Em, I'm home."

"I'm in here," Emzara called from the sitting room.

Part of the renovations included moving their sitting room away from the front door. Puzzled that Emzara had not come running to greet him, Noah dropped his bag on the floor and hurried to the room on the opposite side of the wall on his left. "You won't believe . . ." Noah stopped when he saw several people in the room.

"Welcome back!" Several voices mingled together in greeting.

Tubal-Cain stood before him. "Great to have you back."

"It's good to be back. Although, I didn't want your face to be the first one I saw when I got home." Noah chuckled as he scanned the room. To his right, Adira, Zain, and Kmani sat on one of the large cushioned benches, but he had eyes only for Emzara. As his beloved approached, he held his arms out wide.

Emzara engulfed him in a massive hug, her familiar fragrance washing over him as he closed his eyes and cherished her touch. "I missed you."

"And I missed you too." As he pulled away, he saw three more guests. To the left of where Emzara had been, reposed Elam and Zedakal, with a very young girl sitting on her lap. "What a pleasant surprise. I didn't expect you to be in town." He took Emzara's hand and followed her to her recently vacated spot. She sat and scooted close to Zedakal, giving Noah space to sit beside her.

"So what's everyone doing here?" Noah asked as he settled in to get comfortable.

"We couldn't turn down Emzara's offer of evenfeast to celebrate your return," Zain said. "And we wanted to surprise you. Looks like it worked."

"It sure did, and I look forward to that meal as well." He leaned forward and turned to Elam. "I was just near Zakar a couple weeks ago. What are you doing in Iri Geshem?"

Elam pointed at Zain. "I had some business with Zain this week, and when I heard you were returning soon, we decided to extend our stay. Emzara was kind enough to offer one of your guest rooms to us. My father sends his greetings as well."

"Please give my regards to him and the others in your village when you return," Noah said.

"I will."

Emzara patted Noah's knee. "I needed some company since you were away so long. Besides, they brought their daughter, and I couldn't pass up the opportunity to play with her." She held her arms out to the little girl. "Come see Memma?"

Elam's daughter's green eyes sparkled as she smiled with a drool-covered fist against her mouth. She leaned forward for Emzara to catch her.

Emzara hugged the child. "Noah, say hi to Rayneh. Rayneh, can you say 'Noah'?"

Rayneh played shy and buried her face against Emzara.

Noah gently placed his hand on the child's head and stroked her wispy, light brown hair. "It's great to meet you, Rayneh." He looked at her parents. "Congratulations on another beautiful child. She's adorable. I didn't know you were going to have any more."

Elam and Zedakal had met about ten years after she moved to Iri Geshem with Garun's family, when, as an aspiring seamster, Elam accepted Zain's offer of an apprenticeship at Noah's recommendation. He and Kal bonded deeply during those years when he lived with Noah and Emzara. Noah thought back to the many things they had in common. Both had been kidnapped when they were young. Both had scars on their upper arms resulting from efforts to blot out the awful marks burned into their flesh. And Noah had played a role in rescuing both of them, although much more directly in Elam's case. After Elam finished his apprenticeship, they moved to Zakar, where the people were ecstatic to learn she was Aterre's sister. The Creator blessed them with nearly two dozen children, all adults by now, so this little one surprised Noah.

Kal smiled. "We didn't either, but we're thrilled to have her."

Noah loved Kal's smile. In it, he saw Aterre again. Though he sometimes struggled to remember exactly what his friend looked like, some of Kal's expressions refreshed his memory. Noah touched Emzara's arm. "Well, I'm very pleased you're all here, and I look forward to catching up with everyone. But if you don't mind giving us a moment, I need to speak with my wife privately."

"Right now?" Emzara's eyes widened. "Is everyone well? Your parents?"

Noah nodded and stood. "Everyone is fine. This shouldn't take long. I have something very important to tell you and I really can't wait."

"Oh, well I have some news for you too." Emzara kissed Rayneh's cheek and then handed her back to her mother.

Kal grinned and nudged Emzara with an elbow.

"Alright." She reached for Noah's hand and he pulled her up.

"Whatever it is, you can just say it in front of us." Zain chuckled and slapped Noah's leg with the back of his hand. "We're like family here."

Noah smirked. "And I plan to tell all of you later, but Em needs to hear it first."

The women whispered to each other and Kal put a hand over her mouth to contain her giggles.

Noah shook his head slightly, feeling as if he had missed an inside joke. *I'll ask later.* "Come on."

Noah led Emzara back through the front room and down the hall to their room. After closing the door behind them, Noah placed his hands on her cheeks and kissed her. He pulled back and looked into her eyes. "I love you. It's so good to be back."

Reddening a little, Emzara said, "It's good to have you back, and I love you too, but what did you need to tell me that couldn't wait?" She took a couple steps back. "Or was your plan just to get a longer kiss?" She grinned.

Noah snorted "No, but I'm not going to pass up the opportunity." He gestured to their bed. "You may want to sit down."

She arched an eyebrow and slowly sat on the edge of their sleeping pallet. "I'm ready."

Noah let out a deep breath. "This is going to sound very strange, but I can assure you it's true."

Emzara cocked her head and squinted, clearly confused.

Noah swallowed and glanced at the floor. "He spoke to me, Em."

"Who?"

"The Creator."

Her eyes snapped wide open. "What? Are you teasing me?"

Noah held her gaze. "No, He truly did."

"What do you mean?"

Noah shook his head. "I'm not really sure how to describe what I saw." Without warning, his eyes welled up. "It was surreal — the most amazing thing I've ever experienced. He was terrifying and beautiful at the same time."

Emzara reached forward and placed her hand on his arm. "What did He say?"

"He said He was going to destroy the world with a flood because of all the wickedness."

She covered her mouth. "What? When?"

"He didn't tell me." Noah sat down next to her and lightly rubbed her back.

Emzara lowered her head, stared at the floor, and spoke slowly. "What will happen to everyone?"

Noah grimaced. "I wondered that too, and I've been thinking about it the past two weeks." He turned to face her. "He told me something else too. He said I need to build an ark."

Emzara faced him. "A boat?"

"Yes, it'll be a big one, but I'm not sure how big."

"Larger than the ones you already make?"

"I think so." Noah bit his lip. "He said that He would send animals for us to take on board."

She straightened. "How many animals?"

Noah suppressed a smile. "I don't know."

"Wait." Emzara gestured to Noah and then herself. "Us? We'll be spared? Why? What about our friends and everyone else?"

"Believe me, I've been trying to understand His message, and we can talk about that later. But Em, there's more." No longer able to hold it in, Noah grabbed her shoulders as his volume increased. "He said that it'd be for those animals, along with you, me" — he gave her a quick peck on the cheek — "and our sons and their wives."

Emzara's jaw dropped and she put a hand to her chest. "Our . . . sons?"

"That's what He said." Noah chuckled. "So I guess that means the flood won't happen for a while since . . ."

Placing a gentle finger over his lips, she smiled and her glistening eyes danced. "Maybe not as long as you think." She grabbed his hand and placed it on her stomach. "We already have one on the way."

Her midsection bulged slightly and he stared at her, dumbfounded. "How long have you known?"

"Since right after you left." A tear streaked down her face. "You don't know how hard it was not to be able to tell you until now."

Noah hugged her tightly. "Praise the Most High. He has answered our prayers." The strange behavior of the women in the other room suddenly made sense. "So all our guests already know, don't they?"

She pulled back and wiped the corners of her eyes with her fingertips. "Yes. They're here to celebrate with us."

Noah kissed her again. "Then let's go celebrate."

Chapter 28

"It was so good to see everybody again. And Elam and Kal — what a surprise." Noah leaned close to his wife. The flickering light from the oil lamp picked up the sparkle of her eyes as the two sat on their favorite overlook by the sea. Though it was too dark to enjoy the view of the water other than the occasional crest of a small wave, his ears stayed attuned to the rhythmic splashing below them. Near the docks to their right, workers loaded and unloaded crates from large seagoing ships his company built. The lights from the city and the harbor dimmed Noah's view of the evening sky. "It's even better to see you."

Emzara snuggled in close and breathed out a happy sigh. "I've missed you. So much has happened while you were away." She put her hand to her midsection and smiled as she slowly shook her head.

Noah wished he knew a way to prolong the evening and simply take in her nearness.

"And your experience is beyond anything we've imagined." She paused and her voice turned somber. "But your news about the flood made it more difficult to enjoy the time with our friends. Did the Creator say anything else about it?"

"He spoke of how wicked this world had become and that He was grieved that He made people. Can you imagine the Most High being grieved?"

"Why shouldn't He be?" Emzara shrugged. "We're saddened by it too."

"I don't know. I suppose I imagined that He wouldn't have emotions like we do." Noah stared at one of the smaller boats in the harbor, where two men busily pulled their fishing net out of the water. Now commonplace, fishing was once unimaginable. Noah dropped his gaze as he recalled the first time he saw someone eating fish. King Lamech's impudence had deeply troubled him at the time, but over the centuries, Noah had grown accustomed to the idea and it rarely bothered him anymore. Suddenly that old revulsion rose to the surface. "But you're right. Man has rejected the Creator in every conceivable way. Why shouldn't He grieve? And why shouldn't He send a flood?"

Emzara started. "How can you say that?" She looked up into his eyes. "Our friends follow the Creator. Why should they be killed?"

Noah stroked her hair above her ear. "I asked Him what would happen to all the people." He thought back to his meeting with his Maker. "Actually, I didn't even ask the question. I simply thought it, and He knew my mind."

Emzara's eyes widened. "What happened?"

"He asked me . . ." Noah gulped, "He asked, 'Do you believe that I will do what is right?' "

"What did you say?"

"What could I say? How could I begin to disagree with the One who knows my thoughts? The One who made me? Of course, I believe that He will do what's right."

In the dim light, she turned her large brown eyes toward him and the softened, higher pitch of her voice foreshadowed her tears.

"So Adira, Tubal-Cain, Kal, Elam . . . Rayneh. . . . Can they come with us or will they just . . . be gone?" She clung to him.

"I don't know what's going to happen." He groaned. "The promise was for us, our sons, and their wives." Ever since receiving the Most High's message, the weight of it had settled on his shoulders like a massive wooden ship beam. His mind fumbled with the knowledge of what the future held and all the details yet unknown, although sharing it with Emzara lightened the burden a little.

"Our lives have been marked by seeing loved ones die. And now you say there's much more to come? How can I bear this?"

He hugged her to himself. "I don't know." Tears rolled down his face and his chest tightened. "It's not easy." She sobbed in his arms, and all the emotion that he had kept locked inside for weeks finally broke free.

After some time, she took in a shaky breath, and he peered into her face, wiping her tanned cheeks with his thumbs.

"Em, God told me not to be afraid and that He loves me." Noah looked up and briefly closed his eyes. "He also confirmed that what we heard about my grandfather's father is true."

Emzara returned a thankful half-smile and rubbed the wet trails on his face with her fingertips. "That's amazing, but. . . ."

"Here's what I have to believe. We know from what happened with Greatfather Adam that even though the Creator warns of death, He's merciful in the outcome. We don't know what that will look like for this situation. Maybe He'll allow our friends to join us, but even if He doesn't, I know we can trust Him. We have to."

She nodded slowly.

"We should take comfort that the flood must be many years away."

"So what do we do until then?" She put her hand in his and his pulse quickened.

"We start by enjoying the time we have with the people we love, and we think about how we'll complete the task that lies ahead."

"We're not alone in this you know."

Noah touched her midsection and smiled. "I know." He stood swiftly and brushed off his garment. "Do we still have that young bleater?"

She rose, tilting her head as her eyebrows came together in the middle. "Yes."

"I know it's late, but let's consecrate our actions before the Most High through a sacrifice and seek His direction."

Emzara clasped her hands together and nodded.

Chapter 29

As Noah walked backward with his hands on Emzara's slightly rounded abdomen, she rolled her eyes. "Are you ever going to hold my hand again?"

"You've had 450 years of that. Right now, I need to be ready in case he kicks."

"I haven't even felt that yet, so I think you'll have to wait a little." She picked up her pace, causing him to stumble slightly. "It's good to have you home, but we'll never make it to the shipyard at this rate."

With an exaggerated sigh, Noah fell into stride with her and placed an arm around her back. "It's good to be back." He looked up at the familiar milknut trees, and she followed his gaze. The massive shoots at the top of each trunk boasted dozens of long, slender leaves that waved like graceful fingers and provided a comforting canopy overhead. She loved how the early morning light pierced through the foliage to dapple the soft forest floor below.

"It's nice to have company again on the way to work."

"You've had him with you." Noah tipped his head toward her midsection.

She smiled. "True. Although not quite the same."

"Well, I grant you I may be a better conversationalist than he is."

"You keep saying 'he.' So you're pretty sure this is a boy?"

Tears formed in the corners of Noah's deep brown eyes. "I'm positive."

"I still can't believe the Creator actually spoke to you."

"Nor can I."

"I don't want to consider all that stuff right now, but tell me what you're thinking about this ark." Emzara kept her voice soft, still in awe of having a mission from the Most High and still trying to wrap her mind around all it portended.

"Well, I think God's placed us in a perfect location. We already have the shipyard and all the tools and materials we'll need. We're right on a harbor, which should be perfect, and we have many skilled people who could help. It's almost like He planned this."

She grinned at him before turning somber. "And I like that we won't be traveling — it's less risky for the baby." Noah reached up and squeezed her shoulder, drawing her closer to him. Fresh emotions from the loss of their first child welled up from deep within her. "But now we have a second chance."

"More than that. The Creator said 'sons.' "

Her smile returned. "Sounds like we'll have our hands full."

"And not just with them, but with animals. Lots of them. You should love that part."

She clapped her hands together. "It looks like studying them all these years will be useful after all." She marveled at the Creator's foresight. During their travels, she had always wanted to stop whenever they sighted unfamiliar creatures, in order to draw pictures of them and document their habits. And before it was shut down to make space for the expanding city, Emzara had helped out at a farm dedicated to treating injured animals. "It's as if the Creator's been preparing us all our lives for this."

"I was just thinking the same thing."

"Extraordinary." She drew the word out in awe of the Creator's wisdom and her responsibility. "Do you realize that this will have to be bigger than any ship you've made so far?"

"Much bigger. I've always wanted to build bigger boats, even back when I was your father's apprentice, and I've had success. Think about the breakthrough we had a century ago when I learned that wood pegs can make the hull stronger than anything we'd tried before that. It seems like the Most High has every detail worked out."

She squeezed his hand. "Remind me of this if I forget to trust Him."

"Of course."

"You've already started thinking out the plan for building it, haven't you?"

Noah's grin gave away his answer.

"I thought so."

"I'll need to construct some scale models to learn which proportions will be best. There's still a lot to figure out." Noah flexed his hand, revealing his eagerness to begin.

He stared at the ground silently for a few moments. "The last thing my grandfather told me was that he saw in me the same spirit that his father had. He encouraged me to warn people of the Creator's judgment." Noah looked up at her. "This impending flood gives me an urgency to tell others about Him and His ways."

She stopped and faced him. "Will you say anything about the flood to them? To our friends?"

"I — I don't know. Probably not yet. It's still too new. But I'll do my best to persuade people to follow Him."

"Count me in."

"There you are!" Tubal-Cain's loud, frantic voice cut into the peace of their walk as he ran toward them from the shipyard.

Noah tensed. "What's wrong?"

"Word's just getting out. Three of our council members were found dead this morning in the town hall."

"What?" Noah's and Emzara's startled responses mingled into one cry.

"Zain?" Noah asked.

Tubal-Cain nodded grimly. "He's one of them."

"No!" Emzara's scream muffled as Noah pulled her against him.

Noah's chest heaved shakily.

Emzara sniffed. "And the other two?"

"Kanael and Te'arek."

Noah shook his head as Emzara tried to absorb the information. *How could three people die at the same time, unless —*

"Adira was talking to Maiava when I left to see if she could learn any other details. But, I think it's obvious that this was no accident."

Emzara gasped. "Those are the last three members committed to the Most High."

Noah took in a long breath. "Does Kmani know yet?"

"I don't know, although . . ." Tubal-Cain stopped as Adira rounded the side of the old office building and rushed toward them.

"Maiava couldn't say much," Adira tried to catch her breath, "but she was able to tell me in private that it looks like they were poisoned during or after the council meeting last night."

"Poisoned?" Noah asked.

A loud clanging of deep tones from the town's emergency gong grabbed the group's attention.

"Guess we're being summoned to the crier's post." Tubal-Cain turned as he spoke.

"Stick together," Noah said.

Emzara walked alongside Adira as they followed Tubal-Cain's long, hurried stride while Noah brought up the rear. They marched up the hill toward Sarie's and found a large crowd had already gathered at the broad intersection. As the city's population increased, they had implemented a series of outposts by which news could be disseminated quickly. The council dispatched runners to inform the citizens gathered at each station.

Tubal-Cain led them up against the wall of the former bakery. He and Noah strained to see over heads, but the tightly packed crowd made any visibility impossible for Emzara. Glancing back over her shoulder, she pulled Adira close.

"Make way," a loud voice shouted ahead of them.

She turned her eyes up to the small platform that had been built about eight cubits off the ground between two large poles. Before long, the speaker climbed the rungs of the left post and stood above the crowd.

The gathering hushed as they waited.

"The words of Ashur, councilman of Iri Geshem. 'Tragedy has struck our great city.' " The crier's perfectly enunciated words carried over the assembly without being yelled. "Three of our cherished council members died mysteriously last night: Zain, Kanael, and Te'arek. As difficult as it will be to mourn for them, you need to know that we may all be affected by more than just grief." He paused to allow the crowd time to process.

Carefully, the messenger produced a small scroll from his wrap and held it above his head. "I have a message from the master healer." He unrolled the document and cleared his throat. "I have examined the bodies to see how all three could have died at the same time. There was no sign of violence, and I have concluded that they all had the same strange illness."

Emzara pressed herself against Noah, feeling reassured by his nearness. She imagined the high-pitched, nasal tone of the healer as the crier relayed his words.

The citizens murmured and many tried to back away from each other only to bump into the people behind them. A woman's voice called out, "Will it spread to others?"

"He wasn't sure, but he added a precaution. Ah, yes, here it is. 'If anyone has had contact with any of the deceased in the last week, they should go home immediately and remain there until the master healer declares it is safe to come out. Make sure you bathe in a blend of warm water, salt, shavings of milknut fruit, and three leaves from a red orb plant. If you experience any sudden pains or convulsions, hang a white cloth from your front door and a healer will be sent to you.' "

The crier rolled the scroll up and slipped it back into a pocket. "Following the private burial today, there will be an official week-long mourning period concluded by a gathering seven days from now in the square. That is all."

Questions immediately filled the air, and the messenger instructed the crowd to ask them in an orderly manner. At the same time, the gathering began to disperse. Emzara followed Noah as they weaved through the onlookers, and before long, they were on their way to the shipyard with Tubal-Cain and Adira.

"I don't believe it," Tubal-Cain said.

"Neither do I." Emzara shook her head. "I don't like this at all."

"Sickness?" Adira rolled her eyes. "Why would they gather everyone together only to tell them they need to avoid contact with each other?"

"With Zain gone, who will lead the council?" Emzara asked.

"Probably Ashur." The blacksmith squinted and clenched his jaw. "I suspect he's behind all of this somehow."

Emzara held up a palm. "So do you think the master healer is part of some conspiracy?"

Tubal-Cain shrugged. "Could be. He'd do what Ashur says if he thinks it's in his best interests. But maybe they were poisoned so that their deaths look like an illness."

Adira ran her fingers through her hair, pushing it behind her shoulders. "It's all a lie. Who's ever heard of such a silly cure? There's something they aren't telling us."

"Obviously, they intend to replace the three council members with people who agree with their wicked ways." Tubal-Cain slammed a fist into his open palm. "Zain didn't deserve this. He was a good man."

Emzara knew her husband's silence meant he was deep in thought. "Noah? What do you think?"

He shifted his focus from the road before them and held her gaze. "This changes everything." Noah grasped her hands.

"What do you mean?"

With a grim look, he glanced at Adira and Tubal-Cain. "We can't stay here. It's not safe for us."

"Where will you go?" Tubal-Cain asked.

Noah sighed. "I'm not sure. Probably Iri Sana at first, but I don't know if I want to stay there either."

"Just until things settle down, right?" Emzara said.

Noah shook his head slowly. "I can't see that happening. I'm afraid we won't be coming back."

"But this is our home." Emzara pulled her hands away from him. "We can't just give up and move away when something bad happens."

"Em, once the mourning period is over, Ashur and his followers will have complete control of the council." Noah stroked his temples. "Do you really think they'll allow followers of the Creator to just go about their business? They'll make it illegal to serve the Most High, and you know what that means?"

Emzara imagined some of the horrors she had heard about from cities where Nachash worship flourished. Shivering as she pictured herself going through unspeakable torture, she beheld Adira for a moment before turning back to her husband. "What's your plan?"

"We have a week. It'll take a few days to load a boat with the necessary supplies, and I think we'll need two of them." He pointed to her midsection. "You'll leave town with our son when the first one is loaded and head to my parents' house. I'm sure Garun and Laleel would be willing to go with you."

"What about them?" Emzara faced her long-time friend. "We can't leave them here."

Adira glanced at Tubal-Cain. "Most of our children are around here, so we'll stay put for now?"

Tubal-Cain nodded curtly.

"But if what Noah says is true, then you'll be in danger." Emzara swallowed hard.

"Maybe not right away," Tubal-Cain said. "Ashur's afraid of my father. I doubt he'd do something to us. If things turn out as poorly as you anticipate, then perhaps we'll join you in a short while."

Adira grabbed Emzara's arm. "Promise me that you'll stop in Iri Dekkel and tell our son what's happened. Tell him not to visit here until he gets news from us."

"That's a better plan," Noah said. "Em, instead of going all the way to Iri Sana, go to Purlek's and wait for me. We can travel together from there."

Emzara sniffed and her lower lip quivered as she watched her husband. "And when will you leave?"

"As soon as the second boat's loaded." Noah kissed her head. "I should be well on my way before the mourning period is over."

"Do you think they'll guard the bridge to make sure no one leaves?" Tubal-Cain asked.

"I don't think so, but if they do, there are ways around that." Noah turned his head to make sure no one else could hear their conversation. "The hinges on the lift need to be replaced and require the care of a certain blacksmith. Of course, it makes sense to work on it at night so you aren't interrupting normal business traffic."

"And if a certain boat happens to come along while I'm working on it?" Tubal-Cain asked.

Adira put a hand on his chest. "Then you pretend like you didn't see it."

Chapter 30

Iri Geshem — Noah's 499th year

I'd prefer that you come with me." Noah looked the elderly man in the eyes. "But I understand that you want to stay close to your family."

Bakur leaned his 810-year-old frame against the outer hull of one of the ships under construction. "I'm sorry to see you go, but I understand why you must. So what becomes of the shipyard?"

Noah slowly surveyed the flurry of activity around him. Over a dozen employees scurried about as they neared completion of another pair of ships for Malrak, a major port to the southwest. As the business had expanded in the past century, Noah had replaced a few run-down buildings and built a large warehouse for lumber, tools, and other supplies. Even more impressive, a giant four-story construction barn butted up close to the sea. Reserved for constructing the 100-cubit-long cargo vessels, this outbuilding allowed the shipwrights to work in any weather, and it contained moveable platforms for easier access to even the tallest portions of the ship.

Noah smiled to mask his pain at leaving it all behind. "If you won't come with me, then it's all yours."

"What is?" Bakur asked.

Noah spread his arms out wide. "All of this. The shipyard. The whole business. The house. It's yours." He pointed to the small river runner that he had been loading all morning. "Except that one, of course."

The old man shook his head. "I never asked for . . ."

"I know, but if anyone deserves it, you do," Noah said. "There's no one else I'd rather see it go to. After all, you helped train me."

Bakur stared off into the distance and a smile slowly crept across his lips. "Those were the days, weren't they?"

"They sure were." Noah placed a hand on his shoulder. "I've already written up the papers in your name. They're in my office."

"I can't believe this is happening — that you're really going through with this. It's all so . . ." Bakur turned his head up as if searching for a word. He shrugged and said, "so sudden." He sighed. "Make sure you add a line to the effect that the business reverts to you if you ever decide to come back."

"I can do that, but it won't be necessary. I have a new calling." He glanced toward the city. "Besides, I doubt I'll be safe here for much longer."

Bakur nodded grimly. "You've made a lot of enemies around here by doing what's right."

Noah had stood against the younger generations' practices for a long time, and a growing number of them resented him for it. Being a successful businessman and occasional member of the council earned him some respect, but based on the snide comments and angry looks, most of the town's burgeoning population was not going to miss him.

"Well, for what it's worth, I'm grateful for your example over all these years," Bakur said. "I'll truly miss you and Emzara."

Noah nodded. "And we'll miss you and many others. We'll get everything finalized later. Right now, I need to finish loading the ship."

After enlisting the assistance of two younger employees, Noah headed for the warehouse to finish the tedious process of moving items to the boat. Two days earlier, Noah had finished loading Emzara's boat with many of their belongings, along with various tools and devices necessary for shipbuilding, though he was careful to leave plenty for the shipyard to run efficiently. She had left with Laleel and Garun the night before last, and he could almost feel the distance between them grow with every moment he delayed.

When most of his items were packed away on the ship, Noah went to his office and stretched out on the nearly vacant floor. Closing his eyes, he smiled as memories rushed through his thoughts. This room had been his second home for centuries. He could have ruminated for weeks on the memories he'd made here, but a knock at the door stirred him from his daydream.

Noah rolled over and pushed himself up. "Come in."

The door opened and Pav, one of the young men who had helped him load the boat, stepped in. "Sir, Bakur said there are guards from the city waiting outside. Everyone is required to head to the city square immediately."

Noah raised an eyebrow. "Did they say why?"

"The memorial celebration for the fallen council members."

"That's not until tomorrow."

Pav shrugged. "It must have been moved up a day for some reason."

"I see. Thank you. I'll be out shortly."

"I'll let them know." Pav turned to leave.

"Pav, wait." Noah gestured for the young man to enter his office. "Did the guards see you?"

"No, sir. I was inside and Bakur told me to fetch you."

"Great. How'd you like to earn three weeks' pay for a short errand?"

The young man nodded excitedly. "What do you want me to do?"

Noah slipped a gold pikka from the leather band around his neck. "Wait in here until everyone's gone, and then take my riverboat to the old docks."

Pav's eyes followed the golden disc in Noah's hand. "On the river? And what if they stop me at the bridge?"

Noah nodded. "You shouldn't have any trouble, but if they ask where you're going, just tell them your boss wanted you to take it for a short ride on the river. If they tell you to get to the ceremony, ask them to let you use the old docks so you can get to the square faster." Noah flipped the pikka to Pav. "I'll make sure you receive two more if you complete the task."

"I will. Thanks. I'll stay out of sight until the guards are gone." Pav headed to the next room.

Noah adjusted his wrap and took a deep breath, contemplating why the council would have changed the timing of the ceremony. Bowing his head, he focused on his recent encounter with the Creator, and a sense of awe and responsibility washed over him. *Creator, I promised I would serve You. Help me to remain true to my word and faithful to You.*

Moments later, Noah marched down the long hallway and stepped outside. Over at the main building, a guard directed his employees toward the road while two more approached from Noah's right. Each sentry sported a leather jerkin under a bronze chest plate and shoulder covers along with a long dagger in a sheath hanging from the left side of his belt.

"Noah," the man on the left said.

Spinning to face them head on, Noah said, "Morning peace."

"Sir," the guard said without changing his stoic expression. "We have orders to take you to the council right away."

Noah tilted his head and smiled when he recognized the speaking guard as Elnach, a grandson of Ashur and Navea. "For what reason?"

Elnach shook his head. "The council chairman didn't say. He just told us to find you and bring you to them."

"The chairman?" Noah asked. "They've already selected a new leader?"

The guard nodded. "Ashur. He wanted you to join them for the memorial."

Noah pursed his lips and turned toward town. "Then I shouldn't keep your grandfather waiting."

They led Noah on the shortest route to the city's central district, which took them through Iri Geshem's old city square. These days he typically avoided the area altogether. He hated the increasing violence and blatant immorality, and he struggled to block the vile images that it burned into his mind. Sadness and disappointment washed over Noah as they passed through the area. Ashur's old inn served as a brothel, and rumors persisted that he still owned the place despite his public denials. The ancient town hall stood in disrepair while functioning as a shop selling idols and potions designed to enchant their users. Rickety shelters leaned against many of the buildings, and a foul stench filled the air from the garbage and human waste dumped in the open square. Shaking his head, Noah tried to comprehend how so many denizens lived in this squalor and how his beloved city had come to this.

People still milled about — taking their time to get to the memorial. A woman, obviously from the brothel, almost bumped into him as she laughed with her male companion. Noah quickly sidestepped her, but in the brief moment they exchanged glances, her eyes told a story of misery. In a darkened alleyway, two ragged young boys sat, their heads bent low. Noah had often offered jobs and mentoring to those in need, though few had accepted over the years, most choosing to continue searching for worldly ways to numb their pain. *Oh, Most High, surely You didn't create us for this. Use me however You will to show them the life that comes in following Your ways. And God, if that means . . .*

"Going to the memorial?" A confident voice interrupted Noah's prayer. "You'll need one of these." Holding up a small animal idol, the salesman started his pitch. "With so much death around, Zsanom is the only one to protect you now."

Noah turned away and held his arm out, refusing the offer. He picked up his pace, eager to break away from this environment.

The guards grabbed Noah's elbow and turned him onto the broad street that led straight to the central district. Now beyond the malodorous area, Noah took in a deep breath of fresh air, trying to clear the disturbing effects from his spirit. Hundreds of citizens marched toward the square in the distance; most stepped aside for Noah and his armored escorts.

The sounds of construction grabbed Noah's attention as they neared the massive theater, where crowds frequently gathered to be entertained by plays and other activities. Initially, the dramas showcased talented performers from around the world acting out epic adventures or gripping tragedies. In his days on the council, Noah often took Emzara to the shows, where they enjoyed the best seats in a section reserved for council members and dignitaries. But Noah stopped attending many years ago. In the past few decades, most of the performances had degenerated to the point of focusing on coarse jesting and sexually immoral behavior. Recent renovations expanded the theater even more to allow for sport and often featured warriors who fought to the death to entertain bloodthirsty audiences.

Noah beheld the newest construction project attached to the theater's southwest side. Roughly the size of the shipyard's largest barn and featuring extremely thick stone walls, the addition spread up half the outer wall and around the outside of the theater. A stone ramp dropped below ground through a large tunnel. *That must be the new entrance to the lower levels Zain told me about.*

They ambled past the arena and under the imposing gate that led into the central district. Tens of thousands of people moved about the expansive square as they waited for the ceremony to begin.

"Over there." Elnach nudged Noah and pointed toward the new town hall, a towering edifice that dwarfed all the other extravagant buildings around it both in size and elegance. The sunlight reflected off the hall's white stone façade causing Noah to shade his eyes with his hand. A sprawling balcony jutted out from the third floor, allowing those on the terrace to look over the entire square.

Elnach led Noah to a reserved section on the ground that featured about 25 rows of benches. It was roped off and guarded to prevent any unauthorized admittance. Beyond that area, an immense crowd had gathered. Noah was ushered to a seat near the middle of the reserved section, giving him a perfect view of whoever would address the crowd.

"Why so close?" Noah asked.

Elnach shrugged. "I believe many of the business owners will be in this area." He and the other guard turned and marched back the way they had come.

From high above, a metallic clang sounded twice, alerting attendees to get ready for the ceremony to begin. Fashioned by Tubal-Cain, the huge bronze disc hung at the top of the town hall and could be heard throughout Iri Geshem. *Where is Tubal-Cain?* Noah scanned the crowd but did not see any of his friends. He recognized some of the people around him, but at best they were merely acquaintances. The wife of a man who owned a tavern in the old city scowled at Noah. Apparently, she still held a grudge against him from when he, along with the majority of the council, rejected the initial proposal to allow the establishment of such drinking halls in town. Noah shook his head. *That must have been 200 years ago, and it was changed soon after that.*

The metal plate was struck again. On the platform above, five council members dressed in traditional white garb strode to the edge of the terrace and dropped into their ornate seats. Four spots remained empty; one belonged to Ashur, and the replacement council members would fill the other three. Ashur walked to the middle of the group and gestured with his arms for the crowd to be silent.

"Citizens of Iri Geshem, thank you for arriving on short notice to honor the lives of three faithful servants of our city. This past week has been very difficult for all of us." Criers stationed strategically throughout the square echoed each line of his speech so that everyone heard the proceedings. "This tragedy has affected each one of us. We've lost dear friends and tremendous servants of our great city, but we know that they would want us to move forward and take every opportunity to ensure that Iri Geshem has a bright future."

He motioned to his fellow councilors. "We've been in constant meetings throughout the week, deliberating on what to do next. We decided to replace our fallen members so that your council would have every advantage as we make important decisions. So please welcome your new council members."

Although he had anticipated that the new elders would not be followers of the Creator, Noah's heart sank as he watched his concerns become reality. He did not know the first woman mentioned, but the serpent markings on her arms told him enough. The man was a wealthy merchant and the other woman was an apothecary who peddled the intoxicating substances often used in Nachash worship. Both had repeatedly stood against the previous council's efforts to maintain the Creator's ways in the city, and they made no secret of their contempt for Noah.

Another clash from the bronze plate rang out. Music filled the air from all directions as shouts resounded from the north side of the courtyard, causing Noah to turn. A large wagon pulled an enormous object toward the middle of the square by a team of six lunkers. Having seen a similar event in Havil in his youth, Noah shook his head, knowing full well what rested beneath the cloth. He spun back to glare at Ashur, only to see the chairman looking straight at him with a wicked grin. Noah scanned the crowd for an escape route, but he realized that dozens of guards now surrounded his position.

Once the lunkers stopped, Ashur spoke again. "Today is a monumental day for Iri Geshem. We will finally cast off the restrictive rules of those who follow the so-called Creator. Today, our marvelous city becomes even greater as we officially dedicate it to the mighty Serpent, Nachash."

As the covering dropped from the stone serpent, cheers erupted from the masses. Gold glimmered in a long line along the back of the figure, and red stones filled its eye sockets. Similar to the idol in Havil, the stone abomination stood roughly twenty cubits tall, with its body coiled at the base and its head erect, as if poised to strike.

When the people finally quieted, Ashur continued. "The new council's first act is designed to foster unity among our citizens and loyalty to our true god. When you hear the music play, you will bow down to Nachash.

All who refuse will be arrested and will face banishment or worse." He stared directly at Noah. "We cannot permit such treasonous acts to go unpunished." Ashur held his arms up high. "Are you ready?"

A deafening shout instantly sounded from the populace, and a chill swept through Noah. At the same time, a confidence he had never known before surged through his body. The hairs on his arms and neck seemed to stand and yet he struggled to repress a smile.

Ashur lowered his arms. Instantly, drummers throughout the courtyard beat on their instruments in rhythm. People all around Noah spun to face the idol and hastily dropped to the ground in obeisance.

Defiantly, Noah folded his arms across his chest and refused to budge, keeping his back turned to the serpent god. Ashur's lust for wealth and control stirred feelings of pity inside Noah. Nevertheless, he knew Ashur's disobedience would soon be punished. *Creator, be with me and guide my actions. May these people realize that You are the Most High and that the Serpent is the Great Deceiver.*

The music paused as Ashur held up a hand and looked around the square. "Did you not hear the music?"

Noah followed Ashur's gaze around the square and noticed a few dozen people standing.

"You will have one more chance to honor Nachash," Ashur said. "If you refuse to bow, you will be arrested promptly."

The music started again, but Noah stood tall, sticking out like a taroc next to a group of buzzbirds. Ashur grinned at him, as did several other council members as four guards approached.

The captain spoke. "You were ordered to bow!"

Noah raised his voice. "I bow only to the Cre —" A sharp pain exploded in the back of his knees, dropping him to the ground. Noah looked up and realized it was Elnach who had struck him.

"Bow!" Elnach held a staff above his head, ready to deliver another blow.

Noah stood quickly despite the searing pain in his legs. "The Creator is the Most High!"

Another blow to his legs caused his knees to buckle, but he caught himself before hitting the ground. As he tried to right himself, he glimpsed a fist just before it crashed into his face. Suddenly, he fell backward and everything faded to black.

Chapter 31

Noah raised his bound hands and pushed them against his head to quell the throbbing that gripped his attention the moment he regained consciousness. He carefully opened his eyes, trying to take in his unfamiliar surroundings. Daylight streamed in through a thin opening at the top of the stone wall to his right. He cringed after taking in a breath of the stale, pungent air.

"You're finally awake."

The familiar voice slowly registered in his head. *Tubal-Cain.* Noah rolled onto his left side to face his friend. "They went after you too?"

The blacksmith rested against the wall, each arm stretched to the side by ropes tied to his wrist on one end and a ring in the wall on the other. His head sank. "And Adira, but I don't know where she is. They arrested dozens of people."

"I'm sorry. We all should've left with Em."

"It's not your fault, Noah. We knew the risks, but we wanted to stay near our children and their children." Tubal-Cain sighed. "I just never imagined things could change so rapidly."

"We should've seen it coming, though. Ashur's been trying to get control of the council for decades."

"And in his first move, he arrests everyone who would dare oppose him. Ruthless."

"Ara warned me about him so long ago, but I don't think even he ever imagined it would come to this." A sharp pain stung Noah's leg as he attempted to stretch it out, a painful reminder of the blows from Elnach.

Wincing, he forced himself into a seated position and leaned against the wall opposite Tubal-Cain. "Speaking of arrest, do you have any idea where we are? This isn't one of the holding cells near the town hall."

"No, it's not." Tubal-Cain lifted his head and looked toward the wooden door on the far side of the room. "That's the only way in or out. I think we're in the lower level of the old theater. It sounded like there was some cheering a while ago, but it was pretty muffled in here."

Noah's eyes widened as a cruel thought formulated. "And we're going to be part of the entertainment, aren't we?"

"That seems like a strong possibility."

Twisting his wrists, Noah tried to slide his restraints off. "Any chance of us breaking out of here?"

Tubal-Cain shook his head. "Not likely. I've tried."

Noah fell still as hopelessness washed over him. Then he smirked. "Well, you'd better hope they don't make us fight to the death. I think we both know who'd win that one."

Tubal-Cain snorted. "Only because I'd let you."

"And I'd never fight you." Suddenly serious, Noah shifted his weight, trying to find a comfortable position. "No matter what happens today, I want you to know how grateful I am for your friendship over the years. I couldn't ask for a better friend, and I know Em feels the same way about Adira."

"And we think the same about you and Zara, but don't get too mushy. Besides, I don't think Ashur would have the guts to kill me if he thought it would upset my father." Tubal-Cain glanced up and his eyes glittered with unshed tears. "To be honest, I'm worried that he'll want to make an example of you."

Approaching footsteps captured Noah's attention.

"He's in this one." A man peeked into the locked room through a small opening near the top of the door. "One moment." Metal pieces clinked together before the latch slid out of its place. The door opened and two guards carrying torches entered the cell.

The man on the right pointed to Tubal-Cain. "There he is."

As the guards stepped to either side and placed their torches in the sockets on the wall, a woman dressed in a long black gown walked between them, holding her chin high and shoulders back. The left side of her head was shaved, but her dark black hair hung down behind her right arm, which bore the unmistakable emblems of Nachash. A high-ranking soldier followed close behind her. She cocked her head to the side. "Tu?"

Noah's heart sank and he quietly dipped his head, hiding his face from Naamah. He watched Tubal-Cain from the corner of an eye.

Tubal-Cain's head flinched backward. "Amah?"

She let out a mocking laugh. "Ah, brother, it's been a long time."

"Yes, it has. What are you doing here?"

Naamah raised her chin. "Haven't you heard? This city belongs to Havil now, and it's time for them to meet their princess and high priestess."

"What? How. . . ."

"You'll know soon enough."

"Where's my wife? Is she safe?" Tubal-Cain fought his restraints.

"How should I know?" She bent down in front of him. "I'm sure we'll find her, and if you cooperate, I can guarantee her safety."

"Cooperate?" Tubal-Cain leaned back. "What do you want?"

"That's for Da to decide." She snapped her fingers and turned to leave. "Guards, take him to my father."

Noah dipped his head even lower, but a man's armored legs soon filled the edge of his view. A strong hand grabbed his chin and forcibly twisted his face upward. Recognition filled both captor and captive at the same moment. *Nivlac!*

A wicked smile opened on the guard's lips. "One moment, Princess. Look what I found."

She turned and fixed her gaze on Noah. Her mouth widened in a slow, sinister smile as she recognized him. "I'll be there soon," she said over her shoulder, without taking her gaze from Noah's face. "I'd like to have a few moments to talk with my old friend Noah before he makes his debut in the arena."

"Naamah, don't do this," Tubal-Cain said as the guards untied the ropes from the wall and bound his hands together.

"It's not up to me. Perhaps you can persuade the king to spare his life."

Noah looked past her to Tubal-Cain. "Don't worry about me. Honor the Creator no matter the consequences."

Tubal-Cain climbed to his feet with the guards' assistance. "I will. Farewell, Noah."

"May the Creator keep you."

"Enough!" Naamah stiffened and faced the guards holding Tubal-Cain. "Get him out of here."

The two sentries pulled the rope binding the blacksmith, leading him out of the room while Nivlac took up a post near the door.

Naamah laughed derisively. "Ah, Noah. This certainly looks familiar. Just you and me. And your life in my hands again." She paced in front of him. "And to think, you could've prevented all of this. You and I could've ruled Havil and the rest of the world together, but you were too self-righteous and too naïve. Tell me, where is your wife now?"

Silently thanking the Creator that Emzara was safe far up the river, Noah said nothing and kept his head down, only able to see Naamah's feet as she stopped in front of him. He recoiled when her hand touched his cheek.

"Still intimidated by me, I see. Very well. Perhaps she'll be in the crowd, cheering you on as you face your death." She pivoted. "Help him to his feet."

The dry ground crunched beneath Nivlac's footsteps. He grabbed Noah under the arm and pulled him to his feet.

"That's better," Naamah said. "Look at me."

Noah stared at the ground until Naamah snapped her fingers. Nivlac grabbed Noah's hair and yanked his head back.

Naamah stretched her arms to the side and slowly spun around. Her attractive form had diminished little over the centuries, but somehow she seemed to have aged much more than her contemporaries. Her eyes lacked the beauty and spark that had inhabited them so long ago. Her face was wrinkled like that of someone a century older, though she tried to mask it with various paints and dyes. "Do you regret your decision now, Noah?" She brushed his cheek with the back of her hand and then gently slapped him. "What a shame. We could've accomplished so much together, but today will be your last, and I'll continue to be the most powerful person in the world."

A surge of confidence rushed through Noah. He straightened, drew back his shoulders, and stared defiantly at her. "I will not die today."

One side of her lips curled up and she unsuccessfully tried to stifle a laugh. "You amuse me. But I promise you, you will die today."

"I don't think so." Noah shook his head. "But even if that happens, the Creator will bring me back to life."

Naamah's jaw dropped and she stared at him. "The Creator? After all this time, you're still trying to serve a defeated God? Most of the world follows Nachash now. He has overthrown your insignificant God." She snickered and strode away before turning and marching back. "Tell me, Noah. What makes you think you'll live beyond this day?"

Something in her expression and tone showed a tinge of doubt. Noah's confidence rose even more. "Because I haven't finished the task He has given me."

"The task? The Creator gave you a job to do?"

Noah wondered if he should remain silent, but his desire to see everyone follow the Creator won out. Still, he did not want to give away too many details. "Yes. He's going to destroy this world with a flood. Only a small number of people will be spared."

"Let me guess, you're supposed to be one of those people."

Noah nodded.

A vicious grin curved Naamah's lips. "Well, this day just got better. Not only will your life come to a spectacular end in the arena, but so will belief in your weak God when the people see your demise."

"And when you're proven wrong, then what?" Noah asked. "The Serpent is a fraud, Naamah. Turn to the Creator while —"

She slapped him. "Don't you dare address me without my proper title! I am the high priestess of Nachash, and you'll soon learn the meaning of true power." She spun and walked to the door.

He watched her go, saddened by her eagerness to follow the Great Deceiver. Nivlac held the door open for her, and a massive human frame appeared on the other side of the opening. The top of Naamah's head barely reached his waist, and his torso and head remained a mystery because they were higher than the door frame. Each of the giant's legs measured about as large as Noah's whole body.

"Your father is waiting for you." The man's deep voice rumbled through the cell just before the door shut.

Is that what I'll face in the arena? Noah took in a deep breath before slumping to his knees and stretching forward. *Creator, my life is in Your hands. I believe You'll rescue me today because I trust You to fulfill Your plan. I don't know how You'll do it, but I ask that others will have the opportunity to hear the truth about You.*

Chapter 32

Naamah walked swiftly beside her gigantic guard, rage fueling her steps and allowing her to keep pace with him. What was it about Noah that always made her feel powerless? She no longer felt any attraction toward him, but his words still sliced through her and made her feel helpless. The lack of control she felt around him was the same as when her then-beloved father brought home a second wife all those hundreds of years ago. *Really? You're not going to die today?* She smirked. *We'll see about that.*

A gaping door stood at the end of the wide passage, but the hulking figure at her side opened up a smaller door to their right, which led to a snaking path up to the main platform. Approaching Tu, who waited by the entrance with his armed escort, she tossed her hair behind her back with a flick of her head and straightened her shoulders.

"What's going on, Amah? Why are you and Da here?" His old pet name for her sparked something from deep within, but she squelched it.

Four guards accompanied them through the smaller exit; two led the way while the other two followed. Her giant companion left her side in order to enter the arena from a route more suitable for his size.

"We took over the town. Well, it was handed over to us. No battle necessary." She allowed Tubal-Cain to walk beside her and he leaned his head occasionally to avoid the low ceilings. "The king plans to make Iri Geshem our northern capital."

"Come on, Noah's not here, and you don't have to brag in front of me."

She leveled a cold look at him. "I'm not kidding. Once you see him, you'll know the truth."

He shrugged. "So what does he want with me?"

"You're his son, why shouldn't you share in his greatest achievements?"

"He's always left me alone before now."

"Well, you're not young anymore. Maybe he thinks it's time you started showing loyalty to your family."

"Oh, I'm not young anymore, huh?" His face lit up with his unique grin.

Naamah kept her visage expressionless, hoping to hide her thoughts from him. *Oh, Tu, when's the last time I've seen a genuine smile from anyone? I didn't realize how much I've missed you.*

"You know," he said, "you're not so young yourself." He winked at her. "And what's this new look you've got going on?" He pointed to the intricate design on her shoulder, where embedded ink interwove with lines of delicate scar tissue to form twisted vines and snakes in the branches of a Sepha tree. She had endured countless needle pricks and fine knife work to shape the image and raised skin, which covered her shoulder and a good portion of her arm, and extended down her back. Yet she had received it so long ago that she had almost forgotten it was not naturally part of her. "Nachash has been very good to me all these years."

"Pardon me for saying so, but I don't believe that. You still look beautiful, sister, but the look in your eyes and the wear around them tell me a different story. You seem wrecked by Nachash."

Anger flared again, and she sneered. "How could you say that? Don't you realize I could have any man in this arena if I so chose? But I doubt that anyone in this place is worthy of me."

He groaned and shook his head, but the pity in his eyes drove her onward. "I have more power than ever before. In moments, and with barely a nod of my head, people run to do my every whim: whether that's to sentence someone, to start a new project, or to simply call someone to bring me a piece of exotic fruit from the south country. I have it all."

"You seem to. But you've forgotten the most important thing, that which makes life truly meaningful."

"And what's that?" She spat the words at him.

"You've chosen to ignore the Creator and His ways. Instead, you're a slave to your own passions and pride."

"Enough! The Creator is a weak God worshiped by weak-minded people desperate to justify their own failure to rise in this world. You will speak no more to me about this, and if you know what's good for you, you won't breathe a word of it to Da." She turned away slightly and bit her lip, frustrated that she used an informal name for their father in this setting. It was a sign of weakness that he flustered her, but if he noticed, his unchanged expression did not show it.

Naamah stepped in front of him and held her head proudly. Seeing the sunlit entrance ahead of them, she was glad his opportunities to harass her had come to an end.

One of the guards hurried out through the exit to announce their arrival to those seated in the place of honor. After he returned, he motioned to the guards in the rear. "You two, escort the Prince and Princess of Havil to their waiting areas atop the platform." The soldiers instantly obeyed, grabbing Tubal-Cain's restraints and forcing him forward as Naamah followed.

The back wall temporarily blocked their view of the sizable audience, but Ashur's annoying voice welcomed the people to the dawn of a new era of prosperity and peace. He pontificated on how the King of Havil had arrived just in time to save them from whatever evil killed three of their leading citizens. "And now, give your king the honor due to his greatness."

A deafening roar split through the arena, making her ears ache, while reverberating through her chest. Soon the voices quieted, and Naamah imagined the king's fist raised high, commanding their attention.

Lamech's voice thundered through the crowd. "My people, as your first king, I'm indebted to your loyalty. Let us celebrate the peaceful transition and the prosperity to come." A slight pause followed before he yelled, "Let the games begin."

The crowd erupted again. Having witnessed it in Havil and a few of the other cities they controlled, Naamah could picture the scene clearly: a small company of captives shuffle their way into the center. Once the guards return to safety, a door opens, allowing whatever wild beast lies behind it to come and prey upon the hapless victims. As elsewhere, the roar of this crowd revealed their enjoyment of the sport. She sneaked a sideways glance at Tubal-Cain, who was still heavily guarded. With his eyes closed, his broad shoulders quivered as his lips moved silently. Even the sentry fumbling to untie her brother's bonds failed to interrupt his focus.

You haven't seen anything yet. She laughed low in her throat, thinking about how powerful she was compared to him, that even this death sport had little effect on her emotions.

"And now, my people," King Lamech called out, "I give to you Nachash and unity."

From their place behind the platform, Naamah and Tubal-Cain followed their cues and entered through the heavy brocade fabric that draped on either side of the open doorway. The deafening applause thundered again as she confidently took her place on the king's right. The newly unveiled statue of Nachash towered above them to her right.

"Let me introduce you to two people whom you may have already met. The first is Naamah. She, my only daughter, is high priestess of Nachash, and quite a sight to behold. Am I right?" He paused, letting the crowd show their approval.

The volume of praise filled her heart, and she breathed in the moment, holding her fist high in the air. As they chanted her name, she twirled and sashayed a bit, accentuating her best features in a spontaneous dance, spurring the crowd into more of a frenzy.

"The next . . ." the king waited for silence, "the next is my oldest son and heir, who has lived among you as one of your own for centuries. Your favorite blacksmith, Prince Tubal-Cain!"

Amid cries of delight, a guard directed Tubal-Cain to sit in the large throne made for him on Lamech's left. He leaned toward the king and shook his head slightly, "You know I want none of this."

"Quiet, you fool!" The king scowled at his son. The vehemence of his words caused the tight curls of his coiffed hair to dance about his shoulders. "You will do as I say."

"My good people." He straightened the crown on his head. "Tubal-Cain and Naamah are brother and sister, they are my children and they will demonstrate before you their loyalty to Nachash and their unity to this new, wonderful nation. Bring forth the sacrifices!"

Two scantily clad, stone-faced women came forward, each with a baby in her arms. They stood in front of the towering serpent statue, its golden head held aloft, forked tongue ready to receive innocent blood.

Lamech gestured to a guard who quickly handed him a knife. He held it out to his son. "And now, here is my son to offer the first official sacrifice of Iri Geshem, the northern chief city of Havilah."

The color drained from Tubal-Cain's face, and he folded his arms across his broad chest, refusing to take the dagger.

Shock rippled through the crowd, slowly silencing their cheers.

Come on, Tu. It's just one baby. Naamah tapped her foot on the stone flooring.

Anger churned in their father's eyes as he stood and approached Tubal-Cain. "You will do as I command."

Tubal-Cain held his head high. "People of Iri Geshem," his voice rang out as clearly, if not clearer and louder, than the king's, "I am not a prince of Havil. I am but a servant of the Most High, and He never asks for the blood of a child. Only the Great Deceiver demands the sacrifice of a baby."

The people jeered and shouted their disapproval.

Lamech, in his anger, whirled and stood before his throne once more. When the crowd quieted, he spoke loudly. "If your squeamish, sensitive nature cannot handle the demands of sacrifice, then at least bow before Nachash."

Unfazed, Tubal-Cain shook his head. "Never." He turned to the crowd. "Friends, I beg you, turn from your ways. Remove the shackles of fear and bondage brought by Nachash and embrace the one true God, the Creator."

Naamah watched the unfolding power play between her father and brother as both tried to sway the masses to their way of thinking. *Just bow, you fool.*

"My son, you talk of fear." Lamech rubbed his hands together. "You say your worship of the Creator frees you from fear?"

"Yes."

The king held out his arms. "Good citizens, he lies. Bring out his wife!"

Tubal-Cain gasped as the guards brought Adira to the center of the stadium and one of them shoved her. With disheveled clothes and hair, she staggered and fell to her knees.

"She will die if you do not bow." The king flashed a grin at Naamah before fixing his gaze on his son. "Surely you fear that!"

"Stay true to the Creator, Love!"

The plaintive cry of the bound woman annoyed Naamah, and she hissed. "Just bow! Don't you see that you could lose everything?"

He pierced her with his eyes. "Rejecting my Creator would be the worst loss of all."

The crowd yelled out a variety of taunts. "This is unity?" "You can't even control your own offspring!" "We want blood!"

"Tu, she will die if you don't bow." Naamah's voice squeaked in desperation. *Ugh, why do I feel so powerless?*

"You have one more chance to show your loyalty." Lamech narrowed his eyes on his son.

Tubal-Cain stood silently.

"Very well." He held up one finger toward a small entryway into the arena. "Bring it out."

A pithoct entered the area, snarling and tugging against its restraints, which were held by a pair of strong warriors. The beast bared its two long upper teeth, locked its eyes on its prey, and roared.

Why wouldn't Adira tell him to bow? Now she's made Da look bad in front of all these people. I hope it's a slow and agonizing death for her. Naamah watched the proceedings in front of her intently, hoping to catch the full measure of pain and justice.

"Listen to me! As your king, I know what you want and what you need. Nachash will have his unity and his blood. Not even my son will get in the way of that."

Alarmed at the undertone of pure hatred in his voice, Naamah turned just as her father lifted the sacrificial dagger he still grasped. His hands quivered only slightly before driving it into the lower right side of her brother.

"No!" The scream escaped Naamah's lips before she could stop it. *Tu! How did it escalate to this?*

Adira shrieked and ran toward them.

Tubal-Cain slumped against the railing, keeping his eyes on his wife.

"A kingdom cannot allow such treason to exist." Lamech stepped forward, bent down, and lifted Tubal-Cain's legs up and over the railing. "Die with your wife, Traitor!"

Naamah fought to control her emotions as she watched her brother fall into the arena and hit the ground with a thud just as the guard released the furry beast. It took every bit of her self-control to resist charging her father to push him over the rail as well. She glared at the back of the king's head with all the hatred she could muster. *Someday, you'll die for this.*

The beast slowed as it seemed to contemplate which of the two victims it preferred first. Keeping its distance, it circled around the couple, stalking them, as Adira tried to shield her wounded husband. Finally, it charged.

Tubal-Cain ripped the dagger from his side, scrambled to his knees, and pulled his wife down behind him. As the beast leapt, Tubal-Cain yelled and jabbed the blade upward as the pithoct struck him. The animal moaned as it collapsed on its target. Screeching, it hopped awkwardly to the side before stumbling, a dark red spot growing on its white-furred chest. Lying on its side, the creature kicked its legs for a few moments and then stopped moving.

Tubal-Cain remained motionless as well, except for the barely noticeable rise and fall of his chest and a slight turn of his marred face to look at his wife. She knelt at his side and pulled his wrap away from the dagger's previous location. Blood oozed from the gaping wound, causing her to slump over him and wail. He struggled to lift his left arm and drape it over her.

Unable to watch his demise, Naamah turned away. Seething rage increased with each breath.

Tubal-Cain's wife screamed in agony, and it echoed through the arena, causing some to laugh while others looked on in shock.

Having heard similar cries many times before, Naamah knew her brother's life had just ended. *Tu! How could you be so stubborn and ignorant? How foolish to give your life for nothing.*

"Take her," Lamech said to the giant guard, who had just entered the arena, while pointing at Adira. "Put her with the next batch of prisoners."

Naamah glared at her father. His smile showed his delight in the turn of events. *You wanted this to happen all along.* She paused in her thoughts and looked up at the giant serpent next to her. *O Nachash, grant me strength and wisdom to exact revenge on him.*

Chapter 33

Noah lurched forward and stumbled to keep up as the enormous guard yanked the rope tied about his wrists. The immense man easily covered four stairs at a time, practically dragging Noah up the steps. Above the pounding in his ears from his heartbeat and his panting for air, Noah still easily discerned the roar of the crowd in the arena.

They reached level ground and stopped in what had been one of the four large foyers in the theater's early days. Remodeled over the years, the cavernous room now seemed to serve as a staging area for whatever bawdy entertainment happened to be on the schedule. Huge timbers stretched upward to support the sloped ceiling, which also served to hold hundreds of spectators above it. Racks of weapons and armor lined the wall ahead. To their right, countless shelves of colorful garments and headwear rested behind three reflective metallic panels.

As they approached the large iron gate that led to the arena floor, the room grew lighter, allowing Noah to finally take a long look at his giant escort. Rumors of giants in Havil and other places abounded, but he had assumed the tales were merely exaggerations of tall individuals. The reality proved to be more impressive than the stories. The man easily surpassed six cubits. Musclebound like Tubal-Cain, only much larger, the man pulled Noah as if he exerted no effort at all. His left fist, roughly the size of Noah's head, clenched the rope, while his right hand swung freely. Iron armor covered his chest and midsection. A long, thick spear hung across his back and strapped to his belt, and a massive sheathed sword rattled and swayed along with its owner's loping gait.

To avoid the discomfort, Noah fought to keep up. "Will they even give me a weapon to fight you?"

The giant stopped before the gate and angled his shaved head down toward Noah before snarling. "I wish they would. You'd make a good meal."

Noah turned away in disgust. Was the man simply trying to scare him or did he really eat people?

A deep, rumbling laugh escaped from the titan's mouth. "I'm told they have something special planned for you."

Noah grinned. "So does the Creator."

The giant's free hand moved with blinding speed to grip Noah around the neck. With just one arm, the oversized man picked Noah off the ground and raised him until they were face-to-face. Huge, hate-filled, bloodshot orbs glared at him, and for an instant, fear surged through Noah's body.

Noah felt as if his eyes would pop out of his head — that is, if his head did not separate from his body first. With breathing or screaming an impossibility, he kicked and swung his arms wildly to break free, but striking at a stone wall may have been more effective.

"Don't you ever speak of the Creator around me." He spat in Noah's face and tossed him to the ground.

Gasping for air, Noah wiped saliva from his face with his shoulder. He groaned and struggled to stand, hoping to avoid being dragged again.

As a roar resounded from the crowd beyond the gate, the giant glared at Noah. "Time for you to die."

Noah cleared his throat, trying to collect himself. "Not today." He had imagined those words coming out stronger than the hoarse whisper that escaped his airway.

The huge man snorted before he bent over and grabbed the gate with his free hand. With metal creaking and groaning in protest, the giant heaved the iron bars above his head in one swift motion until it latched in place.

A crowd buzzing with excitement roared as Noah's attendant stepped out of the shadows. He yanked the rope, causing his captive to stagger before falling to the ground. The giant laughed as he dragged Noah across the arena floor.

The afternoon sunlight assaulted Noah's eyes while the hardened soil scraped his arms and legs as he flailed about, unsuccessfully trying to scramble to his feet. Finally, the man stopped. Noah peeked through the dust cloud around him only to see the giant looming over him.

"Get up, morsel." The deep voice bellowed above the cacophony. The colossus drew his large blade and stuck the point of it in Noah's face. He scowled and then quickly severed Noah's bonds. He sheathed his weapon and walked back toward the gate.

Noah unsteadily stood and glanced around. Several thousand people packed the benches throughout the stands; most jeered him with curses and other vile taunts. He spun around to face the reserved seating, knowing it was where Naamah, Lamech, and others who sought his death would be located, but a blood-soaked wrap on the ground beneath them grabbed his attention. A moment later, he realized a body lay beneath the garment.

Moving a few steps closer, Noah stopped and his stomach tightened when he recognized the lifeless eyes of Tubal-Cain staring back in his direction. He clenched his fists and fought the simultaneous urges to scream and weep. Laughter from the audience barely registered in his ears as his pulse quickened and his neck burned with anger. Gathering himself, he let his eyes drift up to the platform above. *God, please repay the king for this evil.*

Seated on a throne, dressed in a glimmering, gold-flecked robe, and wearing a large, ornately designed golden crown, King Lamech raised a hand and the crowd noise subsided to a murmur. Ashur, Navea, and the other council members sat behind him on the elevated platform in smaller and less decorative chairs. Naamah stood beside the king, but her earlier amusement had vanished. Glaring at her father as he stood to speak, she seemed pale and ill. On a large pedestal at Naamah's right stood a golden serpent idol nearly twice the height of a man.

Lamech directed a finger to the arena floor. "Noah, my old friend, it pains me that we meet again under such conditions. You have been charged with a capital crime against your own city. They say that you refuse to honor our chief deity, Nachash. Tell me Noah, are you guilty of such treason?"

Noah thought of the Creator's promise to give him sons and to flood the earth. He dusted off his arms and cleared his throat as conviction filled his mind. "I'd rather commit treason against the Great Deceiver than deny the Most High, the Creator of heaven and earth."

Angry shouts and obscenities streamed from the audience as Lamech raised an eyebrow. He waited for the crowd to fall silent before he spoke. "Noah, you have just condemned yourself to death, but because I am a merciful king, I am willing to give you another chance." Lamech turned to the iron gate and with his hand beckoned someone to enter the arena.

The giant returned, but this time he pulled seven captives in tow. The gate slammed shut behind them, and a pain struck Noah's heart as he recognized Adira, Elam, Kal, and even little Rayneh among the prisoners. Adira stared blankly at the body of her husband as she walked behind the towering man. Kal fought against her bindings to hold on to Rayneh, who cried out to her mother and father for help. Attempting to rush to her side, Elam tripped when the guard tugged the rope, eliciting uproarious laughter from the crowd. Finally, the procession stopped some 15 cubits to Noah's right, and the audience awaited the king's words.

Lamech ordered the giant to remove the binding ropes from the prisoners and then held a hand out toward Noah. "As I said before, I am a merciful king, but even the most compassionate leader cannot allow sedition to undermine his rule. I will give you one more opportunity to do what is right." He pointed to the large idol near Naamah. "Kneel before Nachash now and proclaim your allegiance to him. If you refuse, not only will you face a terrifying death, but you will condemn these seven people, including one little child, to the same fate. What will it be, Noah?"

Noah shook his head slowly at Lamech, astonished by the depths of his wickedness. A fleeting thought encouraged him to obey the king to spare his friends. He could always plead for the Creator's forgiveness later. But he quickly dismissed the pragmatic idea. The king could not be trusted to keep his word about sparing them, but more importantly, Noah would never deny the Most High. The God he had recently encountered was far more terrifying than anything Lamech threatened, and more deserving of devotion than any other.

Elam shouted encouragement to Noah, urging him to stand for the Creator. The colossal guard immediately silenced him with a swift backhand that sent Elam tumbling.

Creator, what I do now, I do for You. Please show these people Your power. Noah let out a breath and stood tall, holding Lamech's gaze. "You speak of mercy but know nothing of it. It will not be my hand that kills these people today. King Lamech, you and you alone will be guilty of their blood." Noah turned to the crowd and shouted as loud as possible. "I serve the Most High, the Creator of all things. Before Him alone will I bow, for only He is worthy."

"And I, as newly appointed king of this city" — Lamech walked closer to the platform's edge — "cannot allow Nachash, the Splendor of the World, to be disrespected in such a way. If your God does not let you kneel to another to spare the lives of your friends, then the Creator is a cruel monster." An evil grin streaked across his face. "And speaking of cruel monsters." He turned to Naamah and chuckled.

Dread settled in Noah's stomach. What vile scheme could trigger such an amused response?

Naamah stepped forward and leaned against the rail. "Just think, you could've been sitting up here by my side, but now . . ." She scoffed and then held her arms out wide, raising her voice for all to hear. "Moments ago, Noah told me that he wasn't going to die today." Laughter broke out in the audience, and when it quieted, she continued. "Then he said that even if he did die, the Creator would bring him back to life."

An eruption of insults and jeers rained down on Noah. People he recognized and had treated kindly over the years now mocked him for his faith and clamored for his blood.

Naamah waited several moments before gesturing for the crowd to listen. She smirked at Noah. "You still think you won't die today?" She laughed and then nodded to her father.

Lamech signaled to the guards standing above the large wooden double-door gate on the opposite end of the coliseum from where Noah had entered. The loud clacking of the gate's massive latch popping open drove the spectators into a fevered pitch of excitement.

Noah stared at the gate, his mind racing to figure out who or what would soon emerge from the other side. *Most High, my life is in Your powerful hands.*

A thunderous roar shook the wooden doors and echoed through the stadium. Having heard such a roar only a few times in his life, Noah cringed. His thoughts returned to the night he and Aterre had fled from the carcass of a dead earthshaker as a grendec approached. *Oh no.* Terror gripped Noah and his body went rigid. Suddenly, the same peace as when he encountered the Creator washed over him. Noah's dread instantly vanished. He took a half step forward as if readying for battle.

As the crowd anticipated the monster's entrance, the giant laughed behind him.

Noah glanced at Naamah. "I will not die today." He kept his words quiet enough so that only she and those in her immediate vicinity heard.

Naamah raised her eyebrows and waved to the guards above the gate.

In the stillness of the moment, Noah spoke loudly as he turned to face each part of the crowd. "People of Iri Geshem. Nachash is the Great Deceiver and the old stories are true. Just as he tricked our Greatmother Eve, he has misled the world, and now you, into following him. The Creator is the true God, and He is going to wipe this world out with a flood. Denounce your false god, turn from your wicked practices, and serve the Most High."

Laughter and jeers mixed in abundance for a brief moment until an earsplitting crash flung the massive wooden doors wide open. Only the beast's head emerged from the shadows at first. Perched more than eight cubits in the air, the gaping maw displayed dozens of long bony daggers. The grendec's greenish-yellow eyes locked onto Noah, and the creature stepped into the arena, revealing gold and jewel-encrusted covers on the two large horns above its eyes. Two absurdly small arms dangled from its torso, while brown and gray scales rippled over unbelievably powerful leg muscles as the horned grendec took three large steps in Noah's direction. Its lengthy tail swayed wildly behind it, striking the wooden door on the left and splintering one of its panels.

Noah stared in wonder at the mighty creature, but remained calm. *Almost too calm.* With no fear at all, he wondered anew how the Creator might rescue him from his deadly foe.

Only about 40 cubits away, the beast stopped, lowered its head, and looked directly at Noah. Opening its mouth wide, it let loose the loudest roar imaginable, mingling with the cries of the audience.

Noah flinched at the sound before taking a step toward the daggertooth. The creature twisted its massive head one way and then the other. Without warning, it rose and faced the crowd opposite the king, eliciting screams from some of the people sitting in its view. Its nostrils flared and fury grew in its left eye. The grendec charged the audience, the ground seeming to shake at each step.

Noah drew back as he recognized the danger. The arena had not been built to exhibit such a large creature, so the wall only extended about six cubits up from the ground, putting the front two rows of onlookers within reach of the beast.

As people directly in front of the monster scattered, the grendec rushed in without slowing. Turning its head at the last moment, the animal blasted into the wall, using its massive neck and shoulder as a battering ram. Stone and brick shattered and a section of the barrier — some three cubits to either side of the impact — crumpled to the arena floor, dumping screaming citizens to the ground in the process. The monster snapped its powerful jaws around the body of a man as he fell, instantly silencing his horrific cry. The weakened wall continued to crumble and spill spectators into the arena.

A child shrieked behind Noah. He spun and saw the giant standing over Zedakal, holding the back of her head with one hand while his other hand gripped the handle of the massive spear he had run through Kal's midsection with such force that it stuck into the ground beneath her.

Elam yelled and scooped Rayneh up as he ran with the other prisoners away from the titan toward Noah. Setting his daughter down, Elam directed her to Noah before he hurried to the fallen body of Tubal-Cain and picked up the sacrificial blade that lay beside him.

"Elam, No!" Noah picked up Rayneh and sprinted toward his friend. "There's nothing you can do for her now."

Adira arrived near her deceased husband and dropped to her knees beside him.

"Come on." Noah motioned frantically for her to get moving.

She shook her head and waved for him to leave. "Farewell, Noah. Tell Emzara that I love her." She grabbed Tubal-Cain's hand and held it against her tear-stained face.

The giant withdrew his spear, and Kal's lifeless body slumped to the ground. With blinding speed, the huge man spun and bounded toward them.

Elam finally turned and followed Noah toward the growing crowd of people attempting to flee through the double gate the grendec had entered through. Noah glanced over his shoulder and saw the giant pulling his weapon out of Adira's back as she fell across her husband's body.

Quickening his pace, Noah tried to force the horrific images from his mind. A moment later, a long, bloodied spear zipped between Noah and Elam and lodged itself in the ground. A spine-tingling shout rang out behind them.

Elam looked back and dropped to the ground just as the giant's massive blade flashed over him, hitting nothing but air. In a seamless maneuver, Elam rolled to one knee and swung his own blade behind him, striking his attacker. The blow opened a gaping wound in the middle of the man's large lower leg muscle.

The giant stopped and reached for his leg, allowing Noah, Rayneh, and Elam to decrease the gap between them and the exit. Turning to look back, Noah watched as the warrior looked up from the wound, grinned, and gave chase.

Noah tightened his grip on Rayneh and hurried into the midst of the crowd with Elam right beside them. The horned grendec continued its pursuit of the moving targets, pausing occasionally for a deep, thunderous call.

Without warning, Elam grunted as he fell to the ground, and his weapon bounced out of his hand, landing near Noah's feet. A massive hand clamped around Elam's ankle.

The giant stood upright, dangling Elam upside down by one leg and raising him so that their faces were even.

Rayneh screamed for her father.

Noah set the girl down, shielding her with his body, and picked up the long dagger by his feet, yelling to distract the murderous guard.

Ignoring Noah, the giant opened his mouth wide and leaned in as if planning to take a bite out of Elam's neck. Just before his teeth met flesh, the grendec's massive tail struck the colossus in the back, sending him sprawling forward toward Noah while Elam crashed to the ground.

Instinctively, Noah raised the dagger to protect himself just as the giant slammed into him, knocking him backward and forcing the air out of his lungs as he hit the ground.

Groaning loudly, the guard reached for Noah before yanking his hand back to his side as a howl bellowed from his lungs. The sacrificial blade stuck firmly to its hilt in the giant's side.

Noah scrambled to his feet and then helped Elam stand. "Let's go."

The brute tried to get up, but upon reaching his knees, the large guard yelled and clutched at his side again as he dropped to the ground.

He grasped the handle of the weapon as his own blood dribbled through his fingers. Wincing, he pulled the sword from his flesh and hurled it at Noah, missing his mark by less than a cubit. The weapon clanked harmlessly against the wall. Noah rejoined Elam and Rayneh as they blended with the crowd and hurried out of the arena.

Chapter 34

Emzara sat on the deck of the river runner, her back against the cabin. She turned to look for the late afternoon sun, but the thick fog still obscured it. Whenever it peeked through the mist, it looked more like the moon than the sun. As the craft made its way upriver, she barely glimpsed the ghostly tops of the tall trees along the shore as they moved slowly past.

Clutching the soft, handmade blanket from Adira in her lap, Emzara thought over the events since Noah had made it home up until the moving secret farewell two days ago. Her gaze shifted to the blanket, and tears pricked her eyes as she replayed her last moments with Adira. Following an emotional hug, her friend had handed her the intricately patterned weave. "It's for your new little one. Take it with all the hope and love I'm giving you."

"Zara?"

Emzara peered across the deck and barely discerned the outline of Laleel as the woman approached. Beyond her, Garun kept his back to them as he piloted the boat. Hastily wiping her eyes with her fingertips, she placed the blanket back down on the small wooden chest near her. "Yes?"

"What are you doing?"

"Just thinking, I guess. And enjoying the stillness."

"This is a good place for that." Laleel reached down and touched the spread. "What's this?"

Emzara smiled. "Oh, it's a gift from Adira for my baby." She tucked it into the chest before standing. "I guess I'm being overly sentimental, but I've been going through some of my old keepsakes."

"Will you tell me about some of them?"

Emzara read the care in Laleel's questions and it warmed her. She nodded before kneeling and pulling out a few items from the chest. "Well, this is the eye wrap that Noah wore for our wedding. These are beads from our anniversaries. And this" — she held up an old scroll — "is a letter my father gave to me on my wedding day. It's probably my favorite possession." She sniffed and closed her eyes. "I'm sorry, I'm not usually like this." Emzara tucked her head in embarrassment.

"There's nothing to be sorry about. I'm glad you thought to bring those along." Laleel walked to the railing. "I'm sure it helps. You've had huge changes in the last few days. And bringing something to remember those you love is a good idea."

Emzara joined her. "I'm not the only one going through big changes. I'm grateful you and Garun came with me."

"We wouldn't have it any other way." Laleel rubbed her hands together to warm up. "So how are you feeling?"

"With the baby?" Emzara let out a short joyful laugh. "I'm sorry. It still sounds strange to speak about my own child."

The wrinkles on Laleel's forehead became more pronounced as she smiled warmly. "Yes, with *your* baby."

"Better than I expected. Although, the motion of this ship is getting to me, and I feel sick in the morning."

"I'm sure you know that's to be expected. Your desire to look through those precious things is probably due in part to the baby too."

Emzara smiled as a cherished memory popped into her mind. "That's right. I remember during some of Adira's pregnancies, she would cry while looking through the baby clothing their older kids had worn."

"I was the same way."

Emzara slowly lifted a finger to point at her. "You were the same way?"

Laleel winked. "I guess I just hid it better."

Emzara stifled a laugh and then grew somber.

"What's the matter?" Laleel asked.

"I miss Noah, and I'm worried about him. He should've left when we did."

"He said he'd be on his way before the mourning period ended. They never stopped us at the bridge, so it doesn't seem like there's much to worry about." Laleel gently rubbed Emzara's shoulder.

"I know, but it's more than just Noah. I'm worried about our baby. The circumstances are so similar to the last time I was pregnant."

Laleel raised an eyebrow. "When were you pregnant? I've known you for over four hundred years."

Emzara patted her wrap near her knee to straighten a wrinkle. "It was right before we met. We were sailing to Havil when I lost our child. I was grieving the sudden deaths of two of the people dearest to me."

"Your father and Aterre?"

Emzara wiped a tear as she nodded. "And now things are so similar. Zain was just killed, and here I am on a boat worrying about losing Noah and our baby."

Laleel took a deep breath and grabbed Emzara's hand. "But this time is also very different. You told me yesterday that you have a promise from the Most High that you, Noah, and *your children* have yet to fulfill." She softened her tone and pointed to Emzara's midsection. "I know it's not easy, but cling to that promise. The Creator is faithful."

Emzara remained silent for a while, wrestling inside. *Can I trust You to do what You've promised with all that's going on? What am I saying? Of course, I can depend on You.* She nodded slowly, but then a smile spread on her lips and her confidence rose. "You're right. I may not know everything that's going to happen, but I must believe that Noah will be well. The Creator will protect him."

"Protect him and give you children," Laleel said.

Emzara folded her arms tightly against her body as if hugging herself would keep the warm feelings from escaping. She let out a breath. "I've always referred to Him as the Most High. Well, since that title accurately describes Him, then I know He will make good on His promise."

"And when He does, then you'll tell me more about this promise?"

"When Noah decides the time is right." Emzara yearned to tell her about the flood, but she had yet to grasp all the ramifications of the worrisome news. She forced her thoughts back to the promise of sons. "Oh, speaking of children. We should be pretty close to where Adira's son lives."

"That's right." Laleel turned toward the bow of the ship and called out to her husband. "Any sign of . . ." Her voice trailed off as her eyes followed something in the water.

"What is that?" Emzara leaned in and squinted as they floated past a large wet cloth that appeared to be wrapped around a box or barrel. Near one edge of the fabric, a dark round mass jutted out. As she turned to question Laleel, she glimpsed a human foot at the edge of the cloth on the water's surface. Gasping, Emzara covered her mouth.

Laleel's hand flew to her chest. "I see it. Garun!"

"You'd better come up here," he said. "Something's wrong."

As Emzara and Laleel neared the steering control, Emzara rubbed her forehead. "Did you see that body?"

Garun nodded. "And there was one on the other side too." He angled the boat toward the eastern shore and pointed ahead. "Look there."

Through the patches of fog, blackened silhouettes jutted out from the land. The once proud buildings now depicted harsh angles and missing pieces. The overall landscape reminded Emzara of an animal's lower jaw with jagged teeth, and she instinctively shuddered. Faint wisps of smoke trailed above the destruction.

"Am I seeing this right?" Laleel's voice was a mere whisper. "Is that Iri Dekkel?"

Emzara's heart sank. "Oh no, Purlek."

Garun motioned for his wife to grab the steering arm. "Here, take this." He cleared his throat, but his voice still came out raspy. "Keep it pointed toward the wharf. I've got to slow us down." He hurried back to the mast and quickly dropped the large sail.

"Who could have done this?" Laleel asked as she held the control steady.

"I don't know." Emzara scanned the beach for any survivors.

"Do you know where Purlek lived?"

Emzara closed her eyes, trying to recall from her trip 14 years earlier. "I think I know where his forge is."

"That's right. He's a blacksmith like his father." Laleel peeked over her shoulder and called out. "Hurry up." She smiled at Emzara and spoke quietly. "Or else you'd better find something to hang on to because I have no idea what I'm doing."

Emzara chuckled before bending down and grabbing two pushpoles. She tossed one to Garun as he approached and then moved to the right side of the deck to help him guide the boat safely to the dock. Painted words on a post confirmed they had reached Iri Dekkel.

"Strange." Garun tossed a rope around a mooring. "No other boats. Is that normal here?"

Emzara shook her head. "I don't think so. Maybe they fled."

"Or maybe whoever destroyed the town also stole the boats," Laleel said. "Did you come across any other boats in the night?"

"Just a handful of fishermen," Garun said. "Maybe they went upriver.

"Do you think it's safe for us to be here?" Emzara asked.

Garun nodded. "My guess is that this all happened last night. Some of the wood is still smoldering, but I don't see any flames. Plus, you're with me." He winked at Emzara as he took his wife's hand.

The three stood looking at the burned and gutted remnants of the town. A shiver passed through Emzara's frame. There was something eerie about seeing the remains of what had once been the home to hundreds of people. *Will the whole world look like this after the flood that the Creator's going to send?*

"Where's Purlek's forge?" Laleel asked.

"This way." Emzara led them down the road into town and turned left at the first cross street. A crashing sound to their right jolted them. "What was that?"

Garun nodded in the direction of the noise. "Part of that building just collapsed."

"Do you see any people?" Laleel spun all the way around, scanning the village. "What's happened to them?"

"I don't know, but it can't be good," Garun said.

They continued walking toward the north end of town. Charred remains of homes and shops seemed to be all that was left of Iri Dekkel.

"Is it much farther?" Garun asked. "We shouldn't leave the boat for long."

"We're almost there." Emzara increased her pace and the others matched her. "If I remember correctly, it's just at the end of this road."

The street turned slightly before leading under a grove of large trees lining both sides. The houses stood farther apart in this section of town and appeared to have suffered less damage.

As they crested a small rise in the road before a steady downhill, Emzara pointed. "It's right down — oh no."

The small blacksmith shop she remembered lay in ruins. Three of the walls still stood, but parts of the roof had collapsed. Emzara tried to sprint, but her legs refused to move as quickly as she wanted, no matter how much she urged them.

Garun sped past her and arrived at the forge first. "Purlek!" He pulled two stones away from where the door once stood and called out the blacksmith's name again. He continued shifting the wreckage and calling out.

"Anything?" Emzara asked as she reached Garun.

"No." He pressed on, clearing the entryway.

Laleel picked her way around some debris to the right. "I'm going to check around back."

Emzara peered inside as Garun moved another block. With no sign of Purlek, she stepped back just as Laleel disappeared around the corner. "Wait, I'll come with you." Emzara trekked to the side of the shop and followed a small trail that wove through a copse of large-leafed trees. Keeping her eyes on the rubble, Emzara strained to find any sign of her friend's son.

A cry from Laleel gave her a start. "Garun! Back here!"

Emzara dashed past the trees and found Laleel tugging on a large beam.

"Help me with this. I can't move it."

Tracing the timber from its nearest end to the opposite side, Emzara discovered the source of Laleel's urgency. Under the plank, stones, and other debris, a man's legs extended back toward the building. *Purlek!* An instantaneous sense of grief fled as a surge of energy flowed through her body. She joined her friend and the beam rocked slightly.

Garun soon rounded the back corner of the house. "What is it?"

"He's under here." Laleel leaned back, using all her weight to pull.

"Hold on." Garun quickly examined the scene. "Zara, step back."

Emzara tilted her head and narrowed her eyes, but she obeyed.

He quickly removed two large stones and slid a third one to the side. "Alright, now try."

Together, the three lifted the beam and moved it toward the shop. Then they feverishly worked to clear debris off the man, Garun lifting the heaviest pieces while Emzara, because of her condition, only worked with lighter objects. Finally, the rest of the man came into view. Dried blood fastened some of his dark curly hair to his neck. Scrapes and cuts marred his muscular arms and back. His right leg contorted at an odd angle.

Tears filled Emzara's eyes as she stared at the battered frame of a young man to whom she had been like a second mother. The memory of teaching Purlek to bake bread rushed through her head. Just then a small movement caught her eye. Her imagination must be playing tricks on her. *How can I tell Adira?*

"Is he dead?" Laleel asked.

Garun bent low and gently placed his fingers on the front of Purlek's neck. He bit his lip and looked at his wife. Suddenly, his eyes went wide. He leaned in close to Purlek's face while repositioning his fingers on the man's neck. Garun's jaw dropped. "He's alive."

Chapter 35

A swarm of humanity converged in the staging area under the arena. With no cover of darkness to hide them, Noah pulled his wrap over the top of his head in an effort to prevent anyone from recognizing him. He followed Elam and Rayneh as they fled the arena floor. They passed a woman screaming a man's name as she watched the people stream past her.

Making their way through designated routes, they marched slowly up the large ramp along the outside of the building. Keeping his head down, he listened to the hurried conversations around him. Several people spoke about the grendec, marveling at the creature's strength and ferocity; a few even laughed about the man it devoured. A pair of women wondered if the giant would survive his injuries. Another man made a crude comment about Naamah's appearance.

Finally, the crowd emptied onto the main street. The late afternoon shadows provided slight relief from the heat. Noah pointed ahead and to their left. "This way."

Far behind them, the massive metal plate rang out in a pattern, alerting the guards to prevent anyone from leaving the city.

Elam switched Rayneh to his other arm, and they jogged for several blocks toward the old city square. The tiny girl clung to him, her face buried. Her curly locks displayed a hint of almost gold in some places, if the light caught them just right. "They'll close the gates. What's your plan to get out of here?"

"We need to reach the old docks," Noah said. "If everything went as planned, I'll have a boat waiting there."

Just before the old square, they turned left on a road that led straight to the Hiddekel. Now separated from the arena's crowd, they slowed to a brisk walk. The shock of everything that had just occurred wore off as they walked. Rayneh squirmed and cried for her mother while Elam tried unsuccessfully to calm her. With tears in his eyes, he looked at Noah. "What do I tell her? I don't even know how I'm going to get through this."

Noah shook his head. "I don't have the words to say to bring you any comfort. I'm so sorry about Kal." He stared at the ground and his own eyes welled up. "And Tubal-Cain and Adira." His heart ached and his midsection tightened, threatening to bring him to his knees. Kicking at a stone on the ground, he longed to scream, but the last thing he wanted to do was draw attention to his little group. That final thought helped him refocus on the danger at hand. "I'll do whatever I can to help, but right now we need to get out of the city or we'll be right back in that arena."

Elam nodded. "I know."

They passed the old rundown bakery. Children played a game in the street, paying little attention to Noah, Elam, and Rayneh. Noah cast a look at the shipyard down the road to his right. *I'll likely never see it again.* "Come on. We're almost there."

Jogging again, they moved quickly toward the river. Noah's concern increased with each step because the boat was nowhere in sight. As they neared the docks, his mind raced to consider other possibilities, but the familiar hull of his ship soon became visible beneath a tree branch on the left side of the road. "There it is. We should hurry."

Elam rushed ahead and jumped onto the deck. He set his daughter down and grabbed a pushpole.

Noah loosed the mooring and threw the rope into the boat before hurrying aboard. "Push. I'll get the sail up."

Elam shoved his pole against the shore and grunted as he forced the boat away from the bank.

Noah untied the knot around the sail and hoisted it into place. He tied it off, and a steady breeze soon drove them farther into the river. After pointing the boat in the right direction, he grabbed a pushpole and assisted Elam, but before long the river grew too deep and the poles were of no use.

"Stop!" A commanding voice rang out from the shore.

Noah put his pole down and spotted a group of guards, roughly a hundred cubits away. "Take her below." He glanced at the sail as Elam grabbed his daughter and rushed to the hatch. "Come on, we need more wind."

"Wait!" The guard's voice lost its edge. The blue shoulder cover on his uniform identified him as a low-level officer. "Is that you, Noah?" He leaned forward. "It is! Noah, the shipbuilder, there's no reason to flee. King Lamech enjoyed your actions in the arena so much that he wishes to formally pardon you. Come back with us and you can return to your life at the shipyard."

Noah shook his head in disbelief as they steadily drifted away. "Do you think I'd ever trust that lying murderer to keep his word?"

"Very well. Have it your way." The officer signaled to his men. Each guard pulled a curved bow from his back.

"Stay below," Noah shouted to Elam. "They're preparing to fire at us." As the distance between them and their would-be captors increased, so did Noah's sense of security. He kept the boat aimed across the river as he watched the officer and his men. Typically, the vessel should be driven at a sharper angle, particularly in this wide area with its slow-moving current, but the pressing concern at the moment was to move out of the archers' range before heading north.

Each guard fastened a string to his bow and nocked an arrow. They raised their weapons and directed them at Noah. "This is your last warning. Turn back, or we'll fire."

As the officer dropped his hand, Noah dove behind a shipping crate. One arrow whistled overhead while two struck the hull. A third collided into the opposite side of the crate while a light splash indicated that another had fallen short of its target.

Now nearly halfway across the river, Noah peeked around the box just in time to see two guards move along the row of archers, lighting the tip of each new arrow already nocked. Ducking down, Noah prepared for another volley. He hoped they were beyond reach after two fizzled in the water, but the splintering of wood to his left dispelled that notion as a flaming arrow lodged itself in the hull. Noah peeked around the corner just as two more buzzed past the boat. With a thump, a third one hit its target.

As the guards reloaded their bows, Noah assessed the damage. He peered over the side and noticed a burning substance covered the area around the arrow. He dipped his hand into the water and splashed some onto the flames, causing them to spread. Confused, Noah watched as the liquid seemed to feed the fire. Before dropping behind the crate again, Noah checked their trajectory. They were drifting too far down the river and straight toward the eastern part of the city. It would soon be too late to sail beyond the gate and past the city wall.

Another round of arrows launched, but only one found its mark, igniting a small crate. Noah emptied it and tossed the box overboard. The blaze danced on the river's surface without extinguishing. Shaking his head, Noah hurried to the steering mechanism and angled the craft to the northeast. Looking back, he watched a few fiery missiles drop harmlessly in the water, but one flew directly over his head and ripped through the sail. The tiny hole would have been of little consequence, but the gooey material from the arrow stuck to the canvas and burned wildly.

Making some quick calculations, Noah spun the boat to allow the current to carry them to the eastern bank. The wind momentarily pushed the sail and they picked up speed until the fire damage tore the material apart. They would have to take their chances in the city. He looked back toward the distant shore as the final few arrows fell short.

The guards hurried down the river road toward the bridge.

"Elam! Come up here."

"Are we out of range?" Elam asked as he poked his head above deck. He glanced at the sail. "Oh no. What do we do?"

"There's no time for me to raise the spare. We need to reach the shore as soon as possible and then run." He pointed to the guards. "But we'll have to hurry. Grab a pushpole and get ready. How's Rayneh?"

"She's scared, with good reason. She doesn't really understand what's going on." Elam grabbed the pole and stood near the edge of the deck.

Smoke poured from the back and side of the craft as the flames continued to chew away at the hull. The boat coasted ever closer to the bank. While no guards waited on the eastern shore yet, the archers had arrived at the bridge and started across.

"We should be shallow enough by now," Noah said.

Elam shoved his pole deep into the water. He grunted and the vessel veered slightly to the left. "Just barely." He repeated the process multiple times as the guards closed in.

Noah grabbed the other pole and together they drove the boat toward the beach. "Get your daughter."

Elam dashed down the short flight of stairs and reemerged with Rayneh in his arms.

"Brace yourself." Noah grabbed a large box to avoid losing his balance as the boat slid to a grinding halt. They all pitched forward with the landing. "Come on."

Noah grabbed a sack of food and two small bags of gold piks and pikkas before splashing down into the knee-deep water. He turned around and took the little girl from his friend, allowing Elam to jump off the boat.

"Where are we going?" Elam asked as they hurried to the shore.

The soldiers were about halfway across the bridge now and Noah picked up his pace. "You'll see."

A middle-aged fisherman stood on the beach and looked quizzically at them. He set one end of his pole on the ground and placed his hand above his eyes, squinting as the fading sunlight reflected off the water.

Noah looked away and sprinted up the road. After reaching an intersection, they turned right and headed into an older section of the city down a street lined with fruit trees. Thankful for the deepening shadows, Noah led them toward one of the few farms that still stood within the city wall. An old, tattered shed occupied a small piece of land near the side of a large white stone house. A few cattle grazed in the small pasture. Sneaking around to the right, Noah and Elam ducked under a fence. Noah led them behind the outbuilding, where they pulled back one of the wood panels and slipped inside. Fumbling in the dim interior, Noah found a ladder and climbed up to the second floor. He reached down and lifted Rayneh up and waited for Elam to join them.

Noah directed them to the large piles of hay stashed around the room. "We can hide in those until late tonight."

"Where are we?" Elam asked.

"It's Cada's farm. Aterre used to work here." Although it was now too dark for her to see it, Noah smiled at Rayneh, wishing for all the world that she could have met her uncle.

Chapter 36

A pair of guards searched the entire lower level of Cada's old shed. One of them tipped over a shovel just before declaring it all clear, and Noah held his breath, fearing the noise would wake the sleeping Rayneh. But the little girl continued her slumber. For some reason, the guards never checked the hay loft. Perhaps they were unaware of it. Noah let his breath out in a silent sigh of relief as he remembered Elam's decision to pull the ladder up to the second floor.

Noah waited a long while after the guards departed. "They're gone." He peeked over the edge and carefully lowered the ladder. "We'd better get moving to where we can get out of the city while we still have the cover of night."

Elam nodded and cradled his daughter close as Noah made his way down the rungs. Noah hoped that her dreams provided some peaceful respite from the pain and confusion of the day's events.

The two men took turns carrying the sleeping child as they darted through alleys, hid behind trees, and snuck around buildings. Rayneh stirred occasionally but never fully awoke.

After arriving at the familiar home just before the deepest dark, Elam quietly slid the key into its slot and gently opened the door. Noah handed Rayneh to him before stealing one last glance down both directions of the street. He slipped inside the house behind Elam, closed the door, and breathed a sigh of relief.

"Kmani." Elam spoke just above a whisper as he moved through the sitting room. "Kmani, it's Elam. Are you still awake?" He paused and tilted his head as he listened for a response. He moved to the hallway and stopped. The door at the end cracked open and faint light seeped through the gap. "Kmani, it's Elam."

The elderly woman froze and stared down the hall, her eyes searching the darkness. She pulled a lantern around her rotund frame and held it up, illuminating her smile as she spotted her unexpected guests. "Elam. Noah. What are you doing here?" She increased the lamp's brightness. "Putting that key we gave you to good use, I see."

"Sorry for waking you, but we need to get out of the city." Elam pulled the key from his pocket and handed it to her. He hugged her with his free arm. "I don't think I'll need this again."

"Guards stopped by earlier looking for you and they searched the house. Here, let me take her." Kmani held out her short arms and took Rayneh, who jostled a little before nestling up against her. With a tip of her head, she gestured back down the hall. "Downstairs."

Noah stepped to the side, allowing Elam to move past him and open the entry between the sitting room and dining area. After Kmani walked by, Noah followed them to the stairway and closed the door behind him.

"How are you doing, Kmani?" Noah and Emzara had stopped over to comfort the grieving widow the day before Emzara left town, and he had been stunned at how calmly she seemed to be handling Zain's murder. She told him that although it was painful, she was not surprised by it, given the city's descent into all sorts of evil activities and the fact that her husband had long been at the forefront of the resistance against them.

"Each day is difficult," she said as she reached the bottom of the stairs and handed him the lamp. Noah used the flame to light a second lantern near him on the wall. The cellar instantly seemed larger as the glow illuminated the space. The room served as a storehouse for their textile supplies as well as a cool environment in which to keep food preserved longer. He turned his attention back to Kmani.

"We'd been together for more than 700 years," she said. "I'm grateful for the time the Creator gave us, but at the same time — and I don't know how else to describe it — it seems like half of me is missing." She tilted her head and frowned toward Elam, who sat on the floor against the wall, his head buried between his knees as he wept quietly. She covered Rayneh's ear and looked up at Noah. Grimacing, her voice came out just above a whisper. "Kal?"

Noah pursed his lips. "Kal, Adira, and Tubal-Cain were all killed in the arena." He closed his eyes before the tears escaped. "Tubal-Cain was gone before they brought me out, so I don't know how it happened."

"The king stabbed him for refusing to worship Nachash, but he didn't die right away." Elam wiped his eyes and took a deep breath. "He killed a wild beast that was meant for Adira before succumbing to his wound. We were forced to watch it all through one of the gates."

A knot formed in Noah's midsection as the terrors of the arena flooded his mind again. His bottom lip quivered as he thought about Tubal-Cain being killed by his own father. "That's the second time he's taken the life of my best friend." Self-pity nearly engulfed him, but, glancing at Rayneh, he suppressed it. Yes, another dear friend was lost to him, but the little girl would grow up without her mother, and Elam would never see his wife again — at least not in this world. *How would I feel if that happened to Em?* He cast a sympathetic look at Elam.

"Come now." Kmani tapped Elam. "There'll be plenty of time for that later, and you're right to do it. But not now. Those guards may return at any moment, and you need to get your little girl out of here." She caught Noah's attention and gestured to a large shelf unit holding all sorts and colors of fabric. "Behind that."

Noah nodded. "Do we need to move the whole unit?"

Kmani shook her head. "No, the bottom half of the middle section pulls out, but it's heavy. Just pull some of the material out first. I can repack it later."

"You aren't coming with us?" Noah hung the lantern on a hook near the shelves. "Aren't you in danger here?"

She smiled. "I think Ashur prefers to let me suffer in my grief for Zain. Besides, if he wanted to kill me, I'd already be dead." She adjusted her hold on Rayneh. "Don't you worry about me. Zain made arrangements in case something like this ever happened. I'll head to my son's place in a month or so."

"I'm sorry it's all come to this."

Her eyes glistened in the low light. "So am I."

Noah grabbed a pile of folded linens from the large bin before him and set them on a table to his side. He repeated the action two more times before Elam joined in the work. With half the container emptied, the two men pulled it away from the wall.

Elam snatched the lantern and held it in the recently vacated space, revealing a dark drape hanging from the back of the shelving unit. "It's behind this?"

"Yes," Kmani said. "Just push it to the side."

Elam slid the curtain to the side and then ran his hand along the wall, searching for the small hollow that served as a handle. Once he found it, he slipped a finger behind the little opening and pulled back. A door, lower than Noah's waist, swung open, exposing a couple of steps down to a hidden tunnel that Zain had dug out shortly after building the house nearly a century earlier.

"And this will take us under the wall?" Noah asked.

Kmani nodded. "Yes, take the lantern with you. There's an abandoned shack up against the woods about 200 cubits past the wall. When you reach the end of the tunnel, just look for the door above your head. It's built into the floor of the shed and hidden behind some debris in the corner. Before you open it, listen to make sure all is still."

Elam kissed the old woman on the forehead. "Thank you for everything."

She teared up afresh. "I know you're overwhelmed by all that's happened, but be strong for your daughter." She rubbed his shoulder. "I'll miss you all very much."

Blinking back tears, Elam said, "I love you. You and your husband were wonderful mentors to me. I hope we'll see you again." He turned and crawled backward into the opening. "Don't worry, Noah, the tunnel is taller once you get inside."

Noah hugged Kmani. "May the Creator keep you safe."

"And you as well." Kmani gently handed Rayneh to Elam. "Be careful, and get as far away from here as possible."

Noah waited for her to move out of the way before following Elam into the tunnel, carefully holding the lantern off the ground as he ducked under the low opening. After a few steps, the ceiling allowed him to stand, although not to his full height. "Noah, take this." Kmani reached down and handed an empty waterskin to him.

"Thank you." Noah mustered a smile that tried to convey half a millennia of gratitude. "Oh, I almost forgot." He pulled two gold pikkas from a small pouch. "Please make sure that a young man named Pav at the shipyard gets these."

Kmani nodded and a tear dripped off her cheek. "I will. Farewell." She sniffed and closed the door.

Noah held the light aloft and studied the tunnel before him. A handful of scraggly roots poked through the dirt ceiling above. Wooden beams stretched from the floor to the top every five to six cubits, and a crossbeam connected them along the ceiling. A few streaks of water appeared on the clay that formed much of both sides up to Noah's shoulders. He walked past Elam. "Let's go."

Keeping his head down, Noah led the way through the tunnel. After approximately 60 cubits, the passageway veered left. Just beyond the turn, a tree root had forced its way through a section of the wall, spilling enough dirt to block nearly half of their route.

"We must be under the forest," Elam said. "That means we're past the wall."

"I believe so. It shouldn't be too much farther. Stay quiet until we're sure no one is in the shed."

A few uneventful moments later, they neared the end of the tunnel. Noah dimmed the light and stopped before the ladder set into the left wall. Glancing up, he spotted the hatch. He put a finger to his lips, reminding Elam to be silent.

Rayneh wriggled in Elam's arms, trying to get comfortable. He stroked her head and held her close. After a long silence, he spoke in a whisper. "Noah, if something happens to me. I want you and Emzara to raise Rayneh as your own."

Noah smiled and touched the little girl's cheek. "We'd be honored. But don't talk like that. We're going to make it."

"You think it's clear up there?"

Noah shrugged. "Well, let's find out. I'll go up first." Noah carefully slid a latch that unlocked the door above him and then slowly cracked it open. He climbed the ladder and peeked through the gap. With no sign of intruders, Noah finished his ascent, which led him to a small area behind a wall of crates. A gap between the crates and the far wall opened up to the rest of the shack. He squeezed through the breach. Confident that they were alone, he retraced his steps back to the tunnel exit. "It's all clear." Noah stooped low, set the lamp on the floor, and took Rayneh from her father.

Elam climbed up the ladder and closed the door. "It's safe?"

"I think so. I'll take her for a while." Noah nodded to the far wall. "You can get past the crates over there."

After retrieving the lantern, Elam followed Noah's directions, and they soon reached the front door. "Where do we go from here?"

"North, through the woods. We need to avoid the main roads at least until we're a long ways from the city. And keep the light dim."

"Good idea." Elam took a deep breath. "Are you ready?"

Noah nodded and then closed his eyes. "Creator, please protect us. We thank You for helping us get this far and pray that You'll lead us safely through the rest of the night."

Elam patted Noah on the shoulder and then opened the door. The men stepped out into a glade, hurried across the clearing, and entered the forest. They walked through patches of woods intersected by swaths of fields. When the lights of Iri Geshem could no longer be seen, they slowed their pace a little.

They reached a road marked by deep wagon wheel grooves. "If I'm not mistaken," Noah said as he pointed left, "this road leads west to Kadzen."

"That's the first town on the river, right?" Elam rubbed his tired eyes.

"Yeah." As the threat of death seemed less imminent, the stress of the day's events started to take its toll. Noah stretched his neck and shoulders. "We could go that way and take the river road until we find a boat heading north. But for now, I think we should stay off the roads. After the sun rises, maybe we can find the old trail along the eastern edge of the forest. It'll be a little out of the way, but we should be able to move faster. And I really doubt that troops will be sent that far to find us."

"They probably think we're still in the city. I'm sure glad Zain built that tunnel." Elam yawned. "Let's go with your plan, but I'd like to rest a little first."

Noah motioned to the forest across the road. "Let's find a place in there to hide."

They scampered across the path and down a short hill into the woods. A small stream babbled before them. Noah leapt over it and then filled the waterskin. Both men drank from it before Noah topped it off again and slung it over his shoulder.

The forest offered little resistance due to its sparse undergrowth. While this allowed them to move steadily, it also afforded them very few places to hide. As the eastern sky developed a faint glow, signaling the coming dawn, Noah pointed to a grove of large trees where the brush grew thicker. "That looks like a good place."

Elam found a level piece of ground near one of the trees and reclined. After taking Rayneh, he adjusted his wrap to cover her tiny frame. "I'm glad you're still resting, sweet one. We'll get through this together."

Noah set the lamp, bag of food, and water on the ground. Reclining against a tree a few cubits from Elam, he wrestled with all that transpired in the past day. He remained silent as Elam sniffled, giving his friend some privacy as he grieved an unimaginable loss. Iri Geshem's addiction to violence had now claimed the lives of so many people that Noah loved. Yet, even though the vivid images of brutality remained fresh, his focus stayed elsewhere: the peace and boldness he possessed in the midst of the most terrifying moment of his life. *The Creator protected me and gave me the courage to warn the people.*

Settling his head on his crossed forearms that rested on his knees, Noah closed his eyes to pray. He thanked the Most High for watching over him in the arena and asked Him to protect Emzara, Laleel, and Garun as they traveled the river. *God, please comfort Elam as well.* Noah's prayer continued until he nodded off. His head jerked up before he let it down on his arms again. His thoughts drifted to Emzara and their unborn child, and then sleep overtook him.

"On your feet!" A sharp voice rang out. It seemed distant at first, but Noah quickly realized it did not originate in a dream. "Up. Now."

Noah opened his eyes and his heart sank. A spear was pointed directly at his face only a fingertip away. *Why did I fall asleep?* He blinked hard and his eyes adjusted to the bright morning light. *Elam?* Noah looked over to see two guards standing over his friend with spears aimed at him. Noah slowly raised a hand. "I'm getting up." As he carefully climbed to his feet, he held out both hands. "We're unarmed."

"What about him?" The guard pushed his spear closer to Elam.

"He's only carrying his daughter," Noah said. "Please don't harm them."

The guard gestured to the man on his right. "Get them up."

As a soldier bound Noah's hands behind his back, two others prodded Elam to his feet.

"Sir, what about the girl?"

"Let her father carry her, but bind him around the waist," the man in front of Noah said. "We'll let the captain decide their fate."

Only then did Noah realize why their accents sounded strange. The half dozen soldiers wore red and black uniforms bearing the unmistakable emblems of the famed Nodite army.

Enjoy a glimpse of Book 3 in the compelling Remnant Trilogy

Chapter 1

Iri Geshem — Noah's 499th year

Turning her head to dodge the brilliant reflection of sunlight off the glimmering façade of Iri Geshem's town hall to her right, Naamah marched toward the guest mansion reserved for foreign dignitaries. Jaw set in an angry line, she twisted the oversized iron bracer covering her left arm from elbow to wrist and stared at its intricate patterns.

Led by Nivlac, a quartet of guards flanking her increased their pace to keep up. Even after her many protests, they still accompanied her. Iri Geshem's seedy characters always posed a slight threat, but the soldiers had remained on high alert since the day before. A mixture of outrage and grief had overtaken the town after the debacle in the arena and the chance remained high that someone might seek revenge for loved ones lost. Still, being surrounded by overprotective men at all times did nothing to improve her mood, and she maintained a stony silence throughout their trek.

Two soldiers manned the doors into the residence. Normally, the gold trim along the frame, a sign of Havil's influence in this city, would bring her happiness, but she was in no mood to be amused. The guards pushed the doors open and stepped inside as she approached.

The bearded man on her left nodded. "Welcome back, Princess."

Ignoring him, Naamah stormed ahead into the spacious foyer. She glanced around, hoping there would be no delay. To her right, a small group of people spoke quietly around the low table in the sitting room. They fell silent at the sight of her, but she turned away without acknowledging them. The lavish dining hall to her left sat vacant except for a servant girl preparing the place settings. Besides Nivlac, the guards remained near the door.

Naamah moved to the stairs and ascended to the second floor. She turned left and hurried to her guest room at the end of the hall.

"Princess." Nivlac gently touched her arm. "Is there anything I can do to help?"

She opened the door, jerked away from his touch, and glared at her loyal guard. "Just wait out here."

He drew himself upright and faced the hallway. "As you command."

Naamah shut the door behind her and tossed her green-hemmed cloak on a bench. She slid her shoes off and dropped onto the bed. As she loosened the strings on the bracer, regret and sadness filled her entire body. *How long has it been since I've felt this way?* She adjusted the metal and retied the cords, fitting it more comfortably, even though it was clearly made for a man's large forearm. Studying the remarkable craftsmanship, her thoughts raced back to her brother's final moments in the arena. She shook her head in an attempt to rid herself of that memory. Thankful for the opportunity to spend some time in Tubal-Cain's shop earlier in the day, she stroked the one memento she had found to remember him by.

As she repositioned herself, an object pressed against her stomach. Withdrawing the small dagger from the pocket of her wrap, Naamah held it in front of her eyes and slowly twisted it about. For a brief moment, the thought of plunging it directly into her own chest raced into her mind. She raised the knife and gripped the handle with both hands. Taking a deep breath, she recalled her father's smile as Tubal-Cain died. She lowered the blade and inserted it into its slot in the bracer. *Not while Da is still alive.*

As she stared at the armband her brother had crafted, Naamah said, "And I'll wear this until he's dead." She fell back onto the bed and closed her eyes. *Why wouldn't you bow, Tu?* Her lip quavered and she squeezed her eyes tight, successfully preventing a tear from escaping. *All because you came to this city with Noah.*

Gathering her wits, she sat back up and gazed out the large window to her right. In her mind she watched the giant drag Noah into the arena, leaving him standing helplessly beneath her as the grendec entered and the crowd roared. No matter how many times she replayed the next moment, the outcome never changed. Brimming with a quiet confidence, Noah looked at her and said, "I will not die today."

Her heart pounding, she clenched a fist and slammed it into the bed. "How did he know?" *What if he's right? What if the Creator is more pow* — "No!" Impossible. Noah was just lucky. *No matter. He'll soon be back in our custody, and there will be no escape. How dare he try to make a fool of me in front of everyone!*

Naamah stood and moved to the reflective plate on the wall. She ran a hand through her hair, pushing all of it over to the right. After straightening her gown, she held up her left arm to examine how the bracer looked on her. A hint of a smile grew on her lips as she focused on the hilt of the dagger. *I like it.*

A knock at the door ripped her attention away from her reflection. "Not now, Nivlac."

The door creaked open. "Princess, the king told me to update you on the search." The voice was not Nivlac's.

Naamah gasped, but briskly straightened her shoulders and lifted her chin. "Enter."

A guard stepped into the room and knelt before her. Keeping his head down, he said, "Every exit to the city has been blocked since yesterday. As you know, we stopped him from fleeing the city by boat. Our —"

"Where is he?" Naamah tapped her foot.

The guard hesitated and dropped his head even lower. "Still no sign of him, but he must be in the eastern part of the city. Our men have been searching every home."

Naamah grabbed a small vase off the shelf beside her and smashed it onto the floor, shattering it into dozens of pieces. "Find him!"

The man flinched. "Yes, Princess."

Glaring at the back of the man's neck, she slid the dagger partway out of the armband. Letting out a breath, she replaced the blade with a clinking of metal. "You weren't sent out to come back empty-handed. Return without him again, and you'll be fed to the grendec."

He nodded. "Yes, Princess."

"Get out!"

The soldier stood and bowed before spinning around and hustling out of the room.

Naamah kicked a clay shard across the floor. *Tubal-Cain is dead and Noah's free.* "Ah!" Her breathing quickened as her anger kindled. Trying to shake the image of Tubal-Cain's bloodied corpse from her mind, she paused and let it fuel her temper instead. She scratched an itch near the top edge of the bracer, the irritation increasing her rage even more. Her eyes locked onto the handle. "This comes off today."

Stepping carefully over shattered pottery, she reached for her shoes and pulled them on. "Nivlac!"

He stepped into the room, and his eyes darted from the mess on the floor to her. "Yes, Highness."

Controlling the tone of her voice, Naamah asked, "Do you know where my father is?"

"I believe he's in a meeting with leaders from the city."

Biting her lip, she contemplated how to take revenge. *Yes, that should work.* "Very good. That's all."

Nivlac nodded. "Would you like me to inform the king that you'd like to see him?"

She strode past him. "That won't be necessary. Follow me."

Rushing down the hall, Naamah allowed the memory of Tubal-Cain's murder to drive her forward while ignoring all the warnings that rang inside her. *I don't care if this is a deadly mistake. It's worth the risk.* As she reached the middle of the passage, she turned left and pushed the double doors open, then stepped confidently into the spacious meeting hall. The city's council members reclined on lush cushions around a low table loaded with colorful fruits and vegetables along with a variety of meats. Skimpily clad male and female dancers twirled and twisted near the musicians on the far side of the room.

Seated at the opposite end of the table, her father handed a tray of food to a young woman dressed in a tawdry outfit standing at his side. His eyes lingered after her as she stepped away. Only when the girl had disappeared through the servants' entrance in the corner did he turn to face his daughter. "Naamah, please join us."

Nivlac remained at the door as she glided around the council members and stopped about ten cubits before the king. As she bowed her head slightly, she glimpsed the hilt of the dagger at her wrist. She raised her voice for the benefit of everyone in the room. "Father, why did you murder Tubal-Cain?"

The music stopped and Lamech raised his eyebrows. "Murder?" He snorted. "That's called justice, my dear. He disobeyed direct orders from both of us. He needed to be punished for his treason."

"But he was your son, and my brother!" Her tone grew sharp and accusatory. "You never should have put him in that situation."

"He sought to undermine my rule." The king raised a finger and pointed at her. "And you'd better watch yourself."

"Pah! Are you threatening me?" Naamah stepped closer, defiantly challenging his authority and anticipating a blow to the face as he had dealt her several times before. But at over 700 years old, he was weaker and slower than he had once been. He would never see the dagger until she had planted it deep into his chest in an act of self-defense. "Without Nachash's followers, your rule would crumble."

Anger burned in his eyes as he glanced at the council members, many of whom wore shocked expressions. He stood and took a step toward her. "If you ever speak to me that way again —"

"What? You'll kill me just like you've killed your son?"

"Enough!" Lamech raised his hand to hit her, but he froze when the twin doors burst open.

Jolted by the interruption, Naamah turned to see two guards dash into the room just as she placed her hand over the bracer.

"Sir!" The guard who entered first dropped to a knee, and his companion followed suit. "Please forgive the interruption. I bring a critical message from Commander Tsek!"

Behind the Fiction

Just like in the first book in the Remnant Trilogy, *Noah: Man of Destiny*, the initial part of this non-fiction section, *Questions and Answers*, is designed to address certain questions that readers may think of during the story. Many of these issues will be apologetic in nature. That is, in this portion of the book, we will respond to numerous challenges raised by skeptics and critics. The goal is that these novels will also help you defend the truth of Scripture.

You may have noticed as you read the novel that several things didn't line up with what you may have expected. This was done on purpose to help break certain stereotypes about Noah and the pre-Flood world that many Christians assume are from the Bible, but aren't actually found there. We want you to see clearly what comes directly from the Bible and what comes from traditions people have developed over the years.

The second feature in this non-fiction portion is what we call *Borrowed from the Bible.* Since the Bible only includes scant details about Noah's life and times, we must use artistic license to flesh out his story. We certainly do not wish to be seen as adding to Scripture and want the reader to understand that these are works of fiction, with the exception of the few details that come straight from the Bible. In some places we curbed the amount of artistic license taken by drawing from other biblical accounts instead. In *Borrowed from the Bible*, we highlight certain events and customs in our story that will be somewhat familiar to those who know their Bibles.

The third special feature is entirely unique to this series. We had the incredible opportunity to work behind the scenes at the Ark Encounter for the past few years. Tim was involved in the planning of nearly every exhibit and was responsible for writing or overseeing all of the content while K. Marie took part in designing various aspects of several spaces on the Ark. We wanted to use our experience to bring this series to life in a creative manner. As such, many of the objects and animals described in the book are on display in the Ark Encounter, so visitors to the theme park can see part of what Noah witnesses in our story. The *Encounter This* section lets the reader know what these items are and where they can be found.

We hope you've enjoyed reading about what may have been, while learning to better discern between fact and fiction.

Answering Questions Raised By the Novel

SPOILER ALERT! Many of the answers to questions in this section reveal key points in the storyline of the novel. If you have not read the story first, some of these details will spoil important events in the book.

How long were Adam and Eve in the Garden of Eden?

In chapter 7, Garun told Noah that the first man and woman were in the garden for only a few days before being banished. This was new information for Noah, and likely for many of our readers as well. Many Christians assume that Adam and Eve spent quite a while in the Garden of Eden with the Lord before they sinned and were subsequently banished, but does the Bible support this notion?

In keeping with our approach from the first book to steer clear of popular ideas not specifically found in the Bible, we decided to introduce this topic to encourage readers to closely consider the biblical text. The truth is Genesis does not tell us precisely how long Adam and Eve lived before they rebelled, but it does give us some parameters to make an educated guess.

The Bible provides an upper limit to the amount of time that passed before man's first sin. Adam and Eve had their son Seth when Adam was 130 years old (Genesis 5:3), which took place after Cain murdered his brother. This figure cannot be the upper limit since we must first allow enough time for Cain to grow old enough to offer sacrifices and kill Abel. Let's assume a minimum of twenty years for those details, which would bring our upper limit down to about 110 years.

With the maximum time limit set, let us take a look at the lowest amount of time they could have been in the garden. Adam and Eve were created on the sixth day of the creation week (Genesis 1:26–27), and at the end of that day, we are told that everything was "very good" (Genesis 1:31). God rested on the next day, a day that He blessed and sanctified (Genesis 2:1–3). We can be quite confident He did not curse the ground on that day. So the earliest Adam could have sinned would have been on the eighth day.

There is a strong reason to believe they were in the garden for a very short amount of time. Our first parents were perfect when they were created. That is, they had no defects or flaws that would prevent them from having children. On the sixth day, God told them to be fruitful and multiply. Since they were married from the start and capable of producing children in obedience to God's command, how long might it have taken before Eve conceived a child? It seems likely that this would have taken place within the first few months.

We know that she did not conceive a child until after they were expelled from the garden. This is the order in which the biblical narrative is explained — expulsion from the garden in Genesis 3:23–24, and Eve conceives a son (Cain) in the next verse, Genesis 4:1. But we can also be pretty confident about this because if she had conceived Cain prior to eating the forbidden fruit, then Cain would probably not have been born with a sin nature, which he obviously had.

So with all of these details considered, it seems like Adam and Eve would have been in the garden for a very short time, perhaps less than a month, before they rebelled. The view passed down to Garun in our story is based on this line of reasoning.

Some Christians object to the brief timeline before sin because they say that Adam and Eve had to have time to walk with God in the garden. While this idea of our first parents walking with God is commonly taught, the fact is that the Bible never explicitly teaches it. Nowhere does the Bible claim that Adam and Eve walked with God in the garden, and yet many Christians have taught this idea as if it came right from Scripture.

In all likelihood, this notion is based in some way on Genesis 3:8, which states, "And they heard the sound of the LORD God walking in the garden in the cool of the day . . ." (NKJV). It seems like many people have just remembered some of the wording in this verse and assumed that it says Adam and Eve walked with God. But that's not at all what is going on here. This verse appears immediately after our first parents rebelled against the Creator. They are not taking a leisurely stroll with God; they are hiding from Him as He comes to announce His judgment.

Much more could be discussed on this subject, but those details are far beyond the purpose of the original question. However, if you would like to learn more about the arguments for and against this idea, please read Tim's article, "Did Adam and Eve Walk with God in the Garden?" and the many comments that follow it, at http://midwestapologetics.org/blog/?p=1349.

Did anyone live longer than Methuselah?

In our story, Garun told Noah in chapter 7 that one of his ancestors, Ma'anel, a son of Adam, lived for 985 years. It is not uncommon to hear Christians claim that Methuselah lived longer than anyone in history, but that is not necessarily the case.

The Bible tells us in Genesis 5:27 that Methuselah lived a total of 969 years, and it does not mention anyone living any longer than that, so it is possible that he had the longest lifespan of any human. However, the Bible only gives us the age at death for a tiny fraction of the people who lived prior to the Flood. From Adam through Noah, there are only ten people whose lifespans are recorded, and yet there may have been many millions of people who lived prior to the Flood. So it is certainly possible, if not rather likely, that someone outlived Methuselah.

Of course, Ma'anel is just a fictional character. The Bible mentions that Adam and Eve had other sons and daughters (Genesis 5:4), but it only names Cain, Abel, and Seth. For more details about whether people really lived so long, please see the back pages of the first book in this series, *Noah: Man of Destiny*.

As part of this conversation in the book, there was a reference to King Lamech seeking to live a thousand years. The king also voiced his idea to the council of Iri Geshem in chapter 6. This goal fits well with his boastful character, but there was another reason to bring this idea into the story. God warned Adam that he would surely die on the day he ate the fruit from the tree of the knowledge of good and evil (Genesis 2:17). Just what did God mean by saying Adam would die that *day* when we know Adam lived for 930 years? Biblical commentators have proposed several ideas about how Adam may have died in some sense that day. Certainly, his relationship with God was instantly marred by sin. Many Christians refer to this as spiritual death. There may have been physical implications as well in the sense that Adam's body would now endure sicknesses and other ailments, so to some degree, he began to die on that day.

Not as popular as these first two views, some have proposed that God meant Adam would not live a thousand years, since elsewhere the Bible explains that to God a day is like a thousand years (2 Peter 3:8). We definitely would reject any attempt to insert a thousand years whenever the word *day* is used because the context frequently rules out such a possibility, as it does for the days of creation in Genesis 1 and the days that Joshua and the Israelites marched around Jericho (Joshua 6). Nevertheless, it is interesting to consider how it might fit in some of the places where the term is used in the context of judgment, as it is in Genesis 2:17. While this view may be unlikely, we thought it would be interesting to see the wicked King Lamech hold such an idea and strive to defy his Creator in a unique manner. The reader can probably guess whether the king will be successful in this endeavor.

Why would Noah's culture use a judicial concept not mentioned until after the Flood?

In chapter 11, one of the men in the crowd, Ethlin, accuses Garun and Bedin of murdering two people in Iri Geshem. Consequently, he believes that they deserve to die for their crime. The idea that the punishment should fit the crime is popular throughout the world, but it is not mentioned in the Bible until shortly after the Flood. In Genesis 9:6, the Lord told Noah, "Whoever sheds man's blood, by man his blood shall be shed; for in the image of God He made man." So why did we put this concept into the pre-Flood world?

The answer to this question is probably rather obvious. The concept seems to make pretty good sense in many cases. If someone steals an item from you, then according to this perspective, the thief would need to make restitution in some way. They could return the item, reimburse you for the cost, or replace it at their expense. In the case of murder, then the murderer has essentially forfeited his life.

Did Noah endorse the notion that an idea is true because of how he felt about it?

Postmodernists hold to an idea that views truth as subjective — truth is whatever one wants it to be. We each have our own truth, they say, and there is no overarching truth that is true for every person (besides that statement, of course). This view can often be seen in the way many

Americans talk about religious beliefs. It is not too uncommon to hear someone say, "It doesn't matter what you believe, as long as you're sincere."

This type of argument is also used by some Christians who reject the biblical concept of the lake of fire as a place of eternal torment for the wicked. Since they do not understand how God could sentence someone to this fate or they just do not like the idea, they seek to reinterpret the many passages that teach it. For the record, I am not thrilled about the idea of people I know who will suffer eternally for their sins, but instead of reinterpreting Scripture, I trust that God really means what He inspired to be written in the Bible about those matters. This truth motivates me to share the gospel of Jesus Christ with an unbelieving world. Sincerity or feelings cannot be used as an accurate test for truth.

In chapter 16, while sailing to Havil, Noah and Tubal-Cain discuss the afterlife. You might remember from the first book when we explained why we did not give Noah knowledge of all the details found in Genesis 1–5. As far as we know, Noah and others of his time had not been given clear revelation from God about what happens after death. He certainly could have known that our bodies return to the ground, as God told Adam in Genesis 3:19. This is observable at every burial, so one might assume more of a naturalistic view of death — that there is no afterlife and our bodies decay in the ground. But is that all Noah could have known, apart from direct revelation from God?

Ecclesiastes 3:11 states that God has put eternity in the hearts of men. This is generally understood to mean that man has been given some sense of his own existence beyond his physical life. If this is accurate, then Noah and others in his day may have believed in an afterlife. Also, if Noah knew that God had taken Enoch from the earth to heaven, then he might come to believe that one would enjoy a physical existence with the Creator after this life is through.

This was the rationale behind the discussion between Noah and Tubal-Cain. Near the end of it, Tubal-Cain said that it made sense to him, and he liked it because it would mean their dear friends were with the Creator at that moment. Noah added that he now liked the view even more. Notice, he did not say that he believed it to be true more than he had before, just that he had a stronger appreciation for his view. So in our book, Noah did not subscribe to the idea that something must be true because of how he felt about it.

Were there diseases in the pre-Flood world?

In chapter 14, Naamah spends time in Havil's grand library, the House of Knowledge. While she's there, she reads about Bothar, an important city far away to the north that has been decimated by a strange disease. Readers may remember this city from the first book as the place where the kidnappers were planning to take Elam and the other Zakari children.

Biblical creationists believe that diseases would have been non-existent in the beginning. But over time, due to the effects of sin, which would include genetic mutations, diseases would increase to what we observe today. That being said, some people have asked me if I believe there would have been diseases in the pre-Flood world. Well, we wrote this detail into the book to raise this very issue.

We know from the fossils found in sediments laid down during the global Flood that certain diseases existed at that time. Evidence of cancerous tumors has been found in dinosaur remains buried in the Flood. So if animals suffered from diseases, then humans probably did as well. When we consider how diseases are frequently transmitted in our day, it is easy to see how the same things may have occurred in the exceedingly violent and decadent world prior to the Flood.

Did women suffer miscarriages in the pre-Flood world?

In chapter 16, Noah and Emzara suffered further heartbreak as she lost their first child not long after learning she was pregnant. We know that people of that time would have had fewer genetic mistakes than we do today since they were closer to Adam and Eve, so would women have had to undergo the sorrow of losing a child in the womb?

The Bible does not give any specific examples of women miscarrying prior to the Flood, although by the time God gave the Law to Moses, people were familiar with this concept. The Lord told the Israelites that if they obeyed Him, He would bless them and that no one would be barren or suffer miscarriage in their land (Exodus 23:26). Centuries earlier, after suffering unimaginable personal tragedy, Job expressed that it would have been better for him if he had been stillborn (Job 3:16).

After Adam and Eve sinned, the Lord made a statement that might be relevant to this discussion. He explained that the pains a woman suffered during childbearing would be greatly increased. While miscarriage is not specifically mentioned, there was at least the indication that bringing forth children would be quite difficult.

Many of the people living prior to the Flood were extremely wicked, so many of them surely engaged in harmful practices that might contribute to poor prenatal care, such as violent behavior and an unhealthy diet. Given these factors, it seems quite reasonable to assume that women suffered miscarriages prior to the Flood, although at this point it probably would have been rarer.

Finally, we would like to clarify that the novel does not blame anyone in particular for Emzara's miscarriage. Some people might get the impression that since she was under extreme duress in the weeks leading up to the event that she brought it on herself. While it might be natural to think that way, we did not seek to attribute blame to her. Sometimes terrible things happen in this world without a direct connection to one's own behavior. The fact that she was a sinner living in a sin-cursed world where good things and bad things happen to the righteous and the wicked was reason enough for this to occur.

Would the pre-Flood world endure earthquakes, volcanic eruptions, and other natural disasters?

In chapters 23 and 24, the city of Havil was devastated by a violent earthquake triggered by a volcanic eruption. Is such a scenario consistent with the popular creationist model of a single pre-Flood continent? In other words, if there were no continental plates sliding against each other, could an earthquake have occurred?

The major fault lines, or fault zones, in our world today exist along the boundaries of continental plates. However, there are plenty of fault lines that occur far from continental boundaries. So even if the pre-Flood supercontinent did not have fault zones along continental boundaries, it could have had fault lines in the midst of the land mass.

On the third day of the creation week, the Lord caused dry land to appear. Creationists generally believe God raised the ground up from the water. This enormous amount of geologic activity could have included faults. Residual movement of these faults from the third day could have triggered earthquakes following that time.

Volcanic eruptions occur when molten rock, called magma, forces its way to the surface of the planet. A violent eruption, like the one described in the book, occurs when the pressure in a magma chamber becomes so great that it forces its way through the volcano's conduit and escapes through the vent. While the vent allows for a certain amount of pressure to be released, there are times when the pressure becomes too great for a slow and steady release through the vent. Movement of magma beneath the surface can also cause tremors prior to the eruption. This is why the people in and around Havil were able to see smoke from the volcano and feel tremors in the days leading up to the blast.

Finally, Romans 8:22 explains that "the whole creation groans and labors with birth pangs." The reason the whole world suffers is due to man's sin. So earthquakes, volcanoes, and other natural disasters are almost certainly included in the groaning of the whole creation, and this has been going on since the Lord cursed the ground because our first parents sinned in the Garden. Verse 19 states that all of creation eagerly waits for the time when God will make all things new. In the new heavens and new earth, there will not be any earthquakes or other natural disasters.

Did Noah really believe the earth traveled around the sun?

In chapter 24, we see Noah express a basic understanding of a heliocentric solar system as opposed to a geocentric solar system. He told Tubal-Cain that the earth occasionally moved between the sun and the moon, which caused the moon to have a brownish appearance. Would Noah have known this information given that so many people up until the 16th century A.D. held to the belief that the sun and other heavenly bodies orbited the earth?

It is true that geocentrism was popularly held from the time of the Greek astronomer Claudius Ptolemaus (Ptolemy) in the second century A.D., and it was not widely rejected until the time of Nicolaus Copernicus. However, roughly four hundred years before Ptolemy, Aristarchus of Samos proposed a heliocentric model of the solar system.

We regularly discover that ancient people had a better understanding of the heavens than is generally supposed. Archaeological discoveries throughout the world have shown that ancient people used the stars for navigation and timekeeping, which was one of the reasons God created them on the fourth day (Genesis 1:14). Very early records of eclipses have also been discovered. Incidentally, lunar eclipses demonstrate the roundness of the earth since the moon passes through our planet's shadow, revealing earth's curvature. At the Ark Encounter, visitors can view a globe of the pre-Flood world in Noah's Study.

We cannot be sure what Noah did and did not know on this subject, but based on the discoveries from the ancient world, it is not unreasonable to think that people in the pre-Flood world had a fairly good understanding of the heavens.

Did people really have huge families prior to the Flood?

In our story we mentioned a few families as being rather large. For example, Noah's brother and sister-in-law, Jerah and Pivi, are described as having 31 children and we mention that Tubal-Cain and Adira had 17 children. Is it realistic for a couple to have so many children?

The Bible does not tell us how many children certain individuals had prior to the Flood. Cain's descendant, the evil king in our series, had four children that are mentioned. The men in the line from Adam to Lamech, Noah's father, in Genesis 5 each had at least five children (one is named, and then we are told that they had other sons and daughters).

The novel is actually probably too conservative on the number of children in a given family. A Russian woman from the 18th century is believed to have given birth to 69 children, and she only lived about 75 years. There are more than a dozen women reported to have given birth to more than 30 children in the past few centuries. In the pre-Flood world, men lived much longer lives than they do today, so women presumably did as well. If a woman who lives fewer than a hundred years can give birth to over 30 children, then it is quite believable that a woman who lives for many centuries could have dozens of children.

At this point in our story, Jerah and Pivi are nearly 500 years old. You may recall from the explanation in the first book that we proposed that people during that time would have aged slower. So a 500-year-old person would look similar to a 50-year-old today. Consider that Pivi could have become pregnant from the time she married until she was around 450 years old. That would mean that she had over 400 years to bear children. Even if she had just 1 child every 10 years, she would have had 40 children. The fact that we only gave her 31 kids is probably an underestimation of the size of many pre-Flood families.

Why was God portrayed as a large flame?

Perhaps the trickiest decision we had to make in writing these books is how we were going to depict God when He spoke with Noah. The Bible simply tells us that the Lord spoke to Noah, but it does not say how He did that. Throughout Scripture, God communicated with people through various ways. The following list gives some of these means.

- Appearing as a man to Abraham in Genesis 18
- A burning bush to Moses in Exodus 3
- Still small voice to Elijah in 1 Kings 19:12–13
- In a vision to Isaiah in Isaiah 6
- In a dream to Nebuchadnezzar in Daniel 2

When God appears in some type of physical form in the Old Testament, theologians identify the occurrence as a theophany, from the Greek words for "God" and "appearance." In this case, the Bible does not even say that God appeared at all. He may have simply spoken to Noah without appearing. So there were plenty of options available to us that would have been consistent with how God speaks to people in the Bible.

We chose to use a vision combined with an appearance similar to the burning bush for several reasons. The use of the vision and some of its details will be significant in the third book, *Noah: Man of God.*

Having the Lord appear as a flame tied together several biblical concepts. As mentioned above, Moses saw God as a burning bush, but the bush was not consumed. In our story Noah saw a single flame, but there was no bush or anything else for the flame to burn.

When describing the way God revealed Himself to the Israelites at Mt. Sinai, the Bible states that "the sight of the glory of the LORD was like a consuming fire on the top of the mountain" (Exodus 24:17). This idea is repeated in Deuteronomy 4:24 and 9:3. Also, Exodus 13:21 states that "the LORD went before them by day in a pillar of cloud to lead the way, and by night in a pillar of fire to give them light."

One of the earliest appearances of God in physical form recorded in Scripture occurred when the Lord established His covenant with Abraham, called Abram at the time, in Genesis 15. Abraham gathered the sacrificial animals God instructed him to bring, and then the Lord put him into a deep sleep. God, in the form of a fire pot and flaming torch, passed between the animals that had been sacrificed. Much could be said about the significance of this event, but the point here is that we have another example of God appearing to someone as a fire.

The single flame was essentially an attempt to combine aspects of these ideas while remaining unique. After all, there are differences between each of these appearances, so we did not want to copy any of them in every detail.

Why did God only give Noah part of the details about the Flood and the Ark in this book?

When God appeared to Noah in our story, He described just a fraction of what we read in Genesis 6. Would it not have been better to simply quote exactly what God said to Noah so that someone does not think we were attempting to take away from God's Word?

The short answer is that we will include the entirety of God's message to Noah at the appropriate time. As mentioned in Chapter 26, Noah will hear from the Most High again.

We do not know if the Lord's message to Noah about building the Ark was delivered all at one time even though this seems to be the most natural way to understand the text. However, we need to remember that the Bible does not always include every detail. It is quite possible that God revealed certain aspects of His plan to Noah at various intervals, but when the text was eventually recorded, the writer (Moses) simply put all of the communication into one segment.

This is also the reason Noah did not receive all of the information about the Ark at this point. He does not know at this point how large it will need to be, what kind of wood to use, or any of the other details that God revealed in Scripture. He just knows that he will need to build an Ark large enough for eight people and plenty of animals.

Our decision to divide the Creator's instructions into at least two portions had more to do with storytelling than any clues from the text.

We wanted God's statement about Noah having sons after centuries of childlessness to be an opportunity for Noah to trust God at the heart of his greatest frustration. He had grown discouraged over the years, so he could have responded in various ways upon hearing about having sons. He could have laughed as Sarai did in Genesis 18:12 when God promised that she would have a child in a year's time. He could have doubted the message as Zacharias did in Luke 1:18 when the angel told him that he and his wife would soon have a son (John the Baptist). Instead, we chose to have Noah respond with complete trust in what God told him, which underscores why the Bible identifies him as a righteous man. His confidence in the Lord will continue to grow as he sees the Creator's faithfulness.

Didn't Noah have 120 years to build the Ark? If so, shouldn't God have spoken to him 20 years earlier than He did in the novel?

In our novel, Noah was nearly 500 years old when God first spoke to him. The notion that he had 120 years to build the Ark would mean that God would have spoken to him when he was about 480 since the Flood struck in Noah's 600th year. This idea is a rather common misconception among Christians. I cannot count the number of times I have heard people say, "Noah had 120 years to build the Ark." This is based on Genesis 6:3, but there are at least two problems with this view.

When the Lord gave Noah the details about the Ark, He told him that He would establish a covenant with Noah, his wife, his sons, and his sons' wives (Genesis 6:18). So it sure seems as if the sons were grown up and married when God told him to build the Ark. Since the oldest of Noah's sons was born when Noah was 500 years old (Genesis 5:32), and the Flood came in his 600th year, then Noah would have had much less than 120 years to build the Ark. In fact, he would have had fewer than 100 years to build it, since we need to consider how long it would take for the three boys to be born and to grow up and get married (perhaps 25–50 years), and then subtract that number from 100 to figure out the maximum amount of time for building the Ark (approximately 50–75 years).

The second problem with the idea that Noah had 120 years to build the Ark is that the verse it is based on, Genesis 6:3, is not even about the timing of the Ark's construction. In the first book, we briefly discussed two popular views about the meaning of this verse in which God stated,

"My Spirit shall not strive with man forever, for he is indeed flesh; yet his days shall be one hundred and twenty years." Many people believe it refers to God's judgment on man's lifespan. Prior to the Flood, many of the men mentioned in Genesis 5 lived beyond 900 years. The only two exceptions in the line between Adam and Noah were Enoch (365) and Lamech (777). For God to drastically reduce man's lifespan would indeed be a severe judgment.

Others believe this verse refers to a countdown to the Flood. That is, from the point God made the announcement there would be 120 years before the earth would be destroyed by the Flood. Even if this happens to be the correct view, notice that it would still not mean that Noah started building the Ark at this time. In fact, God commanded Noah to build the Ark 11 verses later.

Finally, in an *Answers* magazine article about the construction of the Ark, I wrote about the following problem in thinking it took 120 years to build the Ark.

> Consider the implications of building such an enormous boat out of wood over the course of many decades. Exposed to the elements, wood tends to warp and decay as it endures heat, cold, and changes in humidity. Imagine trying to complete one part of the Ark decades after another section had been built. The earliest parts of the construction might need repair by the time the Ark was finished.

To read the rest of the *Answers* magazine article, please see "Fantastic Voyage: How Could Noah Build the Ark?" at www.answersingenesis.org/noahs-ark/fantastic-voyage-how-could-noah-build-ark.

Were there really giants prior to the Flood?

In the dramatic arena chapters in our story, Noah encounters a giant guard that would have easily outsized anyone alive today. We depicted Noah as a fairly tall man. While our story never uses modern units of measure, like feet and inches, we decided that Noah should be about 6'2" tall to match how he is depicted at the Ark Encounter. The reason he is that height is based on the 20.4-inch cubit that was chosen for the construction of the Ark Encounter. But even at that height, Noah only reaches the man's midsection. Were there really giants in ancient times or is this idea just a tall tale?

Genesis 6:4 states, "There were giants on the earth in those days, and also afterward, when the sons of God came in to the daughters of men and they bore children to them. Those were the mighty men who were of old, men of renown."

This verse appears at the end of one of the most controversial and misunderstood passages in the Bible, which is one of the reasons Tim decided to write his ThM thesis on this subject. People have long disagreed over many of the details included in Genesis 6:1–4, particularly the identity of the "sons of God" who married the "daughters of men" (Genesis 6:2). Scholars generally adopt one of three views regarding the sons of God. Some believe they were godly men in the line of Seth, others believe they were tyrant kings who viewed themselves as divine, and others believe they were angelic beings who left heaven to marry women. The ministry that built the Ark Encounter, Answers in Genesis, does not hold an official position on the identity of the sons of God. For a balanced overview on this topic, read my article from *Answers* magazine, "Battle Over the Nephilim" at www.answersingenesis.org/bible-characters/battle-over-the-nephilim.

So where do giants fit into this picture? Well, they are often viewed as the offspring produced by the sons of God and the daughters of men. This idea is sometimes disputed as well. Some people will say that the giants were already on the earth when the sons of God and daughters of men had children. However, a close look at the Hebrew language favors the former view. Regardless of one's position on that debate, Genesis 6:4 states that there were giants on the earth in the days before the Flood, and it describes them as "mighty men" and "men of renown."

But does the word translated as *giants* in Genesis 6:4 actually refer to physical giants? After all, many English Bibles use the word *Nephilim*, which is a transliteration of the Hebrew word. Some popular level writings contend that this word means "fallen ones" and comes from the Hebrew verb *naphal* ("to fall"). However, this is unlikely since the Hebrew language follows patterns when a term is used as a basis for another word. Please bear with me for a brief discussion of technical details in this paragraph. In this case, to transform the verb *naphal* into a word that means "fallen ones," the word would be *nephulim*. To convert it into a noun meaning "those who fall" would yield the word *nophelim*. Notice that neither of these terms is spelled the same as the word in Genesis 6:4 ("Nephilim"), and there is a pretty good reason for that. The term *Nephilim* is likely the Hebrew plural form of the Aramaic noun *naphil*, which means "giant."

The translators of the Septuagint, the name given to the Greek translation of the Old Testament begun in the third century B.C., translated Nephilim as *gigantes*. You can probably tell just by looking at it that *gigantes* means "giants." It is interesting that every single Hebrew and Aramaic lexicon that I have examined lists "giants" as the primary meaning of *Nephilim*, and not one states that it means "fallen ones."

When we compare Scripture with Scripture, we find another reason to view the term in question as meaning "giants." *Nephilim* appears two more times in the Bible, and both occurrences are in the same verse. Numbers 13:33 records the words of the spies who returned to Moses and the Israelites after searching the land of Canaan. They said, "There we saw the giants (the descendants of Anak came from the giants); and we were like grasshoppers in our own sight, and so we were in their sight." Both occurrences of the word "giants" in this verse translate to the term *Nephilim*. Notice that they are described as being very large people. Some commentators have argued that the spies were lying about seeing giants in the land because the previous verse states that the spies gave a "bad report." However, the term translated as "bad report" does not refer to a false message but to a true report of bad tidings. Furthermore, the narrator of this passage, Moses, already explained in verse 22 that the spies had seen three giants known as Anakim. In fact, the Bible describes several other people groups in the land of Canaan and surrounding regions as giants: the Amorites (Amos 2:9–10), the Emim (Deuteronomy 2:10–11), the Zamzummim (Deuteronomy 2:20–21), and the Rephaim (Deuteronomy 3:11–13). Since Moses wrote both verses in which the word *Nephilim* appears, and the context of each passage describes some of the physical attributes of these individuals, it makes sense to interpret them consistently as being giants. At the Ark Encounter, we depict a couple of giants in the Pre-Flood World exhibit. We made them to be about the same size as Goliath — six cubits and a span, which is nearly ten feet tall. The giant in the novel is described as being about the same height.

Why did you depict the giant as a cannibal?

Legends and other stories of giants often describe them as having a taste for human flesh. The cyclops Polyphemus from Homer's *Odyssey* is probably the most infamous of cannibalistic giants, but he is not alone. In fact, Odysseus had previously lost his entire fleet of ships except for one when they stopped at the island of the Laestrygonians. The residents of this island were giants who sunk Odysseus' ships by hurling huge rocks at them, and then they speared Odysseus' men as one would spear fish and carried them off to feast on them. The popular story of Jack and the Beanstalk also features a giant with a hankering for human flesh.

In our story, the giant guard is not a very nice character. He made a comment about wanting to devour Noah and then attempted to take a bite out of Elam. What was the rationale in making this guy a cannibal? Was it simply to make him scary and unlikeable or was there a biblical and historical basis for it?

It turns out that ancient Jewish writings also connect giants to cannibalism. The book of 1 Enoch, which is not part of the Bible, was penned sometime between the writing of the Old and New Testaments. Obviously, it was not written by Noah's great grandfather Enoch, although the work pretends to be from his hand. The book describes events prior to the Flood and mentions giants who consumed all the things grown by men, but "when men could no longer sustain them, the giants turned against them and devoured mankind" (1 Enoch 7:1–5). Another popular non-biblical Jewish writing from the intertestamental period, the Book of Jubilees, describes the pre-Flood giants as cannibals. This book has been called "Little Genesis" because it describes portions of Genesis and then adds details. While expanding upon Genesis 6:1–4, the controversial passage about the sons of God and the giants, Jubilees says that lawlessness increased on the earth after the giants were born and that all flesh became so corrupted that "they began to devour each other" (Jubilees 5:1–2). Neither of these books belongs in the Bible because they were not inspired by God, although Jude 14–15 does quote from 1 Enoch.

Where do these ideas come from? Were they just invented to make giants seem more terrifying or might they have a basis in reality? As strange as it may seem, there may be biblical support for this notion. When the Israelite spies returned from searching out the land of Canaan, they said, "We went to the land where you sent us. It truly flows with milk and honey, and this is its fruit. Nevertheless the people who dwell in the land are strong; the cities are fortified and very large; moreover we saw the descendants of Anak there" (Numbers 13:27–28). As pointed out in the response to the previous question, the "descendants of Anak" (the Anakim) were described as giants. Notice that the spies had nothing negative to say about the land itself — they praised it as a land flowing with milk and honey. But then a few verses later, as they are trying to persuade the people against trying to conquer the land, the spies stated, "The land through which we have gone as spies is a land that devours its inhabitants, and all the people whom we saw in it are men of great stature. There we saw the giants . . ." (Numbers 13:32–33). What happened in those few verses? Did the spies change their mind about the land itself? Did they say it was a great land and then immediately go back on their word and say that the land was undesirable? I doubt it. Look closely at what they said about the land in verse 32. They claimed that it was "a land that devours its inhabitants," and then they immediately went on to talk about the giants in the land. By using *land* to refer to the land's inhabitants, a figure of speech known as synecdoche, the spies may very well have meant that certain people of the land literally devoured its inhabitants. No wonder the Israelites were so afraid of trying to enter the Promised Land at that time, although they should have trusted that the God who freed them from Egypt through many signs and wonders could have safely brought them into the land (which He did 40 years later).

Commentators offer a variety of possible meanings to the statement about the land devouring its inhabitants, so I would refrain from claiming that the interpretation mentioned in the previous paragraph must be the correct one. Nevertheless, I do believe it makes the best sense of the context, it helps explain why the Israelites were terrified of trying to enter the land, and it offers some intriguing connections to other ancient literature about the location and behavior of these giants. For more details on this subject, please read Tim's blog post "Giant Speculations" available at www.midwestapologetics.org/blog/?p=1139.

Where did you come up with the various people and place names in the books?

Coming up with unique names for the people and places was often a challenge. Obviously, there were some characters taken right from the

Bible, such as Enoch, Methuselah, Lamech, Noah, Tubal-Cain, Naamah, Jubal, Jabal, Adah, and Zillah. However, many of our characters were simply made up, so how did we come up with their names?

Some people have suggested that we should have used names that are common in the Bible, as many other historical fiction novels about biblical people have done. But there were a couple of reasons we did not want to do this.

The first reason we avoided using names from the rest of the Bible is that most of the biblical names are post-Babel. Since God confused the languages of the people at that time, we can be rather confident that the pre-Flood tongue (and pre-Babel for that matter) would have been different in most cases. Most of the names in the Old Testament are Hebrew names, but it is quite unlikely that the Hebrew language existed prior to the Flood. Although some Christians believe it was the original language, I do not find the arguments for this view to be compelling.

When we borrowed a name from the Bible, we typically limited ourselves to names that are found prior to the Babel account in Genesis 11. For example, the names Elam and Ashur (Asshur) are found in Genesis 10:22, and some of the names we chose were slight variants to names in these chapters. Oban is similar to Obal (Genesis 10:28) and Ara is similar to Aram (Genesis 10:23). Some of the place names are right out of the Bible: Havilah (Genesis 2:11), Nod (Genesis 4:16), the Hiddekel River (Genesis 2:14), and Eden (Genesis 2:8).

At times, we simply made up the name based on what sounded like a good name for that character and others were based on names of real people. For example, two of the characters in this book have names that I discovered while watching rugby, so I adapted their names for our characters.

The second reason we often avoided borrowing names from later portions of Scripture has to do with the way many biblical characters are named. You may have noticed that many biblical characters have "el" somewhere in their name. Here are just a few: Israel, Elijah, Elisha, Daniel, Samuel, Michael, Gabriel, and Ezekiel. These two letters are one of the titles for God, so it was common for a person to have a name with "el" as a prefix or suffix. This existed in the pre-Flood world as well: Mehujael and Methushael (Genesis 4:18) and Mahalalel (Genesis 5:12). So we used "el" in some of our names: Parel, Akel, Jitzel, and Elnach (a combination of El and Nachash, an obvious sign that his parents did not fear the Creator). But there is another popular prefix and suffix found in much of the Old Testament that we were very careful to avoid using for our characters. Many biblical characters have part of God's personal name in their own name. As a prefix, it frequently appears in names beginning with a "J" (Jehoshaphat and Jehoram), and as a suffix it typically takes on the "iah" ending (Isiaiah, Jeremiah, and Jedidiah). The reason we avoided this title will be explained in the response to the next question.

Why does Noah only use three titles for God?

You may have noticed throughout the first two books that Noah and others have only referred to God as the Most High, the Creator, and God. The Bible uses multiple titles for God, such as the Almighty (Genesis 49:25), Ancient of Days (Daniel 7:22), and Holy One of Israel (Isaiah 41:14). Another title that occurs frequently is Lord, but we intentionally avoided using it because most English Bibles use it to translate two very different terms. When it appears as "Lord," it is typically a translation of the Hebrew word *adonai*, and it often means "master." Many English Bibles use the word "LORD" to translate God's name, YHWH (Yahweh).

When God spoke to Moses after the Israelites were commanded to make bricks without being given any straw by the Egyptians, He made a very interesting statement. He said, "I am the LORD [YHWH]. I appeared to Abraham, to Isaac, and to Jacob, as God Almighty, but by My name LORD [YHWH] I was not known to them" (Exodus 6:2–3).

What did God mean when He said that He appeared to Abraham, Isaac, and Jacob, but He was not known to them by His name, Yahweh. The most straightforward way of understanding this sentence seems to be that God said the patriarchs did not know Him by His personal name. However, this would be a strange thing to say since the divine name is used 162 times in Genesis, and 34 of those occasions come from someone speaking God's name. It is possible that when Moses wrote Genesis, he inserted God's personal name in several places to replace *adonai, elohim*, or another title for God, but this cannot be proven. Consequently, some commentators conclude that God meant that the patriarchs did not really know God's covenant-keeping nature, while others propose that God's statement should be understood as a question. That is, perhaps

God asked, "... but by My name, Yahweh, did I not make Myself known to them?"

We may not be able to know for certain how this verse is to be understood. However, there is one very interesting piece of information that I have not shared yet, which explains why we avoided using God's name in the novel. We have seen that many people prior to Moses had "el" as part of their name, but there is not a single example of anyone being identified with part of God's personal name prior to Exodus 6:3. In fact, the first time we see someone with part of God's personal name in the Bible is found just 17 verses later, and it happens to be the mother of Moses, Jochebed. Prior to this passage, she was called "a daughter of Levi" (Exodus 2:1) and "the child's mother" (Exodus 2:8). Could it be that Moses called her by a new name after learning God's personal name? We know that he changed his successor's name to include the divine name when he changed "Hoshea" to "Joshua" (Numbers 13:16). And after the time of Moses, the Bible includes scores of people whose names reflect knowledge of the divine name.

Perhaps they really did not know God's personal name prior to Moses. Since this is at least a possibility, we decided to refrain from naming anyone with part of the divine name, and we also kept people from calling Him by that name. We also did not have anyone call Him "Lord" because of how easily it can be confused with "LORD." At the same time, we realize they may well have known God by His name, but we thought it would be interesting to explore this angle a bit in the story.

Why was Noah so confident that he would not die in the arena, or that if he did die, that God would bring him back to life?

During their brief conversation in the dungeon, Naamah told Noah that he would die that very day. Noah confidently replied that he was not going to die that day, but then he added that even if he were to be killed, the Creator would need to raise him from the dead. Two chapters later, Noah reiterated that he would not die that day.

The source of his confidence that he would survive the arena was his strong faith in what God had told him. He knew that God would preserve his life until he built the Ark and survived the Flood. But he also added one small caveat. If he did die, then God would raise him from the dead. Why did he mention this detail?

This idea actually comes from the life of Abraham, so this idea was borrowed from the Bible, but I wanted to address it here because of its length. Hebrews 11:17–19 states, "By faith Abraham, when he was tested, offered up Isaac, and he who had received the promises offered up his only begotten son, of whom it was said, 'In Isaac your seed shall be called,' concluding that God was able to raise him up, even from the dead, from which he also received him in a figurative sense."

Have you ever wondered why Abraham was willing to sacrifice Isaac? This passage tells us that he concluded, or some translations say he reasoned that God was able to raise Isaac from the dead. What a marvelous picture of faith! Not a blind leap in the dark, biblical faith is a well-reasoned trust in the perfectly good character of the all-powerful Creator.

God called Abraham to do something that most of us would never carry out, yet this great man of faith knew that God had already promised him that the whole world would be blessed through Isaac. Obviously, since Isaac had no offspring at this point, there would be no way for God to keep His Word if Abraham sacrificed Isaac, unless something else happened. Abraham figured it out. He knew that God always keeps His promises, so he believed that even if he sacrificed Isaac, God would need to bring him back to life so that He could fulfill His promises.

We wanted Noah to have a faith similar to Abraham's. Even though he faced a situation that seemed as if it would lead to certain death, he stood firm in his faith and demonstrated why he is called a "preacher of righteousness" (2 Peter 2:5).

Why did you make some of the characters, like Naamah and Tubal-Cain, so different than how many Christians have imagined them?

We have mentioned that one of our goals in writing this series is to encourage readers to take a closer look at Scripture because so many wrong or unsupportable ideas about Noah and the early chapters of Genesis have become popular in the Church. For example, in the first novel, we mentioned rain in a few chapters even though many have been led to believe that it had never rained before the Flood. This allowed us to discuss the issue in the back of the book. In the same way, by countering many of the stereotypes about the biblical characters, we are able to discuss them here and urge our readers to examine the Bible.

Tubal-Cain is often described as a wicked and violent man. The blasphemous 2015 film *Noah* depicted Tubal-Cain as a murderous villain. The late biblical scholar Meredith Kline also described Tubal-Cain's father, Lamech, as a king, but then went far beyond the text in stating that Lamech's "policy was one of tyranny, a tyranny that reckoned itself through the power of the sword of Tubal-Cain more competent for vengeance than God himself" (Meredith Kline, "Divine Kingship and Genesis 6:1–4," *Westminster Theological Journal*, 1962).

We wanted to counter these ideas about Tubal-Cain by seeing him as a man who eventually comes to believe in the Creator through Noah's influence. Although he was raised by a boastful murderer, there is no guarantee that he would have followed in his father's footsteps. Some of Israel's godly kings had wicked fathers. This truth shows us that there is always hope for people who were raised by ungodly parents.

With Naamah, we went the opposite direction. Many Christians believe that she was Noah's wife. A fifth century A.D. writing called the Genesis Rabba identifies her as such. The rationale behind this is that there does not seem to be a reason to mention Naamah in the genealogy, particularly since the text says nothing else about her. While identifying her as Noah's wife is within the realm of possibilities, it certainly is not the only way to understand the biblical text. An ancient Jewish tradition viewed Naamah as a pagan woman who sang songs to idols. Unlike her brother and half-brothers (Jubal and Jabal), no role is ascribed to Naamah. However, her name may come from the Hebrew root *n'm*, which means "to be lovely," or it may be derived from a different Hebrew root that is spelled identically and means "to sing." This is why we made her a beautiful singer who is also an idolatress.

The book of Jubilees identifies Noah's wife as Emzara. Of course, this name is likely just invented by an ancient writer, and it probably means something like "ancestor of Sarah." Jubilees 4:33 states that she was the daughter of Rake'el. While we liked the name Emzara, we did not want to give the impression that we viewed Jubilees as being divinely inspired, so we named her father Ara instead. Finally, if we discover someday in heaven that Noah's wife was Naamah, you can be sure that we will apologize to her for how we portrayed her in this series.

Did the pre-Flood world have large cities with massive buildings and temples?

By the time our story fast-forwards 450 years, Iri Geshem and many other cities are depicted as being heavily populated with huge buildings. But were the pre-Flood cities really like this? After all, these types of cities and megastructures do not seem to appear in historical records until well after the Flood. So why did we describe the cities this way?

There are a couple of points to consider when discussing this issue. First, we have no archaeological record of what the pre-Flood cities were like. These places were entirely devastated by the Flood, so it is highly unlikely that any trace of them will be found.

The second factor to consider is that the Flood would have caused what may be called a technological reset. Apart from what was on board the Ark, all of the world's technology would have been wiped out. Noah's family would essentially restart civilization, but within the next several generations, society would undergo another technological reset at Babel. As people scattered from that place in their various groups, they would have taken what they knew with them. Consider what would happen to a group that had little to no knowledge of agriculture, or if another group knew very little about construction. This is the reason we see multiple civilizations spring up around Europe, Asia, and Africa all around the same time, yet some of these groups were hunter-gatherers and some planted crops. Some people lived in cities while others lived in caves.

With these two factors in mind, we see that we cannot look back to our earliest archaeological records to get a clear view on the pre-Flood society. Since the Bible does not really describe what the cities were like at that time, other than highlighting man's excessive wickedness, we were left to imagine what they could have been like. At the Ark Encounter, we made the decision to portray the pre-Flood world as being somewhat like the classical Greek or Roman cultures, at least in terms of technological achievements. They had civil societies based on laws and were capable of amazing feats, but they were also extremely decadent. So our story will remain consistent with that decision. Since ancient Greece and Rome had massive buildings and temples, we will include similar structures in the pre-Flood world.

Encounter This

Since we worked on the Ark Encounter project, we had the unique opportunity to include details in our story that can be seen in various exhibits. We were also able to influence the design of certain elements so that they connected with our story. If you visit the Ark Encounter in Williamstown, Kentucky, you will be able to see the following items that were included in the story.

Chapter 11: The chapter opens with Noah trying to figure out a way to pass the time while grieving over his tragic losses. He begins carving an animal out of a block of wood, and it is mentioned that the back of a large-eared tusker started to take shape before he put the project down. This carving based on an elephant-like creature modeled after *paleomastodon* can be seen on a shelf in Noah's Library on the second deck.

Chapter 15: In this chapter, Emzara has a nightmare of having her child taken from her, and then she is forced to watch as the child is sacrificed to the serpent idol. While this was just a dream for her, the Ark Encounter depicts a similar scene in the Pre-Flood World exhibit on the second deck. There is a large diorama featuring a pagan temple with people offering their small children as sacrifices to the serpent god.

Chapter 16: While traveling to Havil to find out whether their suspicions about Lamech were correct, Noah is shown working on a map of the coastline they are sailing past. This map and a wider map of the world can be seen hanging on a wall in Noah's study on the Ark's second deck.

Chapter 17: In this chapter, Noah and Emzara witness two strange creatures involved in a clash. Dinosaur lovers may have recognized the creatures being described as *pachycephalosaurs*. These dinosaurs are usually recognized by the large bony crest on top of their skulls. It is generally believed that these were used for sparring with other males, perhaps to earn the right to mate with the females in the group. Two *pachycephalosaurs* can be seen in one of the cages on the Ark's second deck, although they are juveniles at this point, so they have not yet grown the large bony crest.

Chapter 23: In one of the more disturbing moments of the book, Naamah announced the institution of ritual prostitution during their annual serpent ceremony. The people were told that they could engage in a high form of worship by uniting with one of the temple prostitutes. These sorts of religious practices were quite common in the ancient world. The pagan temple diorama from the Pre-Flood World exhibit, mentioned above in the chapter 15 description, shows people meeting outside of some rooms on the side of the temple, and it is apparent that they are there to take part in ritual prostitution.

Chapter 25: While Noah is walking with his grandfather Methuselah, he thinks about the widespread wickedness in the world contrasted with the many wonderful things to see in creation. In Noah's Study on the second deck of the Ark, people can ask questions of the animatronic Noah figure. In two separate responses, he references the world having been such a beautiful place but now had been overrun with corruption. To hear these responses, ask Noah what the world was like before the Flood and why his globe only has one land mass.

Chapter 30: As Noah is being led through the old city square and is distraught over how decadent Iri Geshem has become, a man tries to persuade Noah to purchase an idol from him. Noah puts out an arm and turns away. An illustration conveying this scene can be found in the *Who Was Noah?* exhibit on the Ark's second deck.

Chapter 32: In the dramatic sequence when Tubal-Cain is forced to choose between serving the Creator or saving his wife, we describe a unique creature that is brought into the arena. We called it a pithoct, but the creature being described is known to us today as a *thylacosmilus*. This cat-like animal featured two large saber-like teeth and grew to about the size of a jaguar. They are thought to have been marsupials, so the females may have had pouches. The Ark Encounter features two of these very cool-looking creatures on the second deck.

Chapter 33: After his arrest, Noah is brought into the arena where he encounters two foes that no one would ever want to encounter in such a situation. The guard who drags him into the arena is a giant warrior, but the more terrifying creature is what comes through the door moments later. The "horned grendec" seen on the book's cover is based on a *carnotaurus*, a *T. rex*-like dinosaur with horns on its head. The Pre-Flood

World exhibit on the second deck features a large arena diorama featuring this dinosaur and a giant guard. The arena in Iri Geshem is described as being quite a bit larger than the one shown in the Ark. Also, if you visit the Ark Encounter, take a very close look at the giant in that diorama. One of the authors of this book, Tim, posed for the images used to 3D print the giant, so the character looks just like him.

Borrowed from the Bible

Since the Bible does not give us many details about Noah's life, we needed to use artistic license to tell the story. To keep the story more closely tied to the Bible, we decided to borrow and slightly adapt some concepts found in elsewhere in Scripture and work them into Noah's story.

Major spoiler alert! Do not read this section unless you have first read the novel.

Chapter 23: In the serpent ceremony in Havil, Lamech boasted about killing a young man who wounded him. Of course, this plotline goes all the way back to the first chapter of the first book and forms the basis of Aterre's tragic story. He was the young man who wounded Lamech in self-defense. This boast of Lamech is taken directly from Genesis 4:23–24.

Chapter 23: During the same speech mentioned above, in response to being called a murderer, Lamech boasted about being the most powerful man in the world, although he was unable to finish his sentence because a violent earthquake interrupted him. This concept of judgment immediately falling on a boastful king is found in the Bible. In Daniel 4:28–33, Nebuchadnezzar boasted about all that he accomplished even though he had been warned to humble himself, and immediately God caused Nebuchadnezzar to live like a beast for seven years. In the New Testament, Herod Agrippa gave a speech causing the people to hail him as a god. We are told in Acts 12:20–24 that he failed to give glory to God, so an angel of the Lord immediately struck him so that he was eaten by worms and died.

Chapter 25: After our story jumps forward 450 years, we learn that Noah and Emzara are still childless and that they have been praying for a child throughout those centuries. Of course, if you are familiar with the account of Noah in the Bible, you know that he will eventually have three sons. The idea of a barren couple praying for a child is not uncommon in Scripture. Hannah prayed for a son and eventually gave birth to Samuel (1 Samuel 1:10–11). We do not specifically read about Abraham and Sarah praying for a child, but we know they longed for a son, and even though they tried to fulfill God's plan in a different way, Abraham trusted the Lord (Genesis 15:1–6). Our story probably parallels the experience of Zacharias and Elizabeth in the New Testament. She was barren and both were advanced in years. When Zacharias entered the temple to fulfill his priestly duties, an angel appeared to him and announced that his prayer had been heard and that he and Elizabeth would have a son. Unlike Noah in our story, Zacharias did not believe at first and was struck with muteness until his son, John the Baptist, was born (Luke 1:5–25).

Chapter 26: In our story, when God appeared to Noah in a vision, we borrowed several ideas from other portions in Scripture. The Lord opened by saying, "Do not be afraid, Noah, for you are greatly loved." Many times in Scripture when God or an angel appears to a person, the first words often spoken are, "Do not be afraid" (see Genesis 15:1 and Matthew 28:5 for some examples). The line about being "greatly loved" comes directly from Daniel, who was told multiple times by an angel that he was greatly loved (Daniel 9:23, 10:11, 19). Since Noah is described as being righteous, like Job and Daniel (Ezekiel 14:14, 20), we thought it was fitting for Noah to hear from God that he was greatly loved too. Finally, when Noah replies to God, he begs forgiveness for daring to ask a question. We borrowed this concept from Genesis 18 where Abraham pleaded with God to not be angry with him for asking about possibly sparing the city of Sodom on behalf of a certain amount of righteous people that might be found in it (Genesis 18:22–33).

Chapter 26: After the Lord appeared to Noah in our story, Noah tripped over a stone and knocked it loose from the ground. He decided to stack several rocks together as a way of remembering the place where God spoke to Him. Jacob did something similar to this in Genesis 28:18. He stood one stone on end and poured oil on top of it after the Lord appeared to him during the night in a dream. When the Israelites crossed the Jordan River into the land promised to them, God instructed them to take 12 stones from the river and set them up as a memorial to what He had done for them (Joshua 4).

Chapter 31: When the city of Iri Geshem is taken over by the Havilites, one of the first rules they make is that everyone must bow down to an image of Nachash. Of course, the city council made sure that Noah was in attendance, knowing full well that he would refuse to bow and they would have an excuse to arrest him. This scenario is quite similar to the situation faced by Daniel's three friends, Shadrach, Meshach, and Abednego, in Daniel 3. They refused to bow and were subsequently thrown into the fiery furnace. In our story, Noah refuses to bow to the statue, so he is arrested and eventually brought into the arena, presumably to meet his doom.

Chapter 33: In another scene reminiscent of the Book of Daniel, Noah finds himself in the coliseum being ordered to bow before a false god or face what would seem to be certain death. In Daniel 6, King Darius signs a law forbidding anyone to petition any man or god over the next 30 days, or they would be thrown into the lion's den. The entire plot was a setup by the Medo-Persian governors and satraps who were envious of Daniel. They knew Daniel would refuse to follow such a law, and after he continued praying to the true God, they brought him before the king who reluctantly ordered for him to be thrown into the den of lions. The Lord miraculously delivered Daniel, and those who accused him were then thrown into the lion's den. Similarly, in our story, Noah is delivered from a terrifying beast while some of those calling for his death met their own end.

Dear Reader,

Thank you for continuing our tale of Noah's life, as we have imagined it. As you probably know by now, one of our goals in this series is to encourage readers to carefully study the Bible so that they can rightly discern fiction and biblical fact. And the main reason we want readers to examine Scripture is so that they might learn the most important message we could ever tell — the gospel, the good news that Jesus Christ died on the Cross for our sins, was buried, and then conquered death by rising on the third day.

As we explained in the first book, Noah could not have known all of these details since he lived long before they occurred. However, the Bible describes Noah as a righteous man who found grace in the eyes of the Lord. Even though he lived in an extremely wicked world, he faithfully completed the tasks that God gave him, and he trusted that God would remain true to His promises.

We also live in a time when many people are opposed to God's truth. In an effort to make the gospel message more appealing, some Christians teach that trusting in Jesus will make everything better in this life. While God does grant joy and peace to believers, Jesus taught His followers to deny themselves (Luke 9:23) and to consider the cost of following Him (Luke 14:25–29). We are also told that godly people will suffer persecution (2 Timothy 3:12).

In the climactic chapters of our book, Noah and Tubal-Cain refused to compromise their faith in the Creator even in the face of death. Serving God was more important than life itself. The same can be said of those who follow Jesus today. We understand that He gave His life on the Cross for us and grants eternal life to those who trust in Him, so His followers should be willing to give up everything for Him. This commitment to follow Him at all costs is not derived from efforts to obtain salvation. It is rooted in a desire to love and serve Him because He has first loved us and obtained salvation for us (1 John 4:15–19).

What about you? Have you placed your faith in the risen Savior, Jesus Christ, and are you willing to stand for Him no matter the cost? The reward of serving Him makes it all worthwhile.

Jesus said, "Blessed are those who are persecuted for righteousness' sake, for theirs is the kingdom of heaven" (Matthew 5:10).

About the Authors

Tim Chaffey is the Content Manager for the Ark Encounter and Creation Museum. A former pastor and teacher, Tim is also a leukemia survivor and competes in half-marathons with his wife and son while his daughter cheers them on. He has earned advanced degrees specializing in apologetics, theology, and church history. Tim maintains a popular blog (www.midwestapologetics.org/blog), contributes regularly to *Answers* magazine and the Answers in Genesis website, and has authored over a dozen books, including *The Truth Chronicles* series and *In Defense of Easter: Answering Critical Challenges to the Resurrection of Jesus.*

K. Marie Adams has an obsession with words that once resulted in her being grounded for reading too much. Later, it served her well as she worked for many years at a bookstore and as a literature and grammar instructor. Now, as a graphic designer, her love of language goes by the fancy name of typography. K. Marie also volunteers for several ministries dedicated to rescuing young girls from modern-day slavery.

THE REMNANT TRILOGY

BOOK 1

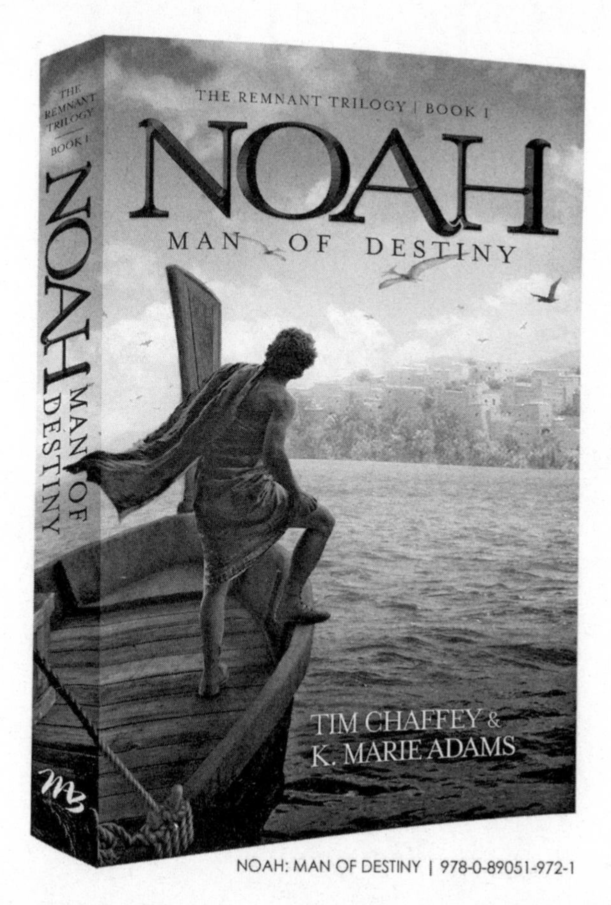

NOAH: MAN OF DESTINY | 978-0-89051-972-1

Most people think of Noah as the man who built a large ship and spent months caring for thousands of animals. But who was he and what events shaped who he would become? *Noah: Man of Destiny* takes readers on a captivating, coming-of-age journey through the pre-Flood world. Noah learns more about the Most High while standing against a sinister belief system emerging throughout the land. Whether escaping legendary beasts, tracking kidnappers, or pursuing his future wife, Noah acquires the skills he will need when God calls him to his greatest adventure: surviving the global Flood. Explore what it may have been like for a righteous man to relate to God before the Bible was written.

Available at MASTERBOOKS.COM & other places where fine books are sold.

— Where Faith Grows! —

40 Reasons Noah and the Ark Still Matter

Though there are mo
books on the Flood i
the creation
movement, There isn
one basic laymen's
book to give answer
those questions aske
all the time. Most bo
are too shallow, too
specific, or too
technical for the
average Christian to
read or get much fr
Most people in pews
could use a book lik
this to give them the
basic answers they
need about the Floo
and the Ark, then th
will be prepared to
into further technica
books or specific bo
from there.

Available at MASTERBOOKS.COM & other places where fine books are sold

★★★★★

THINK

BIGGER

ArkEncounter.com

Williamstown, KY
(south of Cincinnati)